INFECTED

OTHER BOOKS AND AUDIO BOOKS
BY GREGG LUKE

Altered State

Do No Harm

The Survivors

Blink of an Eye

Bloodborne

Deadly Undertakings

Twisted Fate, "The Death House"

The Healer

INFECTED

A NOVEL OF SUSPENSE

GREGG LUKE

Covenant Communications, Inc.

ACKNOWLEDGEMENTS

WHILE THIS NOVEL WAS CONCEIVED and crafted in my own twisted mind, the version you hold in your hand was corrected, improved upon, and polished by many people I consider good friends. In particular, I wish to thank Melissa Duce, Brooke Ballard, Erika Luke, Glen Gordon, and Denise Johnson as beta readers and as sources of information and inspiration, Ben Boyer FNP for medical and geographical advice, and Col. Mike Callahan (ret.) for his aviation expertise.

A special thanks goes out to Phillip Hellewell for his knowledge, expertise, and experiences in Venezuela. He brought an element of authenticity to this story I could not have created alone.

Lastly, I wish to thank my editor, Stacey Turner, who always does a remarkable job of correcting my mistakes before they go public.

CHAPTER 1

"MOTHER NATURE IS A SERIAL killer." Dr. Brandon Udy couldn't remember where he'd heard that quote, nor did he know why it popped into his mind just then, but nearly a decade of experience had taught him it wasn't quite right. A serial killer targets a specific caste of victim—hence the term *serial*. Mother Nature, on the other hand, kills with indiscriminate wantonness. She was a mass murderer of unparalleled accomplishment. No one was more insidious, more creative.

Mother Nature. A mass murderer. No one is more creative . . .

Brandon sat back and removed his disposable gloves. He rubbed his bloodshot eyes, no longer able to concentrate on those prophetic words or on the fungus displayed on his dissection microscope. He'd worked on the new specimen straight through the night, taking only one outhouse break and pausing only once for a snack. He wasn't hungry; he simply needed the energy.

The image in the microscope was sharp and detailed, but the specimen's morphology no longer felt significant to him. Neither did its uniqueness, suspected virulence, or unquestionable deadliness. All he could think about was Goliath, a 150-foot-tall kapok tree, roughly three kilometers from their remote research lab. He had to seek it out, had to reach it before it was too late. Nothing else mattered.

Without shutting down his microscope or storing the specimen in its sealed container, he stood and headed toward the plywood door of their large tent.

"Crikey, you're at it early," yawned his research partner, Julia Fatheringham. "You off to the dunny?"

Brandon didn't answer. It wasn't that he didn't want to. He couldn't. He knew she had asked a direct question; he could see her in his peripheral vision, stepping from their sleeping area. But she registered as an object of minimal importance, nothing more. His immediate focus was on the door. After that it'd be on the narrow trail that led through the rain forest to the thorny trunk of Goliath.

He opened the thin door to a drab morning that seemed to have come without preamble; the ubiquitous cloud cover was opaque and somber. No wind blew along the creek-bed swale. The precipitation fell in a slow, silky cascade. Looking up, he saw the treetops above the canopy swaying to a steady breeze. That was a good sign, though he didn't know why. Dressed in his usual garb—a T-shirt, cargo shorts, and flip-flops—he headed straight for a trail he'd walked a hundred times before, a trail he was now *compelled* to follow.

"Oy. Hold up a tick, will ya?" Julia said, her Aussie-accented voice somehow no longer humoring him.

Her voice sounded close, but he was so intent on his destination that her words didn't slow him a bit. His eyes focusing on the entrance to the shadowy, rain-soaked trail, he let his legs carry him forward automatically, almost as if without sentient command. His mind sparked with snippets of information at every step: the distance to the tree, the ambient temperature and wind direction, the current time of morning, what he had to do when he reached Goliath. Its enormous trunk would be damp from rain and incessant humidity. Regardless, climbing the tree was vital. He would find a way.

"Wait up, B. Where're you headed?"

Julia was just a few paces behind him. He could hear her pushing through the underbrush, trying to keep up. She clearly did not feel the same urging, the same unrelenting compulsion to climb the kapok— hence her banal question. Wasn't it obvious? He was heading to climb the tallest tree in the vicinity. He *had* to. Even if he wanted to stop, he couldn't.

"Come on, Brandon, give it a rest a sec."

He paused when she grabbed his shoulder, although his body strained to continue forward.

"Talk to me, please."

"No . . . time," he heard himself say with considerable effort. Jerking his shoulder from her grip, he resumed his trek in earnest. Time was of the essence—although, curiously, he didn't feel the need to run.

A steady pace would get him there soon enough, and walking would conserve energy. Julia continued pleading for answers as he wended his way into the gloomy interior. He wished she understood his need to do this. It should make perfect sense to her, a fellow scientist.

By the time Brandon reached Goliath, the urge to climb was overpowering. Looking up, he could see where the giant kapok disappeared into the canopy. The emergent layer—his destination—stretched another fifty feet beyond the treetops. Once he was there, all would be well.

"What's going on, mate?" Julia asked urgently, coming up behind him. "You're acting very bizarre."

The base of the kapok was supported by numerous buttressed plank-roots radiating out in several directions. The buttresses rose anywhere from three to ten feet above the ground and sloped away up to twelve feet across the forest floor. They would have made good handholds were it not for the thick, sharp thorns protruding from the bark to ward off would-be grazers.

As Brandon grabbed the top of a buttress to hoist himself up, he felt a dull stab of pain. He thought he heard Julia gasp, but it sounded distant, dreamlike. Removing his hand, he saw blood seeping from a small hole in his palm. His hand throbbed . . . but it didn't seem to matter. Somehow the pain wasn't important. Grabbing the buttress with both hands, he pulled himself over the top and lay across the large plank root. Thorns pierced the skin of his belly. Again, the punctures registered as hurting, but they seemed secondary to his need to reach the top of the tree. Using the trunk for stability, he stood, balancing on the massive root. Multiple thorns punctured the soles of his feet; one sank deep into his heel. Somewhere along the way he'd lost his flip-flops. Pain pulsed up his legs, but his mind overrode the reflex to jerk away from the source. Instead, he wrapped his arms and legs around the enormous trunk and began to shimmy upward. The hard thorns along the bole tore at his chest and arms, his belly and thighs. His flesh shredded; blood ran freely. With morbid efficiency, the thorny protrusions helped him stick to the otherwise slippery trunk.

Julia's calls turned to cries, fearful and desperate. His mind tuned them out, paying no attention to the emotion they may once have engendered.

It took nearly sixty minutes to reach the first branch, some eighty feet up. The thorns were smaller and less dense higher up but still very sharp. He swung over the branch and looked down. In the shadowy gloom below, he saw Julia staring up at him with wide, horror-filled eyes. She'd soon understand his need to climb; in a few minutes it'd be obvious. Steadily ascending from branch to branch, Brandon finally broke through the 120-foot canopy.

Birds left their roosts in raucous annoyance at his appearance; monkeys screeched in protest. At that height, a steady breeze caressed the treetops, drying the sheen of blood covering his face and frame. He climbed a dozen feet higher before the branches of the wide crown became too thin to hold his weight. He needed to get as high as possible. The wind was stronger higher up—that was important. But he could climb no farther.

Constrained to that elevation, he straddled two stout boughs, wrapped his arms and legs around the last section of emergent trunk, and squeezed tightly. Resting the right side of his face against the trunk, he placed a thin, horizontal branch between his teeth and chomped down, resulting in a strange half smile on his face. He sighed and closed his eyes. He'd made it. The steady, late-morning breeze was perfect. He was as high as he could get. All was well.

The soughing wind and gentle swaying of branches was calming. Gradually, his mind dulled; no stimuli triggered response or emotion. His breaths became sluggish, shallow. Steadily, painlessly, his heart slowed to one or two beats per minute. His murky thoughts slipped into a state of emptiness, totally disassociated from his consciousness.

As he released a seemingly endless, wispy lungful of air, an eerie hush fell across the landscape of the canopy.

CHAPTER 2

TORN BETWEEN WAITING FOR BRANDON to climb down or returning to the research tent for help, Julia anxiously paced at the base of Goliath for close to an hour. The weighty emptiness of abrupt solitude pressed down on her, making it hard to breathe.

She had no idea what condition Brandon was in, but it wasn't good. She'd never seen him act this way—like he was hypnotized or something. He never left the tent without saying where he was headed. Neither did she. It was a precautionary measure. Sure, Brandon had often joked about going to the beach or to Burger King, but he made sure he always said *something*. He was insatiably fun, witty, and full of positive energy, rarely doleful, never lugubrious. Sometimes he was a shameless practical joker, but his boyishly unkempt hair and easy smile made it impossible to stay angry at him for long. Besides, underneath his unremitting lightheartedness was a serious researcher, quick of mind and deep of thought. When he latched on to an idea, he'd see it to fruition, often irrespective of food or sleep but never to the point of carelessness.

That's why she knew this was more than a quirky jest. She'd watched him deliberately drive kapok thorns into flesh without so much as a grimace. She'd seen his skin tear, seen his blood pour. *That* was no joke. Instinct told her this was something she couldn't handle alone; she needed to call their coordinator.

"Oy, Brandon! I'm going to radio for help," she called up to the rain forest canopy. "Don't do anything stupid!" As if free-climbing a kapok wasn't already rife with stupidity.

The trek back to the research tent seemed to take forever. Along the way, the angst of the situation bunched on her like floodwaters pushing against a dam.

Once inside the tent, Julia toggled the transmit switch on their two-way radio, signaling the research coordinator at the CIST: The Centro Investigación de la Selva Tropical located in Caicara del Orinoco, a small city some 330 miles northward. "CIST HQ, this is Ascom base, come in!"

The static hiss undulated with a sinuous, high overtone. She shuddered. It was an eerie, spectral noise she'd heard countless times but had never before considered foreboding.

"CIST HQ, this is Ascom base. I'm calling in an emergency. I repeat: this is an emergency! Felipe, are you there?"

No response.

"Criminy!" She tweaked a couple of dials. "Caicara, this is Ascom. Please respond."

A few electric crackles punctuated the unnerving static before a man's voice filtered through. "This is CIST. Good afternoon, Doctor. How can I help you?"

"Oh, thank heavens you're there, Felipe. Brandon's acting very strange. I think he's in trouble."

"You interrupted my afternoon *siesta* just to tell me Dr. Udy is acting strange?" Felipe asked through a chuckle. "He's always acting strange."

Afternoon siesta? Only then did she realize it was almost one o'clock. Where had the time gone? "No, mate. I think he's in *real* trouble. He free-climbed a kapok—without gloves or shoes. There's blood everywhere."

"Geez, are you serious?"

"Too right."

"Okay, listen. Take a deep breath and tell me what happened exactly."

She quickly rehearsed the events of the morning, trying to include every detail but realizing sadly there weren't many. When she finished, there was a lengthy pause over the airway.

"Is this a joke?" he asked with minimal humor.

"No, Felipe. I'm dead serious. He's . . . I don't know. This isn't one of his typical larks. I'm . . . it just doesn't *feel* right, you know?"

Felipe's voice took on a serious edge. "All right, listen, Doc, just stay calm. It's going to be okay. Is he still up there? Up the tree?"

"As far as I know, yes."

"Copy that. Hold on a moment." More empty static followed. The second pause felt like eternity. "Is he studying a fungus that only grows in the canopy?"

"No. Well . . . I don't know. Not recently. I'm worried because he's not responding when I call to him."

"Are you going up after him?"

"I don't know. I think I should, but we don't have any gear on that tree."

"Copy that."

There was more static hiss while she awaited his counsel. Every empty second was agonizing.

"Okay, look, I'm sorry, but I've already got another flight scheduled this afternoon. It's a government thing, so there's no backing out. You understand. But I'll come out at first light tomorrow. I promise."

The finality of his words was like a knife plunging into her gut. "Felipe, *please*."

"Just take it easy, Julia. Listen, Dr. Udy's pretty strong, and he's pretty dang smart for a goof-off. He's probably just . . ." His words trailed off, confirming that he couldn't explain Brandon's bizarre behavior either. "I doubt it's anything serious."

"It's as serious as a heart attack, mate! I saw thorns puncture his skin. He stepped on them with bare feet, for cripe's sake. I . . . I don't know what to do." Julia hated the fact that she was acting so flighty. She was a winner not a whiner. She'd been valedictorian of her class at the University of Queensland and had been Dr. Brandon Udy's first pick as research partner for this expedition. Besides, she'd been in tough situations before and handled them with the stoicism and methodical aplomb of a seasoned field researcher. She'd even captured and tagged saltwater crocks for crying out loud. But *this*! This was unlike anything she'd ever seen before—unlike anything she'd ever *heard* of. "Can't you come right after your other flight?"

"That's a negative, Doctor. Flying into your neck of the rain forest is pretty brutal even in daylight. There's no way I can make it there before nightfall. Sorry. I'll stay by the radio, but there's little more I can do right now."

And there it was: her lifeline had just been severed. She was on her own. Maybe he was right; maybe there wasn't anything he could do just then. But *she* could.

"Fair enough," she said. "You're right, of course. But *I'm* going back out."

"Okay, but be careful. You know that rain forest is no place for a casual stroll—especially with the scent of fresh blood in the air. Be sure to get back in before dark."

"He'd do the same for me," she said with certainty.

Felipe's next pause felt contemplative, as if he was mulling over a way to talk her out of her decision. But she was determined. And doing *something* was better than simply sitting around waiting . . . wondering.

His next transmission began with a long sigh. "Copy that. Please be extra cautious, okay? You hear what I'm saying? The weather looks moderate over Amazonas right now, but there's a big storm on the radar. It looks like a bad one."

"No worries." Julia left the transmitter on in case the CIST called back. She downed a protein bar and a bottle of water and traded her shorts and sneakers for cargo pants and hiking boots. Then, stuffing a small backpack with every essential she could think of, she shrugged it on and went outside. Pausing, she breathed deeply, as much to clear her head as to steel her determination. She set her jaw and narrowed her eyes at the forest. She'd been at this remote location long enough that it no longer seemed strange or alien. That bolstered her confidence.

Ascom base sat in a dense section of Venezuelan rain forest in the state of Amazonas. Lush vegetation abounded. From the emergent layer on top, through the profuse canopy, and down the towering understory to the forest floor, the dark, dank environs were ideal for their field of research: mycology. The moist, spongy biomass of the rain forest floor reeked of decay. Fungi thrived there. Ascom's eighteen-month objective was to isolate the basic biochemical properties of as many new fungal species as possible. They had a small gas chromatograph and colorimeter which gave them a good idea if the isolated biologic compound was new or unique. From there, they would store the sample to be studied later in a full biochemical lab before it was tested on animal cells.

The river swale in which the base sat opened to a narrow yet unobstructed length of sky. The morning's rain had passed, leaving a thin, gauzy layer of clouds veiling the heavens. She knew it was the calm before the storm. If Felipe said a storm was coming, it was.

Six meters away, the perimeter was walled by a dense, dark wall of vegetation. Jagged, gray-green silhouettes harried by a fresh afternoon breeze scratched against each other, sounding like the raspy breathing of some unseen predator.

Julia quickly shook the image from her head. Pushing all fears aside, she unsheathed her knife, set her jaw, and marched into the shadowy undergrowth.

CHAPTER 3

"HOLY MOLEY! I DON'T SEE what all the fuss is about," said Meghan Muir with a roll of her eyes. "So Brandon pricked his finger and got stuck in a tree—now *she's* throwing a hissy fit."

"It sounded like more than a pricked finger to me," Felipe said wearily. He hated responding to anything Meghan said because it always led to the same heated argument and the same aggravating stalemate. It'd been that way since she'd arrived from Stanford University four months ago.

"So what if it *is* a real emergency?" she ranted on. "Serves them right. Little Miss Kangaroo and Dr. Fungus claim they're out there doing good, but all they're doing is looking for the next billion-dollar drug for big pharma. You know that as well as I do. They're both out there taking a bite out of the rain forest, and now the rain forest has bitten back. Well, I say let nature run its course. Let's see how they like the taste of just deserts."

Although Felipe didn't want to take the bait again, he couldn't leave it alone. "It sounds to me like they may need help," he said without meeting her eyes. "Dr. Fatheringham wouldn't call in unless she had to. You know that they're honestly trying—"

"*I* know they're honestly murdering countless species in the name of science," she huffed. "Some of which are undiscovered—and *never will* be discovered—thanks to them. Like I said, if nature retaliates, so be it."

"But that's precisely why they're there: to discover new species—"

"To rip from the forest floor and sell to the highest bidder."

He closed his eyes, wishing he could do the same with his ears. No one ever won an argument with this woman. She debated with emotion instead of logic, citing environmentalist catchphrases instead of verifiable facts. It was best to simply walk away.

Meghan Muir was the result of an ultraliberal, ultra-indulgent upbringing in Marin County, California. After high school, she'd attended a conference in Switzerland on global warming and environmentalism—which made her a self-proclaimed expert. But she had yet to gain any university accreditation and probably never would. After some digging, Felipe had discovered she was on academic probation at Stanford and had been granted a leave of absence, supposedly to conduct field work.

At the insistence of his superiors, Felipe had reluctantly agreed to let Meghan complete a ten-month residency with his department, coordinating in-country research. She claimed the internship met the parameters of a classified university project. Perhaps that was true. But he also knew that her parents had gifted a sizable donation to the university—and some under-the-table incentives to the Venezuelan Interior Department. That was the *real* reason she'd been granted a visa and a position with his department.

Felipe disliked Meghan immensely, but if she left, so would her funding, and that was something his superiors would *not* like. Besides, she never really did anything—destructive or otherwise. She was all talk and no walk. She didn't even like stepping out of their air-conditioned office or getting dirt under her manicured nails. So he simply kept her busy with paperwork, tried to agree with her in principle (though rarely in practice), and continued to fulfill his assignments as best he could. Yes, she was an obnoxious, short-sighted pain in the neck, but at least she was a relatively harmless, obnoxious, short-sighted pain in the neck.

He tugged on his ear. "Listen, I'm going to prep the helo for this afternoon and grab a bite before the next flight," he said, tired of arguing with her. "Call me if anything more comes in from Ascom."

"It's what I do," she said, admiring her nails.

"I'm serious."

"So is deforestation and global warming."

He clenched his jaw. "Look, just do what I ask, please?"

"Like I said, it's what I do."

"For six more months."

"Six *miserable* months," she grumbled, yanking a Sierra Club magazine from her desktop and flipping it open.

Felipe glowered at her without responding. *Just walk away, man. Just walk away.* With a bitter wave of his hand, he left the room.

"Have a safe flight," Meghan called after him in a singsong tone probably meant to irritate him.

It worked.

CHAPTER 4

THE INCESSANT HIGH TEMPERATURE AND humidity grew more oppressive the deeper Julia strode into the jungle. Although she had acclimated to the harsh environment, the draining heat added an edge of frustration to her already harried emotions. The trail felt much longer this time. Shadows encroached from every angle. Every root seemed like a deadfall, every stone a boulder, every depression a crevasse.

Conflicting thoughts assaulted her. Was Brandon indeed playing a prank? No. His injuries and blood were real. Was he stoned? No. He never used illicit drugs, and the only alcohol they had was pharmaceutical-grade isopropyl—which they both knew was potentially deadly to drink. Was he sick? Perhaps suffering from a brain fever? Possibly. But what was the cause? And did such things occur with the speed and complete dominance his had? He hadn't complained about feeling under the weather. He'd been sleeping well and eating normally.

She paused for a sip of water. Sweat stung her eyes.

Was he delusional, then? Evidently. But again, what was the cause? He'd never exhibited such aberrant behavior before, and he wasn't on any prescription medications. She would know if he was. Even though they slept in separate bunks, being with someone 24-7 made it difficult to hide *anything*. He ate what she ate; he drank what she drank. The only medicaments they had were in the first-aid kit, and last time she checked, they were all accounted for. So his sudden fugue wasn't pharmaceutical in nature. Was it caused by some other chemical? A parasite maybe? A bacterium or a virus?

For a fleeting moment, she regretted not going to medical college after graduating from the UQ, as her grandfather had wished. She knew a lot about medicines from her graduate studies in Atlanta. Her PhD focused on such information.

Emory University was where she'd met Brandon. They were both in the biochemistry department. She was finishing her dissertation; he was working on a post-doc. Because they each studied mycology, the department had placed them in the same lab and encouraged cooperative research. They'd hit it off from the get-go. Within eight months they had coauthored a brilliant grant proposal to study the biochemistry of rain forest fungi. Five months after that they were awarded a generous stipend from a research branch of AstraZeneca. And six months later, they found themselves sharing the tented lab in Venezuela.

Winks and nods accompanied predictions that their isolation would lead to more than *scientific* discovery, but they took it good-naturedly and played along. Privately, they'd made a pact to not entertain any romantic proclivity or opportunity. They were scientists first and foremost. They had serious work to do, important research to conduct. The fact that they were both single, in their midtwenties, and had similar interests did not enter into the equation . . . initially.

Pushing the unfinished admission aside, Julia continued toward the giant kapok, detailing everything that might reveal why Brandon had climbed it. *Ceiba pentandra* was the tree's scientific name. It was a bio-diverse ecosystem of its own, being home to numerous birds, frogs, snakes, monkeys, sloths, and countless insects. It also provided a substrate for bromeliads, orchids, ferns, and other epiphytic plants. A unique sampling of opportunistic fungi also made the tree home, from its plank roots to high in the canopy. Was that what Brandon was looking for?—an undiscovered ascomycete?

Reaching the base of Goliath, she looked up but could not see him through the leaves and branches. "Oy, Brandon? Brandon? Can you hear me up there?"

Frogs and insects silenced at the sound of her voice, a few monkeys screeched their annoyance, but no human noises filtered down from the crosshatch of branches.

She tucked her lower lip under her teeth and whistled shrilly. "Oy, Brandon! You still up there, mate? Are you okay?"

A few more screeches echoed down from the canopy but nothing else. She huffed and shrugged off her backpack. Examining the tree, she struggled to keep her nerves steady. Brandon's blood still glistened on the trunk, but it was much darker now, well on its way to congealing. A shiny green leech feasted at the base of one glob.

She sat on the ground and pinched the bridge of her nose to force herself to concentrate. She felt strangely vulnerable. The weight of unexpected solitude pressed down on her. Random forest sounds immediately closed in around her—some *very* close: the rustling of small things moving through the leaf litter, the chitinous chittering of hundreds of insects, the trickle of water cascading into a small depression. But again, no human sounds other than her own coarse breathing. Tipping her head back, she heard the restless keening of a breeze high in the canopy. Felipe's storm was coming in fast.

Knowing darkness would engulf the area in a few hours, Julia considered preparing a small fire between two large plank roots. Her pack held a flint and steel. Building a fire would ward off predators and mosquitos and add a measure of comfort she desperately needed. But even with a cozy fire, Julia knew she'd be fidgety. She couldn't simply wait at the base of the kapok until Felipe showed up, yet she couldn't return to the tent either. Brandon needed her help, of that she was certain.

Approximately forty-five meters from the giant kapok was an enormous fig tree. While not as tall as Goliath, it nevertheless rose more than 130 feet from the forest floor, cresting well above the canopy. They had built an observation platform near the top from which they could study the growth of epiphytic plants and fungi. Perhaps she could see Brandon from there.

Julia made her way to the fig and buckled into a climbing harness dangling from above. She secured her pack around her shoulders and began her ascent. By the time she reached the small platform, dense, bloated clouds darkened the sky.

She attached a safety line to her belt and took a moment to catch her breath. Between the smallish leaves of the kapok dome, Julia could just make out Brandon's shape clinging to the emergent trunk. A sodden wind blew steadily at that height; her partner swayed in concert with the branches, almost as if he were part of the tree.

"G'devening, Dr. Crazy Man!" she yelled, trying to keep her tone light.

Silence. Brandon didn't move a muscle.

She lifted a pair of binoculars to her eyes, but keeping the narrow field of vision on her partner proved impossible; she only caught glimpses of him.

In the end, the gathering storm won out. Soon, rain came down in a steady, obfuscating veil. Julia decided to hunker down on the small deck and wait out the night. The platform had a small retractable canvas awning, which she unfurled. She'd be safe up there. Wet—but safe. Brandon would be all right too. He *had* to be all right. And tomorrow's dawning would reveal everything. She hoped that the revelation would bring good news. Regrettably, in the pit of her stomach, she sensed it wouldn't.

CHAPTER 5

JULIA'S WATCH ALARM BEEPED AT 6:00 a.m. An endless blanket of clouds made the sky lumpy, allowing only sparse, gray light to settle over the steamy canopy. But at least the rain had moved on. With great impatience, she watched Brandon's form gradually materialize from the mist-shrouded gloom. He was still curled against the tree; a score of thin branches appeared to radiate from his dark form. The prickly shape reminded her of a sea urchin. He must have slipped into a very deep sleep to endure such a horrible night. That was good. He couldn't have been very comfortable . . . but at least he hadn't fallen.

As daylight slowly penetrated the ebbing mist, Julia forced herself into action. She stood and stretched. It felt good to get her blood circulating. Below her, the rain forest awakened in cadence with the rising sun. The raucous competition of monkeys foraging for breakfast was noisy enough to wake the dead. Yet Brandon still hadn't moved. A flock of budgies landed close to him and began a session of grooming and socializing. They didn't seem the least bit bothered by his presence. That wasn't normal. Budgies were skittish by nature.

Julia's trepidation inched higher as random breaks in the clouds allowed shafts of sunlight to highlight Brandon's perch. He looked rigid, paralyzed, maybe even . . .

She shook her head aggressively, fighting negative thoughts with every scrap of logic she could muster. Brandon was simply in one of his quirky moods. He'd seen something in his microscope that piqued his curiosity, some epiphytic fungus or lichen that demanded round-the-clock observation. She'd known him to zero in on an idea so intently that the world ostensibly vanished around him. He was that absorbed, that driven. She found his passion and love of research quite stimulating—even attractive. That's partly why she'd followed him to Venezuela. Field research required a willingness to shed all creature comforts for your study. Well, he'd certainly hit that mark last night.

The more she reasoned away his inexplicable behavior, the more her heart lifted. She began to feel foolish for having called Felipe in such a panic. Brandon was obviously onto something big. No wonder he'd been so tenacious.

Cupping her hands around her mouth, she sang out to him. "Oy! G'day, you big sleepy koala!"

The budgies took off in a flurry of blue, green, and yellow. Brandon didn't move. She blew her shrill whistle twice. "Hello-o. Brandon? I'm over here on the observation platform."

Still no answer. No movement.

Her angst returned with a vengeance. Something *was* wrong. Retrieving her binoculars, she focused on her research partner. The lingering morning mists blurred his image; his outline dissolved into the silhouette of the tree and vice versa. She wiped the binocular's lenses and zoomed in on Brandon's back, hoping to detect its rise and fall—an indication he was still breathing—but the gentle swaying of his perch made that impossible.

"This is useless," she grumbled to herself. Then, to Brandon, she yelled, "I'm going to call for help. Be right back!"

Unhooking from the safety line, she secured her harness and rappelled to the ground in a matter of seconds. She stepped out of the climbing gear and jogged back to the tent.

The radio no longer emitted its soft, steady hiss. With sinking affirmation, she realized she'd left the lab on full-run all night. They faithfully shut down all but essential equipment every night to save battery life. Their lab had two solar arrays with hexa-junction photovoltaic cells in a convex honeycomb pattern—a design that amassed nearly all wavelengths of light with up to 60 percent efficiency. But when it was densely overcast or raining, energy only trickled in. At night they had to rely on battery backup alone. Inside the lab, they used low-voltage LED lights and monitors, but their high-tech microscopes and communications systems consumed power rapaciously. To leave such equipment on all night was tantamount to in-field suicide. They had a small, gas-powered generator, but they'd sworn to use it only in dire emergencies. They wanted to keep the area as pristine as possible, leaving a near-zero environmental footprint.

Julia scoffed. The urgency of this situation rendered that ecological goal moot. She switched everything off and ran outside. Ensconced in a box next to the latrine, the generator cranked out eight kilowatts. It took several tugs on the pull cord—and not a few choice words—to start the thing. It sputtered and gasped and finally roared to life with offensive volume.

Back in the lab, Julia switched on the transmitter. "CIST HQ, this is Ascom base, come in."

Nothing.

"CIST HQ, this is Ascom base! Mayday, mayday. Come in please. Felipe, are you there?"

She looked at her watch. 7:50. Someone *had* to be awake by now. *Come on!*

"Caicara, this is Ascom. Mayday, mayday, you bludgers! Can anyone hear me, or do you all have your heads in a dunny hole?"

"Whoa, take it down a notch, princess," Meghan's voice replied. "We can hear you even without the radio."

"I'm calling in a mayday, you dill. Do you even know what a—"

"I know what a mayday is, sweetie. But don't worry—there's still time for tea and cookies before you begin your reign of terror today."

Julia closed her eyes and pinched the bridge of her nose, hoping to quell a pulsing headache. Meghan Muir—how she loathed the woman! Meghan seemed to *enjoy* butting egos, so Julia did everything possible to avoid conversing with her. She knew Meghan's head was scientifically bereft, but the staunch extremist always managed to raise her ire—and that bothered Julia more than what the woman actually said. Perhaps it was the *way* she said things: always condescending, always with feigned compassion and an air of moral superiority.

Steeling herself, Julia said, "I'm not mucking about here. This is an emergency, Meghan. Brandon's in serious trouble."

"Why? What's he done now?" Her supercilious tone came through without restraint.

"Nothing, Meghan," she said through gritted teeth.

"Then why's he in trouble?"

Julia released the transmit toggle and screamed. She then took a deep breath and toggled again. "He's very, very sick. We need helo evac immediately. Is Felipe there?"

Meghan's exasperated huff filled the speaker with distortion before she called out: "Felipe, sweetie. The koala queen needs you."

Julia knew Meghan had intentionally held the transmit toggle open just to goad her. She bit back the desire to tell Meghan off and looked around the lab, trying to focus on something else. The gloomy interior was claustrophobic. The air was musty and thick. It felt like a tomb.

The radio crackled. "Sorry about that, Doctor. I was grabbing some breakfast."

"How quickly can you get here?" she asked without preamble. "Brandon is even worse."

There was a telling pause before he responded. "Is he still alive?"

Julia wanted to say "of course," but she couldn't form the words. Her throat closed off at the possibility. Felipe's question was spot on. *Was* Brandon still alive? She didn't know for sure. He simply appeared to be sleeping. But no one sleeps *that* deeply . . . unless they're sick— especially atop a 150-foot tree. Still, Brandon hadn't complained about feeling ill. He *had* mentioned a dull headache the past couple days, but that was it.

Living in the dank tropics always carried the risk of contracting a bizarre disease, particularly for visitors who hadn't developed resistance to indigenous contagions. Poisonous bacteria, plants, parasites, and fungi abounded. Many species were catalogued, but it was estimated that just as many were as yet undiscovered. Brandon was usually very cautious with the toxins contained in the fungi they studied. She was too. They faithfully wore gloves when collecting and examining specimens. Masks too.

Her gaze fell on Brandon's dissection microscope.

"Julia? You still there?" Felipe's voice buzzed through the speaker.

"Um . . . yeah. Give me a sec," she said, slowly rising to her feet.

"Standing by," Felipe acknowledged.

Brandon wasn't wearing gloves when he climbed the kapok. Had he worn them while at his microscope? Yes. There was a discarded pair off to one side of the unit—right next to his thick notepad, Emory University pen, and ever-present bag of licorice nibs.

She stepped to the dissection scope and slipped on a fresh disposable glove. The unit had shut off when the power failed. She switched it on. Refusing to be intimidated by ominous portents, she patiently waited for the screen to focus. Pinned to the dissection plate was a pale, cylindrical fungus, roughly fifteen centimeters in length. Brandon had sliced it along the length of its body and opened the sporangium—the tiny sac at the tip containing the spores by which it reproduced.

Had Brandon *intentionally* opened the sac? Or had it burst on its own?

Julia didn't recognize the particular species, but its morphology resembled a . . . a what? Using a probe, she lifted a corner of the body to examine the skin. She frowned. It had all the characteristics of a cordyceps: an aggressive, parasitic fungus that in some species—

"Criminy," she gasped. Her mind instantly leapt to a single, horrific conclusion. "But that's . . . impossible," she whispered, barely above a breath.

Julia quickly covered her mouth and nose with a paper mask. Staggering back to the radio transmitter, her feet felt as if they weighed fifty pounds each. Her heart slammed against her sternum; her throat was suddenly very dry.

Toggling the transmitter, she had to swallow several times before she could speak. In a tense, quavering voice, she rasped, "Get me out of here."

"Sorry. I didn't copy that, doc. Say again."

"Get me out of here STAT. I think we have a possible Code Red here."

"What was that? A Code Red, you say?"

She swallowed again. "Yes. We have a possible Code Red. Repeat, a very possible Code Red. I think Brandon—"

The radio suddenly went dead, the image on the monitor shrank to black, and the tent plunged into dark, eerie silence.

It took a moment for Julia to realize the generator had stopped. She ran outside to check it. Nothing looked awry. Opening the fuel tank, she peered inside.

It was empty.

CHAPTER 6

"WHAH, WHAH, WHAH," MEGHAN CRIED, imitating the nasal whining of a spoiled brat. The immature noise grated on Felipe's nerves. She'd undoubtedly perfected the sound growing up. He knew she hated all researchers and tourists, but that was no reason to downplay something as critical as this.

"It sounds like it's a real emergency, Meghan," he said, quickly glancing at the day's logbook. "Let's gear up and go."

"You *can't* be serious," she said, somewhere between indictment and disbelief.

"I'm very serious," he said resolutely. "Dr. Fatheringham wouldn't call in a Code Red unless she meant it."

"She said a *possible* Code Red."

"We treat all Code Reds as if they're real—you know that."

"Really. And how many have you had?"

He paused. "Only two. But both ended in someone's death—"

"But not thousands of deaths. That's what a Code Red means, doesn't it? Something highly dangerous with uncontrolled contagiousness? Some threat that can wipe out entire populations, right?"

"Yes," he said, surprised at her depth of knowledge.

"And did either of your previous Code Reds have that outcome?"

"No. But that's besides the point. Until proven otherwise, we still need to treat it as one. So are you coming or staying?"

"*I'm* not going anywhere. As I said yesterday, if the rain forest decides to fight back, I'm not getting in its way." She picked up a bamboo fan and waved it in front of her face with slow, regal strokes. Her cold, blue eyes held his with a glare of smug superiority. "Go chase your Code Reds or Pinks or Greens if you want. It's time for my break."

"We're talking about saving the life of a fellow human being here," he said angrily.

"So? A wise man once said, 'The needs of the many outweigh the needs of the few.' If Dr. Fungus dies, think how many other species will be saved."

Felipe gawked at her. He'd been a sci-fi fan as a child and recognized the quote from a *Star Trek* movie. "I believe it was Mr. Spock who said that."

She gave a quick nod. "Like I said: a *wise* man."

"A fictitious man, a character in a TV show—" He stopped abruptly, knowing the argument would only go downhill from there. Meghan cocked her head, eyebrows raised in challenge. "Never mind," he grumbled. "Stay by the radio. I'll call if I need help."

"Don't do anything I wouldn't do," she said with a long wink. "I know how much you like the little hussy—I mean Aussie," she quickly corrected as if her slip had been accidental.

Felipe knew better than to respond. He didn't like Meghan—that was a given—but until that moment he didn't realize how much he truly despised her. Exiting the office, he struggled to refocus his thoughts. He needed a clear head to fly into the Ascom site.

Stepping out into the gray morning, Felipe headed toward the helo pad. He loved flying more than anything else, and he took any opportunity he could to cruise over the vast and varied landscape of Venezuela.

At the impressionable age of nine, Felipe moved with his family from Caracas, Venezuela, to Lamesa, Texas. His dad worked as a ranch hand outside of Lamesa while the family lived in town and gained their citizenship. The move had just about crippled him. The anxiety of facing the unknown had always frightened Felipe. Moving to a country where he didn't speak the language was bad enough. Worse, he had no friends, no memories, nothing to which he could find familiarity. Luckily, a few kids in his school spoke Spanish. That helped. But they were still all strangers, and because of that, Felipe always chose activities that kept him away from crowds.

At fourteen he began learning how to fly helicopters. The ranch foreman used them to inventory and drive the cattle. By the time he was seventeen, Felipe had logged enough hours to earn his pilot's license and passed the exam on the first try. Flying came naturally to him, but he wanted to do more than simply count cows. His break came when he turned twenty-two. His dual citizenship, bilingual skills, an associate's degree in business from Howard Community College, and his ability to fly helicopters landed him a job with the Venezuela Interior Department. He'd been in Caicara ever since, managing the Centro de Investigación de la Selva Tropical.

Felipe approached his helicopter with an emotion that could only be described as love. As a thank-you for expanded drilling rights, the state oil company, Petróleos de Venezuela, had gifted the government a fleet of helicopters. Felipe had convinced the Interior Department that he specifically needed an MD600N—a quiet, lightweight, eight-passenger, single-engine bird with NOTAR anti-torque technology. Having no tail rotor made the craft a bit sluggish in agility, but it also meant less prop noise and less chance of chopping things to bits in your blind spot. He'd made a few modifications to it, including beefed-up, extended landing skids which allowed him to land in dense shrubbery and up to three feet of water if need be. He'd also requested installation of an enlarged fuel tank, which gave him a cruising range of close to 350 miles. He called it his *colibrí*—his hummingbird.

Felipe yelled "clear" to the nearly empty tarmac and started the powerful Rolls-Royce engine. As the six-bladed rotor began to turn, he checked over his gear. Much of it was rescue oriented because tourists, researchers, and even seasoned trail guides often met with disaster in the tangled confines of the Amazonas rain forest.

This rescue could easily prove extra challenging. Julia's Code Red could mean anything. When her radio blacked out, he had to assume the worst. A second glance into the passenger hold confirmed his gear was in order: first-aid supplies, a collapsible evac-stretcher, blankets, climbing gear—even a thick plastic body bag and a fireman's respirator. He'd been reluctant to buy the respirator when first outfitting his operation, believing it was tempting fate. Now he was glad he had it. The things Ascom studied were highly contagious. No sense taking chances.

Tightening his safety straps, he checked his instrument panel and briefly consulted a map.

Situated on a tributary of the Rio Casiquiare, Ascom base was actually in the northern extreme of the Brazilian rain forest yet still well within Venezuelan borders. The Rio Casiquiare joined the Rio Negro to the Rio Orinoco, and was unique because it flowed both north to south and south to north depending on the levels of its two "parent" rivers. Tributary streams formed and disappeared in synchronicity with the weather, as did safe landing sites. Felipe knew almost every major mountain, waterfall, swale, gorge, and river by heart, but it never hurt to refresh one's memory with a map.

The current forecast was for a partly cloudy day with a chance of rain—pretty much as it was 300 days every year. He plotted his course, transmitted it to the Interior Department in Caracas, did a quick check for birds, and then lifted into the patchy sky.

Flying south over the Guiana Highlands, he rehearsed everything he knew about the Ascom team. Dr. Brandon Udy was intelligent but mischievous. He loved telling jokes and pulling stupid pranks. His claim to have a "rotten" field of study always made Felipe chuckle. Brandon exhibited teenaged enthusiasm for his research and was known to radio in simply to express excitement over a new chemical or protein they'd isolated from a mushroom growing on the side of their latrine.

Julia Fatheringham was intense but approachable. Felipe liked talking to her because she made Ascom's procedures and findings understandable. Hers was the hand that had penned their application to study fungi in his rain forest. He guessed she'd also written most of their grant proposal. She was physically fit and surprisingly pretty for a field researcher. The female scientists he'd met before weren't necessarily ugly, but they rarely warranted a second glance. Julia, however, looked like she could have been a TV star. And she wasn't afraid of getting dirt under her fingernails. She said digging through the decay and muck was simply part of studying fungi, molds, and all things rotten. Plus, her Australian accent and turns of phrase were disarming. He'd liked her instantly.

Tuning his headset to Ascom's transmitter frequency, he radioed: "Ascom base, Ascom base, this is CIST helo. Come in."

The faint hiss of empty radio waves was the response.

"Ascom base, this is CIST helo in route. ETA, approximately 2.5 hours. Do you copy?"

An abrupt click punctuated the static.

The voice was Julia's, but it sounded flat, distant. "Felipe. Yeah."

"Hola, Doctor. Are you okay?"

"Um . . . yeah. No worries."

He frowned and adjusted the receiver. "Say again. 'No worries?' Please explain."

"No . . . worries."

He didn't know what to make of the short reply. It usually meant there was nothing to worry about. But the *way* she said it suggested that something was very wrong. "Listen, Doctor, I'm on my way. Does Dr. Udy still need help?"

"Um." There was a lengthy pause. She definitely did not sound normal.

He almost preferred last night's anxious, fear-laced voice to this eerie, flat monotone. "I repeat: this is CIST helo, Ascom base. Talk to me, doc. What's going on down there?"

"I . . . I don't . . . I . . . can't understand."

Julia had never before sounded so confused, or so . . . disconnected. It frightened him. Something *was* wrong. Seriously wrong. "I'm increasing my speed. I think I can get there in just about two hours, but I'll have to top off at La Esmeralda. Do you copy?"

The radio offered nothing. The static-infused pause filled him with angst.

"Do you copy, Julia?"

Hsssssssss.

"Dr. Fatheringham?"

"No . . . worries."

CHAPTER 7

FELIPE SLAMMED THE THROTTLE FORWARD, pushing the helicopter to 180 mph. The turbocharged engine roared as if in delight. Luckily, Felipe had a generous tailwind which would hopefully extend his mileage. Little more than an hour later, the Guiana Highlands' south ridge passed below him, opening to a vast expanse of lush Amazonian rain forest.

He radioed the small airstrip to the south. "La Esmeralda Airport, this is CIST helo Romeo-Quebec-two-five-niner-six-one out of Caicara del Orinoco. Come in."

The response was immediate. "Hey, *buenos días*, Felipe. What brings your sorry *nalga* over *la mesa*?"

Talking to Ricardo Paz, the only air traffic controller at La Esmeralda, always brought a smile to Felipe's face. Because the remote airstrip handled only occasional daytime traffic, the native Venezuelan's radio chatter tended to be very casual. Felipe followed suit.

"*¿Qué tal*, Paz? I'm answering a call from Ascom. Have you heard from them lately?" Anytime Felipe authorized a rain forest excursion, he made sure the locals got involved both as a courtesy and in case the team needed help.

"*Nada*. At least not since I took in some supplies about . . . oh, I guess a month or more back. Why?"

"Dr. Fatheringham called in a mayday."

"*¡Caramba!* What happened?"

"She said Dr. Udy began acting strange last night then climbed to the top of a kapok freestyle."

"*¡Qué mal!* You *never* see the natives do that, man. Is he okay?"

"Don't know."

"Then why the mayday?"

"Don't know that either. Dr. Fatheringham didn't say anything other than it was a possible Code Red."

"Is she okay?"

"Unknown. But I think so."

"Ay caramba." There was a slight hesitation before Ricardo continued. "What can I do to help, *amigo*?"

Felipe didn't know *what* he needed. He sensed the danger at Ascom was more severe than someone stuck up a tree. Both scientists were thorough to an extreme—in their studies and in their technique. They could handle just about any small incident or accident. Julia once received a nasty cut that became infected, but she was able to combat the malady with medications on hand. They had a small apothecary for just such contingencies. So if Brandon was sick, Julia would either give him something or would radio for a specific remedy. But she hadn't mentioned anything other than Brandon was "acting strange."

And now so was she.

"I don't know yet," he told his friend. "Maybe it's just a brain fever." He didn't know why he guessed a brain fever. Although rare, he'd seen such jungle illnesses before. "I'll find out when I get there. I'm bypassing La Esmeralda, heading straight to Ascom; ETA, thirty minutes."

"*¡Santa Madre!* You must be pushing it. How is your fuel?"

"A few bars above zero, but I think I can make it. I'll top off on the return trip."

"That's cutting it close, man."

"I know."

"Okay, amigo. I prime the pumps for you."

"Thanks, Paz. CIST helo out."

Felipe looked at the low, dark clouds, remembering that the weather forecast for the territory north of the Guiana Highlands was rarely indicative of the weather to the south. If it started to rain heavily, he'd have to slow down so as not to overfly the site. While his colibrí flew just fine in the rain, his visibility would be greatly hampered.

He dropped to two hundred feet over the canopy and kept his focus on the horizon. His GPS indicated Ascom base was dead ahead: thirty miles and closing. He toggled his radio transmitter.

"Ascom base, Ascom base, this is CIST helo on approach. Do you copy?"

He waited for an answer he feared would not come. He didn't know *why* he feared such a thing. It was a gut feeling, an instinct honed from years of rain forest rescue. The radio's static hiss was steady and flat.

"Ascom, this is Felipe. I'm only a few minutes out. If you can hear me, hold on. Do not leave the lab. Repeat, do not leave the lab. Do you copy?"

A click interrupted the static as if someone was about to transmit back. But the radio remained hollow; no voice came across the airwaves, no indication that someone was at the microphone. As soon as the hiss returned, he asked, "Hey, Julia, is that you?"

Nothing. Not even another click.

"Dr. Fatheringham?"

Felipe kept his eyes peeled for a neon-orange flag on Ascom's aerial . . . *There!*

Roughly twenty minutes later he throttled back, dropped into the tributary swale, and hovered over the Ascom base facility. Nothing looked amiss. Two folding chairs collapsed and skittered away in his prop blast, but the large tent, portable latrine, generator, and storage shed were just as he'd last seen them. A flock of rainbow macaws flapped away at eye level; below, a stout capybara scurried into the underbrush. Felipe maneuvered his helicopter to a small clearing upstream and landed. His fuel gauge was just touching zero, but he guessed he still had enough for about fifty miles if he didn't push it. Crossing himself, he prayed he had a bit more.

Even before the rotors stopped spinning, he crawled into the passenger cabin, belted on a gun holster, checked the clip in his Glock 9mm, and hopped out of the helo. He quickly made his way up the narrow riverbank to the lab. Pausing behind a growth of broadleaf plants, he scanned the lab site. Any number of things could have happened to render the scientists mute: they were simply away from the radio; they were sick and couldn't respond; or worse, they were under duress from drug traffickers or some native tribe who had captured them or killed them or both. Regrettably, Venezuela had the highest kidnapping rate in South America. A disturbing number of those abducted were tourists.

Seeing nothing untoward, he called out, "Hello, Ascom base!"

A few animals voiced a reply but nothing human.

"Dr. Fatheringham? Dr. Udy? Are you there?"

A fat drop of rain slapped the thick broadleaf beside him, followed by a dozen more in a *rat-a-tat-tat* pattern around him. Above him, the clouds were congealing into a gray, distended mass. In another minute he'd be soaked. He withdrew his handgun and stepped into the clearing. A harsh clap of thunder slammed into the swale, making him flinch.

"Hello the camp!" he hollered again.

No one answered. He saw a wall of rain moving quickly over the jungle canopy, heading directly toward the base. Dashing to the entrance of the main tent, he placed his ear against the plywood door, listening for any sign of life inside. He heard only the thwacking of raindrops against the canvas roof. A moment later, the deluge roared in, pounding heavily on the dirt of the small clearing.

Felipe quickly pushed through the doorway in a crouched position and swept the interior over his gun sight. It was dark inside. *Must be running on batteries.* A perpetually morphing screensaver bled across a computer display, a refrigeration unit hummed quietly, a clock ticked from a central support pole, and an oscillating fan buzzed atop a bookshelf lined with bottles and other laboratory clutter. The place wasn't lifeless, but he saw no signs of the living.

Taking a deep, calming breath, he cautiously lowered his gun. Treading lightly, he headed toward the sleeping nook at the far end of the tent. Seeing no one through the mosquito netting, he dropped to a knee. Dirty clothes, a pair of flip-flop sandals, and some books occupied the space under the bunks, but no researchers. A small food preparation area next to the sleeping quarters was also devoid of life.

Pausing at the glass-door refrigerator, he saw numerous stacks of petri dishes filled with slimy-looking substances. Each dish was labeled with a colored biohazard sticker. A key on the side of the fridge identified the corresponding virulence—red: extreme hazard; yellow: high hazard; blue: medium hazard; green: low hazard. Below the petri dishes were two shelves of clear baggies containing mushrooms and other collected samples. They too were labeled with warning stickers. He was relieved to see that most of the stickers were blue and green.

Turning back to the lab, he holstered his Glock and moved to the computer with the colorfully morphing screensaver. A cable ran from the computer to a dissection scope directly beside it. Pinned to the dissection plate lay a fungus in mid-examination. Nudging the wireless mouse, Felipe brought the screen to life. It showed an image of a glossy, pale fungus. Magnified, it looked like a section of a bleached hot dog that'd been sliced from the middle to the tip, exposing a dusty mass of what looked like moldy yellow pollen. Next to the scope lay a clear plastic bag with an identical specimen—

Felipe drew a sharp breath and stepped back, knocking over a folding chair. Abrupt comprehension widened his eyes wide with fright. He quickly removed a handkerchief from his pocket and covered his mouth and nose. Julia's words roared in his mind: *This is a possible Code Red.*

He didn't know what kind of fungus was under the scope, but that didn't matter. He knew it was deadly. The plastic bag with an identical sample was labeled with a bright red biohazard sticker.

CHAPTER 8

HIS GAS MASK! WHY DID he forget his gas mask? *Idiot.*

Holding his breath, Felipe stumbled out of the tent. Heavy rain pummeled the campsite, creating a dark, simmering field of mud. He made it to the center of the clearing before dropping to his knees. His face and clothes were instantly peppered with brown-black splatter. Sucking in lungfuls of wet air, he barely noticed how filthy he'd become. He was more worried about how long he was going to live. Entering a lab under a possible Code Red without biohazard protection was not only careless; it was stupid. It was the mistake a rookie would make, not him.

Felipe's mind filled with rapid-fire conflicts. Julia hadn't said to wear a bio-suit. But maybe she wasn't aware of the extent of contamination. He should have checked first. He should have taken every precaution. So why hadn't he? Maybe because he was so focused on his fuel level? He had pushed his colibrí, knowingly burning fuel at a wasteful rate. But when Julia called in a Code Red, he knew it was serious, so why hadn't he heeded her warnings?

He looked at his mud-soaked hankie. Had it done any good? Was whatever Julia had warned him about airborne? If so, then it was too late. She would be infected. And so would he. Did that mean they'd suffer the same fate as Dr. Udy—whatever that fate may be? Would she randomly climb up a giant tree for no apparent reason? Would he?

The kapok tree!

Staggering to his feet, he searched for a trailhead in the direction of the enormous kapok he'd seen before landing. Julia had said the tree wasn't far from the lab. But "wasn't far" according to a field researcher could mean anything within a day's hike. He quickly found two sets of rain-filled footprints at the entrance of a well-worn path. Gathering his resolve, he started forward. He didn't know if this trail would lead to the right kapok tree—there were dozens in this area—but he couldn't just stand around waiting. Julia was missing now. She *had* to be with Brandon. It was the only logical explanation.

The deeper Felipe penetrated the rain forest, the thicker the vegetation became. He was panting heavily by the time he found a large fig tree fitted with climbing gear. The tree was obviously not the kapok, but he knew the team had fitted several trees with ropes and that one of them was near the big kapok. He hoped that's where he'd find Julia.

Catching his breath, he called up to the canopy, "Hello? Julia? Can you hear me?"

The patter of rain and a few bird calls were his only answer.

He growled deeply and shadow-punched the air. His lack of information tried his patience. He couldn't help them if he couldn't find them.

"Helloooo!" he yelled angrily.

Rather than running from tree to tree, blindly guessing his way through the undergrowth, he decided to climb the fig for a better perspective. Having assisted with several rain forest rescues, he was familiar with the ropes, harnesses, and hardware, and within thirty minutes he was on a small platform near the top of the tree. Neither scientist was there.

The rain had passed as quickly as it had come, leaving a slowly dissipating mist in its wake. When Felipe's breathing calmed, he heard a faint noise—a cry or moan of sorts, one unfamiliar to the forest. It sounded like the private, anguished sob of a woman.

Leaning out as far as he dared, he concentrated on a kapok about fifty yards away. Was Brandon still up there? Had Julia climbed it too? It took nearly ten minutes for the soft breeze to clear the air enough for him to see two figures in the boughs of the kapok—both human, both Caucasian.

"Doctors?" he yelled.

Neither person stirred.

Felipe wished he had binoculars and a megaphone. He stepped onto a bough and cupped the sides of his mouth. "Hello, Dr. Fatheringham!"

Slowly, one of the shapes raised their head. It was Julia. She appeared to be looking below her, searching. She wore what looked like a blue paper mask, the disposable kind health-care workers often wore.

"I'm on the platform in the fig. Over here!" he called, waving an arm.

She pulled the mask from her mouth. "Felipe!" Her voice was rife with anguish. He could almost see her trembling.

"Are you okay?"

She put a hand to her ear. "What?"

The breeze must be dampening his words. He cleared his throat and enunciated each syllable: "Are—you—o—kay?"

She shook her head. "No," she sobbed.

"Just hang on," he said, preparing his gear to repel from the tree.

"Felipe."

"I'm coming. Just hold on—"

"Felipe." Her voice cracked. "Brandon has been taken."

CHAPTER 9

MEGHAN HAD FLIPPED THROUGH THE same Earth Liberation magazine a dozen times. She'd read all the articles—even the ones that she could care less about. Huffing loudly, she tossed it across the room and slammed her head back onto her pillow. She'd napped—at best—only three hours. It was the humidity. The weak AC helped a little but not enough. Even the perpetually spinning ceiling fans seemed to mock her with inefficiency. She was miserable. She'd been miserable ever since she'd arrived in this backward country.

She hated this place. The travel brochures had lied. *Venezuela: land of pristine rain forests, five-star hotels, gorgeous coastlines, and the world's tallest waterfall.* Well, that part was true; but what it didn't mention were the million mango trees dropping smelly fruit that rotted immediately, the hundred-bazillion hideous, disgusting bugs present day and night, the unbearable heat, the oppressive humidity, and the constantly crappy weather. Some days were so thickly muggy she could barely breathe. Even worse, the wretched conditions of this third-world country wreaked havoc on her complexion. Her skin no longer glowed with health; it glistened and dripped with perspiration. Her pores were oil factories. Her hair—ugh! Frizz city. Don't even get her started on that.

She was used to the cool temperatures and mild humidity of the Bay Area. The weather made sense there.

Yet in spite of the unrelenting bad climate, Meghan did love the beauty of the rain forests. She loved nature, loved animals, loved the diversity of the world's forests and oceans. She was convinced the earth's ecosystem was heading for a total meltdown, not only because of uncontrolled logging and mining, but also because of global warming. Why else would these rain forests be so miserably hot and humid? The entire planet was getting way too warm. She was certain the sweltering temperatures would kill every plant and animal in rain forests around the world. Sure, many people claimed it was *always* hot and humid in the tropics, but she pretty much saw through their lies and corporate cover-ups. Yeah, the tropics were warm, but not like this! Year-round temps *and* humidity in the high nineties was just . . . well, it was just ridiculous. Such high heat *had* to be the result of lumber and oil companies slashing and burning thousands of acres every day. One website estimated that the planet was losing up to thirteen million hectares every year! She had no idea what a hectare was, but it sounded like a lot.

Ever since high school, Meghan had crusaded about the negative impact of humans entering such a pristine, delicate habitat to conduct "scientific studies." *Scientific studies, my eye.* Luckily, a growing number of areas were now protected by compassionate Hollywood movie stars who knew a thing or two about environmentalism. You could trust what they said. They were idols, constantly in the public eye; they would never say anything that wasn't true. And just like her Hollywood idols, Meghan saw right through the scam of rain forest "research." It was nothing short of the wanton and immoral exploitation of life. To her way of thinking, such research was no better than a virus discovering new ways to consume and extinguish one natural resource after another with no thought for the future.

The long and short of it was that humans were not humane. They were all selfish and short-sighted. Admitting she was a member of mankind was degrading, humiliating—because *man* was not *kind*. More than once she wished she'd been born a dolphin instead of a human. Working at the Centro Investigation de la Saliva el Tropical— or however it was pronounced—only solidified that wish. Humans had put the environment in irreparable peril. The earth was dying; the miserable conditions here proved that.

Meghan rolled off her bed and started a cool shower. Seeing her reflection in the mirror made her want to cry. She was a mess. She used to be outrageously gorgeous. Now she looked like a discarded Barbie. She needed to get back to cooler temperatures. She desperately needed several sessions with her personal trainer and her aesthetician. Why wasn't anything good happening? Why weren't her leads revealing what she needed to get her out of here? She'd come to Venezuela with a sole purpose in mind. Yes, her current plan went against many of the ideals she championed, but sometimes you had to do things you just didn't like to do. Some people might call her a hypocrite. That didn't matter. She needed money. She had to do what she had to do. But it had yet to happen, and she refused to admit it may *never* happen.

Huffing in frustration, she turned from the mirror and entered the shower. Standing around moping about the lack of opportunity would accomplish nothing. The CIST was the perfect venue from which to find exactly what she sought. It would happen; her psychic had promised her as much. She simply needed to keep busy . . . and presentable. You never knew when a break would come. The pathetic conditions here were something she'd vowed to endure the day she arrived. She had to. She had no other option. It was a vital step in her plans. Powerful people were watching her. Powerful people were funding her. Powerful people didn't like to waste their money.

This was a mess even her parents couldn't bail her out of. Her success was a matter of life or death.

CHAPTER 10

BRANDON'S BEEN TAKEN? FELIPE WONDERED. Taken where? He could see Dr. Udy sitting just above Julia's perch. Did *taken* mean he was dead?

"Stay there!" he hollered. He quickly rappelled from the fig and searched for the path to the kapok. The partly sunny sky allowed intense sunlight to bake the canopy, creating a greenhouse effect in the understory. Large bodies of steam wandered the forest floor, probing every nook like ghostly predators searching for prey. He tried not to think about that and pushed on.

Roughly five minutes later, he stood at the base of the giant. Climbing ropes trailed down from above. At least Julia had used proper technique. He hoped that meant she hadn't acted as "strangely" as Brandon had—whatever that meant. She'd thought this through. Maybe things weren't as bad as he suspected.

"Hello, doctors! Can you hear me?"

"Yes," her voice filtered down.

"I'm coming up. Are the lines secured?"

"Wait. Do you have a mask?"

His previous fears returned, like fangs gripping his throat. Red biohazard labels, exposed fungus spores, possible airborne contagions. "I have a gas mask back in the helicopter," he shouted, unsure it would do him any good now.

"You better get it."

"First, tell me if you're all right."

There was a lengthy pause that filled him with worry. He waited a few moments, staring into the vaporous emptiness above him.

"Julia?"

"Yeah. I'm unsure about that. I . . . we have to get Brandon down from here."

The angst in her voice was a bitter mix of remorse and resolve. *Get him down?* Did that mean he was still alive? He hoped so.

"What did you mean, 'Brandon was taken'?"

A choking sob preceded her answer. "He's gone. He's—he's dead . . . but . . ."

But what? How was there more to being dead? He waited, but nothing more was offered. "I'm sorry to hear that. All right. We'll just take things one step at a time. Can you lower him down with your gear?"

"No. It's—I need—I—I can't. It's too fragile."

It's too fragile? Julia wasn't making sense. She sounded close to losing control—a state Felipe thought he'd never hear in her. Better to just help her and stop asking for specifics.

"Okay. Why don't you come down first? We can discuss the situation without yelling back and forth, and—"

"No!" she snapped. "I—I can't leave him like this. I won't."

There was no changing a tone like that. "Okay then. Secure the ropes. I'm coming up. No arguments."

The climbing ropes remained motionless at first. Then, little by little, they jostled and bobbed a few inches.

"Julia?"

"Go get your mask while I make sure these will hold. Get some gloves too."

"You sure? It'll take me an hour to get there and back."

"Please. It'll be much safer for you. Oh, and don't go in the lab. You got that, Felipe? Do *not* go into the lab!"

Too late. "Copy that," he said with little enthusiasm.

Returning to his helicopter took about forty minutes. He grabbed a climbing harness in addition to his mask and gloves. Pausing, he considered taking one other piece of equipment—the plastic body bag. If Dr. Udy was dead, they'd have to put him in *something*. Stuffing the bag into his pack, he jogged back to the kapok.

By the time he got there, darkness encroached throughout the understory. Clouds were forming again. The ropes hung motionless. He tugged on them, making sure they were secured.

"Julia? I'm back. Are you still okay?" he called, struggling to catch his breath.

"Yes."

"Great. I'm coming up now."

"Are . . . are you sure you want to?" Her voice was distant, unsure.

"I am."

"Do you have a mask and gloves?"

"Yep."

"Okay. Come up. But be ready."

"Ready . . . for what?" he asked, hedging.

"Something horrible. I hope you have a strong stomach."

CHAPTER 11

FELIPE CLIMBED SLOWLY. HIS ENERGY was drained, but his sense of urgency kept him going. The higher he got, the weaker he felt. He hoped it was from exhaustion and not from whatever he may have inhaled in the lab. The thorns of the kapok were smaller higher up but were just as bothersome. By the time he was directly below the two researchers, his gloves were matted with blood—whether Brandon's or Julia's or even his own, he didn't know.

Julia sat motionless across from Brandon, her head bowed, her shoulders slack. Her eyes, puffy and red from crying, had a hollow, vacant stare. Her paper lab mask was stained dark with moisture, her blonde hair a tangled mess.

"Hey, Julia," he said, pausing to catch his breath. "Sorry it took so long to get here. You still okay?"

She looked at Felipe with an expression of total loss—and then anger.

"Stop! What do you think you're doing?" she snapped. "Don't be a dolt. Put your mask on this instant!"

Felipe's gas mask dangled behind his neck. "Oh, right," he said, slipping it on. "It's hard to breathe in this thing. There. Can you hear me okay?"

Nodding, a tear trickled down her cheek. "Please. Don't come any closer."

From where he sat, he could see that Brandon was covered with dried blood, but he saw no open wounds or cuts. He couldn't see the doctor's face.

"Can you tell me what's going on? Are you certain Dr. Udy is . . . is gone?"

"Yes." Her tone was weak, filled with surrender.

"Do you know how he died?"

"I do."

Felipe adjusted his position, removed his gloves, and shook out his hands. His forearms burned from the climb. "You said he was *taken*?"

"Yes. Infected. So put those gloves back on."

He did. "Infected with what?"

"A fungus. It took over his brain."

Took over his brain? "Oh. I'm so sorry."

She nodded an acceptance. After a minute, she again looked down at Felipe, as if just noticing he was there. "You're a mess."

He looked over his filthy, rumpled clothes and shrugged. "I slipped in the mud, but it's okay. Another storm comes, and I'll be clean again."

She gave a weighty sigh and smiled. "Thank you."

"What for? I haven't done anything yet."

"You came."

A twinge of guilt clenched at his chest. "Yeah—too late. I should have come last night."

"No," she said, returning her gaze to Dr. Udy's motionless body. "It wouldn't have mattered."

"Still . . ." He kept his tone gentle but loud enough to be heard through his mask. "How can I help get him down?"

Again, there was no answer. He knew she'd heard him, so he waited patiently. Julia's previous comment still puzzled him . . . and sent a chill along his spine. *A fungus took over his brain.* How could she tell? Did he have some kind of rash? Was there blood coming from his ears, his nose? How did she know it was a fungus and not something else?

Felipe leaned to one side for a better angle. Dr. Udy's face remained hidden by his body and the trunk of the tree, but it looked like he was biting on a branch.

Julia sighed with despondent surrender. "I guess there's no reason to delay it," she said, unfastening her harness.

"Wait. I brought an extra," Felipe said, shifting his pack from his back. "Just in case."

Julia managed a smile. "Brilliant. I'm glad one of us is thinking straight. Thanks, Felipe."

Rising cautiously to his feet, he passed the gear up to her.

"You'll have to climb around the other side to help secure him. Try not to touch his skin," she warned, even though he was still wearing gloves.

"Okay." Felipe didn't like dead bodies. He'd extracted victims who'd had accidents—falling from trees, drowning, and such—but he'd never air-lifted a person that had his *brain taken over by a fungus*. Again, he wondered how she knew. "So, is it okay to touch his clothes?"

"Can't be 100 percent sure, I'm afraid." She paused, closed her eyes, and exhaled heavily. "The vector could be anything. So . . . if you don't want to help, I understand."

"No, no, I want to help. I'm just confused, is all. I, um . . . I'm not much of a scientist, I'm afraid." He hated feeling ignorant, but he couldn't begin to understand the depth of this biology. "What's a vector?"

Julia offered a weak smile. "Sorry, mate. I'm just whacked. A vector is anything that transmits the fungal spores—clothing, skin, fur, feathers, body fluids, even the wind."

"I see," he said, moving to a higher branch, closer to Brandon's body. "Okay, so how are we going to—" Felipe's voice gagged in his throat. His stomach convulsed as he fought the urge to vomit. His grip faltered, and he thrashed about, wildly scrambling for a hold.

"Careful!" Julia cried.

Shakily securing his position, he closed his eyes and mumbled a fervent prayer in Spanish, crossing himself twice. The impulse to throw up was almost overpowering.

"Shhh. It's all right, Felipe," Julia said softly. "Try not to jostle him. You might break the stroma."

Felipe swallowed hard and breathed deeply through his mouth, trying to mute the scream and the bile threatening to erupt from his throat. He had no idea what a stroma was, but he guessed it must be the hideous, glistening, mottled protuberance growing from the nape of Dr. Udy's neck.

CHAPTER 12

It took a full ten minutes before Felipe felt like his stomach wasn't going to lurch past his tonsils. Julia sat patiently, staring off in the distance. She looked physically drained. Her emotions were probably not far behind. Felipe guessed she'd already gone through the shock he now felt.

"*¡Santísima—María!*" he gasped, still swallowing against a gag reflex. "What is that thing?"

Julia spoke in a voice devoid of emotion. "Technically, it's a sporangiophore, a reproductive growth from the fungus."

"A fungus? You mean like a mushroom?"

"Yeah. I'm guessing it's a cordyceps fungus, but I'm still not positive." She shook her head. "If it's what I'm thinking, I've never heard of one infecting a human . . . at least not like this."

The hideous thing rising from Dr. Udy's collar stood about four inches perpendicular to his neck. It was cylindrical, roughly an inch in diameter, and rubbery-looking. Its skin was a sickly beige color, mottled with blotches of green and black. It was glossy, not from rain or mist, but from mucus glistening along its surface. With consummate pity, Felipe was glad that Dr. Udy *was* dead.

"What did you call that—that tube thing?"

"A sporangiophore. It's like the stamen on a flower. In mycology, we call it a stroma."

That didn't help. "Is it dangerous?"

"No, not usually. Not at this stage anyway. Look, Felipe," she said with resignation. "I'll explain it all when I know more. Let's just get him back to the lab, all right?"

"Right, right," Felipe said apologetically. "Sorry. So what do we do now?"

"We need to unwrap him from the trunk." Julia gently tugged at Brandon's rigid arms. His fingers were interlaced around the tree in a death grip. "If this stiffness were simple rigor mortis, then, depending on the actual time of passing, we should be able to move him in a few hours. But if it's caused by the fungus then . . . I really don't know."

"Why is he biting a branch?"

"Again, I don't know."

Bolstering himself, Felipe quickly assessed the situation, trying desperately to ignore the growth on Brandon's neck. He tugged a few times on the man's arms with no success. "Okay, so his arms are too stiff to bend. Do you have a saw in camp?"

Julia frowned at him.

"The branches. We could cut the branches and lift him away."

"Ah. Brilliant. But we have to be extra vigilant so as not to break the stroma. Like I said, I have no idea how this thing's spores are vectored."

"What if it *is* airborne?"

She offered a small smile. It looked forced. "No worries. You're wearing your mask. Besides, this one hasn't developed a sporangium. That's the sac that forms on top of the stroma and releases the spores. Since there isn't one, you can't have inhaled any."

Felipe swallowed hard. "And if I already have?"

Her smile dropped. "When?"

"I, um . . . I'd already been inside the lab, looking for you."

Her shoulders slumped. Her look of dismay deepened. "Did you touch anything?"

"Just the door. Both sides."

She thought for a moment. "Right. Just don't go back inside. You may be fine. There's no telling if this was even caused by something in the lab. He could have contracted it in the field."

Felipe exhaled hard, wishing he could find comfort in her guesses.

Julia continued, "There's a handsaw in the storage shed. Brandon may have touched the equipment in there after being infected, so use gloves at all times."

"What about you? Aren't you worried about being infected?"

"It's . . . too late for me," she said, failing in her attempt to keep a fatalistic tone from her voice.

Felipe didn't want to accept her defeatism. He'd learned in situations such as this that a positive attitude is often the difference between life and death. "It's never too late, Doctor."

"Yes, I'm afraid it is. I've most likely inhaled the spores in the lab or in the field . . . or whenever *he* came in contact with them. I've been with him nearly 24-7. I have no idea how long he's been carrying this . . . parasite. But it's a good chance that if Brandon was infected . . ." Her words trailed off, but the conclusion was obvious. She reached out and gently touched her former partner's stiff shoulder.

Felipe continued to keep his eyes on Julia and away from the dead man . . . and the thing growing on the dead man's neck.

"Okay. You stay put," he said. "Don't do anything until I get back."

She didn't respond. Her eyes were again distant, unfocused as she continued to stare blankly at Brandon's infected corpse.

Rather than waiting for a reply, Felipe slid down the ropes to the rain forest floor. Thunder rumbled deeply, threatening their brief stint of clear weather. Heading away from the kapok, he prayed the next rain would wait until they got the body inside.

Before looking for the handsaw, Felipe headed to his helicopter and switched on the radio. "La Esmeralda Airport, this is CIST helo Romeo-Quebec-two-five-niner-six-one, come in."

The static buzz was short-lived. "I still here, amigo. What did you find?" Ricardo Paz responded.

"*Ay Dios*, it's worse than I expected. This is a confirmed Code Red. Repeat, a confirmed Code Red. No one comes in without my say-so. You copy that, Paz?"

"Wow. *Sí*, I copy."

"I'm gonna see what I can do here. Stay by your radio. This may take a while."

"Okay sure, but, *¿qué pasó?* How bad is it?"

"Dr. Udy is dead. He's . . . he's . . ."

"He's what?" Ricardo pressed.

Felipe didn't know. He'd already forgotten most of what Julia had explained—other than she had no idea how the thing was spread. "I don't know, man. He's definitely infected with a fungus of some kind. Dr. Fatheringham is still looking into it. But it's bad, amigo."

"And what about the *bonita* doctor?"

"So far she's fine, just tired. I'll keep you posted. Stay by your radio."

"No *hay problema*, amigo. La Esmeralda out."

Returning to the camp with the evac stretcher, Felipe went straight to the small storage shed. An assortment of tools dangled from pegs; a few other items, including a one-man kayak, leaned against an inner wall. The handsaw hung directly in front of him, as did two coils of nylon rope. Filling his pack with as much as it could hold, he tried to keep his mind focused on helping Julia, but the image of the glossy fungus growing on Brandon's neck dominated his mind. Julia said the fungus was highly infective and definitely fatal. So . . . was *he* infected?

Don't go there, Felipe. Stay focused.

Dusk had arrived by the time he made it back to the kapok. He forced himself to stay calm. He was Julia's only chance of survival. Even though she'd said it was too late for her, at least she was still alive. For how long was anyone's guess. But it was better to be proactive than to simply sit around waiting to die.

Leaving the stretcher at the base of the tree, he hooked on and began to climb. It seemed the ultimate irony that, while he was climbing toward the heavens, he felt like he was crawling down to hell.

CHAPTER 13

RICARDO PAZ WAS A SIMPLE man. He only had the equivalent of an elementary grade education, but he was life-smart. He'd experienced a lot in his thirty-six years, and it had aged him considerably. While he loved learning new things, he loved to gossip about those things even more. It didn't matter if it was news of a new mango salsa recipe or the latest dirt from the local shaman's wife. Paz was the hub of all information in the area, and he did his best to pass on every juicy tidbit.

Born and raised in La Esmeralda, he'd earned the job of airport controller because he could speak English better than most others in the region and because he had a basic understanding of electronics. Yet, even though La Esmeralda was the capital of Alto Orinoco in Amazonas State, it was still a fairly small settlement. It contained only about a hundred homes, a school, a clinic, and the airstrip. Certainly nothing to get excited about.

That's why news of this nature put him on the edge of his seat. He'd heard Felipe sound nervous before but never like this. Felipe's voice was filled with . . . well, terror. The controller wondered if he should call for help. Had Felipe radioed Caicara yet? Would they send help? Felipe hadn't *requested* assistance yet, but if one person was already dead . . .

He decided to take the first step. "CIST HQ, this is La Esmeralda Airport. Come in."

Waiting impatiently for a response, his mind began to fill with portents . . . and opportunities. He repeated his call. "CIST HQ, this is La Esmeralda Airport. Come in, please!"

"I hear you loud and clear, Ricky. What's up?"

It was Meghan. She was even worse than Paz when it came to using improper radio technique, but her informalities were from ignorance and apathy, not excessive friendliness. She always came across as bitter and agitated, like someone had put red ants in her pants. She was never fun to talk with, but that didn't really matter to Paz. They had met once, and he'd been in lust ever since.

"Hola, Meghan. Hey, I got some bad news. We have a situation here."

Her response was preceded by a disgruntled huff. "What situation?"

"Felipe is at Ascom base. He say Dr. Udy is dead."

Another pause. "And the bad news?"

Paz couldn't believe his ears. Did she really just say that? Perhaps he had misunderstood.

"I repeat: Dr. Udy is dead. Do you copy?"

"I heard you the first time, Ricky. Did the rain forest get him, or did his subordinate kangaroo finally take the crown for herself?"

Paz stared slack-jawed at the radio. For someone so pretty, Meghan sure did have a cold heart. "I, um, I don't know. Felipe has not given any detail. I just want to alert you to the emergency situation. This is a confirmed Code Red."

"So you said. I'll get a *piñata* ready. Do we want balloons too?"

Now he was frowning. "A good man is dead, Meghan. You should show more resp—"

"I'm sorry. Are we still talking about Brandon Udy? Because I thought you said a 'good' man."

Paz took a deep breath. "*Cuidado*, señorita. He is with Jesus now, and Jesus is listening always. You never know when the Lord will call you back—"

"Well, if he does, I simply won't answer," she snapped. "Now, is there anything else? I need to run into town for some supplies before it gets too dark."

His frown deepened. "Is there someone else to run the radio?"

"If anyone happens to be here when someone calls, I guess."

"But . . . is that not your job when Felipe is away?"

"Sometimes. I don't have my contract in front of me, so I'll have to get back to you on that. Adios and out."

The click and following hiss echoed in the small control room at La Esmeralda Airport. Ricardo sat for nearly a minute before he realized his mouth was still open. Was she joking? He knew she didn't like tourists roaming through the rain forest. She liked researchers even less. But this was a man's life they were discussing!

Ricardo had heard many stories about Meghan from Felipe. Some of her beliefs were *muy loco*. Worse, she was spoiled and shallow and loved complaining about, well, everything. She came from a wealthy family. She could go anywhere and do anything she wanted. So why was she spending time at the CIST in the middle of Venezuela? Felipe said a big university had sent her, but he also had his doubts about that. And about her honesty.

Turning to his desk, he wrote a quick note. Something didn't feel right—and yet, it also presented a window of opportunity. And Felipe was right in the middle of it. He sealed the note in an envelope and stepped outside. A group of children always played near the airport. The cement runway was the best place to ride bicycles. Because there was so little air traffic, he let them ride as much as they liked. Calling to a boy of about thirteen, he handed him the envelope.

"Raoul. Take this to Marco in El Desvío," he told the boy.

The boy hesitated. "It will be dark soon."

"You can stay with your cousin there and return tomorrow."

Raoul look at his feet. "But . . . but Marco frightens me."

"He frightens everyone, but he is harmless. I tell you what. Take this letter to him, be quick and tell no one, and when you get back, I'll give you a hundred *bolívares*."

Raoul beamed. "Okay. Thanks."

"Excellent. Now off you go!" he said, clapping his hands in encouragement.

CHAPTER 14

JULIA RIGGED A BASIC PULLEY system with Felipe's equipment before sawing away the branches Brandon clung to. While trying to show the utmost respect for her deceased partner, it was hard to keep personal feelings from breaching her resolve to remain focused. That was especially difficult when removing the branch from his mouth. She took extra care not to disturb the stroma growing on Brandon's neck. It was the key to everything.

She abseiled in tandem with Brandon as Felipe lowered him from above. Once on the ground, she unfastened the equipment and sent it back up.

Night had settled in the understory. Sitting at Brandon's side, Julia used her torch to examine the parasite. It didn't look precariously delicate, but you could never be sure with fungi. Carrying Brandon back to the tent without jostling him too much would be a challenge. It might actually help that his body was still quite rigid; it'd be less awkward. But she wondered why he was so stiff. It didn't follow standard biochemistry. In typical conditions, rigor mortis lasted about thirty hours from beginning to end. But when someone dies after intense physical activity—such as climbing a 150-foot kapok—the process is accelerated. Take into account the high temperature of the rain forest, and Brandon's rigor should have loosened hours ago. But it hadn't. It was just one of a hundred questions she needed to answer.

And the questions kept coming.

Closing her eyes, she self-consciously rubbed the back of her neck. She felt nothing odd there, but that didn't stop her hands from trembling. Her body ached from crown to heel. Her throat was raw. Cradling her throbbing head between her palms, she fought the tears threatening to resurface. She thought she'd used them up last night. How many tears could the human body produce, anyway? She couldn't remember. It'd been so long since she'd felt so physically drained, so emotionally battered. The last time was at her parents' funeral. She was only eleven.

Julia Fatheringham had grown up in Capalaba, just outside of Brisbane. A tomboy from the start, she spent most of her childhood exploring the creeks, billabongs, and shorelines in that area of Queensland. She'd had a wonderful childhood . . . until *it* happened. She vividly remembered coming home from school one day to find two police cars and her poppy's Jeep in her driveway. Poppy Fatheringham held her tightly as he explained that her mum and pop had been killed in a traffic accident. A truck driver high on hallucinogenic mushrooms had broadsided them at a highway intersection. The depth of shock was more than she could bear. Being an only child, she'd been very close to her parents. They both worked long hours so they could live in neighborhoods with higher-ranked schools. They continually encouraged her to rise above their blue-collar status through education and good grades. Early on, she'd developed an insatiable thirst for learning. But when they were suddenly taken, it was as if all their encouragement had been for naught. *Their* hard work had gotten *them* nothing. Emotionally, she closed up, shut down, and withdrew from everything and everyone. No kid should have to go through what she did.

Because her grandpoppy was the closest living relative, social services granted him custody. Julia moved to her poppy's modest home in Frog Tree Pocket, a remote, quiet suburb of Brisbane. Her poppy took charge of selling her parents' house and belongings, settling with the trucker's insurance, and establishing a trust fund for her.

It took a full year of counseling and gentle persuasion to pierce the defensive shell that had formed over her heart. Her poppy continued her parents' wishes, saying the best way to honor their memory was to excel in all she did. One of his oft-quoted aphorisms was, "Don't wait for opportunity's door to open; grab the knob and open it yourself." And she did just that.

With his love and encouragement, she rapidly progressed through the Australian education system, graduating a full term ahead of her class in spite of her time off. Granted a full scholarship to the University of Queensland in St. Lucia, she was able to attend college while still living with her grandfather.

Then, shortly after she accepted her master's diploma, her poppy passed away. He'd been growing steadily weaker; it wasn't a big shock. Gratefully, he'd died peacefully in the night. After his funeral, she decided to get away from Australia for a time. She'd had enough of death and sorrow. In going through Poppy's files, she discovered that the trust fund he'd established was huge. She could have easily lived off the interest alone. Instead, she applied for the doctorate program at Emory University in Atlanta. It took only one month before she was accepted. Her first, second, and third years had been a breeze, full of discovery and excitement. Her fourth year had started even better. It had all been very healing.

Until now.

Julia opened her eyes and looked at the peaceful half-smile on Brandon's face. Why did God feel it necessary to take away everyone she cared for? It wasn't fair. She'd lived a life of learning and sharing. She helped others when she could. She'd cared for her poppy during his final days on earth. There had to be an explanation for the injustice—just as there had to be an explanation for Brandon's strange infection. The coincidence was not lost on her. She'd lost her partner to the effects of a mushroom, just as she had her parents.

She shook her head, as if trying to force the negativity from her mind. *Stay focused. Stay positive. You can do this.*

Willing her scientific mind to take charge again, she bent to examine the fungus more closely. Of primary concern was its virulence. It had yet to form a sporangium, but the one in the lab clearly had. Was she infected? Was Felipe? If so, how long did they have to live?

"I'm coming down now," Felipe called from the darkness above.

"Oy, don't drop a stone in the dunny," she called back with forced cheeriness.

"What?"

"Don't land so hard you make a mess of things," she explained.

"Oh, right. I'll try not to."

Looking back at Brandon, she didn't voice, *And don't land on my infected mate.*

CHAPTER 15

ALL OF FELIPE'S TRAINING AND experience didn't help ease the shock of what was happening. It was like something out of a horror movie. He'd seen his share of injured people and even a few dead bodies. He'd set broken limbs and cleaned festering sores. He didn't enjoy any of it, but it'd become part of his job. This, however, was unthinkable.

Not wanting to show a lack of machismo in front of Julia, he kept busy winding up rope, packing gear—anything to keep his fear in check. But carrying an infected corpse through a dark forest rife with quivering shadows and worrisome noises created its own level of fright. They lifted the body onto the stretcher and headed back. The short trip seemed to take forever.

Finally reaching the lab, Felipe took a moment to collect his nerves as Julia cleared off the center table. Dr. Udy's body lay on the floor. Felipe tried not to look at it, but his eyes kept drifting down to the horrible pale thing attached to his neck. It actually looked bigger now, like it had already grown another centimeter. Felipe closed his eyes and made the sign of the cross on his chest. ¡Ave San Pedro!

"Right. Let's do this," Julia said in a clipped voice.

They lifted the body to the table and positioned it on its side. The corpse's back was to Felipe, bringing the repulsive growth much closer to him. He took two steps back and vigorously wiped his hands on his shirt—even though he was still wearing gloves.

"There's hand sanitizer by the sink," Julia said, nodding in that direction. "You might want to use it after you wash up."

Moving to the sink, Felipe removed his mask, washed his face and hands, then slathered his hands and forearms with the alcohol-based gel. Once cleaned, he replaced the mask. Julia followed suit, replacing her soggy mask with a fresh one and donning some latex gloves.

"Right," she said, reaching for a pair of scissors. "Let's remove his shirt to get a better look at this."

Felipe tugged on his ear. "I'm not sure I want a better look."

"It's gotta be done, Felipe," she said, carefully lifting Brandon's shirttail. Peeking underneath, she said, "Nothing seems to be attached. Brilliant. Let's do this."

Cutting slowly, she started at the shirt's hem and sliced up to the collar. When the fungus was fully exposed, Felipe saw that it didn't grow *on* the nape of Brandon's neck; it grew *from* it. The disgusting thing had erupted *through* his skin, leaving a thin crust of blood at its base. No longer able to suppress the caustic roiling in his gut, he stumbled to the sink, ripped off his mask, and threw up.

"You okay there, mate?" Julia said without looking up.

He rinsed his mouth with some water before replacing his mask. "Yeah, sort of. So . . . what's next?" he asked, studiously averting his gaze.

"I probably should classify this specimen," she stated, not sounding very sure. "Brandon was examining a cordyceps just before he . . ." She didn't finish her thought.

"Is that what this is? A cordyceps?"

She shook her head. "I'm not sure. Maybe. Look, you can stay and assist if you like, but I think it best if you let me handle it. No need to risk both our lives."

Grateful for the reprieve, he nodded. "Okay. I'll take the stretcher outside."

"Brilliant."

The nearly cloudless sky allowed a blanket of stars to illuminate the clearing. The moon had not yet risen, but there was enough ambient light to see without a flashlight. Felipe removed his gas mask and sucked in lungfuls of air, expelling each with forced velocity, hoping to eject whatever bug might have invaded his system. The fresh, moist air felt great, but his stomach still churned. Part of him wanted to fire up his colibrí and fly away as fast as possible, but another part wanted to stay and help. It was more than his job; he wanted to help *her*. There was no denying his attraction to her. But he doubted she'd ever give someone like him a second glance. Perhaps if he could somehow prove himself indispensable . . .

Leaning the stretcher next to the doorway, he peeked through one of the screened windows. Julia was at the dissection scope, studying the sample with the red biohazard tag on it. He watched her use a scalpel to slice through the rubbery-looking fungus. She seemed to have nerves of steel. So did he—when it came to flying. But stuff like this scared the crap out of him. He wished he had the courage to stay in the lab with her. He wished he had the confidence to be more than just a government liaison to her. *Oye! Don't be a coward*, he scolded himself. *Show her what you're made of.*

Donning his mask, he stepped back inside. "I'm going to update the CIST from the helo. Is there anything specific I should request?"

"A miracle," she said, keeping her eyes glued to the scope.

"You got it. Oh, and I'll try not to drop the toilet on the patio . . . ?" he said in an awkward attempt at levity.

"Don't drop the dunny on the deck," she clarified.

"Oh, right."

"Oy, be a chum and switch on the coffee pot first, would you please?"

"Sure."

Felipe moved to the kitchenette and toggled the coffeemaker's switch to ON. As he was leaving, he glanced at Brandon's corpse. Julia had cleaned the area around the growth, making its eruption look even more revolting than before. The fungus glistened under an overhead work lamp, its pale, mottled skin looking like mold growing on old meat. Thin mucus pooled underneath it.

Feeling his nausea rise again, Felipe turned to leave—then recoiled. He stumbled back with a gasp. A hideous reddish bulb began sprouting from the tip of the stroma. He could actually see it growing!

CHAPTER 16

"*¡AY DIOS!*" FELIPE SWORE SHARPLY.

"What's wrong?" Julia asked, still looking through the microscope.

"It's moving!"

"What's moving?"

"The fungus."

She huffed and looked up. "Not likely, mate. It's not a myxomycete."

He frowned at her.

"Sorry. A myxomycete is a slime mold," she clarified. "They're the only molds capable of controlled locomotion."

Felipe pointed; his finger trembled. "Okay, maybe not moving, but it's growing. Look at the tip."

Julia stood and moved to Brandon's body. Sure enough, the end of the stroma had split and was now developing a full-fledged sporangium cap.

"Crikey," she whispered. "I've never seen a fungus grow so quickly. That's unbelievable."

The sporangium ended up being roughly the size of a lime, only reddish-brown in color, very porous, and smelling more like rotten meat than citrus.

Felipe was visibly shaken. "I'm going to start the helo. We're getting out of here, now."

Julia turned to him. "We can't do that, Felipe; not until I can figure this out. We're quarantined. Like I said, no one in or out."

Felipe firmly stood his ground. His hand shifted to his sidearm. "Dr. Fatheringham, I came here to get you out, not solve a mystery."

Julia took a step back. She didn't know why he had a gun in the first place. She had no idea what kind of gun it was, but she had little doubt it was loaded. This situation was already tenuous; bringing a gun into play would only make things worse.

She'd known Felipe for about a year now, but most of their interactions had been via the radio. They'd only met a couple of times. He'd always been professional in their dealings, having a stringent attitude for policy and procedure. He encouraged the discovery of new things in "his" rainforests. He said it was good for his country and good for science. She'd never guess he'd resort to violence.

"Listen, Felipe," she said steadily. "I truly appreciate you coming out here. It was a big risk, I know, and it's completely my fault you're in this mess. But we can't risk spreading this to others. So until I get a better handle on it, we both need to remain calm."

He remained frozen, his eyes glazed with anger and fear.

"Think about it, mate. What if something this deadly *did* get out into the public? What if this infection spread to a city the size of Caracas? Think of the devastation it could cause. And the panic. And what if some infected bloke carried it out of Venezuela into international territories?"

Wide-eyed, Felipe looked again at Brandon's lifeless form and swallowed hard. "Yeah, that *would* be bad."

"It would be catastrophic," she affirmed with a hollow tone.

After a long pause, he dropped onto a folding chair without drawing his sidearm. "But . . . what if I'm infected?" he asked his empty hands. "I was in here without a mask."

"Oy—don't think that doesn't cross my mind every three seconds," she said, pulling a chair next to his. "Look, here's what I think. Your exposure has been minimal. It's unlikely you have anything to worry about."

"But you're not certain."

"No. Not certain. From what I've seen so far, Brandon collected an ascomycete that somehow crossed species. I don't know how he was infected—" She paused to steady her suddenly shaky voice. "But I believe it's only recently been growing in him."

"How do you know that?"

"Well, for one thing how fast it's grown. See, most fungi grow a network of mycelia—kind of tiny roots growing under the surface—before sprouting a fruiting body."

"So that *thing* is spread *inside* his body?"

"Yes. I don't know how extensively, but it apparently got into his brain."

Felipe's eyes registered renewed horror. "Why would he want to study such a thing? Is it worth a lot of money?"

"I haven't a clue."

"Could someone hurt others with this, like they've done with anthrax?"

She frowned, wondering why she hadn't considered that possibility. She was certain Brandon wouldn't have entertained such nonsense.

"Could it be in my brain?" Felipe continued in a tentative whisper.

She offered a soft smile. "Not likely," she hedged. "Look, mate, I've had significantly more exposure than you, and I feel fine."

"Yeah, but you look terrible."

She smirked. "Thanks a lot," she said, punching him in the shoulder.

He grinned then took a deep breath and let it out slowly. She leaned over and took him in a firm hug. She felt him stiffen in surprise and could almost feel the blush rise in his neck and face. It made her smile.

Straightening, she said, "Do me a favor. Take the torch and have a lookabout outside. Look for anything like plants or fungi samples lying about. Also, fill up the generator with petrol if you would. I have a feeling I'll be up late into the night with this."

"And . . . that?" he asked, nodding at Brandon's corpse.

She turned to her former partner and wrapped her arms around herself as if warding off a chill. "This is what he'd want me to do. This is what he'd do were the situation reversed. Go ahead and radio a message to the CIST and have Meghan forward it to the US consulate. Brandon had family that should be told."

Felipe nodded and exited the tent.

Tuning up the radio in his colibrí, he dialed in the needed frequency. "CIST HQ, this is CIST helo. Come in." He glanced at his watch. It was almost ten thirty. Surely a night owl like Meghan would be awake. He scowled. If she was, she'd probably be at some club in Caracas. "CIST HQ, this is CIST helo at Ascom base. Come in, please."

The scratchy, monotonous tone gave nothing in reply.

Felipe cleared his throat. "CIST HQ, this is Felipe Pascal at Ascom base, transmitting with the hope that this is being recorded. I have an update on Ascom's mayday situation. Yesterday's Code Red is confirmed. I repeat, the Code Red is confirmed. I am officially declaring Ascom base a biohazard hot zone. An immediate and complete quarantine is in effect. So far we have one fatality attributed to an infective agent of unknown origin. Dr. Brandon Udy is dead. A parasitic fungus infected his nervous system. Dr. Fatheringham thinks it's a cordyceps fungus, but she hasn't confirmed that yet. Route of infection: unknown. Virulence: unknown. Please immediately advise US consulate of the event. That is all for now. CIST helo transmitting from Ascom base, out."

Julia took a few moments to compose herself after Felipe left. She had no idea how infective this fungus truly was, but until she could examine it in-depth, she had to assume the worst. The trouble was, they were dangerously ill-equipped to study such an obviously lethal organism. What she needed was a BSL-4 lab, a bio-safety facility with highly filtered ventilation systems, ultraviolet and chemical decontamination systems, an autoclave and incinerator, and a self-closing, self-locking, double-door entry-exit. What *they* had was a titch above a BSL-1 facility, not much more than your average college biology lab.

Julia downed a bottle of water without pause, both out of thirst and frustration. If the fungus was airborne, it was too late for advanced BSL protocol anyway. Still, that didn't mean they couldn't warn others. She just hoped that Meghan would forward Felipe's message.

CHAPTER 17

MEGHAN LISTENED TO THE MESSAGE with a grin running ear to ear. She loved the panicked tone in Felipe's voice. She loved the danger potential in the message. She loved that she was the only one who would ever hear it. Pushing a few keys, she erased the new message and then permanently deleted the recycle file.

The message was exactly what she'd been waiting for. It was the reason she'd come here in the first place. After she'd returned from her European excursion, she'd seen a program on the History Channel about mushroom hunters. The program highlighted everything from chanterelles and truffles to morels and magic mushrooms. However, the one that caught her attention was a cordyceps—what the narrator called the "caterpillar fungus." He said in the last decade, the price of cordyceps had risen more than 900 percent. In the mountains of Nepal, some cordyceps hunters were known to sell their harvest at $1,000 an ounce. The Nepalese ate the fungus for its near-miraculous health properties. So did many other Asian cultures. She'd also seen programs about the countless species of fungi in the Amazon rain forest. Putting two and two together, she knew she could cash in on the fungal treasure trove if she just kept her ear to the ground—or, in this case, the radio.

Sneering, she thought, *Dr. Fungus must not have cooked his fungus enough. Oh well. Served him right.* Frankly, she didn't care what any buyer did with the fungus—as long as she was able to secretly cash in on the profits. And since this one was extra deadly, it must mean it was extra strong. And *that* meant it was potentially a gold mine. She could get out of this miserable country within days!

Quickly freshening up, she slipped on a pair of snug shorts and a low-cut tee, and drove to the local police station. She chose the skimpy outfit not only because it was still hot and muggy outside—even at ten thirty in the evening—but because she had a particular rendezvous in mind.

She pulled into a slot at the Caicara municipal building and quickly stepped through the door marked *La Policía*.

"*Buenas noches*, Señorita Muir," the young man behind the counter said with a disarming smile. His name was Carlos de la Montoya. He was in his early twenties, a rookie police officer and a local soccer star, tall, dark haired, and dreamy eyed. A definite hottie at any time of day, in his well-fitting uniform, he was totally gorgeous.

Slinking up to him, Meghan said, "Hi, Carlos." She leaned over the counter, smiling when his eyes flitted to her cleavage. "Say, sweetie, I really need to send my mom a message. Can I use the Internet again, pleeeease?"

Carlos folded his arms. "Señorita Muir. You know I not supposed to do that."

He had the cutest accent too.

"Please, baby? It's very important." She glanced around, just to confirm they were alone. "Momma gets so worried when I don't check in every day, and I forgot to do it this afternoon."

He'd let her use their service before. The official stance at the municipal building—in particular the police department—was that their Internet was for official government use only. No exceptions. To make sure no one abused the policy, they changed the password each week. Carlos was Meghan's way around that safeguard.

Skirting the small counter, Meghan sat on his desk, making sure her leg pressed against his. She took his hand in both of hers. "It'll only take a minute, sweetie. Just a quick message to let her know I'm okay. I'm not getting any reception on my stupid cell phone."

"The CIST has no Internet?"

Using her index finger, she traced a random pattern along the back of his hand. "Of course it does, silly. But that mean old Felipe won't let me send personal messages. He monitors *everything*. I have no privacy at all. It really sucks."

The young officer tapped a key on his terminal, deactivating the CCTV in the room, then stood and slipped his hands around her waist. "And after?"

She smiled coyly. "I'm free all night."

"*Bueno.*"

When he began kissing her neck, she gently pushed away. "The password?"

With a plaintive sigh Carlos plopped into his chair and logged onto the Internet. He then moved to the door to watch for anyone coming their way.

Meghan accessed a private e-mail account, *MM@stp.org: Meghan Muir @ Save the Planet.* She grinned at her cleverness. Muir wasn't her real surname. She'd taken the title in homage to John Muir, one of America's first great environmentalists. Even though most people referred to John Muir as a "conservationist," Meghan was confident that, given the opportunity, he would have embraced the extreme environmentalism championed by her organization.

Her message read:

New material found. Code Red potential confirmed. Very hopeful.

She reread her message and clucked her tongue in satisfaction. Wishing she had more details to offer, she embellished her message with a few false leads.

Highly infective organic organism. Fully bio-compatible. Twenty confirmed deaths. More expected. Confident this is something very valuable.

She was good at padding the truth.

Meghan wanted to make a difference in the world. She wanted her name and face posted on the heroes board of all the big environmentalist movements, perhaps even on the cover of the Sierra Club magazine. She was very photogenic, after all. Her cosmetic surgeon had made sure of that. Notoriety, fame, and glory were destined to be hers. Move over Gore, DiCaprio, and Redford. *She* would save the planet! If she had to do some things that were repugnant—like spending time in this godforsaken country or stooping to private "interviews" with men of influence and wealth—then so be it. She'd done so before. Men were so easy to manipulate. Granted, it hadn't been much fun . . . until now. Her interactions with Carlos seemed more of a fringe benefit than a manipulation. He was so dang hot! But she'd gotten careless in Switzerland. This e-mail wasn't so much about getting famous; it was about money.

She added one more request then pressed Send.

Before logging off she decided to check her CIST e-mail. A new message from Ricardo Paz awaited.

Can't reach you by radio or phone. Felipe said to stay available. Info coming any minute. It sounds bad.

She issued a nasally, "Whah, whah, whah," and typed: Back in a minute. Don't get your tacos in a twist.

Meghan closed her links and stood. "All done here, sweetie, but something's just come up. I gotta run."

Carlos returned from the door and glanced at his watch. "I am off in one hour," he said with a hopeful glint in his eyes.

"Oh, baby, I'm so sorry. Turns out I gotta get back to the office," she said, running her fingers through his dark hair. "Rain check?"

When the look in Carlos's eyes turned angry, she stepped up and kissed him full on the lips, pressing her body against his. Feeling him relax and give in to the embrace, she knew she had won. It always worked.

Meghan exited the building, but she honestly regretted leaving. Carlos was *so* much fun to be with. Still, she didn't want to miss this opportunity to capitalize on Ascom's misfortune. And on her future.

CHAPTER 18

FELIPE WANDERED THE CAMPSITE IN the starlight looking for . . . what? He simply did not know. Julia said to look for plant samples. Well, they were in the middle of primeval, virgin rain forest. There were plant samples everywhere you looked!

He wasn't a scientist or a field researcher—and never planned on being one. The interactions he'd had with them in the past solidified that resolve. Many of the researchers he'd met were condescending; some were downright rude. They looked down on him, treating him as little more than a taxi service. Felipe tried to live the golden rule of "do unto others." If they were disrespectful to him, he gave them minimal help and was brutally stringent on regulations, liberally giving citations and charging exorbitant fines. If they were nice, then he was equally nice, helping above and beyond what was required of him, often turning a blind eye to minor infractions. *Treat others the way you wish to be treated*—that was how his parents had raised him. Regrettably, he found most people to be selfish, uncharitable. And egocentric scientists were among the worst.

Although nearly cloudless, the vacuous sky rumbled with warning. Another storm was closing in. Felipe found a container of petrol in the shed and filled the generator's tank. He picked up scattered debris around the camp and stowed what random articles he could find. By the time he was finished, half of the sky was blocked behind heavy black clouds.

Once again donning his foul-smelling mask, he went back in the tent.

Julia had her head on the table next to the dissection scope. She was fast asleep. He stared for a moment, taking in every aspect of the woman, wondering. Could he ever have a chance with her? She was beautiful and brilliant. He was plain and simple. She was a scientist with an advanced college degree. He was a bush pilot who'd graduated from a community college. He was bilingual, but she could speak science. They were both in good shape, but she was exactly the same height as he. Back in Texas, girls preferred taller men. Back there, a girl like her wouldn't look twice at him. But it was different here; she was different.

He gently brushed a loose strand of hair from her face. She didn't move. In fact, he wasn't sure she was even breathing. A jolt of concern raced through him. The expanding and contracting of her ribcage was almost imperceptible. He held two fingers to her neck to feel for a pulse. It was there, faint but steady. Even though sweat beaded on her forehead and neck, goose bumps covered her arms.

"Julia?" he said softly. When she didn't respond, he gently shook her shoulder. "Dr. Fatheringham? Are you okay?"

She moaned, very softly, as if making the small sound took monumental effort.

Carefully, Felipe leaned her back and lifted her from the chair. He might be short, but he was strong. He carried her to her cot and covered her with a thin cotton sheet. The material would help absorb her sweat and keep the chill from her skin. He wiped her face and neck with a cool washcloth. She breathed steadily and deeply, giving no indication she knew he was there. No doubt she was utterly exhausted, considering all she'd been through.

Felipe secured the mosquito netting around her cot then positioned a fan to gently blow through it. Surrounded by the slowly shifting mosquito net, she looked ethereal, like an angel, like the paintings and statues he'd seen in the cathedrals of Caracas. Even disheveled and grimy, she was beautiful.

Thankfully, the storm outside was a gentle one. The soft patter of rain thwacking against the canvas roof was soothing. He hoped it'd help her sleep. In spite of the adrenaline-rushing events of the past few hours, he felt fatigue getting the better of him. Like Julia, his body craved sleep. But there were still a few things he needed to do.

He found a box of blue paper surgical masks—the kind Julia had on—and switched his respirator for a paper one. He hated the claustrophobic, rubbery stench of his fireman's mask. He figured if Julia was confident using a paper mask, that would be okay for him too.

Powering up Ascom's transmitter, he quietly radioed La Esmeralda Airport. Luckily, Ricardo Paz was still awake.

"*¿Qué tal*, amigo?" Paz answered. "What's happening out there? You okay?"

"Yeah, I'm fine. Dr. Fatheringham is resting now," he said softly. "She seems okay, but she's not sure whether she's infected or not."

"Infected? You mean with the same thing that killed Dr. Udy?"

"Possibly. She's not sure yet."

"Caramba! How long was he sick?"

"Again, she's not sure. It seemed to come on very fast, so not long. I'm letting her rest. As soon as she's able to get back to work, I'll let you know what she uncovers."

"But if he was sick, why did he climb the big tree?"

"I have no idea. Dr. Fatheringham thinks his brain was infected."

"*¡Qué mal!* You want me to send help?"

"Negative, Paz. The quarantine still stands. Do you copy that?"

"Sí. I copy."

"Good. I tried to call Meghan at the CIST earlier, but she didn't respond, so I left a message. We need to notify the American consulate that Dr. Udy is dead from natural causes. I'll send information as I get it. But be sure everyone understands this base is a Code Red quarantine. *Entiendes*, amigo?"

"Sí. No problem."

"Thanks, Paz."

"Be careful, my friend. Do not put your life in danger," Paz said sternly. "Get out as fast as you can. La Esmeralda out."

"Don't put my life in danger?" Felipe repeated softly as he turned off the transmitter. "Too late."

CHAPTER 19

THE INCOMING E-MAIL WAS ENCRYPTED. Mantis ran it through an algorithm on his tablet. It was a simple program, requiring only a couple of button taps. Although he used advanced computer systems and software models at his work, he liked to keep his personal computing simple. Because of his deformity, it made such tasks easier.

The message talked of a wonderful opportunity. The details were uncertain, but the possibilities looked promising. Code Red potential, the message had said. Unknown species. Very deadly. Additional money needed to collect. Cannot progress without it.

Bruja.

Additional money needed? For promising but uncertain details?

How many times had he heard that before? Bruja was a contact he'd obtained through a connection from a fellow sympathizer. Because of the illegal nature of their transactions, Mantis had always kept their identities and correspondence encrypted and untraceable. That limited his exposure, but it also limited his knowledge of Bruja and her activities. Of note, she was always requesting more money, supposedly for materials needed to fulfill her assignments. It was the same old story: tons of input, little to no output.

Mantis hissed in frustration and chewed on his lower lip. He had nothing concrete to offer those in power over him. Not yet, anyway. And that was not a healthy position to be in.

Mantis was a mercenary who specialized in ecotage, a term coined from the word *sabotage*. It was the next generation of ecoterrorism, focusing on punishing those who destroyed the environment for profit. Ecotage subjected select individuals to the worst nature could offer:

Legionella bacterium, anthrax spores, Ebola and Armageddon viruses—his faction had no qualms about using any of it. The organization to whom he'd sworn allegiance was called Green Blade. They were (self-proclaimed) the most insidious.

Mantis scoffed. There were many such organizations, past and present, but they were all so short-sighted, so hypocritical. EarthFirst! drove metal spikes into the bark of trees to break the chainsaws used in the logging industry. But more often than not, the spikes would break through the bark, piercing phloem and cambium layers and sometimes even the heartwood, thus introducing vectors of infection that would kill the tree anyway. Earth Liberation Front members were arsonists, setting fire to the businesses and homes of CEOs who polluted the environment with chemicals and other byproducts of industry. But for some reason, ELF chose to overlook the many tons of carbon thrown into the atmosphere from their fires, along with the sulfur dioxide and nitrous oxide that caused acid rain. Shepherds of the Sea used large ships and fast-attack boats to harass fishing vessels by ramming them, fouling their nets, and even firing incendiary bombs onto the decks of whalers. But they used thousands of gallons of diesel fuel and gasoline processed by refineries that did even more damage to the environment than the harvesting of a few sea creatures.

It was a pity such organizations were so myopic. They simply did not have the grander, enlightened vision of Green Blade. Green Blade's ecotage didn't leave a harmful environmental footprint like the others. Okay, so they did send soldiers into restricted areas, and that took fuel and resources; but they always made sure to do so with prudence. No flagrant expenditures or tactics deleterious to Mother Earth. No demands for redress or blatant media exposure. No extortion. No coercion. Everything they did was what Nature would do. Everything they used was what Nature produced. They simply *enhanced* the delivery of Nature's weaponry. And they were always looking for new weapons.

"No flagrant expenditures" meant that Green Blade was tightfisted; they questioned every dollar. That made Bruja's repetitive demands for more funding very dangerous. The powers-that-be were known to cut off all funding and ties if they suspected embezzlement or the slightest personal extravagance. In more than one instance, Green Blade was rumored to employ their unique style of ecotage to "remove" a mercenary who was using faction funding for personal gain. One man died after mysteriously contracting an aggressive strain of flesh-eating staphylococcus found only in Thailand. He'd never been to Thailand. Didn't matter. In a matter of weeks, he literally rotted away. Of course, Green Blade denied any involvement . . . but everyone in the organization knew better.

Personally, Mantis could care less. He wasn't an extreme environmentalist, nor was he a heartless capitalist. He had other plans, better plans. He cared about the environment but no more than he cared about himself. He'd joined Green Blade because he needed their influence and resources to carry out his plans. He just wanted to be sure he wasn't the next "accident." That's why it frustrated him that he had to rely solely on a contact he knew so little about. Yet those were the constraints of total anonymity.

Absently massaging his deformed hand, he fought the negative thoughts assaulting him. *Bruja*, Spanish for *witch*, was the perfect code name for the agent he was dealing with. They'd never met. He wasn't even certain his contact was a woman, but the person surely acted like every other female he'd ever dealt with. He wished he could dump her and recruit a new contact, but he didn't have the time; his contract was almost up. Besides, the information she'd provided thus far was enticing. He felt it was exactly what he needed.

With his good hand, he typed:

You have already exceeded estimated funding for your station with no viable results. It's time for you to produce.

Request denied.

Mantis.

He hit Send then stood and walked to the large picture window in his high-rise lab. Six stories below, the streets of Seattle bustled with evening rush-hour traffic. Too many people had fallen in love with the beauty of the area. And he hated people. A childhood counselor had told him he suffered from agoraphobia, but that wasn't quite right. He wasn't *afraid* of crowds; he merely abhorred them.

Beyond the city lay the wind-whipped waters of Puget Sound. The sight always took his breath away. This was one of Nature's masterpieces. Nowhere on earth did the weather, seasons, and terrain create such a glorious tableau. Mantis's throat tightened at the grandeur of it.

Reflected in the glass, his green lab scrubs superimposed on the scene like a heavenly apparition. Mantis felt compelled to protect this region, felt obligated to safeguard its pristine beauty. It was up to him.

Mantis hoped Bruja's element would be the discovery that would finally elevate him into the upper echelons of Green Blade. His ascension thus far had been mediocre at best, even though he worked harder than anyone he knew. Well, he didn't actually know other members of Green Blade. Everyone used aliases. Only the top brass knew the true identities of their underlings. But he assumed he was working harder. He always had—even when people said he couldn't because of his handicap.

He filed the message in a ghost folder and went back to his workbench. Bruja would produce. She *had* to. Mantis knew he was meant for greater things. It was his destiny.

CHAPTER 20

THE FACT THAT FELIPE HAD not restocked their diet Mountain Dew only added to Meghan's misery. Nothing seemed to have gone her way that day.

"What do you mean he doesn't have any information?" she growled at Ricardo through the microphone.

"It is true, señorita," Paz responded. "Just what I already said. And I have not left this building since he called."

"Then why did you e-mail me saying you had new information?"

"I didn't say that. I say Felipe said to stay by the radio *in case* he sends new info. He said info can come any minute. That's why I stay here and never leave."

"Really. You *never* leave. What—you just sit there all day playing solitaire?"

Meghan was livid. Not only had she wasted the entire day bored to tears in Felipe's tiny office, she'd missed out on a potentially great evening with Carlos. The hottie knew some awesome clubs just a few hours away in the tourist sectors. It was always worth the drive, especially to her favorite, Sawu Las Mercedes in Caracas. While Meghan loved the planet, she also loved the wonderful things that came from it: tequila shots and rum coolers on a white sand beach; dancing to the latest reggae and ska; swimming in pristine, turquoise tide pools—clothing optional. Such things made life more tolerable and definitely more enjoyable. She loved eating fresh swordfish and Caribbean lobster, even though such sea life was overharvested. Okay, so maybe she was more of a fair-weather environmentalist. These people didn't need to know that.

"No, Señorita Muir, I do not play solitaire," Ricardo grumbled. "I make panpipes for the tourists. This job pays very little."

"So you admit working for The Man isn't all it's cracked up to be, huh?"

There was a pause. "What 'man'?"

"Never mind. Look, I need real-time information, okay?"

"Then perhaps you should stay by your radio and you might hear some." The accusation in his voice was clear.

"Read my lips, Rico Suave," she bit back. "You do your job your way, and I'll do mine my way. *Muy comprendo*?" She knew her Spanish was terrible, but she didn't care. She needed information, specific details that Paz seemed reluctant to give. She suspected that the irritating little man was either hiding something or was just plain ignorant.

After a lengthy pause, he said, "Sí, señorita. I do my job. No *hay problema*."

"Good. Now then, when *exactly* was Felipe's last transmission?"

"About twenty-two-hundred."

"In English."

"About ten o'clock. About two hours ago."

"And what exactly did he say?"

"I told you already. Dr. Udy is dead."

"Yes, but did he say how or why?"

"Sí, um . . . he say his *brain* was infected."

Meghan's mouth involuntarily twitched in a brief smile. She scooted closer to the radio console. "His brain was infected?"

"Sí."

"Infected with what?"

"He didn't say, but he thinks the señorita doctor may be infected too. That is why no one goes in until he gives the 'all clear.'"

Meghan's mind was spinning. She glanced at the wall clock. It was a few minutes after midnight. "Are you going to stay up all night waiting?"

"I will be by the radio, sí, but not awake. But it's okay. I am a light sleeper."

She hated the idea of staying up doing nothing. She *should* have taken up Carlos on his offer. She swore softly. "Okay, got it. You radio me the second you hear anything. Do you understand?"

"Sí, Señorita Muir. I understand. La Esmeralda out."

Meghan quickly switched frequencies and hailed the research camp. "Ascom base, Ascom base, this is CIST HQ. Come in."

She waited as the hiss-laced whine undulated like the intro to a fifties sci-fi movie.

Ugh! Why didn't their camp have Internet capabilities—or better yet, cell phone coverage? Why did she have to wait so long for everything she needed? Back in the States she could get *anything* instantaneously. Why did she ever agree to this stupid assignment?

She closed her eyes and pinched the bridge of her sculpted nose. She knew why she'd come here. She'd made some seriously bad choices while in Switzerland—most of which weren't really her fault. But if her parents found out, she'd be dead. Well, not dead but certainly cut off from the family fortune. She needed to cover her tracks, and this seemed like the best way to do it. But if Ascom base didn't answer soon, she'd have to admit to her debtors she had nothing to offer. The man she'd met in Switzerland was one of the top researchers at Bayer AG out of Germany. During the conference, their liaisons became very . . . *personal.* By the end of the conference, he'd written her a check for a cool one million US dollars based solely on the research she claimed she was heading. Eight weeks after the conference, the CEO discovered her lie and demanded repayment. It wasn't the first time such a thing had happened to her. Her parents had said if it ever happened again she'd be cut off.

Think, girl! There had to be some way to find out what the Aussie princess was hiding. Ricardo wasn't much help. And there was no way she was going to ask Felipe for anything. She needed someone who knew the area personally and who could—

Carlos! Of course. Her mind churned with fresh ideas. He was a native; he'd lived here all his life. That meant he knew the country. He'd mentioned he'd explored the rain forests as a boy. Maybe he knew a way to get to Ascom's location without anyone else knowing . . .

At the file cabinet, Meghan pulled out the thick folder labeled *ASCOM.* Thanks to Felipe's nearly anal-retentive detailing, she had the exact compass coordinates of the camp, a topographical map, and a plot showing the two trails and one stream accessing the facility. Dr. Fungus and the Aussie princess had chosen a very remote site, for sure. The stream squiggled its way all through the jungle, but eventually it flowed past a small village—El Desvío (however that was pronounced)—a few miles away. And if Carlos had friends in that village . . .

Meghan smiled and began brushing out her hair and freshening her makeup. She knew where his apartment was. Carlos was in for a surprise visit tonight. Meghan would make sure he enjoyed it as much as she would.

CHAPTER 21

FELIPE NEEDED REST, BUT HE was afraid to go to sleep. The whole scenario was right out of the *Twilight Zone*.

Glancing at Dr. Udy's shirtless body, he wondered if he should simply leave it as it was. What if the fungus released its spores as Julia said it might? Would she breathe them in during the night and in the morning have some hideous thing growing out of her neck?

Scrounging around, he found a large plastic trash bag. He couldn't help but grimace as he carefully slid it over Dr. Udy's head and neck. The fungus seemed even bigger now; the spore sac was the size of a baseball. The containment wasn't perfect, but it was better than nothing. He didn't know what else to do.

Felipe's stomach growled. After seeing the fungus and throwing up, he thought he'd never eat again, but the constant exertion of the past few hours had renewed his appetite. He was now starving. The lab had a kitchenette, but there was no way Felipe was going to risk eating anything in that tent. Maybe he had a candy bar in his colibrí?

Switching off all the lamps and monitors, he watched the lab instantly plunge into unnerving darkness. Julia would be safe until morning. As much as he wanted to stay with her, he wasn't spending any more time in that tent than necessary. He'd sleep in the helicopter. There was plenty of room in the passenger hold. While perhaps not as comfortable as a cot, at least he wouldn't be staying under the same roof as a fungus-sprouting corpse.

Heading toward the door, he paused at the dissection microscope, wondering what Julia had found. She'd spent hours there before falling asleep. Had she discovered anything before exhaustion took over?

Hazy moonlight eked past the window flaps enough to highlight an open notebook. Pulling a penlight from his pocket, he clicked it on and illuminated the page. The writing was blocky—not at all like a girl's handwriting. Must be Brandon's notes, he reasoned. None of it made sense. He flipped to the previous page, hoping for something he could understand. What he read made his blood chill.

New specimen. Found thirty meters from camp, growing from a dead capuchin monkey. Yellow spores found on hands, feet, and lips. Unknown fungus. Suspect cordyceps sp? Unilateralis? Multiformis?

Sporangiophore 11.5 cm length. 1.8 cm diameter.

Morphology consistent with o. unilateralis. Species only found on insects. Highly infective. Creates "zombie ants."

Method of infection into monkey host? Unknown.

Transmission? Unknown. Spores airborne in nature? Possibly.

New species or a mutation of o. unilateralis? Possible cross speciation—Insect to primate? To human?

Am I already infected?

Dear God, I hope not.

Felipe stopped breathing. He'd been in some frightening situations before. He'd seen some pretty nasty infections come out of the rain forest; he'd heard about even more. But to think *this* could already be inside him frightened him like nothing else ever had.

He crossed himself and began reciting every catechism prayer he could remember as he exited the tent.

CHAPTER 22

CARLOS ANSWERED THE DOOR IN Levis and a form-fitting tank top. The surprised look on his face was exactly what she had hoped for.

"Meghan. Um, can I help you?" he stammered.

She gave him her best flirtatious smile. "You can start by inviting me in. The mosquitoes out here are brutal."

"Um . . ." he hedged. "I have a guest."

"Then send him away. We have something very important to discuss."

He looked back over his shoulder. "But it is already late. Can we talk tomorrow?"

"Nonsense. Look at your watch, silly. It already *is* tomorrow. Besides, this is important. I'm sure your guest will understand," she said, pushing past him.

On the sofa sat a young Hispanic woman about Meghan's age, perhaps a bit older. She wore a plain blouse and a faded skirt. She was cute, but she paled in comparison to Meghan. Sizing her up in a glance, Meghan judged her to be about five three, 115 pounds, flat chested, and pencil legged. Her hair was thick and well brushed, but the cut was simple and unflattering. She wore no makeup that Meghan could see. She was, at best, average. Meghan was a goddess compared to her. Of course, Meghan was a goddess compared to most women. There were two open beer bottles on the small coffee table and a soccer game playing on the television. This would be no problem.

Walking up to the woman, Meghan extended her hand and flashed a smug smile. "Hi. I'm Meghan. Are you Carlos's mother?"

The woman frowned. "*¿Su . . . madre?*"

"No? Well, I hope you're not his housekeeper, because," she paused, glancing around, "you're obviously being overpaid."

The woman's eyes flitted from Carlos back to her. "*No entiendo, señorita.*"

"She is a friend," Carlos explained, coming up behind Meghan.

"A friend?" Meghan said, feigning shock. "Oh, I am so sorry. I didn't know you were on a date."

Carlos shrugged. The way his lean form moved under the snug tank top emboldened her. A cheer rose from the TV set along with the announcer drawing out the word *goooool!*

Feigning excitement, Meghan sat uncomfortably close to the young woman, pinning her against the arm of the sofa. "You're watching soccer? Who's playing tonight? I just love soccer, don't you? All those men running around in those short shorts," she rambled nonstop, knowing full well Carlos's friend didn't understand her. "Are you for the green jerseys or the white jerseys?"

The woman tossed her a confused smile. "*Lo siento,* señorita. No entiendo inglés."

"Meghan, what are you doing?" Carlos asked.

She looked up with another flirtatious look. "Saving you from a boring evening, sweetie."

"We are enjoying ourselves fine."

"Really?" Meghan smirked. "Well, why have this?" she blatantly gestured to the woman beside her, "when you could have this?" she finished, sensuously outlining her sculpted torso.

The young woman, clearly understanding the gist of what Meghan said, stood abruptly, grabbed her purse, and marched to the door. Carlos stepped behind her, rattling off plaintive-sounding sentences, but it did no good. The woman opened the door then turned and glared at Meghan. She hissed a string of Spanish words Meghan couldn't translate but clearly understood, then exited, slamming the door behind her.

Reaching for one of the beers, Meghan took a generous swig. "Now that we've gotten rid of the trash, let's have some real fun."

"I cannot believe you did that," Carlos said evenly, dragging his hand through his dark hair.

"I cannot believe you'd invite her into your apartment. Surely you can do better, Carlos, baby."

"She is a friend."

"*Was* a friend," Meghan corrected with a tweak of her eyebrows.

Carlos sat heavily on the sofa, putting a generously empty space between them. "What do you want?"

She slid next to him and took his hand in hers. "I'm so glad you asked," she said, kissing his knuckles. "I need you to do me a big favor."

"What favor?" he asked carefully.

"A very easy one. One that will make me very happy. One I'd do anything for," she cooed, placing his hand on her cheek.

Even before he answered, the look in his eyes told Meghan that he would do whatever she asked. This really was too easy.

After explaining what she needed, Carlos promised to call a friend of his whom he said lived near El Desvío. He was sure his friend could be in and out before anyone saw him.

"I need you to call him tonight. Right now, in fact. Tell him I need a sample by tomorrow," Meghan said with narrowed eyes. "If it's not here by tomorrow, it'll do me no good."

Carlos sighed and picked up his phone.

Even though the entire conversation was in Spanish, Meghan heard the urgency in Carlos's voice. She felt confident he was fulfilling her request. Sometime tomorrow, with a sample in hand, she could satisfy her creditor's demands. She'd be able to clear her debt. She'd be able to start over with a clean slate. More importantly, her parents would never find out about the mess she'd made.

CHAPTER 23

MANTIS STOOD AT THE SIDE door to a nondescript warehouse on a tiny peninsula south of Seattle. He nervously massaged his gimp hand, though it did little to lessen his angst. A coded keypad was the only illumination under the rusted awning. Few people knew the entrance code: 20200406. It was the date Green Blade planned to release its wrath upon the world. With any luck, he'd be the one to initiate the fury.

Inhaling deeply, he punched the numbers; a click sounded from within the door. He entered and paused as the door swung shut with a metallic *clack*, taking all ambient light with it. It was pitch black inside. He didn't mind the dark. It aided his natural stealth. He was a master of camouflage and fast attack, he reminded himself.

After a minute, a red pinpoint of light centered on his chest. A gun sight.

"Your name?" an electronically altered voice asked.

"Mantis."

"Your purpose?"

"To save the planet."

The laser dot disappeared. "Proceed."

In complete blackness, Mantis walked forward twenty paces then turned to the right ninety degrees and walked another twenty, just as he'd been instructed. When he stopped, a dim green palm reader glowed to life. He placed his good hand on the pad, watched a white bar pass underneath, and heard a faint buzzer sound. A door to the left of the palm reader opened, spilling light into the dark warehouse.

Inside the room, a long, sleek black table stretched out before him. Three men and one woman sat at the far end, two persons to a side.

A glossy, black half-sphere about the size of a basketball sat face down between them. Each person was impeccably outfitted in crisp, austere business attire. They sat straight backed, hands clasped in front of them. Only their heads turned to acknowledge his entrance. One of the men cleared his throat and leaned toward the half sphere. "He's here, sir."

Mounted on a wall at the head of the table was a large flat-screen monitor. It glowed to life with the silhouette of a bald-headed man, backlit by a green, undulating aurora borealis. Reflected light gave only a hint of the man's facial features. When he spoke, his voice was deep and scratchy. "What is your name?"

"Mantis."

"Your real name."

Mantis hesitated. No one was supposed to reveal their true names. But this was the leader of Green Blade, the commander in chief. Was Mantis supposed to give him his real name even though he'd sworn never to do so when on official Green Blade business? The others in the room waited stone-faced, giving no help.

He raised his damaged left hand, showing how it was bent severely at the wrist, forming a clawlike appendage. "I am Mantis, sir."

The bald man chuckled harshly. "Yes. I see."

A section of the tabletop lit in front of the woman. She read it then turned her head to Mantis. "How long have you been a member of Green Blade?" she asked.

It was a silly question. They already had that information. But he answered anyway. "Almost two years."

Another square illuminated in front of one the men. He read it and turned back. "And in that time, what have you done to save the planet?"

"I have marched in Earth Day parades. I have donated my spare time to reforesting hillsides stripped by logging. I have written several letters protesting the slaughter—"

Another square lit up, silencing him.

"What have you done in the name of Green Blade?" asked the third man.

He paused, wondering what they were looking for. Knowing the depths to which these people would go, he decided to go for broke. "I have taken advanced courses on marksmanship—both rifle and handgun. I've earned my pilot's license and am training for my instrumentation

and night-flight ratings. And I am heading up a field study on ultra-
toxic organisms in the rain forests of South America—"

"Is that the same proposal you pitched when you submitted your
application?" the woman interrupted.

"Yes." He wondered where they were going with this line of
questioning.

"The same application we agreed upon twenty months and eight
days ago?"

He swallowed hard, saying nothing.

The faceless image leaned forward, filling the screen. "Twenty
months, Mantis. And what have you submitted for evaluation?"

"I, um . . ." Mantis's eyes fell to the empty tabletop in front of him.
"Well, nothing definitive yet, sir. These things take time, you know.
But I am working on—"

"That is regrettable," the woman said, cutting him off. "Your indus-
triousness showed promise, as did your proposal . . . at first. But your
efforts thus far are dismal and mediocre. Your true work—the weapon
you proposed—has yet to bear fruit."

"Oh, but it will. I swear it will."

"And what have you done with the money deposited in your
account?" the first man asked. "How are you using it to"—he leaned
forward to read from his square—"to 'head up field studies on ultra-
toxic organisms in the rain forests of South America'?"

Mantis was now sweating. He swallowed and pulled at his shirt
collar. Absently massaging his deformed hand, he stammered, "I—I
have two contacts actually—an agent working at Dow Chemical a-and
another working in the Venezuelan jungle. Both are very close to
breakthroughs that will prove to be precisely the weapon Green Blade
needs to command the world's attention."

In truth, he only had one agent working for him—Bruja, in
Venezuela. He had a brother-in-law working at Dow, but they weren't
on the best of terms at the moment because Mantis's sister had moved
out two years ago.

"The weapon Green Blade *needs*?" the bald man asked, putting an
edge on the last word.

"With your approval, of course. It will be very . . . persuasive. I
swear."

There was a weighty pause before the third man's square glowed again. "What is your purpose in coming here tonight?"

"I need—" Mantis choked on the words and stretched his collar again. "I would like to request an extension, please."

The woman's square lit up. "We have already given you one extension. Why should we grant another?"

"Because this time the potential is huge. It's totally natural, totally organic. I have an agent sending me samples as we speak." It was a lie, but they didn't know that.

Or did they?

No. If they knew, he'd never have gotten into the room.

"What is it?"

"A highly infective fungus."

"What is its toxicity?"

"Lethal within twenty-four hours." He didn't know if that was true, but it sounded good.

"Is there an antidote?" the second man asked after consulting his square.

"Not so far as I know. The reports are still coming in."

"Is containment a concern?" he asked.

"No."

There was a deathly pause until all four squares lit up. The board members read them, then each touched a key spot in their square. The bald man looked down as a pale green glow briefly illuminated his face. He looked up and nodded once.

"You have one week," the first man said flatly.

The door behind Mantis clicked open.

"But the samples are coming from South America. From deep in the rain forest. I have no idea how long it'll take to—"

"One week," he repeated.

"Sirs, please—"

"That is all."

Mantis swallowed again. "Thank you," he said before making a hasty retreat.

Outside, the cool night air felt like salvation. To the north, Seattle's evening skyline was poster perfect. The bright, multicolored lights reflecting on Puget Sound, framed by dark pines and basaltic rock, was the stuff of romance, of peace. But Mantis wasn't interested in such frilly nonsense. His life had been spared . . . for the moment. He needed to push harder. He needed to save the planet. He knew he could do it too. He was, after all, the Mantis.

CHAPTER 24

JULIA AWOKE WITH A START. Her eyes flew open, but she didn't move. Something told her to stay as motionless as possible. Someone was in the lab—someone who didn't belong. It wasn't Felipe. She didn't know how she knew that, but she did. She'd heard the lab door squeak open. Someone was using a small torch to move in the darkness. It wasn't pitch black; the dull hue from various LEDs and the moon glow spilling through the windows gave enough light to navigate the lab with minimal caution. But this guy was biding his time, taking a single step then casing the area, then repeating the moves again and again. Was it some tribal scavenger looking for food or trinkets to plunder? No. She'd been there more than a year and had yet to meet but a handful of indigenous people.

From her skewed angle, Julia watched the man examine various lab paraphernalia he moved past. There was some expensive equipment in their lab. She didn't think there was a black market for such stuff, but you never knew. She was about to sit up and confront the intruder when a flash of moonlight glinted off a long machete in his left hand. She tilted her head for a better angle and, in doing so, caused her cot to creak.

The man whipped the light in her direction. He froze with his machete held high in an attack stance. Julia didn't dare breathe. With her eyes squinted almost shut, she pretended to be asleep. Did he even know she was in there? Could he see her through the mosquito netting?

The man marched up to her and yanked back the gauzy netting. She held perfectly still, breathing slowly and deeply as if she were asleep. The man lowered his blade to her neck but didn't touch her. He then slowly brought his face close to hers. She could smell his unwashed skin and clothes; he reeked of alcohol and tobacco. After an agonizing few moments, he backed away and walked directly to Brandon's corpse. The brittle sound of heavy plastic being moved crackled through the darkness as he used the tip of his machete to push back a bag enclosing the fungus. She didn't remember covering the parasite, but maybe she had. She was still trying to wrap her mind around everything that had happened. The intruder flashed his torch at the fungus and whispered something bitterly in Spanish. A profanity? A prayer? Then, before she could do anything, the man raised his machete and hacked off the fungus at the base.

"What are you doing?" she cried, sitting up, yanking the mosquito netting aside.

In two quick steps, the man had the end of his machete against her neck. She winced at the contact, feeling it slice her skin.

"*¡Silencio!*" the man hissed.

"That fungus is deadly, you knob," she said, shrinking from the blade but maintaining her ire. "You may get infected if you touch—"

Using the flat of his blade, he smacked the side of her face. "*¡Cállate!*"

Anger surged within her. She would not be treated this way. Pushing the blade aside, she snapped, "No, I won't be quiet! You just ruined my chances of discovering how my partner died!"

The man paused and chuckled deeply. "*No problema.* There soon be *mucho más.*"

Much more? Much more what? More infections? More deaths? "What do you mean there'll be much more?"

"*Más tiempo.*"

"More time? That shows how little you know. That man was patient zero," she yelled, pointing. "Do you know what that means? It means he's the first person ever to be infected like this. Everything we can learn about how to prevent it from happening again will come from him! That's why—"

Her tirade was cut short when the man slapped her across the face. "*¡Cállate!* No more talk."

The slap stung, but her anger kept her going. She whipped her legs off the cot and leaned forward to stand. "But you must understand—"

This time, her words were cut short by the powerful impact of the man's fist against her cheek. The last thing she remembered were lights flashing around her and the sensation of falling.

CHAPTER 25

RICARDO PAZ AWOKE TO A rooster crowing. The stupid bird always began it raucous calls an hour before sunrise, right outside his bedroom window. It was never a pleasant way to welcome a new day. Today the rooster was perched on the tower roofline, right outside the control room window. The bird was stalking him—there was no doubt. Ricardo covered his head with a pillow. The stupid *el gallo* had to die. There was no other choice. Unfortunately, he'd tried to kill it several times in the past, but the thing seemed to have a sixth sense about impending doom. It always disappeared when he picked up the hatchet.

Ricardo hated mornings, especially when he'd had such a sleepless night. But he knew he had to get up. He had to check in. They were in the middle of a Code Red.

Rolling from his cot, he grabbed his head to keep it from falling off. It pounded insistently. Slowly, he moved to the radio and checked the recorder. No one had called during the night. He wasn't sure whether that was good or bad.

The wall clock read 5:03. He considered calling Felipe but didn't want to wake his friend if there was a chance he'd had as rough a night. Even worse, perhaps Felipe had suffered the same fate as Dr. Udy. Was that possible? With no word one way or the other, he really didn't know.

He got up and starting brewing some coffee. He went to the bathroom, splashed cold water on his face, then pulled a comb through his hair. A few minutes later he was sipping black coffee from a steaming cup, watching the sun peek over the mountains.

Feeling human again, he decided to radio Meghan. He loved irritating her, especially first thing in the morning.

"Buenos días, CIST HQ," he sang, even though it teased his headache. "This is La Esmeralda Airport. Come in."

He turned up the transmission volume and repeated the hail. "Buenos días, CIST HQ. I know you're there, Meghan."

There was no reply. It didn't surprise him. Even *he* usually wasn't up this early.

"Caicara del Orinoco station, come in, come in, come in."

The empty reply boosted his courage . . . and his mischievousness. He took another sip of coffee.

"Mmmmmeghannn," he said in a deep, lusty voice. "*Mi hermosa señorita.* This is the man of your dreams calling."

Nothing but soft hissing came from the small speaker.

"Oh, Meghan, sweet Meghan, my beauty with the long, sun-kissed hair and the body of a goddess and the face of an angel. This is your Latin lover, Ricardo," he said, rolling the *R* in his name with flourish. "Come to me, baby. Come to me, and you shall taste love for the very first time. Come to my bed, and—"

"What?" Meghan replied angrily.

Ricardo fell out of his chair, spilling his coffee. He swore under his breath. "Caramba, Meghan, you scared the crap out of me," he said, regaining his chair.

"Sorry," she said through a yawn, sounding half asleep. "What were you saying? Did you hear from Felipe?"

"Um, no. That's a negative," he replied, relieved she hadn't heard his teasing. "I was wondering if you had."

"No," she yawned again. "But I got in very late last night and haven't checked the recorder. Hang on a sec." There was a lengthy pause before she spoke again. "Nope, nothing."

"Same here."

"Have you tried contacting his helicopter?"

"No, señorita. Have you?"

He heard a scoff. "If I had, would I be asking if you had? Look— never mind. What's your SOP for such situations? It's imperative I reach him ASAP."

Ricardo hated it when people used big words and mysterious combinations of letters. He was a simple man. He'd learned what he needed for his airport job, but he hated all the confusing gringo abbreviations. "What is 'SOP'?" he asked.

"Standard Operating Procedure. Your protocol. What would you normally do in this situation?"

"Oh, sí. I would send someone to the site to see what happened."

"Okay," she said through yet another huge yawn. "Then send someone. Today."

"It is too soon. I can send only someone after forty-eight hours of noncontact," he explained. "Besides, Felipe said no one is to go to the site until he says so."

"Well I'm overriding that order and telling you to send someone right now!" she snapped.

"Overriding Felipe? Can you do that?"

"I just did."

Ricardo knew she didn't have that kind of authority. He could argue the fact, but he knew it would get him nowhere. Felipe had told him that arguing with Meghan was like beating your head against an ironwood tree. But since Ricardo loved irritating her, he couldn't just say "okay."

"But if I leave my airport, who will man the radio? What if someone wants to land here and there is no one to guide them in?"

Meghan let fly a bunch of profanity—some of which he'd never heard before. "Look, I don't care who wants to visit your little slice of hell. Just find some way to contact Felipe or Ascom and find out what's going on!"

He adjusted a knob on his radio, causing a background of static to mix in the conversation. "What? Sorry, I do not copy, CIST. Say again, please."

"You heard me, Ricardo. Get out there now. I order you!"

Hssssss.

"Say again, *por favor*. You want to order something? Like for breakfast? Is that what you want to order?"

"No, you moron. I said—"

He cranked up the interference. "I'm losing you, Caicara."

"Ricardo! Don't you dare hang up on me!"

"I'm sorry, CIST. Must be a storm coming in. I'll contact you later. La Esmeralda Airport out."

He switched off his radio and leaned back, smiling. She clearly did not know he was already on the case. He'd wait a few hours to see if anyone called in. He'd first try to contact Dr. Fatheringham at Ascom, then Felipe in his helicopter if need be. He wanted to get Felipe's opinion on what had happened there—if only for his own amusement. Until then, he needed a fresh cup of coffee. His headache pulsed anew every time that *el gallo estúpido* crowed.

CHAPTER 26

JULIA CRAWLED FROM A NIGHTMARE that had her heart racing. With concerted effort, she peeled her eyes open. Her vision was blurred, and her head and face throbbed mercilessly. Her throat felt raw, like she'd been screaming at the top of her lungs. Gingerly touching the side of her mouth, her fingers brought away a tacky glob of congealed blood.

Pushing through the pain, she rocked herself into a sitting position and pulled back the mosquito netting. Except for a harsh line of sunlight eking around the window flaps, the lab appeared gloomy. Brandon's exposed body caused her to frown; seeing the nub of severed fungus made her cry out. Images of the masked intruder flashed in her mind, igniting her anger. She growled an expletive through her throat pain. She was so livid that all semblance of professionalism vanished. Who would do such a thing? Who would be so callous and—and so stupid? Brandon had clearly died from a bizarre, hideous infection. Why would anyone knowingly risk exposure?

She stood too fast, and her head swam. She supported herself on a tent pole and closed her eyes until the vertigo subsided.

"Felipe?" she croaked, wincing. It hurt to talk.

The low hum of equipment was her only answer.

"Felipe? You in here?"

Still no answer.

Had last night's intruder attacked him too? Perhaps killed him? Resting her face in her palm, she battled a mélange of anxiety, anger, and tears. *Don't jump right to the worst conclusion,* she scolded herself. *Think positive. Solve this mess!*

Donning a paper mask, she fought a gag reflex and moved to Brandon's side. His neck and shoulders were now blanched and mottled with black splotches; his skin was taut from internal swelling. The cordyceps hyphae were clearly filling his body. A dozen or more deep pores dotted his shoulders and spread across the nape of his heck. Each pore—roughly the diameter of a pencil—contained a juvenile sporangiophore ready to sprout. They reminded her of juvenile frogs nestled in the porous back of an adult Surinam toad. The tips were pale, glossy, and just as hideous as the parent structure had been. Was this part of the fungus's natural growth, or was it a result of severing the stroma?

Bitterness and sorrow clouded her judgment. Struggling with her mounting anger, she knew she couldn't take time to examine this new parasitic event. She had to find Felipe and then go after the crazed blighter who'd stolen the cordyceps.

Exiting the lab, she grimaced at the bright morning that greeted her. The ground was riddled with puddles, indicating a storm had passed through in the night. She removed her mask and inhaled the moist jungle air to clear her head and rid her sinuses of death's stink. It helped a little but did nothing to unmuddle her thinking. She hated that. She hated everything that was happening. None of it made sense. Taking another deep breath, she screamed at the rain forest. A brief moment of stunned silence was followed by the rancor of monkeys and birds screeching in reply. She gained strength from the interaction. It signified life.

Focusing past the delirium, Julia made her way to Felipe's helicopter. Pushing through to the clearing, she stopped short. Her breath caught in her chest.

The helicopter was gone.

Clutching the sides of her head, she dropped to her knees and trembled uncontrollably. It was painfully clear that Felipe had abandoned her. When had he taken off? And why? Julia couldn't remember hearing the roar of the helo's engine. But then, she didn't remember much of anything after being coldcocked by the intruder.

Stumbling back to the lab, she switched on the radio. "CIST helo, this is Ascom base, come in." Supplanting the fear in her voice with anger, she hailed again. "CIST helo, this is Julia. Look, I'm not fooling around here, Felipe. Where the crap are you?"

When Felipe didn't respond, she switched frequencies. "CIST HQ, this is Ascom base calling in an emergency. Yes, it's a *real* emergency, Meghan, so answer the bloomin' radio!"

A crackle of static was the only reply.

"Criminy! Okay, look, the situation here is even worse, Meghan. I was attacked last night. And now Felipe *and* his helicopter are gone."

The lack of response was crippling. A feeling of total isolation suffocated her. Even with the loss of her parents and later her poppy, Julia had never felt so alone in her entire life. Her fists clenched into white-knuckled balls of fury. She could barely control the trembling that wracked her entire frame.

Crumpling to the floor, she squeezed the sides of her head and tried not to cry. She could handle an occasional disaster but not when they came one right after the other. After several minutes of extreme focus, she stood up and got to work. Donning her mask and gloves, she gently encased Brandon's corpse in the body bag Felipe had brought and zipped it closed.

She then went back to the transmitter. "Right. This is Ascom base again, transmitting in the blind. The situation here is a confirmed Code Red with numerous complications. We've had a break-in. An unknown Hispanic male cut the fungus from Dr. Udy's body and has taken it. Felipe is missing—not just gone but missing. His helicopter is gone, and he's not responding to my radio calls. He said he was almost out of fuel, but that wouldn't prevent him from answering my hails. I must assume he was hijacked or that he crashed while going for help. Perhaps both. I'm going to go look for the stolen cordyceps. It had formed a sporangium and was ready to shed its spores. It is extremely dangerous. I don't know where I'm headed or how long I'll be gone. Brandon's remains—" She paused and swallowed deeply. "His remains are in a sealed body bag in the lab but are not under refrigeration. His body is in the first stages of decomposition and there are fungal spores growing across his back and neck. Route of fungal infection is still unknown. Immediate evac is requested, but please note whoever comes must follow BSL-3 procedures. I repeat, this is at least a Biohazard Safety Level 3 hot zone. This is Dr. Julia Fatheringham at Ascom base, out."

Julia had several priorities vying for first place. Of paramount concern had to be the containment of the pathogen—the parasitic fungus. There was a possibility the severed fungus would simply die and release inert spores, but that was unlikely. Mold spores were known to remain viable for years, even in a desiccated form. The worst-case scenario was that an entire population—perhaps even all of Venezuela—would be infected. She couldn't let that happen.

Grabbing her field pack, she stepped outside and looked for fresh footprints. Finding some she didn't recognize, she followed them to the riverbank. There, she saw evidence of a boat having beached, with footprints going to and from marks. Because she hadn't heard an outboard motor in the night, she surmised the thief had paddled in. But which way had he come? From upstream or down?

Recalling that the closest village was some twenty kilometers to the north, she dragged the kayak from the shed to the waterline. Checking for leaks and finding none, she stored her field pack in the bow and headed upstream.

CHAPTER 27

"Papa, what is in the bag?" nine-year-old Noely asked her father as he stepped through the entry to their one-room house.

"It is . . . money," her papa answered gruffly.

"Money? Where did you get it?"

"In the jungle. Now stop pestering me. I need to rest," he said, setting the bag on top of a tattered blanket in a corner of the featureless room.

"Can I see it, Papa? Can I see the money?"

"No!" he snapped. "Do not open that bag. Do not even touch it. Do you hear me, Noely?"

"Yes, Papa."

"Noely, stop asking so many questions," her mother said from her chair just outside the doorway. She was mending clothes in the shade of their palm-thatch awning. Mama preferred working outside because it was always so hot in the house. "Go to the cooler and get your father a refreshment. He had a difficult night."

"Yes, Mama." She ran to the side of the house where an old, noisy chest cooler stood under a thatched veranda, where they did the cooking.

Their house was little more than four cinderblock walls with two square holes for windows and two doorways—one in front and one to the cooking veranda—both without doors. The roof consisted of a few sections of corrugated tin, filled in with random sheets of plastic and thatch to keep the rain out. Their beds were two simple mattresses set on the dirt floor—one for Papa and Mama, and one for her and her little brother, Luis.

Noely opened the cooler and reached for a bottle.

"What are you doing?" Luis asked, coming up behind her. He was two years younger than she was but had twice her curiosity.

"Getting a beer for Papa," Noely said, withdrawing a brown bottle and closing the cooler. "He worked hard last night, and he's thirsty and tired, so you'd better not disturb him."

"Papa was working?" he asked, astonished.

"Yes. And he brought home a bag full of money."

Luis's eyes widened. "A bag full of money?"

"Yes. It is in the house. But Papa said not to go near it."

"I've never seen a bag full of money before," he said in awe. "What did it look like?"

"It is just a black garbage sack made of plastic, but it looked very heavy."

"The bag is heavy with money?"

"Yes. Papa was very tired from carrying it. Now stop asking so many questions. I have to take this refreshment to him," she said, stepping to the side entrance. Rapping lightly on the doorless frame, she poked her head inside. "Papa? I brought you a beer."

Papa sat slumped on their old couch with his head back and his legs extended in front of him. "Thank you, Noely," he said softly, as if speaking took great effort.

Noely brought the bottle to her father, all the while keeping her eyes on the mysterious black bag in the corner. "Here you are, Papa. You rest now. I will make sure no one disturbs you."

"See that you do, little one," he said, accepting the bottle. "Before you go, take my shoes off for me. My feet are sore."

As she bent to the task, she noticed something strange. Gently removing his shoes and socks, she asked, "Papa, what is this yellow dust on your pant cuffs?"

Papa crooked one leg up to examine the dust. He dabbed some off and rubbed it between his thumb and index finger. He then glanced over to the plastic bag. Wiping his fingers on his shirt, he said, "It is nothing. Now go and let me rest."

"Yes, Papa."

Pausing at the doorway, Noely saw that Papa had already finished half his beer. The bottle was tipped dangerously to one side in Papa's fingers as he lay slouched with his head tipped back. He was breathing deeply; she knew it would only be a couple of minutes before he started snoring. He might spill on himself.

Gingerly tiptoeing back, she slipped the bottle from his loose grip and set it on the dirt floor beside the couch. She stepped closer to the mysterious bag for a better look. She didn't dare touch it because Papa said not to. But she could look at it, couldn't she? Sure enough, there were splotches of yellow dust around the knot at the top of the bag. That's where Papa had held it. Leaning closer, she grimaced. It smelled horrible—like something was rotting inside. Had Papa gathered fallen mangos along the way?

She glanced back; Papa was still fast asleep. That was good. Papa didn't often get work. Many times their family had eaten only what they could forage from the jungle or beg from their neighbors.

Noely was happy her father had found work. It must have been very good work and very hard work. She'd never seen him bring home a bag full of money before. But why did the bag have yellow dust on it? Was the money also covered with the dust? And why did it stink? Would those things make the money not worth as much?

She had little understanding of money, only that it was needed to buy things. Families with more money bought more things, nice things. She'd never had nice things before. The one thing she'd always wanted was a pair of real hiking boots—the kind she'd seen tourists and soldiers wear. Most of the children in their small village went barefoot. So did many of the adults. Noely always wore an old pair of pink cloth sneakers a missionary had given her. They were okay, but boots allowed you to trudge through the jungle without worrying about snakes and spiders.

Wiping her hands on her thin, dingy sundress, she knelt in front of the plastic bag and stared at it. What did so much money look like? Was it paper money or coins? She didn't remember hearing anything clink or ching when Papa set it down, so it had to be paper money— the pretty kind with lots of colors and pictures of important people. She hoped it wasn't being damaged by the rotting stuff inside.

"Noely," a small voice whispered urgently. It was Luis.

"Shh," she said, gesturing with a finger to her lips. "Don't wake Papa."

The boy tiptoed next to her. "What are you doing?"

She pointed. "The money bag."

"*¡Ave Santa María!*" he breathed, his large brown eyes widening in delight.

"Shh. Do not curse, Luis. It is a sin."

"But Papa curses all the time."

"It is different for adults."

He lowered his gaze, duly chastened. Then, nodding at the bag, he whispered, "Have you seen inside?"

"No, not yet. Papa said not to touch it."

"Then . . . how do you know it is full of money?"

"Because Papa said so."

"Oh. What is he going to do with it?"

That was a good question, especially for a seven-year-old. "I do not know. But when he awakens, I want to ask him for new boots."

Luis's eyes widened a second time. "I want a gun!"

"Shh!" she chastened again. "You're too young for a gun."

Luis immediately began to pout angrily. Noely had seen the expression many times before. It was the look he got just before exploding in a spoiled fit. Standing, she dusted off her knees and cocked her head toward the doorway. "Come on. Let's go outside and catch frogs. We can ask Papa about the money when he finishes his siesta."

Luis's pout softened slightly, but his large eyes still lingered on the money bag. Noely took his hand and gently coaxed him from the house. Outside, she took off in a sprint to the stream. "Bet I catch the first one," she called back.

Caught up in the challenge, Luis bolted after her. That was good. She needed to get his mind off the money bag. When he was distracted, she'd sneak back for a second look. She just *had* to see what all that money looked like.

CHAPTER 28

MEGHAN LEFT CARLOS BREATHING DEEPLY, asleep in his bed. His chiseled chest and abs were exposed; the rest of his frame was barely covered with a light cotton sheet. It was a good look. The hottie was definitely calendar material. Regrettably, the rest of him screamed third-world, minimum wage. His apartment was not only situated in the low-rent district, it was also desperately in need of cleaning and redecorating. She had no desire to be involved with either.

Back in the CIST, Meghan wondered how long it would take Carlos's friend to deliver the specimen. She'd made it clear she needed it immediately. Carlos had relayed the need and said his friend understood. But had he really? She couldn't speak the language, so she had to trust that her message was given the urgency it deserved. Only time would tell—time she didn't have.

She hated involving so many others in her plans, but she had no choice. There was no way she would go into the rain forest herself to collect a poisonous fungus. That was unthinkable. The jungle? The heat? The humidity? The bugs? Nope.

She puttered around the office until ten, then pulled up Carlos's number on her cell and dialed.

"Hola?"

"Good morning, hot stuff. I trust you slept well?"

"Oh, hi, Meghan. Sí, I slept very well."

"That's super. So, have you heard from your friend yet?"

"My friend?"

"Yeah, silly. The one who's collecting the specimen from the Ascom site for me?"

"Oh. No. I only call him last night."

"And?"

"And *nada*. He does not have a cell phone."

"No cell? But you called him. I heard you talking to him."

"Sí. I called the postal center, and they send someone to his *casa*. That is why it took so long. I explained that to you last night."

"Wait. You talked to him in the post office?" she yelled. "With everyone listening in?"

"Sí. Why not? There are few secrets in such a small village," he said with a chuckle.

"This isn't funny, Carlos. This *needs* to be kept a secret."

"Stealing mushrooms from two Americans needs to be a secret? Why? They can always go collect more. The rain forest is full of them."

"I already told you: this one is special."

"Sí, sí. Okay."

"So have you heard from him?"

"No."

She rapidly grew angrier at how lightly he was treating her request. "Look, I want you to call him again, now!"

He grumbled, also sounding angry. "I can call the postal center again, but I doubt he is there. The site you spoke of is many kilometers from his village, and the rain forest is very thick."

"But didn't you tell him I needed it today?"

"Sí. And he said he would try."

"No!" she screamed into the phone. "That's not acceptable. I don't need him to try; I need him to do it."

"He will. As I said, it may take time."

"Why didn't you say that last night before you took advantage of me?"

There was a long pause over the line. "I did not do that."

"Oh really? I seem to remember having all my clothes removed."

"And I remember *you* removing them."

"Look, are you going to call your friend, or do I have to call the police station and tell them you raped me?"

A longer pause followed her threat. "I will call. But it is not my fault if he's not there."

Meghan smiled. "Thank you, sweetie. I knew I could count on you."

She was so close to having what she needed that she was trembling. Carlos's friend would bring back the deadly fungus. Meghan would immediately ship it off to Switzerland, and they would do with it whatever they do with such things to make a billion dollars. Her plans were finally working out. The sample was being delivered. She wished it could be faster, but everyone said the roads through the rain forest were few and poorly maintained. Some were little more than animal trails. Just one more thing she disliked about this prehistoric country.

She snapped open a diet Dew and booted up her e-mail. She didn't care if Felipe got mad. She was so excited that she couldn't make herself wait to use a public terminal.

Sample ready for shipping. Need funds for packaging and transport. Also need address of receiver. This is it, I promise.

CHAPTER 29

MANTIS'S IN-BOX WAS FLAGGED WITH a new message sent in a non-reply format; the sender was identified only by the numerical sequence 20200406. *Green Blade.* He opened the file.

Six days.

That was all—but the message spoke volumes. Six days until he had to produce something or die. So kind of them to send a reminder—as if he really needed one.

He chewed his lower lip in frustration and walked to the picture window overlooking Puget Sound. He needed to clear his mind of Green Blade's intimidation and focus on his end objective. The afternoon was soft and clear. What a perfect world, he thought as he absently massaged his left hand. It's too bad no one appreciated it the way he did. Too bad there were so many greedy, narrow-minded people who ruined it for everyone else.

He leaned his forehead against the cool glass and sighed deeply. Looking down at his withered hand, he smiled. Although his deformity was wrought from a terrible experience, the resultant shape never ceased to intrigue him. It defined him, gave him identity. The hand, bent severely forward at the wrist, had a full thumb, but only half of three fingers and a nub for his pinky. He told everyone he was born that way, that it was a random act of nature. He also claimed the deformity rendered his hand useless. But both statements were lies. The misshapen appendage was actually a disfigurement—the result of one of his father's alcoholic binges. The doctors had tried to repair the horrible accident but with minimal success. "Accident" was another lie; "minimal" was true. While his thumb and half fingers worked reasonably well, they appeared to be nothing more than useless stubs.

His dad was an axe man, a logger for a big company that clear-cut acres of pine in the Olympia forests. The company had all the necessary permits to harvest the trees, but the exploitation still left scars on the mountainside that took decades to fill in. Even at a young age, Mantis (his parents called him Jimmy back then) recognized the ugliness of the act.

Shortly after his eighth birthday, Jimmy discovered a ball-peen hammer in Dad's toolbox. It was much smaller than the large claw hammer hanging on the pegboard above the workbench. This hammer looked like a kid-sized tool, only it was made with a real wooden handle and a real steel head. His curiosity was piqued. The hammer end was obviously used to pound nails, but what was the opposite, dome-shaped end for? He hit a scrap piece of two-by-four and marveled at the bowl-shaped dent it made. He did it again and again, making a pattern of indentations that looked like one of Dad's golf balls. He then struck an empty beer can and got the same result. Without thinking, he went around the garage, making small indentations in everything he could find, including his dad's pickup truck.

Dad came home drunk that night, having gone out with his logging buddies. In a mindless rage, he used the ball-peen on Jimmy's hand as punishment—to do to him what he did to the truck. The pain was unimaginable; the amount of blood scared Jimmy half to death. He remembered Dad lying to the ER doctor about the "accident." A heavy metal toolbox had dropped on his son's hand, mangling it. Jimmy knew better than to correct Dad's lie. The doctors were very concerned. They gave him medicine that took away the pain, but nothing could take away the horror of seeing the bloody, twisted mess that used to be his left hand. The doctors said they'd try to fix it but that he needed to be a brave boy. With tears in her eyes, a nurse forced a smile as she added something to the needle in his arm. He fell asleep.

When he woke up, his hand was bandaged like a boxing glove. It hurt, but he knew he shouldn't cry. Dad hated it when he cried. Still, when the bandages came off, he couldn't stop himself. Strangely, Dad didn't seem angry about him crying this time. In fact, he seemed very sad about the whole thing. He pulled Jimmy into a big hug and held him. Jimmy could feel his dad's body shake. It almost sounded like Dad was crying too.

Gaining courage from his father's tenderness, Jimmy asked, "Daddy? If I promise to be a good boy from now on, can I have my fingers back?"

The next day his dad disappeared. Jimmy never saw him again.

The deformed appendage had earned him the nickname Crabs in middle school. He hated the pitiless label. But as the months passed, he found that kids ran away when he wielded his gimp hand like a weapon. That empowered him. In time, he adopted his own nickname, one that carried with it an aura of danger and respect. He became the Mantis. It was perfect. A praying mantis wasn't praying at all. While it's retracted forearms gave the insect a look of supplication, in reality they were coiled springs ready to snatch unsuspecting prey with blinding speed. He was a master of camouflage and attack.

Mantis wasn't really capable of using his deformity as a weapon, but he could certainly do so in principle. People had made fun of him all his life. Even in an era of political correctness and laws accommodating handicaps in the workplace, he still put up with sideways glances of disgust and "innocent" comments about his disfigurement. Outwardly, he'd learned to shrug them off, but inwardly he seethed and plotted while biding his time.

At last, that time had come. Mantis would soon be able to strike.

"See anything interesting out there, Jimmy?" his supervisor asked, coming up behind him.

Mantis flinched. "Uh, no sir. I was just . . . thinking."

"Well, see if you can get back to running your samples and do your thinking on your own time, okay?"

"Yes, sir," he said, ducking his head and heading back to his bench.

Mantis was responsible for testing water samples gathered from numerous collection sites across Washington State. It wouldn't be so bad if there weren't three hundred plus sites in this batch, ten samples from each site. Running a control prior to each test; then testing the pH, specific gravity, specific conductance, and turbidity of each sample; and then recording each result stretched into hours and hours of tedium. If a gross anomaly was detected, the entire batch had to be retested. Their equipment and procedures were state-of-the-art, so most anomalies were usually considered operator error.

So you need to be patient, Mantis counseled himself. *You have a degree in botany. You know these things take time.*

Besides, the latest e-mail from Venezuela confirmed that *his* sample had been collected. Not a water sample—something even better, a sample that could be his ticket to glory. An ultimate weapon. A weapon he would soon present to Green Blade. They would reward him accordingly, and he could quit this tedious job and bask in the adulation of countless environmentalists for his brilliant contribution to ecotage.

Making sure no one was watching, Mantis reopened his mailbox and reread the short message. Six days.

Gritting his teeth, he sent a message to Bruja. Proceed as directed without delay. You'll get your funding.

He then resumed his mind-numbing job—only this time, he did so with a smile.

He paused. Was a praying mantis capable of smiling?

He shrugged. This one could.

CHAPTER 30

USUALLY PAPA'S SNORING COULD BE heard meters from the house. The neighbors often complained. Mama said he sounded like an old boar. That's why Noely was confused when she approached the doorway. She could hear nothing. He'd been snoring when she'd left to wash clothes in the stream and run errands for Mama.

Poking her head through the doorway, she discovered Papa was no longer in the house. And neither was the bag of money.

Finding Mama leaning over a kettle on the cooking fire, Noely asked, "Where's Papa?"

"He had to go to the city, little one."

"So far?"

"Yes. It is part of his work."

"And he didn't say good-bye?"

"He had to hurry. I gave him a quick lunch after his siesta, and he left."

"Where is Luis?"

"He went with him."

Noely's shoulders drooped at the information. Why would Papa take Luis instead of her? She always worked much harder than Luis. As if reading her thoughts, Mama said, "Do not be sad, my angel. They will be back tomorrow morning. I will make a special supper just for the two of us. You can help me if you like."

Although she enjoyed helping her mother cook, the offer didn't totally nullify her disappointment. She *really* wanted to see inside the money bag. With shoulders still drooping, she nodded. "Okay."

"Go in the house and bring me three onions, please," Mama said.

"Yes, Mama."

Entering the house, Noely moved to the back corner where they kept their meager stores. A string of onions hung from a nail in one of the rafters. She grabbed a knife, then scooted over a chair and climbed up. She cut away the bottom three onions and was about to hop off the chair when she noticed the tattered blanket Papa had set the money bag on. It was still sprinkled with the yellow dust she'd seen earlier.

Even though they lived in a house with a dirt floor, Noely knew Mama prided herself on keeping the place clean. Dutifully, Noely rolled the blanket into a tube and carried it out.

"Here are the onions, Mama," she said, handing them over.

"Thank you, little one. What are you doing with that?" she asked, indicating the cloth.

"It's dusty. I'm going to shake it out and wash it." Not only would that get the blanket clean, it would help her with the frustrations of being left behind.

Mama smiled. "Be gentle, Noely. It is old, but it's still a nice piece of cloth."

"I will."

Taking the sheet to the stream, Noely selected a low branch and draped the blanket over it. The yellow dust made a large, faint circle in the center of the cloth. She grabbed a dead branch that forked at the end, and whacked it against the sheet. The yellow dust leapt from the material. Noely turned her head but not before she inhaled some of the yellow stuff. She sneezed and wiped her nose on her dress. The yellow dust smelled like rotten meat. It was a good thing she'd seen it before Mama did. She could clean it up before it stank up their house.

Noely spent a good ten minutes beating the dust from the blanket. She enjoyed the hard work—but she seemed covered with the yellow stuff. Stepping into the stream, she washed both the blanket and her dress then hung them up to dry. She didn't care about being seen in her underwear. Many of the kids ran around in next to nothing. She sneezed again and wiped her nose on her clean dress—this time with a frown. There was blood mixed in with the mucus.

Luis didn't usually like traveling alone with Papa. Papa always walked too fast; it was hard to keep up with him—especially in bare feet. But Luis was determined to do so and not complain about it. Papa hated it when anyone complained—even though Papa complained all the time. Noely told him it was one of those things adults can do but children must not.

Luis was also hungry and thirsty. Papa didn't like to stop to eat. Instead, he occasionally pulled from his pocket a bandana in which he kept a chunk of dried meat. Occasionally, he would share it. The bandana had some of the yellow dust on it, the same powder he'd seen on the money bag. It smelled funny, but it didn't change the taste of the dried meat . . . much.

Finally, Papa sat on a log and opened his water flask. Luis sat beside him and gathered up the courage to ask: "Why are you taking the money bag to the city, Papa?"

"There is a man there who needs it."

"Who?"

"You do not need to know."

Papa took a long drink then rubbed his temples, groaning softly.

"Are you okay, Papa?"

"Yes. I'm just tired. I did not sleep much . . . and my head hurts."

"You should rest, Papa."

Papa scowled at Luis. "What do you think I'm doing?"

Luis did not want to upset Papa by pestering him with more questions, but he was very curious about the money bag.

"I will keep a watch on the trail, Papa, if you wish to take a nap."

Papa stared at Luis with a look of uncertainty. To Luis, it looked like his father didn't understand what he'd said, almost as if he wasn't even sure who he was.

"Okay, Papa?"

Papa closed his eyes and rubbed them heavily. "Perhaps."

"Lean against the trunk, Papa," Luis said, patting the log. "You will feel better soon."

Papa eased himself from the trunk to the ground, setting the plastic bag to one side. Slowly, his head drooped forward, and soon he was snoring softly.

Luis waited a long time before he quietly stepped over to the money bag. The top was loosely tied shut. He just wanted to peek inside. The plastic crinkled loudly when he tried to undo the knot. Papa stirred, grunting. Scooting back, Luis noticed his fingers were covered with the yellow dust from the money bag—a sure sign he'd been disobeying Papa. That meant a thrashing. Sometimes, when Papa was really angry, he'd use his belt. It really hurt.

Looking around, Luis hoped to find a pool of water to wash his hands in. Papa stirred again; his snoring became sharp and staggered. He was waking up. Quickly, Luis stuck his fingers in his mouth and sucked off all the dust. It tasted horrible—like something too old. But he'd rather taste something horrible than feel the sting of Papa's belt on his backside. Papa groaned and stretched. Luis turned his back to him, licked his palms, and wiped them on the inside of his shirt.

"What are you doing?" Papa asked harshly. "Are you touching the bag?"

"No, Papa. I'm just resting."

Papa glanced at his watch. "It's late, but I need a few minutes more rest. You watch the trail like you promised, then you can rest."

"Okay. Papa?" Luis winced a little on the bitter taste in his mouth. "May I have a drink of water?"

Papa handed him the flask. "Just a sip."

Luis took a small drink. The bad taste didn't go away.

CHAPTER 31

JULIA HAD KAYAKED COUNTLESS TIMES in her youth. A kayak was the perfect conveyance for maneuvering through dense overgrowth and up narrow tributaries. Plus it was quiet. She could approach animals to within one or two meters before they fled. She loved it.

Regrettably, today's outing was anything but a pleasant excursion. Hampered by pain, anger, and dread, her progress felt pitifully slow. She had to accept that. If she rushed, she could miss something, some vital clue. Resting, she forced herself to breathe slowly, deeply, listening for anything that did not sound indigenous to the rain forest. It did little good. After only a moment, her mind drowned out all sounds, beleaguering her with questions.

Why had the intruder taken the fungus? Was she going in the right direction? Was there the same element of danger now that the stroma had been severed? She knew the answer to the third question even as she asked it. Quite often the fruiting body didn't release its spores until it was separated from its hyphae. A favorite experiment of hers in her childhood was to slice the crown from a common *Laccocephalum* mushroom then place it undisturbed on a piece of white paper. The next day, she would carefully lift the crown from the paper to find a perfect circle of spores, patterned exactly like the underside of the crown.

Brandon's cordyceps had already developed a sporangium. It was ludicrous to think it wasn't filled with viable spores. If the intruder caused the release of spores, then it was only a matter of time before someone else became a zombie.

She scoffed and shook her head. *Really, Jules? A zombie? Now you're being delusional*, she berated herself. *There's no such thing as zombies.*

But was that completely true? She knew the common term for ants infected with *Ophiocordyceps unilateralis* was "zombie ants." And hadn't Brandon behaved in pretty much the same way?

She wished she could push that terrible memory aside, but she recognized it was key in discovering what had happened. She needed to ascertain the full life cycle of Brandon's fungus, particularly, how it was vectored and absorbed. But that biology was something for a later date. Right now, she needed to stop this new species from infecting anyone else.

As she paddled on, her thoughts turned to Felipe. What had become of him? Why had he left without saying anything? It was clear that he was frightened, but he'd done very well helping get Brandon down from the kapok tree, pushing past his fears. It didn't make sense that he would simply run away.

Or *did* he run away? Perhaps he was coerced, forced to out fly against his will by the intruder?

She stopped paddling as a new possibility entered her mind. What if Felipe was party to the theft? Hadn't he asked her if something like this could be used intentionally? Hadn't he speculated what something like this could be worth? If he was involved, she could paddle until doomsday without gaining any advantage.

She shuddered. *If something like this gets out, doomsday will be sooner than anyone thinks.*

Julia paddled on. As the sun rose higher, the humidity amplified exponentially. Sweltering heat waves shimmed off the slow-moving tributary. Mosquitos harassed her relentlessly. Her sweat-soaked clothing chaffed against her skin with every stroke. Her entire body ached. Pausing only to take an occasional sip of water, Julia kept her eyes focused on the riverbanks. After nearly three hours of paddling, she was exhausted and extremely woozy.

Then, rounding a bend in the stream, she came upon a half dozen children splashing along a cleared section of shoreline. An older girl in a sundress sat on the shore watching them. The children immediately halted their play and gawked at Julia as she drifted slowly toward them. Her light skin and blonde hair were a novelty in the Venezuelan rain forest, and she hoped it would gain her some advantage in communicating with them. Instead, they all looked frightened, ready to bolt.

When Julia tried to talk, her parched, swollen throat closed up. All that came out was a rasping wheeze. She swallowed and tried again. "Hola, *niños*," she croaked in a raw, scratchy voice.

Panic-stricken, the children fled the water and disappeared up a trail, screaming, *"Una bruja! Una bruja!"*

The girl in the sundress, however, stood but didn't run. Taking the girl's courage as a good sign, Julia pointed at her throat. *"Muy malo. ¿Mucho dolor, sí?"*

The girl nodded.

As her kayak touched the shore, she noticed the girl had blood crusted on the front of her upper lip. "Are you okay?" she asked.

The girl frowned and tipped her head to one side.

"¿Está bien?" she tried again.

"Sí," the girl responded warily.

Julia fought for the Spanish words she needed. *"¿Ayuda,* por favor?"

The girl shifted her weight. "Sí. *¿Está usted enferma?"*

"No. No, I'm not sick," she said as she stowed her paddle. "But I need—" She cleared her throat again and smiled weakly. *"¿Hablas inglés?"*

"No."

"Drat!"

"Pero, *mi madre habla un poco de inglés."*

"Your mother? Brilliant. Can you take me to her? Um, *¿dónde está tu madré?"*

The girl pointed up the trail along which the other children had fled and rattled off a string of Spanish. Assuming the girl was going to take her to her home, Julia dragged the kayak up the embankment.

"Gracias," she said, following the girl into the jungle.

CHAPTER 32

JULIA FOLLOWED THE LITTLE GIRL along a well-used trail to a small village comprised of several cinderblock and tin houses, most with just a single room and perhaps a patio on which to cook and wash. A wide dirt road with clear tire tracks led away from the village. Julia estimated the village had a population of no more than two hundred people.

"*¿Ésta es El Desvío?*" she asked. She'd seen the name on a map back in the lab.

The little girl nodded. "*Sí.*"

Everyone stopped to stare at the blonde woman walking through their pueblo. Many of the women gasped; a few children ran away. For a fleeting moment, Julia wondered if she didn't look presentable. She ducked her head and followed the girl to a small house not far from a stream that fed the river. A middle-aged woman sat under an awning, mending a skirt.

"*Mamá, esta mujer necesita ayuda,*" the little girl said.

The woman looked up with a cautious smile. "*¿Oh sí?*"

"*Yo no hablo español,* señora," Julia began. "Do you speak English?"

"A little." Her words were heavily accented.

"Brilliant. I need some help finding a man."

The woman frowned. "He do this to you?" she asked, pointing at the side of Julia's face.

"Do what?"

The woman said something in rapid Spanish to the little girl. The girl ran through the doorless entry to the house and returned with a hand mirror. Julia looked into the mirror and drew a sharp breath. The side of her face was purple and yellow from bruising. A two-centimeter laceration angled along her cheek, red and angry. Both eyes were blackened and puffy; the sclera of her left eye was bright red. Crusted blood snaggled in her hair and coursed down her jaw. No wonder the children had screamed at the sight of her.

"Crikey," she whispered.

The woman rattled off some more Spanish, and the little girl fetched a bowl of water and a washcloth.

"Thank you," she said, gingerly wiping her face. "My name is Julia."

"I, María. This, Noely."

"Noely?" she asked the girl. "What a beautiful name."

María translated what Julia had said to her daughter. The little girl blushed prettily.

"This man. He you husband?" María asked.

"Heavens no," Julia answered, wincing at the sting of cleaning her wounds. "He attacked me last night at our camp upstream. He was Hispanic, late forties, roughly 170 centimeters tall, 150 kilograms. He had a large machete."

María scowled. "What he wear?"

"I couldn't tell. It was very dark. A T-shirt and jeans, I think. He spoke some English."

"What he do?"

"He stole something from me—something very deadly. He's in great danger."

"¿Y éste?" she said, again motioning at Julia's face.

"He hit me when I tried to stop him."

María then looked over Julia's lithe torso and legs. "¿Y no mas?"

"No. No, he didn't try to . . . assault me. Do you know him?"

"Quizás." She spoke again to Noely, and the girl sprinted into the house. Returning, she carried with her an old 5x7 photo in a battered frame. "Is this man?"

The picture was of the woman standing next to a man of equal age. Julia could detect similar features, but she couldn't be certain it was the same man that had attacked her last night. Then it came to her. Last night's intruder might be this woman's husband. The photo had been taken many years ago.

Julia shook her head. "I don't know. Maybe. It's hard to tell."

María's eyes narrowed as she read Julia's attempt at lying. A fleeting smile pulled at one side of her lips. She lowered her eyes and shuffled one foot. "Entiendo. *Es mi esposo.* He a good man, but not much smart. He can be . . . *odioso.* Hating?"

"Hateful? Mean?"

María caressed the photo. "Sí," she said softly. "Especially when he drink."

"I'm so sorry."

The woman waved away the apology. "Me also." She handed the photo back to her daughter and instructed her to take it back inside. "Mi esposo gone last night. When he come home, he carry *una bolsa plástico.* Something inside, I don't know. He no say."

"How big was it—the bag I mean?"

María pantomimed with her hands.

"Where is it now?"

"*¿Por qué?*"

"It's extremely dangerous."

"Dan-gersos?" she struggled with the word. "*¿Peligroso? ¿Cómo?*"

"It can make him very sick. *Muy enfermo.* He could die."

"Die? *¿Se muere?*"

"Yes."

María looked over at Noely sharply. She again rattled off a string of Spanish, gesturing wildly with her hands. The girl ran to the house and came out a minute later carrying a bulging cloth knotted together by the four corners. Maria handed it to Julia.

"Here food and drink. Mi esposo went that road," she said, pointing. Tears pooled in her eyes as she spoke. "Por favor, señora. *Vaya rápidamente.*"

Her sudden urgency frightened Julia. "Why? What's wrong?"

The tears spilled. "He take my son. Por favor. *Rápidamente.* Go fast!"

Julia nodded. "How long ago did he leave?"

"This morning."

"Thank you, María. I am very grateful," she said, energized by the information. "I'll grab my things from the kayak and then go after them. I *will* bring your son back. I promise."

CHAPTER 33

PAPA HAD OPENED HIS EYES and belched before adjusting his position and returning to sleep. It seemed a very long time before he awoke. When he did, he was grumpy, like he didn't get any rest at all. He glanced up at the darkening sky. He stood and cursed, all the while glaring at Luis.

"Let's get moving. You let me spend too much time sleeping. Now we're late," Papa said, heading off at a brisk pace.

"Sorry, Papa," Luis said, following quickly.

The sky was beginning to cloud up by the time they reached a small clearing a few hours later. Luis could smell the rain coming.

"We will wait here," Papa announced, sitting heavily on a large flat rock.

"What if it starts to rain?"

"Then we'll get wet," Papa said gruffly.

Luis sat beside him. His stomach felt very empty. He was thirsty and tired and his head hurt, but he didn't dare ask Papa for anything to eat or drink. He must wait for Papa to offer instead.

As he rested, Luis watched the tops of the trees. He felt curiously drawn to them. He loved climbing trees. He and Noely would spend hours playing among the branches, acting like monkeys and sloths. But this time felt different. He didn't want to play, just climb—climb as high as he could.

"Are you hungry, Luis?"

Luis startled. "Yes, Papa. Very."

Papa pulled out his bandana. They sat in silence as they gnawed on the last of the dried meat. Normally, Luis loved the salty goodness of the snack, especially the way Mama prepared it. But this time it tasted flat. In fact, it really didn't have much taste at all. Looking around, he spotted a fruiting papaya tree.

"Can I pick a papaya, Papa?"

Papa stretched and nodded.

The juicy fresh fruit was a welcome addition. But even as Luis slurped on the fleshy pulp, the sweetness of the fruit didn't hold the same appeal it usually did.

"Papa, does this taste all right to you?"

Papa wiped his mouth on his shirt. "Yes. It is very good. Do you not think so?"

"It doesn't taste right to me. Neither does the meat."

Papa huffed. "Do not complain so much, Luis."

"Yes, Papa."

They waited quietly, listening to the wind against the plants and the distant rumble of thunder. A few minutes later, a short man appeared in the clearing.

"Hello, my friends," the man called cheerily.

"You're late!" Papa snapped, rising quickly.

"Am I? Didn't we agree to meet here this afternoon? The sun has not set, so it is still the afternoon. Wouldn't you agree, Luis?"

Luis frowned. The man seemed very friendly. Luis couldn't remember having met him before, but the man obviously knew his name. He ducked his head and inched closer to Papa.

"Aw, don't be shy, little one. You're father and I are related. Your mama is my sister. That makes me your uncle. I'm your Uncle Ricardo. Your papa and I often do business together."

Papa grabbed Luis's shoulder and pulled him around front. "Do not be rude, Luis. Say hello to your uncle Ricky."

"Hola," Luis said softly.

The man laughed loudly. "Hello, little man. You have your mother's beautiful large eyes and thick locks," he said, tousling his hair. "Now then, Marco. Do you have the item I requested?"

Papa held up the plastic sack.

Luis was confused. "Papa? You're going to give Uncle Ricky the money bag?"

"The 'money bag'?" Uncle Ricky laughed. "Oh how quickly they learn. Yes, Luis. It is a bag full of money. But only if it turns out to be what our customer wants."

"It will be money to me regardless of what your customer wants," Papa said without laughing. "I worked hard for this—and I will be paid in full right now, or you will not have it."

Uncle Ricky stiffened then smiled. "That is what we agreed on, of course. But I first have to see it. That's only fair."

Papa untied the knot and held the plastic bag open to the man. Particles of the yellow dust floated to the ground. A terrible stink rose from the bag. Uncle Ricky peeked inside and frowned deeply. He did not look pleased.

"That's disgusting. Are you certain it's the right thing?" he asked.

"Yes, I'm certain. The woman scientist said so."

Uncle Ricky seemed shocked. "She *gave* it to you?"

"Of course not. I had to take it from her. She was very angry."

"And she did not try to stop you?"

Papa shrugged. "She did. But I—" He paused and glanced down at Luis. "I was able to persuade her to let me have it."

"So . . . no one else saw you?"

Papa looked angry again. "I did not see anyone else there. Besides, I was very careful. Now stop delaying and give me my money."

"Okay, Marco. It is only fair." The man pulled a paper envelope from his back pocket.

Papa opened it and leafed through whatever was inside. His face went from angry to happy very quickly. In fact, he seemed happier than he'd been in a long time. Luis wanted to ask what was in the envelope but knew he shouldn't. If it was important, Papa would tell him.

"It is all there, I assure you," Uncle Ricky said.

Suddenly, a clap of thunder slammed into the clearing. Luis recoiled, wide-eyed.

His uncle looked up at the dark, cloudy sky. "It is getting late, and this storm is about to soak us. Come, Marco. You and Luis should stay at my house. It is safer than wandering the jungle at night."

Papa looked at the sky for a moment before nodding. "Okay. But no tricks."

"No tricks, my brother. This is for Luis."

"All right, then. Just for the night."

"Excellent."

Luis wasn't sure he wanted to go with the man. Something about him seemed wrong. He seemed way too happy for a grown-up.

"But Papa," Luis urged. "Mama is waiting."

"Mama will wait until I tell her not to. Now let's go."

"Come on, Luis," Uncle Ricky said with a wide grin. "I have flan at home."

Luis loved flan, but he didn't feel the excitement he knew he should at the announcement. Instead, he kept glancing up—not at the encroaching storm but at the tops of the trees. It was almost as if they were calling to him.

CHAPTER 34

RICARDO LED MARCO AND LUIS toward his home in La Esmeralda. Had Marco been alone, Ricardo would have sent him on his way . . . or made other, less hospitable decisions. Marco was Ricardo's least favorite brother-in-law. He didn't like the man for several reasons but mostly because he was lazy, ill-tempered, and a horrible father. Yes, he was his sister's husband—but that didn't weigh heavily in his favor either. Ricardo didn't care for his sister. They'd never gotten along. Still, Marco *was* willing to do just about any dirty work for a price. That was as good as any excuse to maintain a relationship. In reality, the only reasons he tolerated the man were Luis and Noely. He loved those kids as if they were his own.

The rain had begun in earnest. Ricardo hated that Marco walked directly behind him. He simply didn't trust his brother-in-law. The man was unpredictable, and that made him dangerous. Worse, he was careless. Ricardo could hear the rain striking the plastic bag as it brushed rhythmically against Marco's leg. He wondered just how dangerous the thing in the bag was—and whether or not Marco had collected the right thing. He knew some kind of fungus had killed Dr. Udy. Felipe had said so, and he trusted Felipe. If Marco did what was asked of him, then the thing in the bag was immensely dangerous. He snuck a glance at the black trash sack then shrugged. It didn't matter; its deadliness wasn't his responsibility. He was asked merely to collect the fungus and ship it as soon as possible.

Ricardo knew one thing for certain: the fungus reeked. It smelled a lot like the *dama del velo*, the veiled lady mushroom. He didn't know the scientific name for it, but everyone knew it by its odor. It smelled like decomposing flesh. The dama fungus was actually kind of pretty, with its brown-orange cap and long white, skirt-like lattice veil. But it's odor? *¡Guácala!* It stank worse than the dead, rotting peccary he'd found behind his house last week.

Rain began pounding just as the lights of La Esmeralda blinked through the jungle foliage. Ricardo could tell Luis was very tired. But the young boy didn't complain. He trudged on with determined resolve. Ricardo was very proud of the kid.

"Not much farther, my family," Ricardo announced. "How are you doing, Luis?"

"Okay," the boy replied.

"Excellent. We'll be inside and dry very soon. Are you hungry?"

"I'm so hungry I could eat an elephant."

Ricardo chuckled. "I will see that you eat your fill, little man. I have some tamales and rice at home. Do you like that?"

"Yes. Very much."

"Then that is what we shall have."

"And flan?"

Ricardo guffawed loudly. "I did promise you flan, didn't I? Yes, of course we shall have flan too."

"Luis," Marco snapped. "You will not eat any of your uncle's food. He works hard for his meals and does not need to waste it on a little boy."

"It is okay," Ricardo said easily. "I have plenty to share."

"We brought sufficient for our needs," Marco grumbled. "But . . . a cold beer would be very welcome."

Ricardo continued to chuckle, but it was forced this time, insincere. "Fine. Beer for you, tamales and flan for Luis."

As they entered the clearing of the town, the downpour strengthened. La Esmeralda was much bigger than Marco's tiny village. Ricardo had visited many times. He also knew that while Marco wouldn't care about the comparison, little Luis would be in awe of its size. He had hoped to show Luis around, letting him meet other children and marvel at the electric lights in their school and airport. Regrettably, the current deluge would make everything hard to see. Better to wait out the storm and show him everything in more pleasant conditions in the morning.

Besides, he needed to report in. His customer was waiting.

CHAPTER 35

JULIA WAS STILL INCENSED AT the argument she'd had with María just before leaving. The woman had insisted that Noely accompany her. She had flat out refused. She was not going to risk exposing the child to deadly cordyceps spores.

"*Entonces*, there are many path," Maria had argued. "Easy to lost. Mi esposo go to La Esmeralda. Noely know the way."

"Why would he go there?"

"He do *trabajo* at town. Um, work, sí?"

Before Julia could argue further, Noely grabbed her hand and pulled her toward the trailhead. *"Vámonos, señora. La lluvia comenzará pronto,"* she said, gesturing at the darkened sky.

Julia was impressed by Noely's lack of fear. It actually made sense to let her lead the way. The girl obviously knew these jungles better than she did.

María gave both girls a quick hug. *"Vaya con Dios*, señora. Gracias. Muchas gracias."

Julia and Noely had been on the path only one hour before the rain hit. The downpour didn't seem to faze the little girl in the least. Her pace was brisk and unrelenting.

The noise of the rain lessened when they entered the understory of the rain forest canopy. Still, it was a constant drone that twisted Julia's orientation. She was soon lost as to points on the compass. The trail split or converged with other pathways several times, but Noely never hesitated on choosing which way to go.

"Is the town much farther?" Julia gasped, struggling to keep up.

Noely glanced back and shrugged.

Did that mean she didn't know the distance or that she didn't understand the question?

As she plodded on, a headache assaulted Julia from every point in her skull. Combined with her already sullen mood, she quickly became cocooned in a depressing funk. Her mind worked scenario after scenario, trying to understand why Brandon had been infected and she hadn't, why anyone would want to steal a toxic fungus, and where the heck Felipe had gone. She found herself clenching her jaw so hard that her teeth hurt. Her fists were clenched to cramping. She stopped dead in her tracks and, closing her eyes, forced herself to calm and relax.

Noely stopped and returned to her. "*¿Esta bien*, señora?"

"Yes—sí." Pointing to her skull, she said, "*Cabeza dolor.*"

"Sí. *Claro*," the little girl said, choosing a fallen log to sit on. "*Mi padre tiene dolores de cabeza todo el tiempo.*"

Julia chose to keep standing. She couldn't allow herself to get too relaxed. It would dull her ability to deduce and reason. More than anything, she wanted four ibuprofen and a dry bed. "Okay, mate. Take things one fact at a time," Julia said aloud to help herself focus. "List the things you know, not what you don't know. First, in ants, *Ophiocordyceps unilateralis* is internal not topical. So it's not like mold growing on bread. Second, not all cordyceps species are deadly; many cultures use it medicinally. Some even eat it on a regular basis, so infection may or may not be via the gut . . ."

Noely sat staring at her with a faint smile. There was no way she understood any of what Julia was saying, but she seemed entertained by it nonetheless.

"But if any of it had *ever* been incorrectly prepared and people were infected, then we'd already know about the *human* zombie effects it created, right?" she asked the little girl, knowing she wouldn't get an answer.

Noely's smile broadened. Julia sat next to her, nestling against her like two best friends. Noely didn't seem to mind.

"Right, so once an ant is parasitized, the fungal spore goes to its brain and prompts it to get to high ground. And not just any high ground—the highest ground possible. So, in Brandon's case, how did the cordyceps fungus know the tallest tree was the nearby kapok? It couldn't have *known*; fungi have no sentient abilities. They have no brain, no ability to reason," she said, tapping the side of her head. "But *Brandon* knew about Goliath. So does that mean the fungus accessed his memory and selected Goliath from a list of local trees?"

Noely began picking dirt from underneath her fingernails and yawned as if she'd lost interest.

"I know what you're thinking," Julia said to Noely. "You're thinking, *Of course not, you ninny. Fungi* can't *do that. And ants don't have categorical memory either. They have instinct and response, not reason.*"

Julia angrily wiped at the water trickling down her brow.

"¿Está bien, señora?"

Julia took a deep breath and let it out slowly. "Yeah. No worries."

"Brain?" the little girl asked, pointing at her head.

Julia smiled. "Sí, Noely. I'm trying to use my brain—but without much luck."

Noely shrugged with a smile of apology and glanced up at the rapidly darkening sky. *"Entonces, debemos darnos prisa, señora. Será oscuro pronto."*

"Right," Julia said, understanding. "We should get moving."

After another two hours, the rain eased up, but it still created a haze that prevented seeing more than a few meters up the trail. The clouds hadn't thinned. More rain was on the way.

"¿Más rápido, sí?" Noely asked.

"Sí, Noely. Más rápido."

The little girl took off at a pace that astounded Julia. She wasn't running—but pretty close to it. Within the third hour night had fallen. Soon, faint pinpoints of light broke through the foliage ahead of them. They rounded a bend and crossed a dirt road scarred with water-filled tire ruts. The thoroughfare twisted a few times before opening to a large swath of cleared land.

Across a cultivated field, she saw a wide river and a small town with semi-modern buildings, electricity, and an airstrip. Even in the hazy, moisture-soaked night, Julia recognized it as La Esmeralda—the airport they'd flown into nearly one year ago.

CHAPTER 36

WITH A PLASTIC CUP FILLED with cheap box wine, Mantis sat at his home computer surfing the Internet. He was looking for the best ways to disappear from society . . . without dying. Green Blade was breathing down his neck. Tomorrow they'd send him a message saying *Five days*. If he didn't deliver in five days, his death was guaranteed.

He had to produce something, anything. Bruja claimed she'd gathered a specimen sample meeting his needs, but had she really? When he'd first contacted her, he'd asked for anything that might prove deadly and highly contagious. Bruja had suggested a few species that were already known to science. That meant there were already cures or at least ways to deal with the infection. He said to keep searching. What he needed was the ultimate deadly bioweapon—a species with a biohazard rating of 4, a BSL-4 substance like the Ebola and Marburg viruses. Did she even know what that meant? Did she have any knowledge of biochemistry to the toxicity of plants and fungi? What if the sample she sent was a dud? He needed proof that it had high virulence and toxicity. True, she'd claimed there were confirmed deaths, but again, where was the authentication? Did she understand the importance of the sample arriving alive? And fully contained? Selling a questionable bioweapon to a vindictive ecotage organization before you even knew it worked was more than stupid. It was insane.

Mantis frowned. He had never received any documentation detailing Bruja's qualifications as a field expert or a botanist. She'd never sent a résumé. He didn't know if he was dealing with a colleague or a counterfeit. He was going off of a recommendation from a contact outside of Green Blade. He needed something verifiable, something tangible. If he didn't have that, Green Blade would be angry. Those who angered Green Blade did not live long. Therefore, he had to find a way to disappear . . . just in case.

Mantis scanned several articles on random bug-out locations in South America and how to prepare for the collapse of civilization. A number of articles highlighted families who had become remarkably self-sufficient—growing their own food, raising their own livestock, purifying their own water—but that was simply too much work, especially for someone with only one fully workable hand. If Mantis needed to disappear, he wanted to do so in comfort. Sure, it would entail money. Lots of money. He had personal savings of about eighteen thousand dollars and his company 401K, which was about three times that amount, but that wasn't nearly enough to live on the rest of his life, even in South America. At least not in the lifestyle he wanted. Then there was the money Green Blade had given him. He'd already spent a considerable amount of that chasing leads for possible bioweapons, but until Bruja, none had panned out. Mantis had secreted away the remaining money in an offshore account under a fictitious name.

With massive regret, he knew he'd spent way too much time planning for the comforts of his future rather than researching his bioweapon. But such research required a lot more money than Green Blade had granted him. Didn't they know that?

Taking a large gulp of his wine, Mantis shuddered at the irony of his predicament. The best source of such funding was from the very people who were demanding results from money already invested. And Green Blade was a heartless creditor. He finished his cup with a hard, painful swallow. A delinquent payment didn't simply mean a compounded interest rate. It meant a ghastly death.

He needed to deliver Bruja's sample to Green Blade in less than a week—which brought him full circle to his original question: what if the organism was a dud? He *had* to find out more. He had to find out if the sample was real. He couldn't simply deliver to them a stinky old mushroom in a Ziploc baggie postmarked Venezuela and say, "Merry Christmas."

He chewed on his lower lip. That brought up yet another concern: delivery. He couldn't risk the sample being confiscated by the TSA or having it destroyed through sloppy handling. He'd taken too many risks already. He cursed.

Mantis stepped to a window and looked out at the nightscape. He watched a passenger jet line up to land at Seattle-Tacoma International, and sudden, profound comprehension enlightened his mind. He realized all the issues plaguing him could be solved with one single, proactive plan of action.

Mantis returned to his computer and switched from researching bug-out locations to surfing for the cheapest flights to Venezuela. He grimaced. The flights were all so expensive! There were one or two that weren't as bad, but they had hours and hours of layovers. Time was of the essence here. He finally found one that had only one layover with medium wait time; he booked it. He then logged into his offshore account and wire transferred a large chuck of money to his personal bank account. Next, he accessed his company's HR website and typed a message saying he was suddenly very sick and would not be in for a few days. Because he worked in a cleanroom environment, the company rarely made a fuss over someone taking a sick day. Better safe than sorry.

Before shutting down his laptop, Mantis checked his personal e-mail. There was a message from Bruja.

I have the sample you need in hand. I can ship it to you overnight for $5,000 American.

Five thousand dollars? Was she nuts? That was ridiculous. He felt his anger flare before another thought tempered it. He smiled and poured another cup of wine. A curious sense of assurance washed over him as he headed to his bedroom to pack. It was a stroke of genius he'd booked the flight when he did. Not only would he personally be able to obtain the sample, he'd also be able to settle matters with the annoying Bruja . . . permanently.

CHAPTER 37

"Eat, Luis! You are embarrassing me," Papa demanded.

With a blank expression, Luis sat staring at his plate of food. It looked delicious, but for some reason he wasn't very hungry anymore. Instead, he felt . . . squirmy. He had all sorts of energy. He certainly didn't want to disobey Papa and make him angry, but he had no desire to eat. There was something more important he had to do.

"Leave him be, Marco," Uncle Ricardo said from across the kitchen table. "He's probably just tired. It is a long hike from your village to here."

"Just a few minutes ago he was complaining about being soooo hungry," Papa grumbled before downing half his beer. "He should eat what you have offered and stop embarrassing me."

"I'm sorry, Papa," Luis said, his soft brown eyes burning with unwanted tears. "I . . . I feel strange."

"Are you sick, Luis?" Ricardo asked gently. "Do you wish to go to bed now?"

Luis glanced from Uncle Ricardo to Papa, but Papa refused to look at him. Not knowing how to answer his uncle, Luis lowered his gaze and felt a hot tear run down his cheek.

"Now he chooses to cry to get his way. Do not be fooled by his act, Ricky. He will eat what you offer, or he will not leave your table."

"Marco, Luis is just a boy. Perhaps he does not feel well because of the long walk from El Desvío. Would you like to try some flan before you go to bed, Luis?"

Luis looked at the eggy dessert dripping with caramel sauce. It *did* look wonderful. He knew he could easily eat two of them, perhaps even three. But now it held no appeal. Something felt more important than any food or drink. He wasn't sure what, but he knew he'd understand once he got outside.

"Answer your uncle!" Papa yelled. "Do not be so disrespectful."

"May I be excused from your table, Uncle Ricardo?" Luis managed to say. Strangely, speaking suddenly took great effort.

"Yes, of course you can, little man. We'll save this meal for tomorrow. It will keep just fine. Don't you worry."

"Why do you encourage the boy?" Papa hissed. "He is too spoiled as it is."

"Why do *you* belittle him? He has not once acted spoiled since our meeting in the clearing," Ricardo said, moving to Luis's side.

Papa finished the bottle of beer and twisted open another one. Luis couldn't remember if it was Papa's fourth or fifth. He couldn't concentrate.

"It's his mother's fault, you know," Papa grumbled. "Your stupid sister."

"My sister is not wise, I agree," Uncle Ricardo said. *She married you, didn't she?* he didn't voice. "But Luis is not influenced by her bad choices. He is a brave, polite boy."

"Yeah, a 'momma's boy.' Look at his tears. Why is he crying? He isn't hurt."

Uncle Ricardo had a strange look on his face. It was like he was very sad, like he wanted to cry too. "He is not hurt *physically*," Ricardo said softly as he gently stroked Luis's head. "There are other ways to feel pain."

Papa took a long drink then belched loudly. Normally, Luis would have laughed. Now it seemed . . . unimportant.

"Fine. Whatever," Papa muttered. "Go to bed hungry. It serves you right for being so disobedient."

Luis felt himself standing. Uncle Ricardo placed his hand on his shoulder, but he shrugged it off and headed to the door. What he needed to do next he had to do alone.

Uncle Ricardo lived next to the airport. Luis had seen the long landing strip on the way in and the tall control tower where Uncle Ricardo worked. The airport also had a tall tower made out of steel bars, like a bunch of small triangles stacked straight up. It was a radio tower, Uncle Ricardo had explained. He'd called it an aerial. There was a red light that steadily blinked on and off at the very top. Luis knew he could climb up to it, no problem. He'd climbed trees about the same height—he and Noely. It was always fun to do. Climbing the tower would be fun, but he didn't feel much joy in the anticipation. He just . . . wanted to climb.

No, that wasn't quite right. He *needed* to climb it, though he didn't know why.

"Luis? What is the matter? Are you okay?" Uncle Ricardo asked, standing next to him on the wide veranda.

Luis heard his uncle's words. He knew he should answer. It was disrespectful not to. Instead, his legs began moving, carrying him into the wet night toward the tall tower.

"Luis? Luis, what's the matter? Luis, answer me. Please."

CHAPTER 38

RICARDO WAS SCARED. VERY SCARED. It was as if Luis was in a trance—like some witch or shaman had put a spell on him. The only thing he'd seen like it was when a young man in town had been bitten by a bat with rabies. The teen had lost his mind, snarling at people, running onto the tarmac regardless of airplanes coming and going. Some men finally caught him and tied him to a cot. The poor boy twitched uncontrollably and foamed at the mouth for hours. Their local shaman could do nothing for him. They'd called Felipe to transport him to Caracas, but by the time he arrived, the young man was dead.

What a horrible way to die. Ricardo swallowed hard. He ran out into the misty rain, picked up Luis, and carried him back to the veranda. He sat the boy on a long bench, praying the child didn't have rabies. Luis wasn't twitching or foaming at the mouth; he simply sat there staring toward the airport with a blank expression.

"Are you okay, little man?"

Luis didn't answer.

"Talk to me, *mijo*. Please."

The boy slowly pointed toward the control tower.

"The tower? You want to go to the tower?"

Luis said nothing.

"Marco!" Ricardo yelled into the house.

No answer there either.

"Come on, son. Let's get inside where it is dry and warm, okay?"

Luis continued to point toward the tower.

"No. It is not wise to visit the landing area at night, Luis. And please do not go back out into the rain, okay?"

Leaving the boy for a brief moment, Ricardo threw open the door and stuck his head inside. Marco was folded over the table, his face in his dinner plate. He was out cold.

"Marco!" Ricardo hollered, moving toward him. "Wake up, you stupid drunk. Your son's in trouble."

Hauling Marco into a sitting position elicited an angry growl that reeked of beer. Marco's face was ruddy, flushed to the point that small blood vessels stood out on his cheeks and nose. Kernels of rice and daubs of refried beans clung to his beard stubble. "Go away, pest," he slurred, jerking from Ricardo's hold.

"Marco, it's Ricardo. You're at my house. Come on, man. Get up." Ricardo removed a nearly empty beer bottle from Marco's grasp and tried to lift him under his arms.

Marco cursed angrily. "Get away from me, dog. I need to sleep."

"Listen to me, you worthless pig," Ricardo snarled in response. "You have to come help your son. I don't know what's wrong with him, but he is acting very sick. He doesn't answer to anything. He may have contracted something."

Marco looked at Ricardo in a confused glare. His eyes were bloodshot and rheumy.

"It's me, Ricardo—your brother-in-law. Luis, *your son*, is not responding."

"Try whipping his behind," Marco huffed, lying his head back down. "He always responds to that."

Ricardo grabbed a pitcher of water and dumped it on Marco's head. The drunk sat up sputtering and cursing, his arms thrashing the air. His eyes were filled with venom.

"What did you do that for?"

"To wake you up. Your son is acting strangely. I think he's got rabies."

"Rabies? Don't be absurd. How could he have rabies?"

"I don't know. Was he bitten recently?"

Marco frowned and rubbed his forehead. "Not that I know of."

"It doesn't matter," Ricardo said shortly with a jerk of his head. "Come look for yourself. We have to get him to the hospital."

"So take him."

"I will. But you need to watch him while I contact—" Ricardo stopped short. *Felipe!* He should have checked in by now, but Ricardo had forgotten due to the excitement of his delivery. "You must help, Marco. Luis keeps wandering away. You must watch him while I call for the shaman and a helicopter."

Marco let out a prolonged, exasperated sigh and staggered to his feet. "Where is he?"

"Just outside, on the veranda," Ricardo said, leading the way.

The two men walked outside.

Luis was not there.

CHAPTER 39

THE RAIN HAD LESSENED TO a soft mist, allowing for a fairly clear view of the airfield. The town was asleep and eerily silent. Julia and Noely followed the muddy road that ran past one end of the airstrip. Julia was exhausted, utterly whipped. Even with the excitement of reaching their destination, she couldn't force herself to walk any faster.

"*Estamos aquí*, señora," Noely said, sounding equally spent.

"Sí. Gracias, Noely."

La Esmeralda was a small town spread across a cleared patch of land adjacent to the bend of a wide, black river. The Orinoco. The airstrip ran the entire length of the town on the opposite side. Most of the homes sat between the airstrip and the river.

Julia and Noely trudged toward a low, white building next to the red-and-white checkered control tower. Not much else could be seen. The haze blurred anything that was not illuminated by electricity.

Passing a small, dark outbuilding, they heard the misty precipitation hiss against its tin roof, sounding like a warning issued from a thousand snakes. The rest of the area was deathly quiet. Nothing moved. Julia wondered if she was too late. Had the entire town been infected already? Were they all in trees waiting for a stroma to erupt from their necks?

As they drew close to the white building, Julia heard two men shouting the name *Luis*. They sounded desperate.

"Luis!" Noely cried, equally desperate.

"Luis?" Julia asked.

"*Mi hermano menor*," she said before running toward the building.

Julia picked up her pace but couldn't break into a run. In the light of a bare bulb yellowed by time and burnt insects, Julia saw the two men standing under a veranda, staring across the grassy field that ran the length of the airstrip. They argued in rapid Spanish, frantic and angry.

She heard Noely call out, "*Tío* Ricky!"

As the men turned toward the little girl, Julia recognized the one as Ricardo Paz.

"Ricardo!" she yelled, finding the strength to jog the last few meters. She was so grateful to see a familiar face that she immediately wrapped him in a crushing hug. Noely had her arms around his waist. Ricardo hesitantly returned both embraces with an awkward chuckle.

"¡Ay caramba, Dr. Fatheringham! What are you doing here?" he asked, gently pushing her away. His expression was a mix of confusion and horror.

The second man ducked his head and went inside the house. Julia didn't recognize him, but she smelled the fermented stench of alcohol in his wake.

"Something terrible has happened," Julia said, wiping unbidden tears from her eyes.

"Sí. You *look* terrible," he said, examining the bruises across her face. "¡Qué mal!"

"No. It's worse than that. Someone stole the fungus."

Noely sat on the bench and rubbed her arms to ward off the chill.

"What fungus?" Ricardo asked, motioning toward the bench.

Julia removed her backpack and sat heavily next to Noely. "Didn't Felipe tell you?"

"Only that Dr. Udy died from an infection and he went to collect the body."

Julia leaned forward and placed her face in her hands—then flinched at the touch. The pain from her head wound seemed amplified by her fatigue.

Ricardo gently turned her face toward the light. He drew in a long breath through his teeth. "Who did this to you?"

"The man who stole the fungus."

"What fungus do you mean? The one that killed Dr. Udy?"

"Yes." Julia pulled out her water bottle and took several long swigs. She then steadied her emotions and rehearsed all that had transpired the previous few days. Ricardo sat beside her and stared with eyes wide and jaw dropped. He kept softly repeating, *"Dios mío,"* and occasionally crossing himself.

"But you did not see the man's face?" he asked after she described the attack.

"No. It was too dark. But he was definitely Hispanic."

"¡Caramba! Is the fungus truly that . . . dangerous?"

"Yes, it's that dangerous. Why do you think I've been chasing the blighter all night?"

"What about Felipe? Did he see this man?"

Julia's throat tightened. "I don't know. When I awoke, Felipe and his helicopter were gone. I don't know where he is. He won't answer his radio."

"I've tried to call him too. Many times. He has not answered." He paused. "Can he be sick too? With the fungus, I mean?"

"Crikey, I hope not." She groaned to her feet and stretched her lower back. "I can't worry about him right now. I need to find that thief and get back the fungus."

Ricardo stood too. So did Noely.

"Are you infected?" he asked.

"No. At least, I don't think so. As I said, Brandon's infection happened very quickly. I was exposed to the fungus for a long time, and I feel fine."

"But—forgive me—you look terrible. And you have not slept all this time?"

She shook her head then nodded toward Noely. "As I said, this little girl led me here. Do you know her?"

"Sí. Noely is my niece, my sister's daughter."

"Brilliant. She brought me here because—" She stopped short as the family connection hit her. "Wait. That bloody thief is your brother-in-law?"

Ricardo blinked hard. "Why do you say that?"

"Your sister told me. María is your sister, right?"

"Sí. But why does she think her husband stole your fungus?"

"I don't know. Perhaps she—"

Both adults flinched as Noely let out a shrill scream. She had moved to the end of the veranda and was staring toward the airstrip. Ricardo was immediately at her side. *"¡Cielos, mija! ¿Qué pasó?"*

Julia joined the two at the corner of the porch. With absolute terror blazing in her eyes, Noely pointed at the tall radio tower. Following her line of sight, Julia saw nothing unusual in the murky night.

"What's the matter, sweetheart?" she asked.

Suddenly, Ricardo looked as frightened as his niece. "*¡Dios mío, no!*"

"What?" Julia cried.

He pointed. "There. At the very top."

Julia could see it now. A red strobe light blinked steadily atop the tall radio tower. A small, dark shape, highlighted by the pulsing strobe, looked like that of a child.

With a sob, Noely choked out, "Luis!" She took off, sprinting toward the tower.

Not again, Julia pled, feeling as if an ice-cold lance had pierced her chest.

"*¡Noely, párate! ¡Espera!*" Ricardo yelled, chasing after her.

Just as Julia was about to follow, something crashed behind her. The second man, obviously still drunk, stumbled through the door. He leaned heavily against one of the veranda supports and threw up. He mumbled something in Spanish then noticed Julia. His head bobbed back and forth as if trying to focus on her.

She was in no mood for introductions or conversation with a drunk, but she had to ask, "Do you speak English?"

His eyes narrowed in suspicion. "*Poquito.*"

"Call for help. *Ayuda médico. Una doctor*, sí?"

The man slowly nodded and stumbled back into the house. Julia turned and followed Ricardo into the dark night.

CHAPTER 40

NOELY WAS ROUGHLY TWO METERS up the radio tower and still climbing. Ricardo scrambled up a couple rungs and grabbed her ankle, preventing her from ascending higher. They were arguing in Spanish. Julia understood very little, but she got the gist of it. High above them sat the small form of Luis. He was perched on a flange just below the flashing warning light; his little arms and legs were wrapped around the superstructure of the tower.

All the angst and heartache she'd suppressed over Brandon's death suddenly surfaced, slamming into her resolve like a tidal wave. She couldn't breathe. Tears sprang up, burning her eyes. On wobbly legs, Julia approached the tower. She had to swallow several times before finding her voice.

"Noely, do not climb up there!" Julia cried.

The little girl was also sobbing, saying something about her brother and pointing to his small form pulsing red in chorus with the strobe light.

"She cannot go up there," she continued. "Ricardo, tell her not to go up there. She'll get infected."

Ricardo's expression was already one of concern. At her words, it switched to sheer terror. "Infected? You mean like Dr. Udy? That is what is wrong with Luis?"

"Yes," she said, wiping away her tears. "Tell her that Luis is very contagious. She cannot go near him"

Ricardo spoke rapidly to the little girl. Noely looked back and forth between her uncle and her brother. She then focused on Julia. "¿Es cierto?" she asked.

"She asked if that is true," Ricardo translated.

"Yes," Julia answered. "Sí, *es cierto*. It's true. Now please come down."

Noely unhooked her arm and allowed her uncle to guide her off the tower framework. Once on the ground, Ricardo indicated that she should stay with Julia. Then he began to climb.

"No, wait," Julia said, stopping him. "You could get infected too. Let me go up."

"Are you immune?"

"I don't know. But I've been around the infection for days now without contracting it, so maybe." She looked up and stepped around the base of the narrow tower, trying to get a better perspective. "Do you have any rope?"

"Sí," he answered. He then rattled off a bunch of Spanish to Noely and pointed toward his house. The girl nodded and ran into the night.

"Why is this happening? Why is my nephew sick?" he asked in a voice filled with angst.

"Oy, I'm still trying to figure that out. I don't even know how Brandon got infected."

"Will Luis . . . be all right?" His concern was deeply apparent.

Julia had to strain against the tightness in her throat. "I don't know, mate," she lied.

Ricardo looked up at the small form a hundred feet above him. A tear coursed down his cheek. Softly, he pled, "Por favor, señorita. Please help him."

"I'll do what I can," she said, knowing it was an empty promise.

Noely soon returned carrying a few well-used bungee cords. She said something that Julia took for not finding any rope.

"Will these work?" Ricardo asked.

"They'll be fine. Thanks."

Julia secured the cords, five in all, through her belt and began ascending the tower. Almost immediately her legs cramped and screamed with fatigue. Her muscles were on empty. She hadn't rested well or had a proper meal in days. The toll on her body had brought her to her breaking point. But an innocent boy's life was at stake, and somehow she felt accountable for what had happened. Using guilt to fuel her endurance, she climbed ten rungs, rested a minute, then climbed ten more. The ascent seemed to take forever. It amazed her that a small boy could have ascended to such an elevation, but she reminded herself that he was a native and was probably used to playing in trees of equal height. Plus, he had the drive instilled in him by the cordyceps fungus. There was no doubt he'd been infected. The scene was all too similar to Brandon's fugue to be coincidence.

The murky haze abated as she continued upward; muted moon glow aided her ascent. Pushing on, she reached the little boy within minutes. Her heart thrummed in her chest—both from exertion and in anticipation of what she'd find.

Gasping for breath, she said, "Luis?"

He fidgeted a bit.

"Luis, my name is Julia. Um . . . *mi nombre es Julia. Quiero ayudarte.*"

No response. Perhaps she hadn't said it right.

She took a deep breath and climbed to his level on the opposite side of the tower. Flashbacks of Brandon's plight flooded her mind. She fought to stay focused and to keep her hands from trembling. Through the lattice of the superstructure she could see the little boy's head pressed against the framework. She reached around and eased his T-shirt away from his neck. No stroma pierced his skin. Yet. She rounded the structure and stood directly behind him, bracing her arms on either side. Carefully, she placed a hand on his frail chest. There was a faint heartbeat—weak but steady.

"Luis, I'm going to wrap some bungee cords around you. Don't be afraid, little mate. I've got you."

She knew the English was lost on him, but she said the words aloud anyway, if only to talk herself through what had to be done. With utmost care, she stretched a bungee around Luis, pulled it snug, then clipped both ends to her belt loops. She repeated this procedure until all five cords were pulling him tightly against her frame. She then unwrapped his legs from the metal framework and peeled his fingers from the crossbars. His grip was tight but not rigid. Holding him with one hand, she began a slow descent.

Ricardo and Noely gazed up at her with eyes wide.

How was she going to explain this to them? Would they think she was at fault? Probably. She felt the same way. It was an irrational emotion—but it was one she could not deny.

"Please stand back," she said as she drew near the onlookers.

"Can I help?" Ricardo asked, taking a single step back.

"Did the other bloke call for help yet?"

He frowned. "What is a bloke?"

Julia huffed. "The other man."

"What other man?"

"The one back at the house, dolt." She couldn't stop her ire from rising.

Ricardo glanced back at his home. "I do not know."

"Well somebody needs to contact a hospital immediately," she said harshly. "This is something I can't fix."

"I will call the medicine man," Ricardo said, reaching to guide her down the last couple of rungs.

"Don't touch me!" Julia snapped. "Call a doctor, not some local shaman. I'm not mucking about here, mate. We need a real doctor."

"Sí. I will."

"And no one is to touch Luis but me. Make sure Noely understands."

Ricardo rattled off a stern sentence to the little girl. She nodded and wiped at her eyes.

"Sí, *claro*," she said softly.

"I need a room where Luis can rest in isolation. That means *alone*. Do you have one?"

"Sí. In my house."

"No. I don't want to risk infecting others in your family."

"But I live alone, Doctor. I am not married. You know this."

She tipped her head toward Noely. "I mean your visitors."

"Ah, sí. In the control tower, then," he said, nodding toward the tall red-and-white building. "There is a room with a cot. He will be safe there."

"Brilliant."

Julia wasn't worried about Luis's safety. Her heart ached with the certainty it was already too late for him. She hated herself for not being more hopeful. It was the first time in a long while that her pragmatic nature was more foe than friend.

CHAPTER 41

Ricardo couldn't believe what was happening. Everything had been fine just minutes ago. He'd been so close to being a rich man; he was certain of it. Now this! There was no way little Luis could have the same horrible infection that had killed Dr. Udy. No way. It wasn't fair.

"Tell Noely to go fetch the town doctor," Julia instructed Ricardo. "And tell her to hurry."

He did, adding a stern warning not to talk to anyone else on the way. No need to get his small town in a panic.

As he led Dr. Fatheringham, who carried his unconscious nephew, into the control tower, Ricardo's mind refused to stop connecting links of condemnation—the end result of which was that *he* had killed his nephew.

No—Luis is not dead! he cried internally. Dr. Fatheringham had said so. Besides, he argued, really it's all Marco's fault. If the drunk, worthless bum hadn't been so careless, his son would not be dangerously sick. If he had done as instructed, he would have collected the mushroom and brought it directly to La Esmeralda instead of stopping off at his house for whatever stupid reason. But that was so typical of Marco. The man was a complete imbecile. Why María had married him was beyond explanation.

Ascending a flight of stairs, Ricardo led Dr. Fatheringham to a small workroom directly below the third-story control room. The room held a long work table, a few folding chairs, an executive desk, and a portable cot.

Dr. Fatheringham unfastened Luis from the bungee cords and laid him on the cot. His face looked serene—as if nothing was wrong and he was simply sleeping through a pleasant dream. His skin was pale and drawn, but that was probably due to the cold rain.

He reached out to caress the boy's hair, but the doctor stayed his hand.

"Don't touch him," she softly said.

"But . . . is he alive? I need to know."

"Yes, he's alive."

He drew a tentative breath. "Then . . . he will be okay, sí?"

"I can't say for sure." She began rifling through a desk drawer. "I need some scissors."

"I will get them," Ricardo said, turning and sprinting up the stairs. He always had a pair in his control room desk. Returning, he watched Dr. Fatheringham cut away Luis's T-shirt.

"What are you doing?" he asked.

"Just checking for signs of the infection," she said, turning Luis on his stomach and wiping his skin with the shirt. "If this is what Brandon had, it will show on his neck and back first."

Ricardo leaned closer. Luis's back looked frail and boney, but that was not unusual for children in that area. While few were starving, many were undernourished. María was a passable cook, but Marco had never earned enough to keep his family well fed. And anytime he *did* bring in a few bolívares, they were quickly wasted on alcohol and cigarettes.

Dr. Fatheringham held a desk lamp close to Luis's neck. "Do you have any gloves?" she asked, poking at the boy's skin with a pencil.

"There are some work gloves out in the hanger."

She shook her head. "Never mind."

In the harshness of the lamplight, he saw small red dots along his nephew's shoulders and neckline. "Are those bug bites or the infection?" he asked, pointing.

The doctor wiped at them with the shirt. They seemed to grow more intense at the touch. He watched her swallow a sob before she answered. "I'm not sure. When will Noely return?"

"If the doctor is in town, they should be back soon."

She looked up sharply. "If he's in town?"

He shrugged. "Sometimes he is called away."

"Time is of the essence here, Ricardo."

He nodded. Clasping his hands behind his back, he again leaned close to his nephew. Luis's breathing was shallow and slow. He didn't seem to be in any distress or pain. Perhaps he was just sleeping off whatever had driven him to climb the tall aerial. He prayed silently, *Blessed Virgin. Please let it be so. Let him live and not suffer.*

"When was the last time you heard from Felipe?" Julia asked, interrupting his supplication.

"Not since he went to Ascom. I talked to him on his helicopter radio, um, two days ago?"

"And nothing since then?"

He shook his head.

"Any guesses as to where he went?"

"No, Doctor."

"Where have you been during all this?"

He unclasped his hands and slid them in his pockets. Staring at the floor, he confessed, "I come in and out. It sometimes happens, you know? I cannot be here all day and night. But I leave the recorder on all times."

"Brilliant. Have you checked that?"

"Sí. But there was nothing from him."

"Crikey! Well, what did he say the last time you chatted him up?"

"He said there was a serious problem at your site—that Dr. Udy was dead from a brain-infecting fungus. He said the camp was quarantined, Code Red."

"But he didn't hint he was going somewhere else?"

"No. He said he was staying with you. Is Felipe—" he paused and gulped. "Is he infected?"

She blew out a deep breath. "I don't think so, but I can't be certain. I have no idea how this fungus cycles through humans. I have some guesses but no facts."

A hopeful smile crossed his face. "So he could be okay?"

"Possibly."

"Then so could Luis."

She looked down at the boy and wiped his neck and back again. "I don't know." Her words clearly lacked confidence. Was she lying?

"If he *is* infected . . . what can be done for him?"

When she looked up, tears filled her eyes. "Nothing."

Ricardo's stomach clenched. He felt like throwing up. His anger toward Marco soared. He hated the pig. How could a father do this to his own children? If Noely and Luis were his, he'd treat them so much better. He wouldn't be so selfish or domineering. He'd give them everything—

His thoughts slammed him against a wall of guilt. Perhaps *his*— Ricardo Esteban Paz's—selfishness *had* brought this on. Yes, Marco had been careless, but the man would not have gone after the stupid fungus if Ricardo hadn't sent him there.

The noise of a door clacking open downstairs startled him. Noely came bounding up the stairs and approached the door to the small room. Gasping for breath, her face was contorted with anguish.

"Is Luis okay?" she asked in Spanish.

"He is sleeping," Ricardo lied. "Did you find the doctor?"

"Sort of."

CHAPTER 42

JULIA TURNED TOWARD THE WINDED little girl. The look in her eyes was pained. She stepped to one side to allow a shirtless man in soiled jeans and ceremonial headdress to enter the room. He sported a wiry goatee, a strand of beads and bones around his neck, and armbands dangling with feathers. His face was striped with swaths of red and black paint. His skin resembled old leather. He looked to be about sixty, but she couldn't tell for sure. He held a black plastic trash bag.

"Crikey, you're jesting, right? *This* is the doctor?" she asked, frowning.

"Sí. He is the town medicine man," Ricardo said.

"I said to get a *real* doctor. Not Voodoo Charlie," she spat with a flick of her wrist.

Without a word, the shaman marched past Julia and knelt beside Luis.

"Don't touch him," Julia cried, shoving her hand between the shaman and the boy.

The feathered man smiled softly, and benevolently moved her hand aside. He then felt for a pulse on Luis's carotid artery and gingerly palpated his neck and back.

"Oy, I don't know what you think you're doing, mate, but this boy is very sick," she said, near the point of breakdown. "And highly contagious."

Ricardo took Julia by the shoulders and gently guided her back a few steps. Succumbing to the effects of extreme fatigue, horrendous anxiety, and little food, she complied. She felt tears trickle down her cheeks but did not have the strength to wipe them away.

"He is very skilled at medicine," Ricardo explained. "You will see."

Feeling numb, Julia collapsed into a chair. She watched the shaman rifle through his rubbish bag. Expecting him to withdraw a magic rattle made from rodent teeth, she was surprised to see him pull out a small bottle of hand sanitizer and a modern stethoscope. He swabbed his hands with the astringent gel and began a cadre of pokes and prods, testing the boy's reflexes, smelling his breath, tasting his saliva, burning a sample of his hair, listening to his heart and lungs. Some of what he did made no sense to her—but at that point it didn't matter. Not only did Julia feel useless, she felt like a failure. She hated that feeling.

After about fifteen minutes, the shaman let out a deep sigh and pulled up a chair next to Julia's.

"Thank you for allowing me to examine the patient," the shaman said in English only slightly accented with Spanish. "I have heard of this malady among the Yanomami natives, but I've never seen it."

Julia blinked. "Say that again?"

"I believe it is a bacterial infection of the brain," he went on. "We need to get him to the hospital. I'd like to start him on sulfamethoxazole right away."

"Hold on a tick—you speak English?"

Ricardo smiled at her astonishment. "I told you. This is the town medicine man. He is very wise."

"How—?" was all Julia could come up with.

"I'll explain everything on the way," the shaman said. "Time is of the essence."

"Sí! That is what she said," Ricardo agreed, pointing at Julia.

"Indeed," the shaman said. "Ricardo, please call Felipe. The sulfa may or may not help. We need to evac this boy to Caracas."

"I do not know where he is," Ricardo said. "He is missing."

"Missing?"

Julia finally found her voice. "I think he's afraid he may be infected with the same thing Dr. Udy was. He flew out to Ascom base three days ago when I called for help. He left without a word. I still don't know why."

"Ah," the shirtless man said, snapping his fingers. "You're Dr. Fatheringham. I am sorry to hear about your loss." The man extended his calloused hand. "I'm Dr. Henry Esparza. Very pleased to meet you."

Julia hesitantly shook his hand. "Likewise, Dr. Esparza."

"Please. Call me Henry."

"Julia. And how did you know about Brandon?"

"Such information spreads faster than a common cold in this area," he said with a slight smile. "You say you think Dr. Udy succumbed to the same bacterium?"

"Yes, but it's not a bacterium. This isn't typical bacterial or viral encephalitis; it's fungal. I'm 99 percent sure it's a form of cordyceps, perhaps *O. unilateralis.*"

Henry blinked hard. "Zombie ants?" he said with obvious surprise. "Huh. I never would have considered that. Are you sure?—because there's never been documentation of it crossing species."

"I wish I was wrong, but I'm pretty confident it is."

"Huh. Well, clearly I'm not as versed in mycology as you are. Was this something the two of you were studying?"

"No. This was a project Brandon was doing on his own—which was a nip away from normal. We always kept track of what we're—"

Suddenly, Luis drew in a sharp breath and let it out in a high, scraping wheeze. Julia, Henry, Ricardo, and Noely were immediately at his side. Dr. Esparza tried to communicate with the boy, but he was completely unresponsive. As if someone flipped a switch, Luis's skin steadily faded to the putrid color of old milk. Noely burst into tears and ran out of the room. Ricardo crossed himself twice then followed after his niece, offering consoling words in Spanish.

Esparza and Julia watched helplessly as the little boy drew a final, shuddering breath then slowly, noiselessly released it.

CHAPTER 43

DR. ESPARZA AGAIN FELT LUIS'S carotid. "He has no pulse," he said, slowly shaking his head. "Lo siento."

"This is exactly what happened to Brandon," Julia muttered.

"Brandon?"

"Dr. Udy. He was dissecting a cordyceps and just suddenly got up and climbed to the top of a kapok."

"*¡Rayos!*"

"When I climbed up to him, he was—" She paused and swallowed. "He was dead and had—" She couldn't continue, knowing what was about to happen to the little boy.

"And had what?" Henry encouraged.

She took a breath. "He had a large stroma, a sporangiophore growing out his neck, between the C7 and T1."

"*¿En serio?*"

"I'm sorry. I don't speak much Spanish."

"Sorry. I asked, 'Seriously?' Because that kind of presentation sounds exactly like a zombie ant."

"Too right. It had all the characteristics of an *Ophiocordyceps unilateralis* infection."

Esparza scratched his head. "*How* did he become infected?"

Julia moved to a window and stared out at the wet landing strip. The sun was already turning the sky a brassy hue from below the horizon. "I don't know."

"What did you rule out? Perhaps we can reach a mutual conclusion."

Julia turned. "Wait—let me ask you a question. Are you really a doctor?"

He gave a wan smile. "Indeed. I graduated from the University of New Mexico medical school, Albuquerque, class of 1984."

She took in his attire—or lack thereof. "Then why the aboriginal togs?"

He fiddled with his necklace. "Ever heard of white-collar hypertension?"

"No."

"It's like this: a person can have totally normal blood pressure, day in and day out, but the minute they enter a doctor's office, their anxiety kicks in and their blood pressure soars. I dress this way because, quite simply, the locals trust me like this."

"And you have no qualms about gallivanting through the rain forest like that?"

"No. Should I?" He chuckled.

Ignoring his question, she said, "Do you work anywhere else?"

"Certainly. There is the small clinic here and a few outpatient hospitals around the area. When I'm there, I wear a shirt and trousers."

Satisfied, Julia moved back to Luis's frail body. "I hate sickness. I hate seeing death."

"It is part of life, Julia," Henry said with practiced tenderness.

"Not when it affects children."

He grunted a soft affirmation. "That is a truth. So, any more questions?"

After a long pause, she tilted her head toward Luis's corpse. "Yeah. How is this possible?"

"You're the mycologist. I can only guess at this point in time. Have *you* reached some conclusions?"

She sighed remorsefully. "Nothing solid."

"I see. Well," he continued, taking charge of the conversation, "if this has happened twice already, it will happen again. Obviously, we must find a way to stop its spread. What can you tell me about it?"

Julia rehearsed the events of the previous days with detached feelings because she wanted to avoid reliving the pain. Then, using the rent T-shirt, she again wiped at Luis's neck and shoulders. "Within a few hours we should see a juvenile sporangiophore erupt about here, on the nape of his neck." The words were agonizing but necessary.

Henry frowned. "When did Dr. Udy succumb?"

"I'm not certain when the actual infection took place. The effects didn't present until three days ago. He died shortly thereafter."

"Three days? I wasn't aware it'd been that long."

She shrugged. "I assumed Ricardo or Felipe would have shared the news. I called in a Code Red, BSL-4 emergency the day after it happened."

He was clearly angered by the news. "I'll speak to them about that."

"Brilliant," she huffed.

As she turned to set the T-shirt on a countertop, a brutal wave of vertigo washed over her. She staggered and collapsed to her knees.

"Julia, you are exhausted," Henry said. "When was the last time you ate?"

"I can't remember."

"And slept?"

She rubbed her temples, not answering.

Esparza pulled a sheet from a nearby cupboard and draped it over the tiny body of Luis. "Let me help you to Ricardo's house and get you nourished and rested."

"But—" she began, gesturing toward the boy.

"I will move him to the hospital." When she opened her mouth, he cut her off. "I will be extra cautious with the body. I'm sure you will agree this building is not suited for such an event. I assure you I will not leave his side."

Julia's shoulder slumped. She was too tired to argue.

"When you are refreshed," Henry continued, "come to the hospital, and we can discuss our options. I assume since you've been exposed to the fungus more than anyone else, you are either immune or it is not as easily transmitted as you think."

She nodded, surprised at how much effort that simple movement took.

Henry practically carried Julia down the stairs and over to Ricardo's house. A bowl of hot soup and some tortillas were prepared as she washed her face and hands in a sink. While she ate, Ricardo made up a bunk in the next room. The minute her head hit the pillow she was out. She was so shattered she didn't even dream.

CHAPTER 44

MANTIS ALWAYS OVERDRAMATIZED THE HANDICAP of his deformed hand when dealing with the public. Playing the pity card gave him a sympathy edge. Air travel was no exception. It had gotten him a free martini on the flight to South America.

Simón Bolívar International Airport was much bigger than he had expected. Knowing Venezuela was still considered a third-world country, he'd thought he'd land in Columbia or Brazil first, then shuttle over to Caracas. Not so. A large plaque on the wall boasted that this airport hosted over fourteen million national and international flights in 2014. Simón Bolívar International was an official hub for South America.

Entering the immigration terminal, he cased the check-in kiosks until he found a middle-aged female officer. Using his gimp hand, he clumsily handed his passport to the woman. She stared at the hand then quickly looked away. With his best sheepish expression, he said, "It's been like that since I was a little boy. Don't worry, it won't bite."

With a look of apology, she took the passport and ran it under a scanner. "Your purpose for visiting Venezuela, Mr. Jones?" she asked in heavily accented English.

"I've always wanted to see Angel Falls and the rain forest."

"It is a popular destination. Do you have a tour itinerary?"

"Unfortunately no. This was sort of a last-minute trip. I got a great deal on a flight, and I left before I could arrange anything," he said, massaging his ruined hand with the good one. A quick flick of her eyes confirmed she'd seen the action.

"Normally, we insist your entire trip is itemized with the tourism board before you enter the country. Now is not a good time for tourists. There is much political unrest."

"Oh?" Mantis cried worriedly, holding his ruined hand to his chest.

Her eyes filled with utter pity. "Sí. But I think we can make an exception."

"Thank you," Mantis said with a heartfelt sigh. "You are very kind."

"I suggest you take a taxi to Caicara del Orinoco. That is where the rain forest tourism office is. They can suggest the best sights and *safe* tour guides."

"Safe tour guides?" Mantis asked with a quaver in his voice, again massaging his gimp hand.

"Unfortunately, yes. Some tour guides are not as honest as others. They take advantage of foreign visitors. Do you speak Spanish, Mr. Jones?"

"Just enough to ask where a bathroom is."

She smiled. "That is important to know—especially if you are unaccustomed to our food. As a caution, do not eat the food from street vendors, and drink only bottled water."

"Noted." Mantis smiled as if it was the kindest suggestion he'd ever been given. "You are very charitable, señorita."

Her eyes crinkled. "You need to work on your conversation skills, Mr. Jones. I am much too old to be called señorita," she said with a blush. "But thank you for the compliment." She pecked a few keys on her computer and continued, "I will stamp your temporary visa to allow for better access than we normally grant unregistered tourists. That way you can visit more unique sights. But please be careful out there."

With watery eyes, Mantis said, "Thank you so much for your generosity. God bless you, señorita."

She playfully slapped his good hand. "Señora."

"Oh, right, right," he chuckled with a lopsided grin. "Señora."

"*Vaya con Dios*, Señor Jones."

Exiting the airport, Mantis felt as if he'd walked into an invisible wall. The heat and humidity were oppressively thick; the air actually felt difficult to move through. He paused and fought to catch his breath. Cigarette smoke and vehicle emissions choked the air. The smell of sweat and animal excrement fouled his nostrils. The airport causeway was crowed and noisy: people yelled, children cried, horns blared, chickens squawked. He even heard the squeal of a pig. His agoraphobia flared. How could people live and work in such conditions?

He approached a brightly colored taxi with a handwritten sign professing the driver spoke English.

"Excuse me? How much is it to get to Caicara del Orinoco?"

"Are you scientist?" the driver asked.

"Yes, as a matter of fact, I am. How did you know?"

"You want to go to CIST, si?"

"Do I?"

"All scientists go to CIST. I can take you, *ningún problema*. You pay dollar or bolívar?"

Mantis patted his pocket with his good hand. Showing his damaged hand to such men usually encouraged them to be less than honest. They liked to take advantage of people with handicaps. And this guy looked money hungry. Mantis braced himself for exhausting tales of the man's sick wife and thirteen beleaguered children.

"I haven't had a chance to go to a currency exchange. Will you take dollars?"

"Sí. Está bien," he said, wheeling Mantis's luggage to the trunk of his car.

When they were on the road, the driver glanced in his rearview mirror and asked, "How was the flight, señor?"

"I slept most of the way."

"Bueno. What do you science?"

What do I science? Obviously this guy's English wasn't top notch. "Fungus."

"Fungus? What is fungus?"

"Mushrooms."

"Oh, sí, sí. I love mushrooms *con mantequilla y ajo. ¡Qué bueno! ¡Es muy delicioso!*"

Mantis smiled. "I agree."

"You have *una esposa*, señor?"

"No."

"You like to nightclub then? You like girl shows?"

"No thank you."

The man shrugged. "Okay. You like eshopping? I can show you best markets. Very cheap."

"No thank you."

"Okay, roger. I live here all my life. Whatever you want, I can get, sí?"

"Super," he said with minimal enthusiasm.

A few hours later they pulled next to an official-looking building with a sign that read *Centro de Investigación de la Selva Tropical*.

"Here is research center," the driver announced. "Everyone call it CIST."

Mantis looked at the small building with a skeptical eye. The headquarters for rain forest research looked like a rundown DMV. Only one car sat in the parking stalls. A windsock next to an empty helicopter pad indicated a negligible breeze. He saw nothing that suggested anyone there spoke English.

The driver unloaded Mantis's luggage and opened the passenger door for him. He quoted Mantis a price in bolívares.

Mantis removed two twenties from his wallet and handed it to him. "Will this cover it?"

"No, señor. That not enough for such a distance . . . and for the especial stop."

He handed over an additional twenty.

"Thank you, señor scientist. That good. But mi esposa—she is sick and cannot feed our many children. She be grateful for *un poquito mas*."

Mantis rolled his eyes and gave the driver an additional Jackson.

"Muchas gracias, señor," he said with a grin. "Enjoy your stay. And be careful."

CHAPTER 45

MANTIS KNOCKED ON THE GLASS front door of the CIST as the taxi drove away. He would have walked right in, but the door was locked. That surprised him. He glanced at his watch: 10:21 local time.

The building had government funding written all over it. Most of the other buildings they'd passed in town screamed third-world cut and paste. There was no signage on the door indicating the agency's hours of operation.

He knocked again and waited.

"Come on, guys," Mantis said under his breath. "It's almost ten thirty for cripe's sake. You've got to be open by now."

His phone chirped with a text message.

Five days.

A courtesy prompt from Green Blade.

He knocked again, this time with enough force to rattle the blinds on the opposite side.

A woman's voice sounded through the door. "Hold your stinking horses. I'm coming."

Stinking horses?

The door was opened by a pretty blonde with disheveled hair and smudged eyeliner. "Yeah?" she demanded.

"Oh. You're—you're American?" Mantis stumbled.

She forcefully rubbed her eyes. "Two points for stating the obvious. What do you want?"

Momentarily caught off-guard, Mantis struggled to remember why he was there. He couldn't help but notice how her colorful silk nightshirt flattered her sculpted figure. The front of the shirt boasted a dolphin appearing to breach from her cleavage. "I, um . . . I need to schedule a trip to Amazonas. I was told by the immigration office that this was the place to do it."

The woman gave him a blatant visual once-over and released an exasperated sigh, clearly unhappy with what she saw. "Fine. Come on in."

The office was Spartan in accoutrements but very functional. A few posters advocating the need for protecting the rain forests adorned the walls. A couple of topographical maps hung behind the large desk. It felt more militaristic than touristy. But that didn't matter; he wasn't there as a tourist. Of more importance, the building was air conditioned. The temperature inside was significantly cooler than outside, even just after ten in the morning. "It feels good in here," he commented.

"It's like a sauna: hot and humid."

He noticed parts of her nightshirt were glued to her figure with sweat. He wondered what someone like her was doing in a place like this—but he wasn't about to voice that cliché. "Well, we *are* in the tropics," he said with a half smile.

"Another two points. You going for a record or what?"

He frowned at her snarkiness, but he chose not to comment on it. "I'm terribly sorry. Did I awaken you?"

"That makes six. Gosh, you're on a roll."

"I apologize, Miss . . . ?"

Flicking back her hair, she said, "Muir. Meghan Muir."

Mantis noticed she wore a cause bracelet stating *Save the Planet*.

"Bob Jones. Pleased to meet you." When she didn't respond, he continued, "I'm truly sorry that I woke you, but my business is rather urgent. As I mentioned, I need to charter a flight to a remote location in Amazonas. Is that something you can help me with?"

Meghan grabbed a can of diet Dew from a small fridge and flopped into an armchair. The motion caused her nightshirt to hike up, but she didn't seem to care. She snapped open the soda and took a sip, all the while staring at him with narrowed, steely eyes. "Why?"

"Why?"

Megan rolled her eyes. "Why do you want to go to Amazonas?"

Mantis guessed his answer would determine the amount of help he got, and he'd seen plenty of clues already. Smiling, he lowered himself into a chair opposite hers. At that angle, not only did he notice plenty of bare skin, but also a colorful tattoo on her upper thigh: an image of the world wreathed in a banner saying *MOTHER*. On the end table sat a stack of Sierra Club magazines and an Earth Liberation periodical. *Perfect*.

He switched his smile to a pout. "The long and short of it, Ms. Muir, is that I have always wanted to see the unspoiled beauty of the rain forest as soon as possible. You know, not where the tourists go, someplace pristine. I figured the best way to do that would be to get off the beaten path. You see, I want to witness nature in its purest form."

There was a lengthy pause before Meghan took another sip and again asked, "Why?"

Mantis bit his lip and gave a deeply troubled expression. "Okay, Meghan—may I call you Meghan?"

Her eyes grew more steely. "People call me all sorts of things."

I bet they do, he didn't say aloud. "Meghan, then," he established. "You look like a person who is astute enough to see through the lies and cover-up of those with ulterior motives. Am I right?"

Another sip, no answer.

"Okay. So I'm going for broke here. If I cause offense, it's only because I am so passionate about nature." He sat forward and cleared his throat. "I am very alarmed about the plight of these virgin rain forests. Did you know almost 5,000 acres of rain forest are lost every day to logging and strip-mining?"

Meghan's eyes lost some of their defiance. "If not more."

"Exactly! Someone has to do something about it. The locals won't do anything because the greedy corporations pay them a year's wages for one week of work—which still isn't much compared to American standards. And the government won't step in because the lumber and oil companies keep buying *them* off—and they have no problem accepting it."

Meghan huffed. "You got that right."

"And it's not just the lumber and oil companies. Pharmaceutical companies are strip-mining the forests looking for chemicals and biologics with which to addict the world—"

"Killing countless species in the process," Meghan finished the sentence vehemently.

"Exactly right," he said, slamming his twisted hand on the arm of his chair, intentionally exposing it to her scrutiny.

Meghan's gaze zeroed in on the deformity and lingered. Mantis slowly withdrew his hand and cradled it against his abdomen as if to hide it.

Realizing she was gawking, Meghan flustered. "Oh—I'm so sorry, Bob. I didn't mean to stare."

Milking the role of the victim, Mantis gave an embarrassed shrug. "It's okay. I'm used to it."

Meghan tucked her hair back and nodded toward his hand. "How . . . ?"

Mantis was prepared for this. He had a selection of stories about his injury for multiple situations—none of which, of course, were true. Massaging his hand, he said, "I was careless. My hand got pinched between a one-ton bulldozer blade and an old-growth redwood when I was protesting the building of a logging road through an Oregon forest."

"Pinched?"

"Crushed," he said, as if it no longer mattered. "I stood between the dozer and the tree, and refused to move. The dozer tried to nudge me away and . . . well, the rest is history."

Now her eyes were wide with admiration. "You took on a bulldozer? Like—like that Chinese dude stopping that tank in Tiananmen Square?"

Mantis allowed a slight blush. "I guess."

Meghan's mouth hung open for a full thirty seconds before she leapt to her feet. "Wait right there, Bob. I'll freshen up and be right back. There's water and diet soda in the fridge. Help yourself."

She gave his knee a flirty squeeze and skipped out of the room.

Mantis sat back with a smug leer. Yep, he knew how to read people. Once Green Blade realized that, they would fund whatever project he dreamed up. And once he delivered the world, they would not only throw money at him, they would worship him.

CHAPTER 46

JULIA AWOKE, TOTALLY DISORIENTED. THE room was tiny; thick stucco slathered the walls. Harsh daylight spilled through an open window. She smelled meat cooking, and her stomach growled. She tried to move and groaned. Her entire body ached profoundly. Her joints felt rusted in place. Forcing herself to sit up, she inhaled deeply through her nostrils. As her head cleared, the images from the previous few days spread across a mental canvas. They didn't paint a pretty picture.

"Hello?" she voiced cautiously, hoping the effort wouldn't provoke the headache poised just behind her temples.

A chair scooted across a floor in an adjacent room.

"¿Señora. Está bein?" It was Noely's voice, right outside the doorway.

"Noely? What time is it? ¿Qué hora es?"

The little girl entered the room. Her face was still tearstained and ruddy. Her puffy eyes were rimmed with dark circles. Her countenance was lifeless, without a trace of joy.

"Tiempo de almuerzo," she said weakly.

Julia recognized the word. "Lunchtime? That sounds brilliant, sweetheart. But what is the time?" she said, pointing at her empty wrist.

Noely shrugged. "No sé. Un momento."

She left, and a few seconds later Ricardo came to the doorway. "Dr. Fatheringham. It is good to see you awake. We were worried about you."

"Thank you," she said, holding out her hand. "Now help me up."

Ricardo gently pulled her to her feet.

"What time is it?"

"It is just after one o'clock."

"Crikey. Why'd you let me sleep so long?"

"You were very tired. You needed rest."

"Well thanks, mate, but I'm fine now. Is Dr. Esparza still with Luis?"

Ricardo's eyes misted. "Sí."

"I am so sorry," she said, taking his hand in both of hers. "Please, I must see him."

Ricardo nodded. Julia was only able to take two steps before her legs gave out and she buckled to the floor.

"Señora!" Ricardo dropped to her side.

"Crikey," she hissed.

"You should rest more. I'll send for the doctor."

"I said I'm fine," she grumbled. "Where is Luis's body?"

"The doctor took him to the hospital."

"I have to see. Please take me there," she said, struggling to her feet.

Noely entered carrying a plate of scrambled eggs, some kind of sausage, and fried plantains. "Señora. *¿Tienes hambre?*"

"Not anymore," she said, holding her stomach. "But thank you."

"You must eat, Doctor," Ricardo said. "You have no strength."

"Por favor, señora," Noely said, holding out the plate.

Julia sighed and accepted the food. Taking a bite of sausage was like flipping a switch inside her. She knew it was a purely psychological reaction, but she instantly felt a surge of energy course through her body. She chewed with intense pleasure and swallowed.

"Muchas gracias, Noely. This is delicious! Muy delicioso."

The little girl gave a wan smile. "Gracias. *Ven aquí*, por favor."

Julia followed Noely into the kitchen and sat at the table to finish her meal. Ricardo joined them after retrieving a glass of mango juice.

"The shaman says he wants to study Luis," Ricardo explained. "He says if Luis died from what you say, it is something he's never seen before."

"That makes two of us." She downed the glass of juice and wiped her mouth with the tail of her shirt. "Will you translate for me? I need to ask Noely some questions."

Noely was at the sink, washing up. She turned at the mention of her name.

"She is very sad about her brother," Ricardo said. "She may not wish to answer."

Julia pulled out a chair and patted it. "Noely, please come sit by me."

The little girl wiped her hands on a dingy towel and sat.

Julia took a deep breath. "I am terribly sorry about your brother." She paused and took Noely's hands in hers. "Please understand that I must ask some questions to help me figure out what's going on. I am not doing it to be mean. I need to prevent it from happening to anyone else. Do you understand?"

She kept her eyes on Noely's face as Ricardo translated.

"Sí. Claro," Noely said with a trembling lower lip.

Julia stared blankly at Noely's hands in hers as her mind tried to determine the best place to start. Of paramount concern was *when* and *where* Luis had come into contact with the cordyceps fungus.

"Was Luis sick before any of this happened?"

"No."

"Did he act fatigued or confused at all?"

"No."

"Do you have any idea what made him climb the radio tower?"

"No."

Releasing her hands, Julia sat back forcefully. "This is going nowhere," she mumbled, rubbing her eyes. "Okay, let's try this: do you know what a fungus is?"

Noely listened patiently to Ricardo's translation. "Yes. We gather them from the forest to eat all the time."

"Brilliant. Okay. Did you recently gather a new fungus? One you've never seen before?"

"No."

"Did you mother or anyone in your village?"

A look of understanding flashed across Noely's eyes. She gave a lengthy answer, using the words *dinero* and *padre* several times, but when Ricardo translated, the answer was simply, "She doesn't know."

Julia tilted her head. "Wait. What did she say about her father and money?"

"Nothing."

She frowned. "Noely said *dinero*. I know that means money."

Ricardo's face twitched with what looked like guilt, but it was gone as quickly as it came. "She said her father had asked her to hunt for mushrooms . . . but that is all. You must be mistaken because you are still very tired," he said with a forced chuckle.

Julia understood enough Spanish to know that she *wasn't* mistaken. Ricardo was hiding something.

"Listen, Ricardo. I need to know if her father brought home a new mushroom."

His eyes refused to meet hers. "She already said no."

It was a lie. She desperately wished she could speak Spanish so she could ask Noely directly. The little girl watched the interchange with a worried expression. Julia wondered how much of the conversation she understood.

"Fine," Julia said shortly. "I must see Luis, then. Where is the hospital?"

"It . . . it is off limits to strangers," Ricardo said hesitantly.

"That's ridiculous. How can a hospital be off limits to anyone?"

Ricardo shrugged.

She felt her former frustrations returning quickly. "I don't believe you. Point of fact, I think you're hiding something from me, Ricardo."

"I do not know what you are talking about, Doctor."

"You don't seem to realize how dangerous this thing is, mate. Your nephew is dead! That fungus killed him. Noely may be infected. *You* may be infected."

Ricardo's eyes widened. He stepped to the fridge and pulled out a beer before moving to stare out a window. "You are not infected," he stated weakly.

When Ricardo didn't say anything more, Julia rose from the table and grabbed the bottle from his hand. "No more drinking. I need you sober. I need you to be completely honest with me. If not for me, then at least for Noely. Her life is in grave danger."

Turning to his niece, Ricardo flinched. "Noely?"

Julia turned to follow his gaze. The little girl was gone.

CHAPTER 47

AFTER FRESHENING UP, MEGHAN CHANGED into a tight-fitting tee and cargo shorts. She grabbed her clipboard and returned to the reception area. Her visitor was skimming through a pamphlet. She wanted to like this guy. Too bad he wasn't better looking. He had no fashion sense at all. Pleated slacks and a T-shirt? And that ancient Club Med powder-blue windbreaker? Like he'd ever been to Club Med. Still, he claimed he felt the same way she did about the rain forest—so that was good. Plus, he seemed trustworthy. His hand had been crushed in the name of environmentalism, after all. You can't fake that. But she needed to make sure.

"So, Bob. Did you have a particular destination in mind?"

"Somewhere in Amazonas. I was thinking maybe La Esmeralda . . . ? Knowing the area as well as you do, I've no doubt you can offer some amazing suggestions."

She smiled. "What do you do for a living?"

He gave a slight recoil. "Why do you ask?"

"It will help me determine what you might like to see." She sat very close to him, brushing her leg against his. "It's okay if you'd rather not say, but since you and I seem to have so much in common, I just wanted to get to know you better. I hope you don't mind."

She watched with pleasure as her visitor swallowed hard and chewed on his lower lip. "My," he gulped, fanning himself with the pamphlet. "I see what you mean about it being like a sauna in here."

"All—day—long," she said with disgust. "It's impossible to get used to. But you look like you're in pretty good shape, so it shouldn't take you long," she said, pretending to admire his physique. There actually wasn't that much to admire. He wasn't fat, but he definitely hadn't seen the inside of a gym in like—ever.

"Thank you. But I really need to work out more. Too many hours at the office makes it hard to get the exercise I should," he replied, trying to puff out his chest like an infatuated schoolboy.

"Well, you look good to me," she said with a coy smile.

He blushed.

"So, what do you do at your office?"

"I own a small magazine. Perhaps you've heard of it? *Tide Watch?*"

"*Tide Watch?*" she said, looking down at her clipboard. "No, I don't think so."

Bob unzipped his satchel and rummaged through it. "Gosh, I'm an idiot. You'd think the owner of a magazine would have a copy of his own product."

Meghan craned her neck to peek in the carryall. She saw an iPad, travel brochures, and paperwork that looked like bank statements.

"It's an environmental periodical that focuses on the plight of the world's coastlines. Did you hear about the recent oil spill off the coast of Santa Barbara? The authorities claim it was a small one." He scoffed bitterly. "One hundred thousand gallons of crude oil dumped into the migratory route of blue whales and gray whales—" His voice caught, and he paused to wipe at his eyes. "The 'official' size of the spill is much smaller, but it always is. Cover-ups, you know?"

She nodded.

"Anyway, my magazine has estimated that it's killed over thirty thousand animals: fish, sea otters, birds, dolphins."

Meghan let out a gasp. "Dolphins?"

"The oil blinds them and clogs their blowholes. Then they beach themselves, and the weight of their own bodies crushes their lungs. It's a horrible death."

"That *is* horrible!" The back of her eyes began to burn. "I feel terrible not knowing . . . but I've been stuck down here for almost a year. I hope you've nailed whoever is responsible."

"We have evidence that proves it was from the unauthorized drilling of a new well. Oh, they claimed it was a break in an existing pipeline, but we know better. My magazine is at the forefront of exposing such crimes against the world's coastlines."

"That must keep you very busy."

"It does. But . . ." Bob paused and hung his head.

"But what?"

When he looked up, his eyes were filled with tears. "It really gets to me, you know? I can only take so much. I actually . . . hate to admit that. It makes me feel so weak. But it's an emotional drain to my soul every time I see Nature suffer."

"Oh, Bob," she said, wrapping him a big hug. Yeah, this guy was real. She had no doubt.

"Anyway, that's why I'm here," he went on with a sniffle. "I want to see as much as I can before it's too late."

"I totally understand," she said, releasing her hug. "But if your focus is on coastlines, why come to the rain forest?"

"Coastlines are being ruined by oil companies. The latest surveys say there are huge oil deposits under the rain forests of Central and South America. Once big oil finds out—" Choking on his words, he paused to wipe his eyes again. "I want to see if I can do something—anything—to stop that from happening."

This guy got better looking with everything he said. It was an unusual experience for Meghan. Usually it took lots of alcohol for her to feel that way. She definitely wanted to do anything she could to help him. "You are a wonderful man, Bob. I'll arrange everything for you. I'll book you to La Esmeralda today. It's an excellent choice—right in the heart of Amazonas. I know the airport controller personally. I'll make sure you're treated with a golden ticket."

"Thank you, Meghan," Bob said with a warm smile. "Thank you so much."

"Anything for a fellow lover of Mother Earth."

Bob scratched his shoulder with his damaged hand. She couldn't imagine how painful it must have been being crushed by a bulldozer. But it didn't deter him from continuing his crusade. She truly admired that.

He gave her a hopeful look. "I wonder if I might log onto your Wi-Fi to check my e-mail?"

Meghan stood and glanced out a window. "This is a government facility, Bob. We're not supposed to allow visitors to use the equipment." She turned and gave him a coy wink. "But I'll make an exception for you."

CHAPTER 48

THEY SEARCHED RICARDO'S HOUSE TO no avail. Noely was not there.

"Oy. Call Felipe, immediately!" Julia ordered.

"I have tried. He does not answer. Besides, he is not the man to worry about."

"Of course he is! We need that helo! Try again and again and again until you get him!"

"But Noely—"

"I'll find her. You go to the tower and get on that radio," she snapped, marching out of his house.

The harsh sunlight was blinding, the air hot but surprisingly clear. Julia soon broke into a sweat as she searched along the dirt streets of the small town, calling out Noely's name. Several people stared at her as if seeing a specter. She knew she looked a mess, but she didn't care. In halting Spanish, she asked if anyone knew Noely from El Desvío. Most responded with continued blank stares. Some ran away. One older woman called her *bruja* and excoriated her with a mouthful of harsh words. Julia said *gracias* and moved on. Guessing Noely had gone to the hospital to be with her little brother, she decided to head there.

The single-story stucco building was painted white and red. It sat roughly two blocks from the landing strip. It was small—no more than 1,500 sq. ft. The outside was partially landscaped but nothing fancy. A wooden plaque read *Hospital de La Esmeralda*; below hung a hand-painted board with the words *Clínica Gratuita* and the hours of operation. Entering, Julia found Noely sitting alone on a sofa in the reception area.

"Thank goodness," Julia sighed, sitting beside her and wrapping her in a hug. "Are you okay, Noely? ¿Estas bien?"

"*Tengo miedo. El curandero no me deja ver a mi hermano.*"

"Lo siento," she offered, giving the little girl a hug. "No entiendo. *¿Dónde está el médico?*"

Noely pointed to a door to one side of the reception counter.

Julia opened the door and called, "Dr. Esparza?"

"Back here," his voice answered.

Stepping to the first door down the hallway, Julia entered a generous-sized room with a drain in the floor. Luis's small body lay on an exam table in the center of room. A sheet covered all but his head and shoulders. Esparza was gowned in a disposable paper apron, latex gloves, and a mask. He had exchanged his aboriginal garb for trousers and a collared shirt.

"I'm very glad you've rested." He nodded to a counter strewn with medical paraphernalia. "Grab a mask over there."

She did as instructed. "I don't think it's airborne."

"Really? How so?"

Despite her best efforts, when she rounded the table and saw Luis, her heart ached. She'd known there was a good chance the boy would end up just like Brandon, but seeing a stroma sprouting from the nape of the child's neck still pained her. Feeling the blood drain from her head, she leaned against the table and drew in several steadying breaths.

"Are you okay?" the doctor asked.

"I will be. Give me a minute."

"I'm sorry you have to see this," Henry said and, after a moment's pause, added, "Again."

"No worries."

"Still, I am terribly sorry not only for your loss, but for the nature of it. I take it you still believe you're not infected?"

"No, it's not likely anymore."

"Anymore?"

"Yes. The gestation of this ascomycete seems very rapid. If I was infected, I'd be up a tree by now."

"And the fungus looked like this one?" he asked, holding his hand to the growth.

"Identical. Brandon's grew to about twenty centimeters before it formed a sporangium."

"That's enormous. Did it release its spores?"

"I assume so. How else would Luis be infected by it?"

Henry looked up and frowned. "Luis was at your research site?"

"No, no. About the third night, someone broke in and stole the specimen."

"And you earned your contusions trying to stop him," he said, eyeing the dark bruises still discoloring her eye and forehead.

"Too right."

"Do you have any idea where it is now—the stolen cordyceps?"

"No. But I suspect Noely does. And perhaps Ricardo too."

Henry's frown deepened. "Ricardo Paz?"

Julia glanced at the door before meeting the doctor's eyes and nodding.

"We are alone here," Henry said carefully. "You can trust me."

She gave a wry scoff. "They say the one person never to trust is the one who says, 'You can trust me.'"

"But in this case it's true," Henry said in a tone just shy of offended. "Dr. Fatheringham, as a fellow scientist and as a doctor of medicine, I assure you I want to help prevent this from happening again. But to do so I need to find out everything you know."

Julia nodded. "Yes, of course."

"Now, it stands to reason that if Luis was infected, Noely could be also. As for Ricardo, I've known him a long time. He's not always the most upstanding individual, but he generally means well, especially when it comes to children."

"Perhaps you've been hoodwinked," she said, pulling up a stool to sit. "Ricardo was translating between me and Noely this morning. When I asked Noely if she knew anything about an unusual fungus, she said something about her *padre* and *dinero*—her father and money— but Ricardo's translation left out both of those words."

"Translation is not always word for word."

"Yes, I know, but when I questioned him about it, he came up with something that didn't ring true."

"Then we should ask her again. Is she still at Ricardo's house?"

"No, she's here in the waiting area."

"What?"

"Yeah, I just saw her."

"Well, bring her in."

"Not a brilliant idea, mate," she said, standing quickly. "She can't see Luis like this. It'd devastate her."

Henry nodded and removed his mask. "You're absolutely right. Come."

Noely was still in the reception area. Henry sat beside her and handed her a sucker from his pocket. She accepted it but didn't unwrap it. He spoke gently to her in Spanish. Julia caught a few words—including Ricardo's name—but most of the conversation passed by her. Noely answered quietly, as if each explanation took extraordinary effort to voice. As the Q&A progressed, Henry's tone grew sharper, more angered.

Finally, he turned to Julia. "Where is Ricardo now?"

"I told him to contact Felipe."

"Is there another man with him?"

"There was last night. I haven't seen him since."

"We have to find Ricardo. The other man is Noely's father. His name is Marco. Ricardo purchased the fungus from him. It stands to reason Marco is the one who stole it from you."

She frowned deeply. "But why?"

"That is what I intend to find out."

CHAPTER 49

MANTIS WATCHED AS MEGHAN CHARTERED a plane with practiced efficiency. She seemed to have a number of connections with government officials in the area—some with dubious strings attached, he was sure. But that didn't matter to him. He only cared about obtaining his prize as quickly and as secretly as possible, and then returning home.

"Doesn't the CIST have its own plane?" he asked.

"Felipe—he's the director—has a fancy helicopter. There aren't many landing strips in the rain forests, thank heavens. Just imagine how much the noise and pollution of an airplane would traumatize the animals."

"Indeed. Where is your director now?"

"Not a clue or a care," she said, leaving her desk and joining him on the couch. "The government has him bought and paid for because he can fly a helicopter. And, as you said, big oil and big lumber have bought and paid for the government. And neither of them give a rat's fat patootie about the rain forest beyond what they can gouge out as profit."

Mantis grumbled. "I hate people like that. Felipe, huh? Just think, with a helicopter he could watch for poachers and wildfires and flooding. Instead he wastes his talents . . . how exactly?"

"He shuttles scientists and tourists into the interior for 'research,'" she said in disgust. "Or wherever else they want if the price is right."

"Typical," Mantis spat with equal disgust. "So is that where he is now? Shuttling some rich dentist to Angel Falls?"

"Oh no. He thinks he's too good for that. No, last I heard from him he was hightailing it to a sight called Ascom base."

"And what goes on there?"

"Research, supposedly," she scoffed. "Dr. Brandon Udy and his snooty assistant Julia Fatheringham from Australia root around the forest floor looking for mushrooms."

"Mushrooms?" he chuckled. "What do they want with mushrooms?"

"Big pharma wants them to squeeze whatever chemicals they can from the fungi to make new drugs." She leaned forward with a gleam in her eye. "But get this: apparently, the good doctor stumbled onto a bad 'shroom the other day. Felipe went to retrieve his body."

Mantis could not stop his eyebrows from rising in glee. *Could this be the same incident Bruja had mentioned?* "His body? You mean he died?"

"Pretty sweet, huh?" she said with a wink.

Mantis couldn't believe she was so indifferent to a man's death. But it caused something to stir within him. He felt deliciously excited! Emotionally and physically excited. He squirmed in his seat, trying to mask his enthusiasm. Feigning the same indifference, he scoffed, "Sounds like it served him right."

Meghan beamed. "I was hoping you'd feel that way. I think anyone who intentionally harms the rain forest gets whatever the rain forest dishes back."

"I couldn't have said it better myself, Meghan," he said, massaging his gimp hand. His mind was churning with possibility. Could this woman be his Bruja? If Mantis believed in luck, he'd consider himself inundated with it. But he didn't. Everything happened for a reason—and that reason was fate, pure and simple. Mantis's fate was to save the planet—same as Meghan's. Only, *he* had an actual plan to do so. Meghan had the emotion and enthusiasm; she simply lacked the brains. *No.* There was no way this ditz was his contact. Nevertheless, the incident she spoke of sounded very familiar. He needed to find out more. "When did this happen?"

"Oh, I don't know. Four or five days ago? Felipe's been gone pretty much the whole time."

Mantis frowned. "And he hasn't been in contact since then?"

"Oh sure, he called in a couple times, but he didn't say much. He classified the site as a Code Red quarantine. That means it's very bad," she explained.

Mantis knew what a Code Red was. "What level of biocontainment do they have?"

Meghan's eyes narrowed. "Why do you want to know that?"

He chuckled. "With any luck, they were sloppy in their work and now everyone raping that part of the rain forest is receiving the same."

"I think it was a B-3 or something. I don't think it was very high," she said, relaxing. "Julia said she doesn't think she's infected, but she wasn't sure."

"When was the last time you heard from Julia?"

"Two, three days ago. She left a message and signed off. Haven't heard a peep since."

Mantis thought for a moment. He was amazed at how closely this incident resembled the one Bruja had reported. Perhaps Meghan *was* Bruja. He knew his Bruja was in this part of the Venezuelan rain forest. Meghan certainly had the resources to accomplish what he had requested. But could she do it without anyone else knowing? He doubted she had that skill level. Again, *no*. Meghan's drive was fueled by emotion, not logic. Emotions led to knee-jerk reactions not fact-based analysis or the ability to plan and execute clandestine liaisons. Of course, she, like he, could simply be a good actor.

He chewed on his lower lip. The only way to find out for sure was to just ask.

He shifted to face her and adopted a serious expression. "Meghan, may I ask you a direct, rather personal question? It's—it's kind of embarrassing."

She smiled, playing the shy coquette. "Why, Bob. We just met," she cooed.

Mantis hesitated. "Look, I know it's kind of sudden, but I sense that you're as passionate about saving the planet as I am." He cradled his ruined hand. "I've proven my dedication—my commitment—by sacrificing part of my body. I'll give the rest if need be."

"I know you would, Bob. Go ahead. Ask me whatever you like."

He cleared his throat. "Are you familiar with the word *bruja*?"

"Bruja?" She frowned in concentration. "No . . . can't say that I am. Sounds scary. Is it a Stephen King book?"

Mantis did his best to read her confused expression. There was no deceit in her eyes, no guile on her face. "It's not a book; it's a name, a title. You sure you haven't heard it before—maybe as an alias?"

"Yes, I'm sure. Why? What does it mean?"

"It means wi—" He stopped abruptly. He didn't want Meghan to think he was calling *her* a witch. "It means 'sorceress' or 'temptress.'"

"Oo." She giggled. "I like that. I might have to insist that everyone calls me Bruja from now on."

Mantis smiled. "If it's not too forward of me, I think it fits you well."

Meghan put her hand on his knee and slowly caressed it. "Why, Bob, if I didn't know any better, I'd swear you were flirting with me."

He ducked his head shyly. "Can you blame me?"

"So . . . why did you want to know if I knew what that word meant?"

"Well . . . this is the embarrassing part. I've been in contact with someone online who goes by Bruja."

"Some international dating site?" she asked, grinning.

"Yeah. Something like that."

Her grin morphed into a leer. "Oh, I see. One of those sites where anything goes but everyone remains anonymous?"

His eyes darted to and fro. "Something like that."

She leaned forward and gave him a big hug. "Oh, Bob, don't be embarrassed. I think those sites are super fun."

He returned the hug with a hesitant pat on her back. "Thanks. So . . . you've never gone by the name Bruja in any correspondence?"

"Nope, but I will now. Do you want to exchange e-mails and cell numbers?"

"Sure," he said, glancing at his watch. "In the meantime, you said my flight leaves soon. Can you call me a taxi to the local airport?"

Her smile faltered. "Um . . . okay. But your flight doesn't actually leave for another two hours."

"I know, but I have some other business I need to attend to that—" He stopped abruptly. "Say, maybe you can help me with it."

Meghan raised an eyebrow. "What other business?"

Mantis removed his wallet, extracted two one-hundred dollar bills, and set them on the coffee table in front of them. "I need a gun."

Meghan blinked in confusion. "Excuse me?"

"I don't mean to shock you, Meghan, but you know how dangerous it is for foreigners to wander around unprotected—especially us Americans. These people we're dealing with will stop at nothing to keep their underhanded butchering of the rain forests a secret, right? If I discover something that could put them in jeopardy, you're darn tootin' I'm going to blow the whistle." He feigned an innocent, puppy-dog look. "I just want to cover all my bases, keep myself safe, you know?"

Meghan considered him warily without speaking. Mantis cleared his throat and added another bill. He saw her mouth briefly twitch up before standing and swiping the bills into her pocket. "Okay. Wait here."

"Thank you. And if we find out that Julia has also succumbed to the fungus, we'll go out for a celebratory drink when I get back."

"I know all the best clubs around here," she called over her shoulder, heading into a back office.

"We'll toast to the mushroom."

"With that kind of news, we'll toast to the whole planet."

What a psychotic ditz, Mantis thought.

CHAPTER 50

WITH HIS ARMS WRAPPED GENTLY around Noely's shoulders, Dr. Esparza rocked gently, shushing her sorrow. He'd asked her a line of brutally honest questions. She was in tears but not sobbing. Her depth of anguish for her little brother had drained her of the energy needed to sob.

"What else did she say?" Julia asked.

"She is ashamed of her father, but she still cares for him. She says it's what Jesus would tell her to do."

Julia understood the girl's loyalty. Raised a devout Catholic, she had been taught to honor her parents dutifully. "But why Marco? How'd he get involved?"

"Marco does odd jobs for Ricardo. Most are . . . well, let's just say they aren't always above the law. This area of the country has almost 80 percent unemployment, and the drug trade in Venezuela is very lucrative. Everyone wants a piece of the pie. Too many of the unemployed are willing to act as mules."

"Mules?"

"They carry drugs from producers in Venezuela, Colombia, and Brazil to Caracas and other port cities, and from there to America and Europe. Marco has spent time in jail for such actions, but . . ."

"But what?"

"Even the local law enforcement turns a blind eye most times. You see, most people here are uneducated. I'm referring to both indigenous Indians and native Venezuelans. The government does not see the need to fund such policing, so the locals do whatever they can to pay for food and necessities. It is simply their way of life. The authorities can only do so much. If they imprison one man, another takes his place. Rarely does anyone spend more than a few days in jail."

"But they are caught with illegal drugs. Isn't that an international crime?"

"It is, but the crime is based on the volume of drug in the courier's possession. The drug lords know this; therefore, each mule is given only a minimum load of product."

Taken aback, Julia looked at Noely and asked, "Is Ricardo a drug lord?"

"Ave María, no. He is perhaps the most educated man in La Esmeralda."

"Present company excluded," she said with a smile.

He shrugged.

"Is he involved in drug trafficking?"

"I do not think so. It would mean his job as airport controller if he was caught. Even so, he did ask Marco to bring him the fungus, though I have no idea why he would want it."

"What?" she cried. "Are you sure?"

"Noely confirmed it. She said her papa was meeting Ricardo to sell it to him."

"But why?"

He shrugged again.

"Does Ricardo have any schooling in science?"

"Not that I know of."

Julia was flummoxed. Her interactions with Ricardo had been few, but they had all led her to believe him to be a decent, hardworking man. Still, she'd never had a casual conversation with him. She didn't know anything about him except that he ran the La Esmeralda airstrip. But Ricardo had never expressed more than a passing interest in what she and Brandon were studying. What in the world would he want a deadly fungus for?

"Henry, will you please ask Noely if her father knew he was collecting something so dangerous?"

The doctor translated.

Noely leaned back against the wall and drew her knees to her chest. She rambled off a long string of soft words, pausing several times to swallow lumps of tears.

"She doesn't know. She says her father is often gone for days at a time. Occasionally he brings home food and supplies, sometimes a few coins. This time he returned with a bag he claimed was full of money. She said the bag stank like something rotten was inside, and the opening of the bag was covered with yellow dust."

No! The sporangium *had* burst. "Did she touch the dust?"

He asked. "Yes. As did her father and Luis. She said it smelled terrible, so she immediately washed her hands."

"Did Luis do the same?"

"She does not know."

Julia frowned. "Where is the bag now?"

He asked. "She thinks her uncle still has it."

Noely lay down on the sofa and curled into a fetal position. She softly mumbled another length of sorrow-etched words. Julia could tell she was not only anguished; she was utterly spent.

"She says she does not care about money or toys or candy. She says she likes living as she does. The only item she's ever wanted is a pair of hiking boots—like yours," he said with a brief smile. "Like a real explorer. But she says she would gladly give up the chance to have such boots if she could have her little brother back." He reached over and gently stroked Noely's hair. "I wish that was something I *could* give her."

"Please tell her how sorry I am," Julia offered.

He did.

Noely sighed deeply and closed her eyes. The scene tore at Julia's heart. She prayed that the sweet little girl would not suffer as her brother had. Or as Brandon had.

Julia pinched the bridge of her nose and tried to concentrate. Things were finally adding up, but she still didn't know why Luis had been infected and not Marco or Noely. Or she. The inconsistency didn't make sense. Then a new thought came to mind. Something deep in Julia's reasoning kept trying to surface—something Ricardo had said.

She had asked him to find Felipe . . . then Ricardo had said . . . what?

Finally it came to her: *He is not the man we should find.*

CHAPTER 51

USING HIS IPAD, MANTIS LOGGED into the Internet at the small airport in Caicara and sent Bruja a message.

Have the sample ready. It will be picked up today.

There was no immediate reply—but it usually took a day to get one. He mostly wanted to make sure his contact didn't send the sample away via some unauthorized, unreliable courier. With something this valuable, Mantis trusted no one.

His plane arrived an hour late. It frustrated him, but he was determined to stay focused. Walking out on the tarmac, his first thoughts were that a mistake had been made. The twin-engine box-with-wings on the runway had more rust on it than paint. He didn't recognize the make. From the looks of it, this one probably rolled off a foreign assembly line. A faded, hand-painted insignia on the fuselage showed a caricature of the plane and the name *Air Amazonia*.

"Hola, señor. *Bienvenidos*," a short man said, rounding the plane. He wore dark aviator glasses and a long goatee that seemed to intertwine with his chest hair. At least his smile seemed genuine.

"Hi," Mantis said. "Um . . . do you speak English?"

"Sí. I espeak as a native Americano."

"Apparently."

"Por favor," the man said, reaching for Mantis's luggage.

He yanked open the passenger door and climbed into the back to store the gear. Exiting, he gestured to the doorway. "*Pase*, señor," he said with a slight bow.

Mantis hesitated. "Uh, what kind of plane is this?"

"A Harbin y-12, señor. It is a classic, no?"

"Is it safe?" he asked with a weak smile.

"Sí, sí, señor. I fly many kilometers every year; no is problem ever. This is a very strong aeroplane craft. You see?" he said, banging his fist against the fuselage.

"So you *are* the pilot then."

"Sí. The very best."

Mantis stepped on the ladder and peeked inside. Tattered and stained with who-knew-what, the interior looked slightly less reliable than the exterior. There was space for a dozen or more passengers, but only four seats were bolted to the floor directly behind the cockpit. The other seats had been removed and the space crammed with numerous boxes and crates—some marked, most not—and several burlap sacks straining with old vegetables. The noxious smell in the confined space was overpowering. Looking forward, he saw a goat sitting on the copilot's chair.

"Yeah, this looks swell," Mantis grumbled. *Is this the* best *Meghan could find?*

"Gracias, amigo. Pick any seat, señor. You are my only passenger."

"Besides the ungulate."

The pilot cocked his head to one side and offered a weak smile.

"The cud-chewer."

When the pilot's smile grew more confused, Mantis impersonated the bleating of a goat.

"Ah, sí, sí. That is Pablo. He is my copilot."

"Great. And your name?"

"Paco, señor."

"Paco and Pablo. Great."

Belting in, Mantis clutched the armrests and did his best to focus on his objective. This is a third-world country, he reminded himself. Everything here is likely to be held together with duct tape and prayers.

Paco clambered in and sealed the door.

Mantis leaned forward. "So how long will this flight take?"

"About three hours, señor, depending on the weather."

The weather. Mantis hadn't considered that. If a storm came up, would a plane this old survive the turbulence? With all the cargo in the back, would it even get off the ground? Was this really the best Meghan could find? He made a mental note to give her a piece of his mind when—and if—he got back. He may even demand a refund. He just hoped she didn't spend the money before he got back.

Paco donned a headset and spoke briefly with the tower. Then, revving the engines, he taxied to the end of the runway. Turning 180 degrees, he shoved the throttles forward, causing the fuselage to rattle violently. The plane lurched forward and quickly gained speed. Mantis had never flown in a twin-engine cargo plane. He was used to flying either single-engine craft with pressurized cabins or commercial jetliners. The extra thrust a second engine gave perhaps helped the flying box to get off the ground, but the vibration it caused was disconcerting. He patted the inside pocket of his windbreaker where the gun Meghan had given him rested, wishing for a moment he'd asked for a parachute instead.

For the most part, the weather cooperated, and the trip was only slightly bumpy. The highlight of the flight was when Pablo rotated in his seat and lifted his tail. Paco quickly reached under his seat and pulled out a plastic shopping bag to hold under his copilot's rear end. The plane immediately tilted to one side and began slipping from the sky.

"Oh for cripe's sake!" Mantis hollered, reaching for the bag. "I'll hold it, you fly the plane."

"Muchas gracias, señor," Paco yelled over the noise of the propellers.

When Pablo was finished with his business, he turned around twice then sat facing forward again.

"What should I do with this?" Mantis shouted, indicating the bag.

"Do not spill it," the pilot suggested.

Mantis glowered at the goat the rest of the flight. Try as he might to concentrate on his ultimate goal, in the back of his mind he kept hearing, *Mantis: master of camouflage and fast attack . . . and holder of goat droppings.*

CHAPTER 52

"RICARDO!" SHE YELLED AS SHE pushed through the control tower door. When no one answered, she bounded up the stairs to the control room. Anger fueled her muscles and ignited her determination. "Ricardo! You'd bloody well better not be trying to hide."

Entering the room she found Ricardo sitting in his chair, staring blankly at the repetitive, circular scrolling of the radar, as if in a trance.

"Oy, mate. I'm going to ask you once, and you'd better tell me the truth. So help me, if you're lying, I'll know it. Did you hire Marco to steal the fungus from me?"

Ricardo remained silent. It was almost as if he hadn't heard her. Julie stormed over and spun his chair to face her.

He flinched reflexively and cursed. "Doctor! You scared the—"

"I don't care," she interrupted. "Did you pay Marco to steal the fungus?" Only then did she notice his eyes were red and puffy, his cheeks streaked with tears.

Ricardo couldn't—or wouldn't—meet her accusatory glare. "It is not my fault," he finally muttered. "Marco was careless."

"That doesn't answer the question."

His hopeless gaze drifted out one of the panoramic windows. "This job does not pay much," he said in a timid voice. "I have . . . obligations."

"Obligations?" Julia huffed. "What about your obligations to Felipe, to Brandon and me?"

He continued to stare, saying nothing.

"Right. This ends here," she spat. "Where is Marco now?"

"I . . . I do not know."

"That's bonkers. You tell me where he is this instant."

"I honestly do not know. He left right after you came."

"Figures. Does he know his son is dead?"

Ricardo's head snapped up. "Dead? *¿Él está muerto?*"

"Yes, Ricardo. Luis died right after you and Noely left. Thank goodness she didn't have to see that. The fungus Marco stole—the one *you* told him to steal—killed him."

"Are—are you sure?" he asked with a pinched voice. "Has el médico examined him?"

"He has a bloody stroma growing out of his skull, you dill!" she screamed, feeling tears again burn her eyes. "I hope he's dead."

Blood drained from Ricardo's face. "Ave Santa María," he mumbled, crossing himself several times. "*Virgen Santísima, por favor perdóname.*"

"No amount of praying will get him back, mate. In fact, if you want to ask God for anything, pray *you* aren't infected too."

He turned a shade paler. "M-me?"

"Yes. If you came in contact with the fungus, you could die a very gruesome death. That's why I need to find Marco and the fungus as soon as possible."

"I swear to you, Doctor, I do not know where he is."

"Fine. If he dies, he dies. Just tell me where the fungus is."

"I do not know that either."

"What?"

"Sí. Marco took it."

Julia stood quickly, causing her chair to topple. "This is insane." She stomped to the radio and stared at the numerous knobs and dials. "How do I call Felipe?"

"He does not answer."

"That's not what I asked. Tell me how to operate this wonky thing—because I bet he listens."

Ricardo nodded and tuned into Felipe's frequency. "His call sign is Romeo-Quebec-two-five-nine-six-one."

She toggled the switch. "Felipe, this is Julia," she said without using the call sign. "If you can hear me, then please respond—" She stopped abruptly. Her previous uncertainties as to Felipe's loyalty reentered her thoughts. What if he *was* involved? Then of course he wouldn't respond.

Just then, Ricardo cried, "¡Ave Santa María! *¡Virgen Santísima me protege de la ira de Dios!*" He was staring out the window, looking like he'd seen a ghost. He crossed himself several times and kissed a medallion hanging on a thin chain around his neck.

Following his line of sight, Julia at first saw nothing. Then—

"Oy! Is that Marco?"

"Sí," Ricardo rasped.

"Crikey," she breathed.

Ricardo dropped to his knees and continued to pray to the Blessed Virgin.

Quickly toggling the transmitter switch, Julia barked, "Felipe, if you can hear me, you must come to La Esmeralda immediately! This is a matter of life or death. Two more people have died because of the fungus: a little boy and now his father. Please, Felipe. Please get here ASAP!"

Feeling her knees weaken, Julie dropped into a chair but didn't take her eyes off the man at the top of the radio tower. She sat mesmerized by the horrific spectacle, wanting to look away but unable. With great effort, she pulled her eyes from Marco and stood.

"Ricardo, get a grip. Call Dr. Esparza immediately," she said with strained composure. "Tell him to meet me at the radio tower."

Ricardo had his eyes pinched shut. He was forcefully whispering one prayer after another. Julia stepped over to him and slapped him hard across his face.

"Ay!" he said, snapping out of it.

Grabbing the scruff of his collar, Julia growled evenly, "Call Dr. Esparza right now. Have him meet me by the aerial. Do it now, or so help me, I'll do more than slap your sorry face."

Ricardo swallowed hard and gave several curt nods.

CHAPTER 53

DESCENDING THE STAIRS AS FAST as her shaky legs would allow, Julia ran to the base of the radio tower. In the light of day, it was easy to see what had happened—there was no second guessing it.

She stood for some time just staring. Marco had reached the top of the tower and was hugging it tightly—just as his son had hours earlier. If the man wasn't dead, he soon would be. Trying to muster her resolve, Julia knew what had to be done, but she couldn't find the strength to move. This was the third time in as many days; her resolve was all but gone.

After a few minutes, Dr. Esparza came up behind her. "*Cielos*. Not again."

"Yes," she said, defeated.

Grasping a rung on the superstructure, Henry said, "I'll go up."

"No. It's too late for him. He's gone, just like Luis and Brandon." She huffed bitterly, kicking the gravel around the tower. Looking up, she said, "Good riddance to that one. He's the bloke who stole the fungus."

"Good. Then perhaps it will end here."

"No," she said, frowning at the corpse a hundred feet above her. "Marco doesn't have the bag with him. We need to find the plastic bag he had. The cordyceps is inside."

Henry's mouth dropped open. "You mean the cordyceps is here? In La Esmeralda?"

"Too right. Henry, you have to get the message to everyone to stay indoors. If any have to venture out, tell them not to touch any plastic bags until I get a chance to inspect them."

He nodded curtly. "I'll get right on it."

"Brilliant. I'll—"

"Señora!" the call of a young girl's voice interrupted her. "*Aquí está la bolsa de dinero.*"

Julia and Henry turned toward the house. Noely stood on the porch, holding a black plastic bag at the end of a stout stick.

"Noely!" Julia screamed. "Drop that bag immediately! Henry, tell her to drop it now."

"She says it is the money bag."

Julia ran toward the house.

Henry chased after her while yelling to Noely. She set the bag down and leaned the stick against the house. Skidding to a stop, Julia dropped to her knees and grabbed Noely's hands, turning them over and back again, looking for yellow spores. Joining them, Henry spoke continuous, consoling words as Julia examined Noely from top to bottom. Tears of fright sprang to the girl's eyes.

Julia couldn't stop her own eyes from brimming. "Lo siento, Noely. Lo siento. Henry, tell her she's not in trouble. I didn't mean to yell at her. She just needs to understand how dangerous that thing is."

He spoke again, and Noely mumbled a reply.

"She understands," the doctor affirmed.

"Thank you," Julia said, rapidly stroking the girl's hair. She gave Noely a fierce hug then sat back on her heels. "I don't see any spores on her, but to be safe she should have a wash without delay."

"She can wash off at the hospital or here at Ricardo's house."

"Brilliant. Have her do it here, now. Tell her to rinse off top to bottom, hands, hair, feet, everywhere. Have her do it right away then meet me at the hospital."

Henry spoke to Noely. The girl nodded and headed into the house.

"Do you have a larger sack we can put this one in?" Julia asked, indicating the plastic bag. "I want to examine this specimen at the hospital if possible."

"Yes, but . . ."

Julia looked up. "What?"

The doctor hesitated. "I do not have biohazard equipment there."

"Then we'll improvise. Look mate, you already have one sporangium growing there. This one has already released its spores. That's where the main danger lies. If I can contain the bag, it'll be okay."

Henry stepped closer to the bag. "There are spores all over it. Look, here . . . and here. This bag is not sealed. Marco may have spread spores from El Desvío to here."

"Crikey. Well let's hope the rain has washed them away. Until we can prove otherwise, our primary concern is to contain this in La Esmeralda. If it gets outside this town, there'll be no stopping it."

"Agreed. You take care of this bag; I'll get Marco down before he grows a strom—"

Henry's words were interrupted by the noise of a twin-engine airplane flying low overhead.

"No," Julia whimpered.

CHAPTER 54

"LA ESMERALDA TOWER, THIS IS Air Amazonia, requesting okay to landing," pilot Paco radioed.

"I saw you coming on the radar, Paco," Ricardo replied. "This is not a good time, amigo. Go home." The fear in the controller's voice tolled through the cabin.

The pilot cast a hopeful glance back at his passenger. The gringo was white as a ghost. And it hadn't even been that bad of a flight. The Americano avoided all attempts at conversation. Even Pablo seemed bored by him. At least he hadn't spilled the plastic poop bag.

Switching to Spanish, Paco joked, "Is it *ever* a good time to visit your sorry village?"

"Your request to land is denied. Turn away."

Paco frowned. "Stop joking around, Paz. I have a passenger with me, and our petrol is low. Now clear the landing strip of your stupid chickens, or we will have shredded *pollo* tonight."

"I am not joking, Paco. There is a terrible sickness here."

"A sickness?" He cast another quick glance at the Americano.

"Yes. It is very dangerous. You should fly to Cacique Aramare."

"That is two hundred miles away. I don't have enough fuel. You know my bird drinks more than a student on spring break."

"Then go to San Fernando de Atabapo."

"Their runway is too short. Besides, I have supplies for La Esmeralda, and this is where my passenger wants to go."

"I don't care. I will not allow your landing. You must turn away."

For a brief moment, Paco considered flying to one of the other locations. He'd never heard Paz in such a frightened state. Glancing at his instruments, he confirmed that both fuel tanks were in the red. "Nonsense, Ricardo. I'm coming in."

Paco reduced his throttle and angled the plane toward the narrow landing strip. Turning toward his passenger, he said, "Hold on tight, señor. The wind from the river always makes this exciting."

The Americano gave a weak smile.

The overloaded plane shuddered as he banked into his approach. Pablo bleated as if excited. The Americano groaned. Paco smiled. He loved this kind of flying. Using his best piloting skills, he set the plane down with only two minor jolts. The wheels chirped on the weathered macadam both times. They came to a stop at the far end of the runway with only two meters to spare. He turned and taxied back to the tower.

"You've got to be kidding," his passenger said, staring out the windshield.

"What is it, señor?"

The man pointed. Following his line of sight, Paco frowned then leaned forward and squinted. There at the top of the radio tower a man clung to the framework.

"Perhaps he must be change the globe?" Pablo wondered aloud. "Or he fixes the transmitter?"

"I don't think so," the Americano said.

"No?"

"No. I'm pretty sure he's dead."

Paco snorted, both in disbelief and fear. Is this what Paz was talking about? "*Rayos*, I hope not." He chuckled. "That is no way to greet a guest, sí señor? I mean to say, it is terrible bad way for to start your adventure here, sí?"

The Americano smiled. He no longer looked frightened. "On the contrary. It is a magnificent start."

Paco parked his Harbin next to the filling station in front of the service hut. Helping his passenger out of the plane, he said, "Thank you for flying with me. I hope you enjoyed your flight, señor."

"It was fine," the Americano said, pulling out his wallet. "Tell me, how long will you be here?"

Paco tore his stare from the man's ruined hand. "Perhaps one hour, I think. I must unload the plane, buy fuel, and then eat some lunch, sí?"

"I may be here longer than that, but I'm not sure. This may be easier than I thought."

"What is easier?"

The man pulled out an American one-hundred-dollar bill. "Will this keep you here until I return?"

Paco paused, considering. "But I thought you stay here long time, señor. One or two days, sí?"

"I thought so too, but if the dead man on that tower has anything to do with what I came here for, I should be back about the same time you're finished. This," he said, fluttering the bill, "is merely insurance." He shoved the bill into Paco's hand.

"It is usually the best insurance," Paco hedged, again glancing to the top of the tall aerial. Could the man up there really be dead?

The Americano placed a second one-hundred-dollar bill in his hand.

Paco quickly determined that he could do everything he needed to do without stepping more than a few meters from his plane. He crumpled the bills into his pocket. "Sí, señor. I will wait right here."

The Americano left his luggage and walked directly toward the radio tower.

¡Usted es un hombre loco, señor!

CHAPTER 55

JULIA LOOKED FROM THE TWIN-ENGINE plane to Henry. "You have more influence here than I do. Go tell whoever that is to scram. This area is quarantined. I'll take this to the hospital," she said, pointing to the plastic bag.

He nodded. "I'm on it."

As Henry headed toward the airplane, Julia examined the black trash bag. It was dingy and streaked with mud. Pale yellow spores rimmed the opening. Worse, it reeked. The stench emanating from the opening was stomach-churning—worse than any fungus she'd ever encountered. Fighting a gag reflex, she grasped the bag on either side of the knot and cinched it tighter. Then, using the staff Noely left, she jammed an end under the knot and lifted it off the ground. A muffled, moist noise slogged within the bag. Julia fought another gag and headed to the hospital.

A middle-aged receptionist sat behind the desk in the foyer. She wore a simple dress and a pleasant smile. Regarding Julia and her package with a curious look, she asked, "Hola, ¿*Puedo ayudarle*, señora?"

"I need to take this to the procedure room," she said, hefting the bag. "Dr. Esparza said I could examine it there."

As the foul odor grew in strength, the receptionist fought to keep her smile. "Oh sí. Pase, señora," she said, covering her mouth and nose with a hankie and waving Julia into the back.

The procedure room had been cleaned. Luis's corpse was no longer there—as if last night's encounter was only a bad memory. *So where is the body?* she wondered. She set the bag on the exam table and peeked in the other room. It wasn't there either. Returning to the receptionist, she asked, "Where is the body of the boy that was brought in last night?"

The woman stepped through the doorway and pointed down the hallway. It was only then that Julia noticed the large chest freezer at the far end, next to what looked like a utility closet.

"The body is in there?"

The woman nodded.

Walking toward the freezer seemed labor intensive. The faster she walked, the slower she seemed to move. It was like walking down a long hallway in a Hitchcock movie. With each step she took, the hallway seemed to stretch in length. And the closer she got, the more her skin crawled. Her hand trembled as she reached for the lid. If the little boy's corpse had been placed within, she knew just what she would see. But that didn't stop her emotions from flaring. It was one thing to see an adult infected with such a parasite. It was something completely different to see a small child so infected. But she had to confirm that what had killed Luis was what killed Brandon. *Ophiocordyceps unilateralis.* A zombie maker.

Taking a calming breath, she opened the freezer lid. A plastic sheet covered what was inside. Pulling it back, a small corpse met her gaze with dead, milky eyes. His stare was one of confusion and accusation— she being the accused. *Her* announcement of Brandon's discovery had killed this innocent child. She closed the lid and slumped to the ground. What she wouldn't give just to pack up and go home, to pretend this never happened. *Poppy, I am at my wit's end.*

Her heart ached to the point of splitting. It thumped painfully against her sternum. Her throat constricted as if clenched in a python's coils. She was supposed to be finding beneficial ways to use nature's wonders, not witnessing its wanton destruction, not seeing innocent children die.

"¿Señora? ¿Está bien?" Noely asked from the doorway.

Julia turned and met the little girl's eyes but couldn't voice any words. Her entire frame shivered uncontrollably. Tears spilled. Noely quickly closed the distance between them and wrapped Julia in a tight embrace. She spoke soft, consoling words Julia didn't understand but recognized nonetheless. She returned the embrace and sobbed.

She didn't know how long they sat on the floor, but Julia suddenly noticed that Noely's hair was wet.

"You washed everywhere?" she said, pantomiming the action.

"Sí. *No estoy enferma*," Noely said confidently. She then asked a lengthy question, pointing at the procedure room.

"No entiendo," Julia said with a weak smile. "But I want to thank you for being so strong." She tenderly scooted an errant strand of wet hair from Noely's pretty face. "I wish I could be as strong right now."

Noely smiled. There was understanding in her deep brown eyes. Julia wrapped her in a second warm hug then stood and led the girl to the reception area.

"Can you watch her until I'm finished?" Julia asked the receptionist.

"Sí. *Será un placer*. I happy to. No problem."

"No," Noely argued. She rattled off a string of sharp words, at the same time motioning at herself and pointing toward the exam rooms.

The receptionist held up her palms as if in a truce. "She say she no sick. She want to help you . . . *¿descubrir?* . . . what is happen. She know her father is his . . . blame?"

"It's his fault."

"Ah sí. She miss Lu—her brother," she said, probably changing her mind so as not to say Luis's name aloud. "She is fault also. She no want more to have sick. She want to help."

Noely's plaintive yet determined look was inarguable. Julia knelt and caressed the little girl's arms. "Please tell her it is most certainly *not* her fault. She is not to blame. I'd be happy to have her help, but I am worried she may *become* infected. And I will not risk that."

Before she could translate, Noely continued in Spanish.

"She say—" The woman paused and smiled. "She say she do whatever pretty doctor say, but she can help. She say she know how her brother be sick."

Noely's expression remained resolute. Jabbing her thumb at her chest, she said, "I help! *Ningún argumento*."

"I'm afraid that is not going to happen," Dr. Esparza said, entering the hospital.

"Why?" Julia asked, turning.

No one answered. No one had to. A Caucasian man Julia didn't recognize stood behind Henry holding a gun to his head.

CHAPTER 56

"WHERE IS THE FUNGUS?" THE stranger demanded.

Julia began to laugh. This new conflict was simply too much on her weakened system. The situation was already so tenuous it felt brittle. Now this. She couldn't help it—laughing was her release from having a complete breakdown. She felt lightheaded with anxiety.

"Please do not laugh, miss," the stranger calmly said. "I am not a patient man, and I do not like being laughed at. I have no problem using any means at my disposal to get what I want."

"Please do what he asks, Julia," Henry concurred.

"Who are you, and how do you know about the fungus?" Julia demanded, ignoring the doctor's request.

"That is none of your business."

"A wombat's bum it isn't. It's *all* my business. That fungus is deadly. It's already killed three people—although I assume you know that."

"Yes, the good doctor here brought me up to speed on our walk over here," the man said with a hint of a smile. "Are you the researcher who discovered it?"

"My partner did. It took his life before he could figure it out. What makes you think you'll fare any better?" she spat indignantly. "What makes you such an exp—"

"Because I have a degree in botany and I am not careless," he cut in. "Now—do I blast a hole through the good doctor's face, or do you shut the hole in *yours* and bring me the fungus?"

"Oy, steady on, mate," she said, holding up her palms. "No need to get obstinate. Look, since you know the fungus is deadly, you'll know it requires significantly more study before it gets out of control."

The stranger smirked. "Having seen the dead man on the radio tower, I believe that goal is moot."

Julia dropped her hands to her sides as if in surrender. "You may be spot on—that's why we've got to find a way to stop it. You're welcome to join me, but you'll have to do so without random threats of violence."

Without a word, the man turned and shot out the glass front door. The receptionist screamed and dropped to the floor. Noely dove behind the counter. Julia's giddiness vanished.

Slowly uncoiling from a reflexive crouch, Julia again held up her hands. "Bludgers! What'd you do that for?"

"To demonstrate that my threats are *not* random. I do what I say; I don't play games."

"Okay, okay. The fungus is in a safe place. But it's probably a ruddy waste of time. I don't know if the spores are still viable."

"Then you shouldn't have an issue giving it to me."

"Right. But if they *are* still viable, then—"

"Then it will suit my purposes even better," he again cut in. "Now," he continued, pressing his gun against Esparza's head, "get me the fungus, and no one will get hurt. Test my patience any further, and this place will resemble a slaughterhouse."

"All right. At least tell me who you are," Julia pressed.

An unsettling, macabre expression crept across his face. "They call me Mantis." With the gun in his right hand, the man held up a deformed left hand. He then pointed the gun at her and added, "As I said, I don't play games—Julia, was it? Now—WHERE IS THE FUNGUS?" he suddenly screamed.

The receptionist let out another scream and began to cry.

"Be quiet!" Mantis yelled at her.

"It's in the back," Julia said with a jerk of her thumb. "In the freezer." She added the lie as a plan quickly formulated in her mind.

Mantis frowned. "The freezer? Why?"

"Because this is the tropics, you dill. It'd decompose in a matter of hours if left out."

Julia saw hesitation in the man's demeanor. Clearly, this thief didn't have the same scientific background she did. Freezing tropical spores would most likely kill them.

"Take me to it," he demanded.

"Stop pointing the gun at me, and I will."

The intruder scowled. He looked around the room, thinking. The receptionist continued to whimper loudly. "Who is this woman?" he asked Esparza.

"Her name is Consuelo. She is my receptionist."

"I don't speak Spanish. Tell her to be quiet."

The doctor did as asked.

"Who's the little girl hiding behind the counter?" Mantis wanted to know.

"Her name's Noely," Julia answered. "She has nothing to do with this."

Mantis snorted at her reply. "Is there anyone in the back?"

"No," both Esparza and Julia answered simultaneously.

"How many rooms are there?"

"One exam room, one procedure room, and a utility closet," the doctor said.

"Okay then, here's what's going to happen. First, the doctor will lock Noely and Consuelo in the utility closet. Then I'll have you show me the fungus."

When he mentioned her name, Consuelo began to wail again, but no one moved.

"Somebody please shut her up," Mantis complained.

All eyes turned to Julia as if she had the power to counter his demands. But she didn't know what to do. At this point she was so knackered, she half wanted to give him the cordyceps and have an end to it. And yet she knew it *wouldn't* end there. With disturbing clairvoyance, she realized this Mantis bloke wanted to *exploit* the lethality of the fungus. *Why* was a question secondary to ascertaining how this man—clearly an American—even knew about the cordyceps. It'd been less than a week since its discovery. She did transmit a mayday, but she doubted Meghan had passed it on. The intruder obviously wasn't part of a CDC advance team. They don't use guns.

Time stood still. Consuelo continued to cry.

Mantis sighed. "I see more proof of my resolve is necessary." Without hesitation, he pointed the gun at Consuelo and fired. The gun's rapport exploded in Julia's ears.

With a sharp grunt of pain, Consuelo fell backward. A splotch of red quickly blossomed across the front of her blouse.

"No!" Henry yelled, moving toward his fallen receptionist. Before he could take a second step, Mantis clubbed him with the butt of his pistol, dropping the doctor to his knees but not knocking him out.

The gunman smugly blew at a tendril of smoke from the barrel. "Now do you believe me?" he asked Julia as if speaking to a child.

"I believed you the first time, you nob," she snarled, rounding the counter to the fallen receptionist.

Eyes wide with panic, Consuelo fought for breath with huge, wet gasps. Blood oozed between her fingers as she clutched her chest. The bullet hole was high and to the right of her sternum.

It missed her heart. Please let it have missed her heart, Julia hoped desperately.

Consuelo blanched in pain as Julia applied pressure to the pulsing wound.

"I'm sorry," Julia whimpered. "Lo siento. Lo siento. Dr. Esparza, I need your help!"

"Everybody just stay calm," Mantis said evenly. "Doctor, you go help your assistant. Julia, you will assist me."

"I will do no such thing," she growled, still trying to staunch the flow of blood.

Before she could stop him, Mantis stepped around the opposite side of the counter, grabbed a handful of Noely's hair, and yanked her to her feet. Holding the pistol to the girl's head, he sneered, "Oh, but I think you will."

CHAPTER 57

MEGHAN HAD WAITED SEMI-PATIENTLY ALL day. She'd given Bob Jones Felipe's reserve gun—well, not given, more like sold it to him. She'd put him on a charter plane and wished him luck. He really was a nice guy, and his heart was in the right place. She felt he cared as much about the environment as she did. She could read it in his aura. Along with her spiritual connection to dolphins came an inner sonar that pinged with compatible ethos. At least, that's what her psychic had told her. She wasn't sure exactly what it meant, but the gist was that she shared a common, mystical bond with other environmentalists. It really was too bad he wasn't better looking.

There was also that thing about being called Bruja. Bob had seemed certain she was his secret friend in Caicara. She had no idea who Bruja could be, but Meghan was confident she was superior in every category. With everything she'd done for him, Bob would no longer need his Bruja.

The wall clock read quarter to four, and she still had no word from Carlos's friend. The man had promised to deliver her the mushroom by this afternoon. Carlos had promised her. Technically, it was still afternoon, but she couldn't wait any longer.

Sprucing herself up, she hopped in her car and drove to the city offices. She hated going out at this time of day. If she were on a beach in a bikini, it'd be fine. But having to get dolled up to chase a promise someone was welching on was not her idea of a pleasant afternoon—ever. When she entered the police station, the afternoon got even worse. Some middle-aged officer with thinning hair and a mustache the size of Cleveland sat behind the desk, picking at his teeth with an uncurled paper clip.

"Hola, *mi muñequita sabrosa*," he oozed, removing the paper clip and using his tongue to suck at whatever hadn't quite dislodged.

"Is Carlos in?" she asked flatly.

"He no work today. But I help you," the man said with a wink.

"In your dreams," she replied, turning on her heel and exiting quickly, knowing the officer's eyes were all over her backside.

She plopped into her car, cranked up the A/C, and drove to Carlos's apartment. The hottie answered the door wearing a faded pair of Levis and a stretchy white tank top. She never got over how well it clung to his chest and abs.

"Hi, sweetie, you got a minute?" Meghan asked, pushing past him.

Sitting on the couch was the same woman she'd seen last time. The woman looked up with a smile, but it vanished instantly. With eyes narrowed to two black slits, she hissed something in Spanish.

"Oh, well it's good to see you too," Meghan crooned. "Listen, I'm here on official government business, so could you please come back later?"

The woman continued to scowl at Meghan as Carlos said something to her. Meghan assumed it was a direct translation. But the woman didn't move.

"Meghan, I cannot see you now," Carlos said, rather sternly.

"Don't be silly, hon." She giggled. "You can see me as clearly as I can see you. Besides, this will only take a second."

Carlos folded his arms. "Say what you have to say, then go."

"But . . . ," she paused and flashed a smile at the woman. "It's a private matter."

"She cannot understand you. She speaks no English."

Meghan huffed and moved closer to Carlos. Whispering, she said, "It's about that thing I asked you to get."

"What thing?"

"You know. In the rain forest? Your friend said he'd bring it to me . . . ?"

"Oh, sí. You mean the mushroom."

"Shhh, not so loud," she admonished, glancing back at the scowling woman. "Call it the . . . the 'item.' It's top secret."

"The mushroom?"

"Yes, call it the 'item.' That way no one will know what we're talking about."

"O—kay," he said, as if hesitant.

"So . . . where is it? You said your friend would bring it to me by this afternoon."

Carlos glanced at his watch. "It is only sixteen hundred."

"No, it's already after four. The afternoon is almost over, and I still have no . . . *item*."

"But—" Carlos stopped short as if in frustration. Meghan couldn't understand why he was being so bullheaded. She'd asked him to do something quite simple. She'd already "paid" him for it.

"Don't make me mad, sweetie," she said with practiced venom. "You won't like me when I'm mad."

"Fine. I will call him, but as before, he may not be there," he said, grabbing his cell phone from a table.

"Carlos?" the woman on the sofa said. "*¿Está todo bien?*"

"Sí," he replied, teeth gritted.

"Geez, I don't understand why *you're* so angry." Meghan pouted. "I'm the one being cheated here."

A painfully awkward silence ensued as Carlos listened to the empty ringing on the other end of the line. "There is no answer."

"Tell him I can't wait any longer."

"But he does not answer."

"Isn't there some other way to get ahold of him?"

"No. As I explain, he live far away."

"Well you stay on that line until he *does* answer. And when he does, tell him I am very disappointed," she snipped.

The hottie let it ring a dozen more times before disconnecting.

"What are you doing?"

"My battery is low. I try again later. I tell him bring the mush—, the *item* to the CIST." He set his phone on the table and moved to the door. "I did what you ask. Now, please leave. I have a guest."

Unsatisfied, but knowing there was nothing else she could do, Meghan stepped over to Carlos and put her hands on his chest. "No, baby, you don't have a guest," she said, rising on her toes to kiss him on the cheek. "You have that," she said, nodding smugly at the other woman.

The woman jumped to her feet, her fists clenched.

"Adios, sweetie," Meghan said, opening the front door. Then, turning, she added, "Don't do anything I wouldn't do."

The door closed none too gently behind her. She lifted her hair off her neck and fanned it. The heat of the late afternoon was insufferable. How could people live like this? She couldn't wait to get her mushroom and leave this miserable country.

From inside the apartment she heard the woman's angry voice yelling at Carlos. He offered a continuous string of calming words. Meghan had no clue what they were saying—but she certainly got the gist of it. And that understanding put a spring in her step as she sauntered back to her car.

CHAPTER 58

JULIA LED THE WAY TO the exam rooms. The appearance of this Mantis bloke and his knowledge of the cordyceps fungus further jumbled the puzzle in her mind, adding at least a dozen more pieces. Nothing was fitting together; nothing added up.

The freezer sat at the end of the hallway, but the distance to it seemed much shorter this time. The whole area smelled fetid, sickly. The drone of flies echoed up and down the hall. Passing the procedure room, Julia glanced at the black plastic bag still sitting on the exam table.

"Ugh," Mantis coughed, burying his nose in the crook of his elbow. "What is that horrible smell?"

"I suspect it's the thing you came here for," Julia answered.

"Is it rotten?"

"Of course it's rotten. It's a fungus, you twit."

Mantis tightened his grip on Noely's hair, causing her to cry out. "I said not to test my patience. Stop calling me names, and give me a straight answer."

"Look, I don't know why it stinks back here. The doctor told me he put the fungus in that freezer there. I don't know its condition. I haven't had a chance to examine it since it was stolen from me a few nights—" Julia stopped short as some of the puzzle pieces suddenly lined up. This man knew about the fungus because he was the one who . . .

"You!" Julia said sternly. "*You* had Ricardo tell Marco to steal the fungus from me, didn't you." It was an accusation, not a question.

"I don't know either of those men," Mantis said.

"But you knew about the fungus. You knew it had killed my partner."

"That would be correct," he replied with a mealy grin. "I know a lot of things. I have many connections all over the world."

"So it *had* to be them," she confirmed. "Ricardo Paz—he mans the airport control tower here. He hired Marco to steal the fungus. Marco thought he could make money from it. I couldn't figure out how on earth he could, but now it all makes sense. He stole it for Ricardo because Ricardo's going to sell it to you."

"Very good, doctor. Now, let's stop stalling and go collect my fungus."

As she stepped to the freezer, Julia's mind was racing. Her impromptu plan from a few minutes earlier hadn't included Noely.

At the freezer, the gunman said, "Now open the lid."

Knowing what was inside, Julia hedged, "Hold on a tic. Let Noely go back to the foyer. She has nothing to do with this, and I don't want her to get infected."

"She'll stay right here," he said, pushing the girl up against the door to the utility closet. "Don't move, or I'll shoot you."

Noely frowned.

"She doesn't understand you, mate. She doesn't speak English."

Mantis pointed to the floor. "Sit."

Noely lowered herself to her knees and sat on her heels.

"Close enough."

As Mantis raised the lid of the freezer, Julia motioned for Noely to behind-crawl toward her. The little girl waited for the gunman to reach in before she scooted forward. When she was directly behind him, Julia indicated she should stop. Understanding instantly registered in Noely's eyes.

Mantis pulled back the plastic sheet and saw the small frozen corpse staring wide-eyed at him. He cried out and, stepping away, tripped over Noely. Falling backward with an angry yell, he slammed onto the tile floor with a grunt. Regrettably, he maintained his grip on his gun.

Julia leapt on top of him, reaching for the gun. "Run!" she shouted at Noely.

The little girl scrambled to her feet and bolted down the hall.

Mantis thrust his hips, arching his back, causing Julia to fly over his head. She landed hard on her shoulder, feeling it momentarily dislocate from the socket. The gunman quickly rolled into a prone position and leveled the gun at her.

"Don't move!"

Julia was frozen in pain. She couldn't move if she wanted to. She cursed her bad luck. Her plan had almost worked. She had hoped to wrestle the gun from him when he was sidetracked by Luis's frozen stare.

"I have half a mind to shoot you in the face," the gunman hissed, struggling to catch his breath as he shimmied to his knees. "You knew that corpse was in there, didn't you."

She didn't answer.

Mantis struggled to his feet. "That was very foolish," he growled, still breathing hard. "Someone will have to pay for your insolence."

Julia was on her knees, gingerly working her sore shoulder. "Too late." She grimaced. "Crikey, this hurts."

"There is no fungus in that freezer, only a corpse."

"The fungus is growing from the back of his head. You have to turn him over to see it. I thought you knew everything."

Mantis scowled. "You must think I'm really stupid."

Wisely, Julia opted not to respond.

"The fungus infected your partner, not a little boy." He leveled his eyes at her. In a dark, even tone he said, "Place your left hand on the floor, palm down."

"Why?"

He stepped up to her and rammed the gun against the side of her head. Slowly, Julia stretched out her left hand to the floor as instructed.

"Do you want your hand look like mine?"

She didn't answer.

"Julia, you are trying my patience." He placed his foot on her hand and pushed down.

She sucked in a breath between her teeth, steeling herself against the pain.

"Do you?"

"No," she grunted softly.

"Louder."

"No!"

"Then no more games," he said, stepping back. "Bring me the fungus."

Just then, Dr. Esparza poked his head around the corner. "Excuse me. I need materials to treat Consuelo. I cannot stop the bleeding."

Mantis jerked his head, indicating the doctor could go to the procedure room to gather supplies. After a moment of rustling about, Henry strode back across the hall into the foyer.

"Show me the fungus," Mantis ordered. "Now!"

Julia wobbled to her feet and led him into the procedure room. The stench was nearly unbearable. She was certain the severed stroma was all but decomposed, but that didn't matter. The sporangium had released its spores. They were the deadly part. Did the gunman know that?

"It's in there," she said, pointing at the plastic bag.

Mantis stepped over to the bag. Even though his face was scrunched from the terrible odor, his eyes shone with delight.

"You might want to don a mask before opening that," Julia said.

"Is it airborne?"

She shrugged. "I haven't confirmed that, but I haven't had a chance to rule it out either."

"How it is vectored? What is it virulence—Its R-factor? 2? 3? 4?"

Julia frowned. "How do you know those terms?"

"I know a lot of things, doctor."

"Then I hope you know you're playing with fire. Crikey, what do you want with the cordyceps anyway?"

Mantis turned to her with a grin. "It's a cordyceps? How interesting . . ."

He put on a pair of latex gloves from the counter and carefully undid the knot at the top. The stench immediately amplified. A faint puff of yellow dust lifted out of the opening and dropped to the floor. Mantis leaned back and waved his hand to dissipate the smell. "Has it always smelled this bad?"

Julia's anger was quickly replacing her fear. "Look, this is ridiculous. I'm not answering any more of your questions."

Staring into the depths of the black bag, Mantis said, "You tried that once and almost got someone killed. Do you really want to try again?"

"I didn't try to kill anyone. You did."

"Oh right, I did *try*," he said, finding some zip-ties in a drawer and sealing the bag. "I promise to do better next time." He moved swiftly to Julia and rammed the gun into her temple. "Put your wrists together. No arguments."

She complied, holding her hands at arm's length.

"Don't move." Using the minimal dexterity of his left hand, he was able to zip-tie Julia's wrists together. "That's better. Now, let's go decide who dies next."

CHAPTER 59

THE FOYER WAS EMPTY. CONSUELO'S blood still pooled on the floor, but her body was gone. Mantis cursed his foolishness for letting the others out of his sight. But he was determined not to make any more mistakes.

"Looks like we're all alone," Julia said with a hint of cockiness.

"No matter," he quickly retorted. "I have the fungus, and I have you. Let's go."

"Not likely, mate. I'm not going anywhere with you."

"I disagree. There's no telling what's waiting for us between here and the airstrip. I need a shield."

"And if I refuse?"

"Then I will kill you."

She huffed. "After what I've been through, I say go ahead, pull the trigger. I just don't give a hoot anymore."

"Oh, I think you do." He gave a wry smile as he lifted the plastic bag and shook it. "Besides, who said anything about *shooting* you?"

She huffed again. "You think I'm afraid of that? I've been exposed to that smelly thing for days now, and I've yet to be infected."

"Then let me rephrase my promise. If you don't cooperate, I will infect this entire town—beginning with sweet little Mogley."

"Her name is Noely. And she's long gone by now," she said shakily as a flash of uncertainty flitted across her face. "You'll never see her again."

The researcher's words were obviously hollow. Mantis knew her threats were mere show. "Yes, of course. There are so many places to hide in this riverside metropolis," Mantis chortled. "No matter. It's a pity everyone here will be dead in a few days. More's the pity any survivors will blame it all on you."

Her eyes narrowed. "How do you figure?"

"Simple. No one knows I'm here, and everyone knows you've been studying rain forest fungi. You see, I've been following your work, doctor. It's very impressive, but you lack vision."

"I do?"

"Yes. The bioweapon potential of this fungus is phenomenal. Imagine the money one could make amplifying it."

Her face lost almost all of its color. *Good*, he thought. *She's finally starting to believe me.*

"How can you be so heartless?" she asked in a whisper of shock.

Raising his damaged hand, he spat, "How can *I* be so heartless? Easy. It's called payback. Payback for all the pain inflicted on me—from my father and from everyone who pretends to take pity on me while turning their heads in disgust. Payback for watching greedy monopolies rape the environment so their CEOs can build absurdly huge homes in Key West and Martha's Vineyard that they'll use only ten days a year."

"Look, I'm sorry for your hardships, mate, but what has that got to do with me?"

Mantis shrugged. "Not a thing. You're merely a means to an end. Now, let's stop stalling and get to work, shall we?"

Using the barrel of his gun, he pushed her toward the door. They stepped out into the sunshine and paused. He looked around for any signs of resistance but saw none. Keeping the gun between her shoulder blades, they worked their way back to the airstrip. The town seemed strangely empty. A few chickens pecking for scraps and the occasional dog tied to a porch were the only signs of life; they saw no people. It was as if all humanity had vanished.

"Where is everyone?" he asked himself aloud.

"Perhaps word is out a madman's in town."

He laughed. "I disagree. A madman would not have made it this far. I prefer to think of myself as an enlightened man."

She scoffed but didn't voice anything.

Rounding a small stucco house, they saw radio tower come into view. A man stood at its base gazing up at the lifeless form still clinging to the top. As they drew closer, Mantis recognized his pilot, Paco. He appeared very jittery.

Pressing his gun to the small of Julia's back, Mantis whispered, "Don't say a word."

"What is happen here?" Paco asked when they stopped a few feet from him. "Is that man honest dead?"

"Yes," Mantis replied.

"How he die?"

Before Mantis could answer, an eerie, almost inhuman howling sounded from somewhere near the control tower. Turning, he saw a man dressed head to toe in the garb of a voodoo witch doctor coming toward them. The man wailed as if possessed.

"What in the world?" Mantis breathed.

"Ay Dios," Paco gasped, crossing himself several times. "Un brujo."

Mantis blinked at the title. This freak couldn't be his contact, could he?

The shaman approached them, shaking a bone rattle with one hand while withdrawing a reddish powder from one of three pouches dangling around his waist. Casting the powder into the air, he did a brief, frenetic dance. His face was smeared with charcoal and blood. His outfit—what little there was—was made from various animal parts, ornamental feathers, and dried strands of long grass.

When the witch doctor came within fifteen feet of the trio, his lamentations reached a fevered pitch. Then, with a final tonsil-bursting screech, he stopped. The ensuing silence was almost as creepy as his wailing. He dropped his bone rattle to the side and dug each hand into its own pouch. Withdrawing a generous handful of red powder in one hand and yellow powder in the other, he cast it toward the onlookers while hissing between his teeth.

Paco dropped to his knees, fervently whimpering prayers in Spanish.

Mantis yanked Julia in front of hm. "What's going on here?" he demanded.

"How should I know?" she said in a terse whisper.

Mantis couldn't believe this was happening. While he gave zero credence to witchcraft, there was something about the intensity with which the shaman performed that made him panicky. Where did this guy come from? What nonsense was he spouting? Could he really be his contact, Bruja? And what were the colored powders he kept tossing in the air?

The witch doctor took three steps closer, glaring at Mantis if he wanted to flay him alive and wear his skin as adornment. He continued to hiss like a deranged snake. Pilot Paco—still cowering on the ground—had all but passed out. The smell of fresh urine came from his direction.

When the shaman was within ten feet, he pointed at Julia and spat out a string of aboriginal-sounding words. Mantis found himself trembling, even though he was the one holding a gun. "You want her?" Mantis asked shakily. "You want this woman?"

The shaman reached into his third pouch.

"What—you want to trade for her?" Mantis asked, lowering his gun.

The painted man nodded then tried to quickly withdraw something from the pouch—a handgun—but the hammer caught on the drawstring, snagging it. Mantis quickly raised his gun, pointing it directly at the man's face.

"Don't shoot!" the witch doctor said in perfect English, holding up his hands.

CHAPTER 60

"What the—?" Mantis barked.

"Don't shoot. Just leave these people, take the fungus, and go," the shaman said, keeping his hands aloft.

It was only then that Mantis recognized Dr. Esparza's voice.

"Slowly remove the pouch with the gun. Don't remove the gun, or I'll drop you where you stand."

The doctor complied.

"Now toss the pouch to me."

He did. Mantis removed the gun and rammed it in the pocket of his windbreaker.

"I'm sorry, Julia," Dr. Esparza said. "I guess I'm not much of a hero."

"You tried. That makes you the best kind of hero," Julia assured him.

"Oh, this is just too touching for words," Mantis groaned. Then, looking at the pilot, he growled, "Get up."

"B-but the brujo," Paco stammered, keeping his eyes focused on the ground.

"He's not a witch doctor."

"Sí, sí, he is."

"He looks like a brujo to me," Julia pitched in.

"Shut up," Mantis snapped at Julia. "Tell him who you are," Mantis ordered the doctor.

Esparza grumbled something in Spanish. Paco eyes got even larger.

"He doesn't believe me," Esparza said with a shrug.

"You tell him," he demanded of Julia.

"I don't speak Spanish."

Mantis yelled in frustration and fired a shot at the ground. "Get up!"

The pilot slowly eased to his feet, keeping his eyes down. "Do not shoot, señor."

"Now listen to me carefully. Are witch doctors magical?" Mantis asked the pilot.

"Sí. Their magic very strong."

"So magical that nothing can hurt them?"

"Sí, señor. Nada hurt him."

Mantis turned and shot Esparza in the leg. The doctor cried out in pain and collapsed. As he writhed on the ground, Paco's look of fear slowly vanished.

"*¿Entonces . . . usted no es un brujo?*"

"No," the doctor forced past a pain-filled grimace.

"See? Now let's go," Mantis said with a jerk of his head.

"Why you have a gun, señor?"

"Encouragement."

"*¿Cómo?*"

"Persuasion, then."

"I . . . I still no understand."

"GET IN THE PLANE!" Mantis screamed, shoving the barrel of the pistol in the pilot's face.

"Ah, sí."

Pushing Julia from behind, Mantis walked briskly out onto the tarmac. Esparza lay on the ground, trying to staunch the blood pulsing from his wound.

"Can't we at least take Henry to the hospital?" Julia asked.

"He'll live," Mantis answered flatly.

The rust-cankered Harbin sat on a gravel holding pad near the end of the runway. Paco opened the fuselage door and lowered the steps. "Please get in and buckle up. I go get Pablo."

"Forget about him," Mantis snapped.

Profound disbelief twisted Paco's face. "What?"

A happy bleating came from a grassy area on the opposite side of the tarmac.

"I call him," Paco quickly added. "*¡Pablo! ¡Ven aquí, Pablo, Ven!*"

Like a well-trained dog, the goat rounded a small shed and ambled toward the plane at a leisurely clip.

"I'm not flying with that disgusting animal again," Mantis grumbled.

"No fly with Pablo? But he my copilot."

"It is a goat, not a copilot! And I'm *not* going to carry his droppings again."

Julia turned to him with an expression of *What the heck?*

"Don't ask. Just get inside," he said, pointing at the open hatch.

As Julia climbed onboard, the goat arrived and rubbed his flank against Paco's leg. "You see? He want to go. No is problem, sí?"

"Sí. No is problem," Mantis said—then shot the goat in the head. The animal dropped to the tarmac without a sound. "No problemo at all."

"NO!" Paco cried. "No, no, no, no!" Slumping to his knees, Paco cradled the goat in his arms. He sat sobbing in Spanish, clearly anguished over the abrupt loss of his friend.

"Get in the plane," Mantis ordered the pilot. "It's time to go."

Face red with tears, Paco scowled at him then spat on the ground. "No! I no fly you anymore." He added to the declaration a few words in Spanish that Mantis took to be insults. He didn't care.

"Is the plane fueled?"

"It is, but I no fly. Why you kill my copilot?"

Mantis rolled his eyes in frustration. "He is *not* a copilot."

Paco spat on the ground again. "He fly better than you, señor."

"Oh, you think so?" Mantis clambered aboard and turned to the pilot. "Adiós, loser." He quickly pulled up the steps and locked the door.

Paco didn't answer. He remained on the blacktop, softly muttering in Spanish while gently rocking the dead goat.

Mantis tossed the bag containing the fungus in the nearly empty cargo area. Even though the bags of old vegetables were gone, their stench remained. The only thing left were some burlap sacks and a pile of strapping cord.

Julia sat in a passenger seat. "Get in the copilot's chair and buckle up," he told her.

The task proved difficult with her hands still bound, but she succeeded with some assistance. He buckled her in and used another zip tie to shackle her wrists to the safety belt.

"Oy, what's that for?"

"To keep you from touching the controls."

"Why would I do that? I don't know how to fly a plane."

"It'll help me focus."

"But these things are cutting off my circulation."

"I don't care."

Mantis tucked his gun in his windbreaker and fastened himself in the pilot's seat. Glancing over the instrument panel, he allowed himself a faint smile. He hadn't flown a twin-engine plane before, but he did have several hours in a SIMCOM training simulator. His main concern was adjusting the prop pitch during takeoff and while cruising. *When adding power, adjust the props first then the throttle*, he rehearsed mentally. Decreasing power is just the reverse. How hard could that be? The rest of the plane functioned the same as a single-engine plane, right?

Besides, everything else was going well so far—better than he'd expected, in fact. He'd arrived thinking he'd have to spend days unearthing his contact while assuming the role of a sightseer. He was certain the greedy Bruja would demand more money. But when Mantis saw the dead man at the top of the radio tower, he knew his luck had changed. The man he met at the base of the tower ended up being the local doctor, and he revealed everything that had transpired in the past few days. There was no question that this fungus was the one Bruja had promised. Now he not only had the fungus, he had the researcher who'd discovered it—and thus everything she knew about it. Plus, he now had a second gun and a twin-engine Harbin. Yes, Green Blade would be very pleased.

Mantis primed the engines and cranked them over. His smile broadened when they both started quickly and gained RPMs. The gauges he recognized all read normal; both fuel tanks showed they were topped off and were flowing in the blue.

"I take it you know how to fly this thing," Julia said over the roar of the engines.

"Of course," he yelled back.

Taxiing onto the runway, he lined up the plane for takeoff. Paco was carrying his dead goat toward the control tower. Glancing up, Mantis saw a man in the controller's window frantically trying to wave him off. He returned the wave with a grin and a thumbs-up.

Julia spoke up. "I don't think we're cleared to go."

"Like I said, I don't care," Mantis replied.

"No, I'm serious," Julia said, bending forward to look out the windscreen. "That's Ricardo. He's the air traffic controller. Look, he keeps pointing up at the sky."

As Mantis leaned forward, a shadow paused over the cockpit. At first he thought it was just a cloud, but the day had only a few fluffy cumulous drifting at high altitude. It might be another plane, but the shadow was stationary.

"Looks like Ricardo wants you to turn on your radio," Julia said, nodding toward the control tower.

Mantis saw the controller pantomiming putting on a headset. Unhooking the equipment from the headrest, Mantis nestled it over his ears. A crackling of static filled the muffs. He adjusted the frequency knob until a clear voice came through. Only—it wasn't the control tower he heard.

"Twin-engine Harbin, this is CIST helicopter Romeo-Quebec-two-five-niner-six-one. I order you cut your engines and stand down immediately!"

"Who is this?" Mantis demanded.

The helicopter skillfully maneuvered from a few feet above the plane to directly in front of it, facing them as it hovered only inches off the ground. The dark-haired pilot looked to be ten years younger than Mantis. He wore dark glasses and a serious scowl.

The radio cracked. "I'm Felipe Pascal, director of the Centro de Investigación de la Selva Tropical, and you're under arrest for robbery, destruction of property, and attempted murder."

CHAPTER 61

"FELIPE!" IT WAS JULIA'S VOICE! But how could that be?

Felipe was focusing so hard on the unknown pilot that he'd missed seeing the passenger. Why in the world would Julia be with *him*?

"Get out of my way," the Harbin pilot demanded.

"Why is Dr. Fatheringham with you?" he asked harshly.

The pilot glanced over at Julia. "You mean Julia? Oh. She's my assistant."

"Not likely, you bludger," he heard Julia yell.

"Shut up," the pilot spat.

"Julia, can you hear me?" Felipe shouted into his mike.

"I'm afraid not, Pascal," the pilot said. "She works for me now."

Julia said something that didn't transmit well. It didn't matter. He knew there was no way she was working with this madman.

"Get out of my way, Pascal," the pilot said evenly.

"Felipe, stop this madman!" Julia shouted.

"I said shut up," the pilot shouted back. "Get out of my way, or I'll drive right through you, Pascal. I swear I will."

"Negative," Felipe replied. "The tower informed me of your attempted murder and other criminal activities, pilot. Stand down immediately, or you will suffer full repercussions from the Venezuelan government."

"You don't scare me, Felipe Pascal from the C-I-S-T. I know all about you. You're not a government official. You're just a tour guide who helps the rich exploit the rain forests for more wealth."

Felipe flinched. How could this guy know *anything* about him?

The cargo plane inched forward then stopped. Felipe drifted his helo back, keeping a few meters between it and the aircraft. Was this guy crazy

enough to ram his colibrí? The Harbin's engines increased in speed, causing it to strain against its brakes. Felipe was willing drop his helo right
there to block the plane, but Julia was inside it—no doubt against her
will. He couldn't risk injuring her in a game of chicken with this madman.

"Last chance to move, Pascal."

Felipe cursed aloud. He couldn't allow this man to escape, nor could
he chance injuring Julia. He cursed again. He hated being so indecisive.

Ricardo had told him everything on his approach to La Esmeralda—
including his own role in the mess under the codename Bruja. Felipe
couldn't believe Ricardo would do such a thing; nor could he believe
how far it'd gotten out of hand. When they were face to face again,
he would rake him over the coals for his involvement. He dreaded
the repercussions Ricardo may suffer from the fallout of this event. It
would mean his job and could mean jail time.

Felipe chastised himself for having left Ascom base when he did.
But he'd been scared. He hated admitting that, and yet it was the truth.
And it'd seemed prudent at the time—

"Have it your way," the pilot huffed.

Without further warning, the Harbin lurched forward. Felipe
slammed down his throttle and pitched his helicopter to one side. He
felt the vibration of the Harbin's twin props as they passed within inches
under him. Rotating 180 degrees, he watched the plane accelerate
down the runway and lift clumsily into the air. Felipe immediately gave
chase—but with waning hopes. The Harbin was an older plane, but it
could still travel at just over 200 mph. His MD600N had a max speed
of around 180. If the plane was empty, the terrorist/kidnapper would
soon be a speck on the horizon.

A *kidnapper*—that's what he was. He was kidnapping Julia—and
that's the main reason Felipe was giving chase. The deadly fungus was
a worry, but it was nothing compared to his concern for Julia. Yet he
couldn't do anything too drastic. Bringing the cargo plane down meant
bringing down Julia too. She might be killed.

"Go harass someone else with your fake badge, Pascal," the pilot
snidely quipped as his wheels tucked inside the fuselage.

Felipe's jaw clenched until it hurt. Julia was in danger—again!
He had abandoned her once; he was not going to do it again. Nor
was he going to trust anyone else to apprehend the maniac when he

landed. Fully fueled, the Harbin had a range of nearly 1,000 miles. The madman could land on any decent airstrip, barter with the locals, and disappear.

No, Felipe determined. There *was* no one else. It was up to him to stop this madman and rescue Julia. Switching frequencies, he informed Ricardo to follow the plane on the radar, then he slammed his throttle to max and gave chase.

CHAPTER 62

JULIA WAS TORN BETWEEN FEELING overwhelming relief that Felipe had returned and being burning mad at his abandonment over the past four days. Where had he gone? Why hadn't he returned sooner? Those were only a couple of the questions to which she'd demand an answer when—and if—they got through this. Her only hope was that he was giving chase.

The plane crabbed to one side as Mantis adjusted a dial on the instrument panel. His take off had been wobbly; his cruising wasn't much better.

"Are you sure you know how to fly this thing?" she asked.

He didn't answer. He was still wearing his headset, so he probably didn't hear her. Glancing around, she saw a second set attached to the back of her headrest. Tucking her lower lip under her front teeth, she whistled shrilly. He turned with a frown.

"What?" he asked, pulling off his headset.

She tugged at her restraints. "The plastic ties are cutting off my circulation. Look." She leaned back and showed him where the bands chafed angry welts into her wrists.

"Stop straining against them."

"I'm not. It's the altitude. My extremities swell when I reach high altitudes."

He continued to frown.

"It's a common occurrence, you know. That's why passenger jets are pressurized."

"Fine," he said, pushing a few buttons. He then released the yoke and straightened his leg to reach inside his pants pocket.

"Is this thing on autopilot?" she asked, worried.

"I hope so."

Julia stared straight ahead, willing the plane to remain level. Focusing on a low mountain range helped, as did glancing at the little plane in the center dial that showed their relation to the horizon. In her peripheral vision she saw Mantis pull a small manicure knife on a keychain from his pocket. He reached over and lined up the tiny blade under the first tie.

"No funny business, Julia. You try anything, and I'll shoot you in the face."

"That's brilliant. Why would I try anything? I already told you I don't know how to fly."

Mantis cut through both ties, eliciting a hiss of pain from Julia each time. She gingerly rubbed her wrists as he retook control of the plane. He fastened his seat belt, pulled his gun from his windbreaker pocket, and set it in his lap.

"Thanks," she said out of reflex.

He didn't reply. He'd already fixed his headset back on his ears. As Julia reached behind her seat, Mantis clenched his gun. She slowed her movements and indicated her intentions. He nodded. As soon as she had nestled on the headset and adjusted the mike, Mantis flipped a switch that activated the unit.

"Can you hear?" he asked.

"Yes."

"Good. Now, what can you tell me about the fungus—a cordyceps, didn't you say?"

"Seriously? Why should I tell you anything?"

"Because it'll go much easier on you if you do."

"And when you get what you want, you'll what—kill me?"

"Perhaps. Perhaps not. We'll just have to see how cooperative you are."

"Well, forget it."

Mantis shrugged and examined the instrument panel.

"Where are you going?" Julia asked.

"Somewhere safe."

"When will you get there?"

"Don't know. I guess when we find it."

"When you find it? You mean you don't know?"

"Well we can't very well go back to Caicara, now can we? Mr. Pascal will have already radioed ahead, so they'll be waiting for us. In fact, every major airport will be looking for this plane, so we need somewhere small and out of the way. I'm thinking somewhere in the Caribbean."

"Blimey. Can you make it that far?"

"I think so. Most planes of this make can easily go a thousand miles or more, depending on the load and the weather. Heck, with a good tail wind, we could fly to Cuba if we wanted."

"Stop saying 'we,' like I'm your ruddy partner. *We* don't want to do anything. It's all you, mate."

He chuckled warmly. "Oh I'm afraid it's *we* until I get some answers."

"And then?"

He shrugged. "We'll see."

Considering her options, Julia sighed in surrender. Perhaps if this maniac knew the sample he had was most likely nonviable he'd change his mind. "Right. What do you want to know?"

"Everything—even your guesses if you don't have an answer."

"Okay. How much do you know about ascomycota?"

He rubbed his chin. "It a class of fungus that many people use for medicinal purposes."

"It's a phylum, actually, not a class—"

"Don't!" he cut in. "I know it's a phylum. I meant class as a culture, not as a taxonomical designation. Don't treat me like I'm stupid."

"Look, you may be somewhat educated, but you *are* stupid. Anyone wanting to mess with that fungus is truly bonkers," she said, cocking her head toward the cargo hold.

"*You're* messing with it," he pointed out.

"I'm *studying* it. There's a difference."

"I plan on studying it too."

"You plan on killing people with it. You're a gobsmacked nutbucket as far as I'm concerned."

He gave her a condescending smirk. "Name calling? Really, Julia? I expected better from you."

"I'm happy to disappoint."

They flew in silence for a time. Julia noticed Mantis didn't fly over 5,000 feet. Either he was afraid to go higher or he was trying to avoid air traffic radar. She didn't know how fast they were going, but they didn't appear to be setting any records. He spent much of the time gazing down at the terrain. The cockpit compass read a N-NE heading.

"How did you know it's used for medicine?" she asked out of the blue. "Cordyceps, I mean."

"I told you I've got a bachelor's degree in botany."

"Brilliant. What do you do with it?"

"I work in a chemical compounds lab."

"Crikey. So you *do* know how dangerous this thing is."

"Yes, it has great potential. I know cordyceps is used for strengthening the immune system and as an anticancer treatment, particularly in Chinese medicine. It was once under investigation after the Chinese women's track team took it and set all kinds of new records in the 1993 National Games. What I don't know is how it creates zombies out of ants. I don't think anybody does. I also know that it's never been known to cross species before." He turned to her with a despicable grin. "I know your Dr. Udy will go down in the history books as being patient zero. At least he was good for something."

Julia stared at the man in shock. How could someone so well-informed have such a low concern for human life? How could—

The static crackle of a transmission sounded in her ears. "Harbin Y-12, this is CIST helo Romeo-Quebec-two-five-niner-six-one. You are ordered to return to La Esmeralda Airport immediately."

Mantis snorted. "And if I refuse?"

"You will be shot down."

CHAPTER 63

"FELIPE!" JULIA CRIED, LOOKING OUT the windows for his helicopter. "Where are you?"

"Julia? Julia, can you hear me?"

"Yes, I can hear you."

"Can the pilot hear me?"

"Yes, Pascal, we can both hear you," Mantis said, as if Felipe was being tiresome.

"Good. Then you should know that I have contacted the Venezuelan Air Force. They are scrambling two F-16s, ETA thirty minutes. They *will* shoot you down, Mr. Jones."

Brilliant, thought Julia.

Mantis smiled at the radio. "Where did you get that name?"

"Bob Jones? Easy. I've been in communication with everyone you've come in contact with since you landed in Caracas early this morning. That includes your contact Bruja. Yes—we even know about that. So listen very closely, Bob: your time is limited. Return to La Esmeralda immediately, and I will call off the air force."

"No, *you* listen, Pascal. I got what I needed, and I have no plans on returning to that worthless little town," Mantis said, sounding very cocksure. "Besides, the Venezuelan Air Force would not send two highly trained attack fighters to bring down a civilian cargo plane because you say it's carrying a special mushroom. And they certainly won't shoot me down if they know I have a hostage on board. Seriously, Pascal, you gotta do better than that. Scrambling two F-16s?" He laughed. "The only thing scrambled here is the egg on your face."

"Then you don't know the Venezuelan government, Mr. Jones. They will stop at nothing to bring down a drug trafficker."

Mantis stopped laughing. "What are you talking about?"

"I told them you stole the Harbin from Paco Alvarado to traffic raw cocaine from La Esmeralda to Trinidad. That is where you're heading, isn't it?"

Julia grinned at her captor. "Sounds like you better give up, mate."

"Shut up."

Julia had little trouble believing Felipe had called the air force—she just doubted they'd make a fuss over a small plane like this. If they did come, she hoped they wouldn't hesitate to force this madman to land—even if it meant shooting the cargo plane out of the sky. Thinking how quickly the cordyceps could decimate a city the size of Trinidad made her sick to her stomach.

Mantis cleared his throat. "What makes you think I'm going to Trinidad?"

"The plane has a personal transponder ID. It shows a Harbin Y-12 with your coordinates heading in that direction. There's nowhere you can hide."

Mantis clicked off the radio and chewed on his lower lip while looking over the instrument panel. Julia could tell he was feeling less sure by the second. Flicking the switch on again, he asked, "What proof is there the air force actually believes you?"

"You'll find out in about thirty minutes. Just remember, I am a trusted government official who spends a lot of time in areas known for drug running. You're not the first trafficker I've turned in, you know."

Mantis's eyes set upon something on the dash and lit up with glee. He gave a forced chuckle. "A trusted government official? Ha! You're a tour guide, Pascal. You fly foreigners to exotic places for a price. And I know you're lying because this plane's transponder has been removed."

"You can't remove a transponder, Mr. Jones. It's against FAA regulations."

"Look out your window, Pascal. We're in Venezuela, not the United States. The FAA doesn't give a hoot about a private plane down here. It probably doesn't even know it exists. Oh—and by the way, my name isn't Bob Jones. It's Mantis."

"Mantis?"

"Yeah. Like the predatory insect. I'm a master of camouflage and fast attack. Did it ever occur to you that my passport is fake? You have nothing on me."

"So you think," Felipe answered, unfazed by Mantis's retort. "I say again, you are ordered to return to La Esmeralda immediately."

"Sorry. That isn't going to happen. Dr. Fatherhams and I are off to Trinidad for some sand, sun, and lots of fun."

"It's Fatheringham, you twit," Julia chimed in.

"Whatever. Listen, I'm tired of this game, Pascal. Go harass someone else." Mantis switched off the radio. He gave Julia a crafty smile. "Hold on tight."

Shoving the yoke forward, Mantis forced the Harbin into a steep dive. Julia felt her stomach rise into her throat. The plastic bag containing the cordyceps lifted into the air along with several other unsecured items. The dense, tropical rain forest raced toward them. Involuntarily holding her breath, Julia braced herself for impact. At seemingly the last minute, he pulled back on the yoke and banked severely to the left. Julia was flattened against the fuselage; a wispy groan escaped her throat.

When she could gather enough breath, Julia croaked, "What in the world are you doing?"

"Heading to Columbia, of course."

"Columbia? Why?"

"Extradition from there is very difficult, I hear—especially when the someone you're trying to extradite has lots of money and power."

"Power? What power do *you* have?" she asked incredulously.

"I have a deadly fungus."

She huffed. "You have a smelly bag of decomposing goo."

"You think?"

"Too right. Most fungal spores are only viable for forty-eight hours after they're released. As a botanist, I thought you knew that."

"I know *that* statement is species specific," he retorted. "It doesn't apply to every fungus. And if yours wasn't still viable, you wouldn't be putting up such a fuss over it."

Julia turned from him. Even worse than the haughty way he said everything and his perpetually arrogant expression was the fact that he occasionally got things right. Looking out the window, Julia watched the plane's shadow dance across at the treetops whizzing by a scant few hundred feet below. A moment later, she noticed something else—something that made her heart leap. A second shadow kept pace mere yards behind them.

CHAPTER 64

STAYING ROUGHLY SIX METERS BACK, Felipe kept low to the trees, flying in their blind spot. If Mr. Jones—Mantis—was skilled enough to know he was being followed, he never mentioned it. In fact, nothing about the man convinced Felipe that he was skilled at anything. As confident as Mantis tried to sound, he seemed to be making decisions off the cuff. Nothing in his flying had demonstrated the competence he claimed to have either. His takeoff had been sloppy; his flying was erratic. He kept changing air speed and frequently drifted off true. Perhaps he had limited time behind the yoke; perhaps he was not used to that model of foreign aircraft. The madman probably didn't even know the Harbin's max airspeed. Whatever the reason, his clumsy piloting made it easy for Felipe to keep up with him.

But all that changed with Mantis's bold maneuver. It was an obvious attempt to evade capture. The kidnapper must have believed his lie about the F-16s. Yet rather than returning to La Esmeralda as instructed, he was now making a run for the Columbian border. That wasn't good. Relations between Venezuela and Columbia hadn't been the best in recent years. If Mantis made it to the border, Felipe would not be able to officially continue pursuit.

Felipe's mind echoed with the man's last words: *Go harass someone else.*

If he harassed this guy enough—dive-bombing him like a sparrow harasses a hawk—he could force him to land before reaching the border. Yes, he was taking a chance that the man was willing to die rather than be arrested, but he knew it was the right call . . . except for Julia. Her being on board changed everything. Would she give her life to stop the madman?

Maybe.

Throttling forward, Felipe quickly closed the distance between them. He had to get directly behind them to remain unseen.

"Harbin Y-12, you are not on the approved course," Felipe radioed. "Please continue your arc and return to La Esmeralda."

There was no verbal response or change in course. Felipe suspected the man had turned off his radio.

With his mind groping wildly for options, Felipe held steady with the plane. Nothing he could think of had a quick resolve. Most choices had devastating consequences. If Mantis increased his airspeed even a little, he could be at the border within minutes. Felipe had to act now.

Drifting to his left and accelerating, Felipe moved his helo level with the pilot's side of the Harbin. Glancing to his right, he got a good look at the terrorist. The man was in his early forties and unremarkable in appearance. Mantis flinched, clearly surprised to see Felipe but smiling in a way that showed he still felt like he was in charge.

After a few moments of silent stare-down, Felipe tapped his headset, indicating Mantis should turn on his. The madman's smile grew into one filled with challenge.

Felipe's radio crackled.

"You're a persistent bugger, aren't you," Mantis radioed.

"Only when it comes to upholding the law," Felipe answered.

"Gosh. That's so patriotic," Mantis said as if overcome with emotion. "But if you start singing 'The Star Spangled Banner,' I swear I'll throw up."

"We're in Venezuela, not the US, remember?"

"And I'll soon be in Columbia, so screw you and your F-16s."

Felipe ground his teeth in frustration. This man was not going to return to the airstrip. They were cruising at just under 160 mph. With a touch of his throttle, Mantis could simply slip away. Felipe wished there was a safe means to force him to land immediately, but the ultra-thick rain forest made that wish impossible. In fact, there were very few options to land anywhere before they reached the Columbian border.

Felipe knew the only possibility would be Puerto Ayacucho, a large city on the banks of the Orinoco River. He flew there for tourists, captains in the rubber industry, and occasionally for the Venezuelan Army and Navy, which had bases there. The port city was considered a gateway to Columbia. Mantis wouldn't intentionally head toward a city with so much military infrastructure—assuming he knew it was there. But if he was intent on escaping into Columbia, he'd make a beeline for the border without regard to finding a landing strip.

Then a second option came to Felipe's mind. "Okay, listen, Mantis. Why are you stealing that fungus? To make money, right? How about if you let me buy it?"

"Money?" Mantis chuckled. "You think I want *your* money? Man, you're even dumber than Julia said you are."

"I said no such thing!" Julia shouted.

"Doesn't matter," Mantis continued. "You haven't got enough money to buy what this thing's worth. Isn't that right, Julia?'

She didn't answer.

"Go on, honey. Tell him what it's worth."

"Don't call me honey, you sick freak," Julia hissed.

Mantis persisted. "Tell him how much I can get for the cordyceps you discovered."

A brief silence ensued. Felipe inched closer to the plane, making sure his rotor was well above the Harbin's propellers. He saw the pilot pull a gun from somewhere and ram it against Julia's head.

"I said tell him!" he bellowed.

"I have no idea," she yelled back. "I haven't assayed its biochemical properties yet."

"That's not what I mean," the kidnapper continued malevolently.

"I don't know what you mean. I don't read minds."

"Well then try and *think* like me."

"You mean like a twisted psychopath?"

"Like an enlightened man," he insisted. "Like someone willing to go to the extreme to save the planet from the pillage and plunder of people like you."

After a pause, Felipe heard Julia reply in a tense voice.

"Holy crikey. You want to *intentionally* infect people with it, don't you? You want to use the cordyceps as a bloody weapon."

Felipe's stomach twisted at the revelation. Having seen firsthand what the fungus did to humans, he prayed he'd never have to see again.

"You see? I told you so," Mantis said, suddenly cheerful again. "I knew you were a smart girl."

"Mantis, you can't," Felipe said, pleading. "Please. You—you just can't."

The kidnapper again gave Felipe a sinister smirk. "Watch me."

CHAPTER 65

PASCAL'S DESPERATE, MANTIS THOUGHT, CONTINUING to smile. *That means I'm doing something right.*

Mantis had no idea how near the border was, but it had to be close. The throttle pushed to the next level, the Harbin's twin engines roared. It would have been a thrilling sound were it not for the increase in rattling and groaning in the plane's fuselage. He suspected the aircraft could go faster, but he wasn't certain it would survive the attempt. Besides, he didn't know how to trim the props for max speed.

His smile widened as he watched the helicopter slowly drift back. Just as he suspected, Pascal's fancy machine couldn't match the Harbin's speed.

"So, *Doctor* Fatheringham," he said, slipping his gun back into his windbreaker. "When did you obtain your degree?"

Julia stared at him as if flabbergasted he would try and make small talk. "I haven't," she finally revealed. "I have enough hours for it, but I have yet to defend a dissertation."

"Well, well, well! So you've been lying to these people. My, isn't that the ultimate in skullduggery."

"I've never *lied* to anyone," Julia shot back. "They just call me that because it's easier to remember than 'doctoral candidate.'"

"If you say so."

"Look, Mantis—Bob—whatever. You can't do this. You have no control over it. How do you know you won't get infected too?"

"I already told you I work in a lab. I'll take the necessary precautions. What do you recommend? BSL-3? 4?"

"I *recommend* you turn this plane to the nearest airport and land as Felipe has ordered."

"Ah, well, you see, therein lies the problem. The only person I take orders from is sitting immediately to your left."

She rolled her eyes. He hated it when people did that to him. He stared straight ahead and bit his lower lip. He was not going to let her intimidate him. He was not going to let her get his goat. *His goat!* He already got a goat. The thought made him snort loudly.

"What's so funny?" Julia asked, glaring at him.

"Nothing. I was just thinking how brave you're trying to be, when in truth, I hold all the cards. You really should cooperate with me, you know. Together, we could be famous."

"You mean infamous."

His smile weakened. "Ha. Good one, Julia," he said, forcing levity into his tone. Was she making fun of him again? Maybe. She looked so angry. No—more than angry. She looked enraged, livid. He wished she'd see things his way. He was sincere in wanting her to join in his success. She was obviously a brilliant scientist. And she wasn't hard to look at either. With a little cleaning up, she'd be downright pretty. But not a fake pretty, like that airhead Meghan. She simply needed to wipe the scowl from her face, maybe give it a good scrub and a little makeup. Her bod wasn't nearly as hot as Meghan's, but it still wouldn't look bad in a swimsuit. The image made him smile.

"You really think this is all a joke?" she asked pointedly.

"I'm more serious than you can imagine," he admitted.

"Then stop this madness before it gets out of hand."

"Really?" he asked, suddenly feeling a little indignant himself. "And what about the madness you're doing to the rain forest? What about the madness big oil and big pharma and big lumber are doing to the entire planet?

"What are you talking about?"

"Oh, don't play glib with me, Julia. I've seen what damages labs like yours can cause. You find something new, something amazing, something you can make a billion dollars with, and suddenly Nature takes a backseat to your bank account. Well, I plan on giving Nature a leg up. 'Stop this madness before it gets out of hand'?" He chuffed loudly. "It *is* out of hand. And it's people like *you* that got it there."

Her acidic glare narrowed to two pinpoints of black. When she spoke, her words came out quietly but with such intensity it was as if she were shouting them. "And you expect me to believe you're doing this just to save the planet?"

He tried to match the intensity of her glare but couldn't. "Yes. Yes, I am."

"You know *nothing* about what you're dealing with. Cordyceps fungi kill everything they infect. Everything."

He chuffed again, this time with much less surety. "What are you talking about?"

"Insects, of course. Not only ants, but moths, butterflies, caterpillars, spiders—even other fungi. It infects them and spreads its mycelia throughout the endoskeleton, liquefying and consuming the non-vital soft tissues. *Nothing* survives its attack. And now that fungus has jumped species. Brandon wrote of it infecting a capuchin monkey. And then it infected him." She stopped to wipe the tears that had suddenly sprung from her eyes. "Save the planet? This new species has infected invertebrates *and* vertebrates. Crikey! What's going to stop it from killing *everything* on this planet?"

Mantis couldn't stop himself from smiling from ear to ear. "I know. It's beautiful, isn't it? That is why we have to study it to find an antidote."

"Bloody bollocks!" she cried. "And what in the name of all that's holy do you think Brandon and I were doing?"

He looked at her face a moment, not liking the tears streaming down her cheeks but reveling in them just the same. Her tears emboldened him, reminding him of why he was here. "The difference is, my dear doctoral candidate, that *you* would get nothing more than notoriety from your discovery. If you're lucky, they may name this new species after you. *Ophiocordyceps fatheringhamis.* I, on the other hand, will rule the world. I am very passionate about this, Julia. It is my responsibility, my mission. And I am willing to give my all for it. Are you?"

Julia's expression froze in a rictus of anger. Her cheeks flushed crimson. Veins bulged in her neck and temples.

Without warning, she grabbed the yoke and pushed it forward. But nothing happened. She pulled it back with the same empty result.

Mantis laughed. "You really think I'd keep your controls active with your hands free? Come on. Give me a little more credit than that."

Releasing the controls, she flipped on the radio switch. "Felipe. Felipe, if you can hear me, drop a stone in the dunny."

The radio hissed as Felipe radioed back. "Say again, Julia."

"Drop a stone in the dunny."

"Are—are you sure?"

"Too right I am."

"Wait—what's a dunny?" Mantis asked. "What does that mean?"

"It means the answer to your question is 'yes,'" Julia said. "I *am* willing to give my all."

A shadow suddenly darkened the windscreen as the loud thumping of rotors beat over the noise of the plane's engines. Mantis saw landing skids poke past the cockpit a moment before they slammed down on the cabin. The rending of metal shrieked throughout the cockpit as the helo pressed down on the plane, forcing it out of the sky.

CHAPTER 66

"WHAT ARE YOU DOING—ARE you insane?" Mantis cried without pause, feeling his seat drop out from under him. Gripping the yoke as best he could with one and a half hands, he struggled to keep the Harbin Y-12 in the air. "Pull up! Pull up, or you'll get us both killed!"

The helicopter skids straddled the cockpit, cocooning it in a lattice of screeching metal. One of the side windows cracked and imploded. Felipe's voice buzzed through the radio static and collision noise, but Mantis couldn't understand him.

"Veer off!" he screamed at Felipe. "Veer off!"

The grinding intensified. Felipe was not pulling up. If anything, he was setting the full weight of the helicopter on the nose of the plane.

Shoving the yoke forward, Mantis dropped the plane away from Felipe, bringing him to within a dozen yards of the treetops. But the separation was short-lived. Felipe matched his descent and repeatedly slammed his skids against the joint between the fuselage and the wings.

Julia's face was blanched white with fear—and yet there was a sparkle of delight in her eyes. This was her idea. Her stupid phrase about dropping a dunny stone meant to ram him out of the sky.

"Call him off," Mantis yelled at her.

She turned to him and smiled. "No."

Wham!—the impact was followed by a deathly groan of metal fatigue echoing through the cabin. The helicopter rode them even lower. The Harbin's belly scraped the tops of emergent layer trees as they passed underneath. The ancient Pratt and Whitney engines began to cough and falter. Their reduced speed called for a different pitch on the props, but Mantis was too busy keeping the plane out of the trees.

"Okay!" the kidnapper cried. "Okay, pull up. I'll do it. I'll do it!"

Felipe lifted away only a few yards from the plane. The down thrust of helo's rotor played havoc with the airflow over the Harbin's wings, causing insane turbulence. It was all Mantis could do to keep the aircraft level.

"Harbin Y-12. Come up to fifteen hundred feet," Felipe said. "Acknowledge."

"Yeah, okay. Coming up to fifteen hundred feet. But give me more space. I have no lift with you that close."

"Copy that."

Felipe's helicopter lifted away but kept pace with their speed. Mantis pulled the Harbin up, all the while cringing at the tortured sounds of metal at its breaking point.

"Harbin Y-12, you are at designated altitude. Level off and hand your gun to Dr. Fatheringham."

Mantis did so without thinking. He knew that one more collision from the helicopter would be catastrophic. The rattling noise the cargo plane made on its flight to La Esmeralda was nothing compared to the unholy groans it was now making.

"I have the gun, Felipe," Julia confirmed.

"Copy. There is an airstrip at San Fernando de Atabapo, approximately forty miles from your position," Felipe radioed. "Change your course left two degrees and run true for approximately fifteen minutes. You are cleared to land there."

"I'm not sure this plane will stay together that long," Mantis complained.

"Then pray that it does."

Mantis glanced at Julia again. She still wore a faint smile. It was a smug, triumphant look—perhaps even condescending. He hated that. He hated her.

Scowling straight ahead, Mantis cursed the Venezuelan helicopter pilot and his skills. The guy definitely knew how to fly. He wondered how someone so young could have acquired so much experience. In the end, that didn't matter. He still had the fungus. He also had a hostage. The cards were stacked in Mantis's favor. He simply needed to wait for the right time to play his hand.

That time came as they approached San Fernando de Atabapo. The small town grew from the shores of an incredibly wide river. What appealed to Mantis was what was possibly on the other side of the waterway.

"Harbin Y-12, begin your descent now," Felipe radioed.

"Okay," he answered. Then, after adjusting his throttle, he leaned toward Julia. "Any idea what river that is?"

"The Orinoco, of course."

He smiled. "Lining up with runway now," he radioed.

"Copy that."

Julia frowned. "Why do you need to kno—" Before she finished her question, she knew the answer. "Felipe! He's going to make a run for it!"

Holding the yoke as steady as he could with his gimp hand, Mantis whipped out the gun he'd taken from Dr. Esparza and pointed it at her face. "Forgot about this one, didn't you?"

She simply glowered at him.

"Hey, Pascal. You still there?" he asked, knowing full well he was.

"Affirmative."

"I have a gun to Julia's head. Back off completely, or I'll blow her brains against the inside of this cockpit."

With disturbing calm, Julia lifted the gun she'd confiscated and pointed it at Mantis. "Belay that order, Felipe," she said. "He *is* pointing his gun at me, but I'm doing the same to him."

"Copy that," Felipe acknowledged.

"The choice is yours, mate," Julia continued. "I'm willing to end this right here, right now. What's your fancy?"

Mantis seethed. Each time he thought he had things in the palm of his hand, it was taken from him by some do-gooder wannabe.

"Julia?" Felipe radioed after a few moments of silence.

"Seems we're at a standoff, Felipe. Perhaps a little encouragement is in order."

The helicopter dropped instantly, slamming so hard into the left wing that Mantis heard a resounding *crack*! The left aileron went dead. The left engine shrieked hideously and began to smoke. Mantis dropped the gun and fought an uncontrollable roll to the right. At the same time, he felt the fuselage slip into a left yaw. He applied more rudder to correct the motion but in doing so lost significant airspeed and altitude. The plane plummeted to five hundred feet before he regained any semblance of control. Powering up only caused more engine shrieking and wing shaking. As if that wasn't enough, the helicopter slammed into him a second time.

"Stop it!" Mantis screamed. "Okay. I'm heading straight to the airstrip. No more funny business."

"Julia?" Felipe again radioed.

"Yeah. I think he's convinced," she answered his unvoiced question.

"Yes, I'm convinced," Mantis cried, still struggling to keep the plane aloft.

Lining up with the runway, the battered Harbin vibrated like an unbalanced load in a spin cycle. Overridden with fear of the plane falling apart prior to landing, Mantis didn't even try for a smooth touchdown; he slammed into the runway so hard that the left wing strut snapped away from the fuselage. With a preternatural groan, the wing buckled and folded, the left rear wheel collapsed. Sparks plumed as the crippled plane careened off the runway into some tall, wet grass along the side of the strip. Lurching to a halt, Mantis barely had the presence of mind enough to kill the engines. Luckily, the plane hadn't rolled. Continuing to clutch the yoke with a viselike grip, Mantis didn't dare breathe until the plane had settled into a deathly stillness.

Amazingly, Julia still had the gun pointed at his head. "Let's exit this health hazard real steady like, right, mate?"

He nodded sullenly. This was *not* how he had planned for things to end. With the angst of the near-death landing subsiding, his mind tried to catalog his options. There weren't many. He cursed inwardly. He'd been so close. He'd almost done it.

Mantis's hand trembled as he unlatched his safety belt. Julia had already exited her seat and was opening the cargo door.

Think, Mantis, think. You're better than this, better than her. You're better than any of these people.

Columbia was just across the river. He was *still* so close. He could *still* do this. He had to. This cordyceps fungus was still a perfect weapon. His weapon. Mother Earth was counting on him. More importantly, Green Blade was expecting him to deliver.

CHAPTER 67

JUMPING OFF THE LAST STEP, Mantis smelled the noxious odor of gas and burning oil. The buckling of the wing had ruptured a fuel line. Fire licked the crumpled wing and surrounding grass. The plane would soon be a total loss, but at least he was still alive.

"Let's get out of here before it blows," Julia said, moving away from the wreckage. She still held the handgun, but she was no longer pointing it at him.

Intense heat was already building. Mantis took a couple steps away from the plane then stopped. "Wait. The fungus. Just let me grab it real quick."

"Forget it. Come on."

He cast a glance at the rapidly growing fire. "But the cordyceps. It'll be destroyed."

"I say let it burn."

"But your research!"

"Forget it," she said, breaking into a jog toward safety.

Mantis was shocked and enraged. All his work was about to go up in flames right before his eyes. How could she do this to him? That fungus was his key to everything.

Stepping back to the ladder, Mantis had hiked himself up just before a resounding *whump-whoosh* pummeled the air. A blistering shockwave slammed into him, launching him from the hatchway as if shot from a cannon. He landed a dozen feet away on his back. The air was punched from his lungs. His eardrums rang with a high-pitched whirring then suddenly muffled as if he was underwater. He tried to move but couldn't. Every muscle in his body throbbed. He smelled burning flesh. His eyes were open, but all he saw was a blurry mix of dark and light hues surrounded by blackness. He thought he heard his name being spoken.

"Help me," he croaked. His voice sounded strangely distant—a bizarre mix of feeling himself speak but his words registering yards away. Giving up on regaining his wherewithal, deciding his pain would be more tolerable if he was unconscious, he closed his eyes and sank into the blackness encroaching from all sides.

Julia was facedown in the damp grass. The blast had knocked her over, but she'd been far enough away to avoid any real damage. Her ears rang a bit, but that was all.

"Julia? Julia, are you okay?" It was Felipe's voice.

She rolled over and tried to sit up but couldn't. Firm hands slipped under her arms and hauled her to her feet. She felt wobbly but was able to maintain her balance. Felipe kept a grip under her shoulders and slowly turned her around.

"Easy now. That was quite a jolt you—*¡Hijole!*" Felipe gasped. "Is that from the crash?"

"You mean these bruises?" she asked, tilting her face from side to side. "They're a gift from Marco—you know, the bloke who came into camp right after *you* left. Speaking of which—" Without warning, Julia slapped Felipe across the face.

"Ow! What was that for?"

"Are you serious? What's the big idea leaving me all alone like that—flying away without an explanation or anything?"

"Oh that." Deep shame crossed his face. "I, um . . ." He paused, looking toward the control tower. Julia followed his line of sight and saw several men running toward them.

"Can we talk about this later?" he asked.

"No, Felipe. I've been stewing about it for days. I want an answer now."

He took a deep breath and nodded. "Yep, you're right, of course. I should have said something, but I . . . I was scared."

"So was I," she exclaimed.

"I know. But you were handling it so much better than I was. I was confused and . . . well, I just figured you were busy studying what had happened, so I went back to my helicopter. I figured I was nearly out of fuel anyway—I'd burnt it all racing to Ascom. There was no way I could fly back to La Esmeralda with the added weight of a passenger and—" He stopped and tugged on his ear.

"Brandon's remains," Julia filled in.

"Yeah. So instead, I hopped over here to San Fernando de Atabapo. I figured I could fill up and then return. I made it here on fumes, Julia. Honestly, my engine cut out just before I landed, and the winds were terrible. I hit pretty hard."

"Was the helo damaged?"

"No, thank goodness."

"So why didn't you came back?"

"That's when that storm hit, remember? You can see they're still trying to get things running again," he said, pointing to a group of men working on a newly erected power pole. The old one was snapped in half.

"I don't recall it being *that* bad."

"It probably didn't hit you as badly because Ascom base is in a deep swale. But here, it's pretty unprotected. The storm knocked out the power before I could fill up. That's why I couldn't send you a message either. All radios were dead—even the national guard's. I sent a man to Puerto España by boat to get a hand pump—but that's 100 miles downriver. It was three days before I was able to communicate with anyone."

"And you couldn't send a runner to me?"

"Be reasonable, Julia. The terrain between here and there is almost impassable on foot. Even the Yanomami call it the 'Forest of the Lost.'"

Julia was tired of fighting, tired of chasing, tired of being angry. Her shoulders drooped. "I'm sorry for doubting you, Felipe. I know this town's about as remote as you can get. I'm surprised it has an airstrip this big."

He smiled. "So I'm forgiven?"

"After the way you drove that dingbat to the ground? Too right, mate."

Felipe stepped forward and wrapped her in a tight embrace. Julia didn't return the hug. She relished the comfort of strong arms, but it still felt awkward. Yes, she'd just forgiven him, but he was still on her "wanker" list.

Julia gently pushed away. "What do you suggest we do with him?" she asked, nodding at Mantis's crumpled body lying a few meters away.

The kidnapper was unconscious but still breathing. Felipe knelt beside him and checked his vital signs. Blood trickled from his ears. Smoke seeped from his hair.

"Barring any internal injuries, I think he'll live."

"Good. I can't wait for him to wake up so I can knock his skull off," Julia spat.

"Agreed," Felipe said evenly.

The airport workers soon surrounded Julia and Felipe. They spoke in rapid Spanish. Felipe fielded all their questions. One man knelt beside Mantis and frisked his pockets. He pulled out a wallet and handed it to Felipe.

"Does he have a legit ID?" Julia asked.

"Well, it shows Bob Jones, just like he said, but it looks fake. This picture is too blurry." He picked at the card as if trying to remove something. "It looks like it was laminated on after the fact; it's not part of the original card."

A passport was found and handed to Felipe. "The passport shows the same name, but he could have gotten it using this ID."

"Do you think that's his real name?"

"Nope. But neither is Mantis, I'm betting."

Felipe gave a bunch of orders in Spanish. The airport workers recognized his authority and quickly responded to his requests. A stretcher was brought out, and Mantis was loaded onto it. The image brought back terrible memories of transporting Brandon's corpse.

Julia began feeling light-headed again. Her neck and back were stiffening up. She'd probably gotten whiplash during the crash landing. "Is there somewhere I can lie down a bit?"

"I'm sure we can find someplace. Are you okay?" The concern in Felipe's voice was genuine. Julia appreciated that.

"I think so."

Again supporting her with his arm, he said, "Let's get you taken care of."

"Thank you, Felipe."

"You're welcome. I'm just sorry I couldn't come back sooner."

She smiled. "This conversation sounds very déjà vu."

He blushed. "Yes, it does."

CHAPTER 68

JULIA WAS PRETTY SURE THE cordyceps was destroyed in the fire. There was no foam-spraying crash vehicle. A town of less than five thousand people, San Fernando de Atabapo was simply too small to have such advanced services. They did have a fire truck, but because the blaze was contained, a group of townsfolk simply stood by chatting and pointing as they watched the Harbin Y-12 burn to a pile of oily cinder and blackened metal. The plane crash was clearly the most exciting thing to have happened in a long time.

Julia lay in a hammock on the veranda of the Venezuelan National Guard. A small crowd stood in the street gawking at her. Low gossip and hushed exclamations filled the air. She was probably the second most exciting thing. With eyes closed she tried to relax, willing sleep to overtake her, but to no avail. Felipe had purchased some ibuprofen and had given her four. It helped with the pain but not with her nerves. There were still several lose ends to tie up, still too many questions left unanswered.

After an hour of unsuccessful slumber, she rolled from the hammock and strolled to the plaza near the center of town. Again, people stopped and stared. She hated being the center of attention. Returning to the national guard station, she asked a couple of children shadowing her to find Felipe. Sitting on a bench on the veranda, she leaned back and closed her eyes, wishing for the thousandth time this nightmare was ended. The soft hiss of a light rain helped dampen the harsh sounds around her.

After a few moments, a female voice said, "¿Señora?"

Julia opened her eyes and saw a stocky woman in a loud muumuu offering her a bottle of beer. "¿Tienes sed?"

"No, thank you," Julia said with a weak smile. "No beer for me. I need to keep a clear head."

"*¿Ni cerveza?*" the woman asked.

Julia shook her head. "No, gracias."

The woman stepped off the veranda and spoke to a teenaged girl waiting there. Julia guessed it was her daughter. They had similar eyes and cheekbones. The girl ran to a building next door and returned with a bottle of Coca-cola.

"Brilliant. That's much better. Gracias. *Soy* Julia."

"Gabby," the girl replied, stepping back out into the precipitation. She didn't seem the least bit bothered by it.

Julia took her time drinking the cola. The sugar and caffeine had an almost immediate effect on her fatigued body. She felt a surge of nervous energy that wasn't totally comforting but was greatly appreciated.

"Wow. You attract quite a crowd," Felipe said, walking toward her.

"Too right," she huffed. "I feel like a sideshow freak. Speaking of which, where is Mantis—or whatever his name is?"

"He's at the local clinic. He's still unconscious, but his ears finally stopped bleeding. The doc says he'll live, but he needs to be seen in a real hospital to get a CAT scan. I've arranged for air transportation."

"Is he in custody?"

"Not really," he said with a shrug. "The local police don't want to get involved with an injured American. They say there's no proof he's done anything other than crashing a plane."

"Don't they trust your word?"

He shrugged again. "They still need proof."

"But what if he leaves?"

"Where's he going to go? He has no means of transportation, and he doesn't speak the language."

She frowned, not liking his answer.

"Don't worry. I've initiated all necessary reports and procedures against him. Once it goes through, he *is* going to be arrested and charged."

"Brilliant," she said with a sigh. "So, why aren't you flying him to . . . to wherever he's going?"

"There's a medevac helo on the way. They have better triage equipment on board than I do." He grinned. "I'm just a taxi service for tourists, remember?"

She gave a soft chuckle. "You're a lifesaver is what you are."

The humor left Felipe's face. "Don't say that. Every time I've come, it's been too late."

"You came in time to stop that madman's insane plans. If that fungus had gotten out—" She paused and shuddered. "I hate to think of how many lives would be lost."

He nodded in gratitude.

"So what about Ricardo?" she went on.

Felipe tugged on his ear. "I'm not sure. His involvement is . . . sketchy."

"Crikey, how can you say that? He's the one who started this whole mess."

"Yes, but he had no idea it'd get so out of hand."

Julia bit back a retort and took a long drink of her cola. Ricardo was Felipe's concern, not hers. She needed to get back to Ascom base and prepare Brandon's body for transport back to the States. Then there was the matter of Marco's body. And Luis's. Before she realized she was crying, she felt a hot tear course down her cheek.

"Hey, it's okay, Julia," Felipe said, sitting beside her. "The real danger's over now."

"No, it's not. I still haven't figured out this thing. And then there're the bodies," she replied softly.

"Tell me what to do."

"Aren't you needed back at the CIST?"

"Not for a few days. Besides, I owe you for the time I wasn't there. Tell me what you need, and I'll make it happen."

She set down her Coke and pulled him into a hug. Gratefully, it didn't feel awkward this time. "Thank you," she whispered.

As Julia freshened up in a locker room inside the guard facility, Felipe had Gabby, the teenaged girl, help him buy some clothes for her. The rags Julia was wearing were past needing a wash; they needed a burial. At the Plaza Bolívar, they were able to find underwear, socks, jeans, and a T-shirt advertising a soccer team from Columbia. He wasn't sure how well they'd fit, but the girl assured him they'd still look good.

Standing at the locker room door, he listened to the shower running. Gabby offered to take the clothes in, but Felipe felt Julia might appreciate some privacy a little longer. Sitting on a wooden bench in the hallway, he and Gabby talked about random topics for almost an hour with no change in the water noise. That worried him.

He knocked on the door. "Julia? Are you okay? We have some fresh clothes for you."

There was no response. He knocked again, louder. "Julia?"

When she still didn't answer, he asked Gabby to take the new clothes in to her, just in case Julia was indecent.

Gabby opened the door. "¿Hola? ¿Señora Julia?" she said, entering.

A moment later, Felipe heard some words being spoken—one of the voices belonging to Julia—and some laughter. He breathed a sigh of relief. Gabby didn't speak English, but he was sure she could relay the gist of her being there.

Gabby came out of the locker room wearing a wide smile. "Julia is a very pretty woman," she said in Spanish. "And her Spanish is delightful."

"Her Spanish? I thought she didn't speak much Spanish."

"Oh, she doesn't. But her accent makes it so you don't even care how bad it is."

Felipe had to agree. "So what took her so long?"

"She fell asleep." Gabby chuckled. "She was lying on a pile of laundry with a towel wrapped around her. I gave her the clothes then helped her with her hair while we talked—or, tried to talk." She giggled again. "I like her."

Again, Felipe agreed. He liked her too.

CHAPTER 69

"DR. ESPARZA! BLIMEY, IT'S GOOD to hear your voice," Julia said into the handset of the national guard telephone. It was a huge relief to hear him simply because it meant he'd survived his gunshot. And he wasn't infected.

"I'm glad to hear yours, Julia!" he responded with equal enthusiasm. "Aye Dios, I feared you were dead."

"Almost. But that's a long story for later. How is your leg?"

"Very sore, but I'll live. Luckily, I know a good witch doctor."

She laughed. "I am *so* relieved. Listen, is Luis's body still in the freezer?"

"No, but he *is* in a morgue bag in a secure place. I'm thawing him tonight so I can perform an autopsy tomorrow."

Julia cringed at the lack of emotion in the man's voice. How could he be so unfeeling toward the gruesome death of an innocent child? It was as if he was simply defrosting a piece of meat to cut into steaks. She shook her head, reminding herself of his profession. Clearly, he had compassion for the small child—and all his patients, for that matter—but he had to remain detached from his emotions to focus on his job.

She cleared her throat. "I don't think that's a good idea, mate."

"Huh. How so?"

"I still haven't delineated the biology of the fungus. There could be more than one mode of transmission. Any examination—especially an autopsy—must be done with utmost bio-containment in mind."

"I see. What do you suggest?"

"Can you wait until I get there? I'd like to assist. I'd like to look for evidence of entry and see how the hyphae are attached to the body and how far they've spread, for starters."

He paused. "Yes, I can do that. But I do not think we have the equipment you may need for such a detailed exam. The dissections I do are very basic."

"Bollocks. Well, let me think on that. How is Noely?"

"She is fine. She is with Ricardo Paz."

"No signs of infection?"

"No, none."

Julia said a quick, silent prayer of thanks. "And Ricardo?"

"He's very upset and feels sick to his stomach from worry, but he's not infected."

Julia huffed. "After what he started, I'm not sure that's good news, but I'll take it as such."

She heard a deep, steady intake of breath. "He is a good man, Julia. He's just a little misguided."

"If you say."

"I do. So, where are you?"

"I'm calling from the national guard station at Fernando de Atabapo."

"What—? Why are you there?"

"It's part of the long story."

"Huh. And the gunman?"

"He's being watched. Felipe has notified the authorities."

"Good. And the stolen cordyceps?"

"No worries there. It got incinerated when the plane crashed. Again—long story."

"I look forward to hearing it."

"Look, Henry, I don't think I can be there by tomorrow. It's late, and I need to stop by the lab site first. Did you get Marco's body down from the aerial?"

"Yes. It is in the procedure room. I put him also in a morgue bag. He had the beginnings of a stroma forming on his neck, just like Luis."

"Is there a sporangium yet? A spore sac at the tip?"

"No. Not when we put him in the bag."

She breathed a sigh of relief. "Brilliant. Okay, keep the bag sealed. If it's possible to get him under refrigeration, do so. But don't put anyone else at risk of infection."

"I will be cautious. May I ask why you are going to the lab?"

"Brandon's—Dr. Udy's—body is there. I need to make sure everything is sealed off and get his body prepped for the flight back to the States."

"I see. Do you need help?"

Julia felt an overwhelming surge of gratitude. "Too right, mate, but I'm not sure what you could do. The area is still under Code Red quarantine. Do you understand?"

"Yes, of course. But perhaps it would be best to bring Dr. Udy's body here. I will call for a plane that can carry all three bodies to the university hospital in Caracas for thorough autopsy and examination."

"Brilliant. Hold the horn a tic, Henry," she said before covering the mouthpiece. She turned to Felipe. "Can we fly to Ascom base tonight?"

She saw him swallow hard. He clearly didn't want to do it. He hemmed and stared at his watch. "There's another storm coming tonight."

"Oy, mate. I know you don't like flying at night. But I trust your skills. And this is something that can't wait."

He finally nodded.

Uncovering the phone, Julia said, "Henry, go ahead and make your calls. Please be sure to stress the infective nature of this organism. We'll be there later tonight."

"Will do. Be careful, Julia."

"Thanks, Henry. You too."

Julia was able to procure an old biohazard suit from the guard facility. The heavy, rubbery-smelling thing was claustrophobic, but it was the best the staff could offer.

Flying to Ascom base filled her with dread. The gruesome aspect of what she'd find didn't bother her as much as the thought of seeing Brandon again. He'd not only been a colleague and mentor, he'd been a dear friend. Now there was no one. She hadn't felt this alone in a long time. In fact, at that very moment, she wanted simply to forget the whole ordeal and return to her home in Frog Tree Pocket.

No, she thought, shaking her head forcefully. She'd be alone there too.

In the inky blackness of night, Ascom base proved incredibly challenging to reach. Thick clouds obscured the sky. Not wanting to

risk hitting any of the structures in the camp, Felipe dropped into the
open space just upstream. Judging the distance to the ground was more
challenging in the dark, and they hit the riverbank with a slight jolt.

"Sorry," he apologized through his headset.

"No worries. Listen, I've mulled this over, and I think it'd be best
if you simply go on to La Esmeralda before this storm hits," Julia said.

Felipe stared at her slack-jawed.

She smiled and placed a hand on his. "Felipe. I know you don't
want to go anywhere near the lab—and I don't blame you. But I can't
expect you to sleep in here, not with another storm coming on."

"Thanks, but I'm not leaving you here alone again," Felipe said
firmly. "I've bunked in my colibrí more times than I count. I'll be fine.
I'm more concerned about you."

Julia looked out into the darkness. "No worries."

Felipe heard the words, but her tone said something completely
different. "Here, hang on a minute." He climbed into the passenger
area and unhooked two walkie-talkies from a holder. "Keep this on
channel two. We can be in constant contact all night."

"Brilliant," she said, climbing out of her seat and donning the thick
bio-suit. Before she exited the helo, Felipe handed her his Glock. "At
least take this with you."

She hesitated. "You know I'm not comfortable with guns."

"You handled one pretty well this afternoon," he said with a grin.

"That was out of desperation."

He eased the gun toward her. "Think of it as extra security."

"From what?"

"The unknown."

With a sigh of resolve, she accepted the gun. "Right."

"Thanks."

Felipe knew that she'd accepted the weapon only to make him feel
better. She was a lot more daring than he was. The unknown didn't
frighten her; it thrilled her. She'd run headlong into a tornado if she
thought she'd discover something new to science.

Reaching into the cockpit, he killed the engine. Closing the door
after Julia hopped out, he sank into one of the passenger chairs. He
wished he was as confident as she was. He envied her tenacity, her
bravery. He was going to need such bravery for the other project he'd

recently found himself involved in. But he had no choice—even though following through might mean losing his job . . . and even his life.

CHAPTER 70

FELIPE WATCHED JULIA SLIP BETWEEN some broadleaf plants and disappear into the darkness. His rotor swished lazily above him as it finished its last few rotations. The hissing of the walkie-talkie scraped along his nerves. The foliage near him whipped in the frenzied turbulence of the encroaching storm. He couldn't see anything else beyond that.

"Right, I'm in the clearing." Julia's muffled voice crackled through the walkie-talkie. Her biohazard face shield prevented clear communication. "Oy, it's a mess. The last few storms must have been beauties. The power is off; I can't see any lights. Maybe the batteries are empty. I'm going in."

"Copy that," he said, dousing his running lights to save *his* batteries.

A minute later she said, "The door is ajar. Can't tell why."

Just then, something slammed against the roof of the helo and scraped to one side—a branch maybe or a large leaf. Felipe flinched, cursing in Spanish. Looking out, he could see nothing but the effects of wind and a few drops of rain. He crossed himself and offered a quick prayer.

"I'm in," Julia radioed. "Should have brought a torch. It's pitch black in here and—crikey! Glad I'm wearing this suit. It reeks worse than a backed-up dunny in here. Ugh. The lights don't work. I'm going to hunt for a torch."

Her voice was sounding more and more stressed. Felipe couldn't tell if she was nervous or just sad. Perhaps it was a little of both. He knew what she'd find in the lab. She probably knew too. But even such foreknowledge couldn't fully prepare someone for the graphic reality of a five-day-old corpse in the heat of the tropics. He'd seen similar. It was an image he couldn't un-see.

Three minutes passed in emptiness. Five.

"Julia? Is everything okay?" he radioed.

"Hang on. Okay. I found a torch. Oy, this place is a mess too."

He tried to comment, but for some reason she continued to hold down the transmit button. He heard a harsh intake of breath and a strained whimper laboring to remain in check. Mixed in the anxious strained tones was a subdued string of the word *no*. The walkie-talkie popped a few times then clicked off.

"Julia?"

A full minute passed before she responded. "Felipe. Crikey. This is—is worse than—" Her words were cut short by a choking sob. The walkie-talkie crackled off again.

"Do you need me to come in?"

Nothing. No response.

"Julia?"

"No. I'm okay," was her forced reply.

"Are you sure?"

"Yes. It's trashed in here. There's evidence of animal intrusion. Maybe human too. Nothing seems to be missing though."

"Be careful," he warned. "There still might be an animal in there."

"Right. I need to step out for a minute. I'll check the generator."

"Copy that."

Felipe waited as patiently as he could. He found it curious that she didn't mention the body. In a way he was glad she didn't. The longer he waited, the tighter his nerves twisted into burning, cordlike knots.

A heavy rain began to slap against his fuselage and streak down his windscreen. He knew it'd be followed by a downpour. Just then, a faint light showed though the wind-whipped foliage. It started out as a dingy, yellow glimmer then grew into a blurry, off-white glow.

"Julia?" he radioed.

"Yeah. I got the generator going. Blasted bollocks, it's pouring out here! Are you sure you want to stay out there all night?"

"I'm sure," he said before even thinking about a response.

"Right." A brief pause. "I'm back inside the lab. If you change your mind, there is an extra cot in here. I'll clean things up as best I can."

"Did you find any animals in there?"

"Other than cockroaches, no. I've got all the lights on. There're some tracks, and the boxes of food are chewed through, but that's about it."

Felipe swallowed. "How is the, um . . . the body?" he hesitantly asked.

"It's still in the bag on the table. I don't want to . . . I probably won't bother with it until tomorrow."

"Sounds good to me. I'll leave the walkie-talkie on in case you need me."

"Brilliant. Have a safe night, Felipe."

"Yeah. You too, Julia." Felipe switched on the colibrí's radio and hailed the tower at La Esmeralda.

"*Buenos noches*, Felipe." It was Ricardo's voice. He didn't sound thrilled to hear from him. In fact, his voice sounded empty, devoid of the excess personality it usually had.

"Hey, Paz. Are you okay?"

"Sí. Are you?" he asked flatly.

"Fine. Look, let's not play games here. It's late, and I'm tired and quite frankly a little scared. We'll discuss your involvement in all this later. Right now I want you to tell Dr. Esparza that a storm is preventing us from making it there tonight. We're staying at Ascom base tonight. Can you do that?"

"Sí. No problemo. Oh—the doctor wanted me to give you a message in case you called in."

"What is it?"

"He say he received a phone call from the national guard station at San Fernando de Atabapo."

"When?"

"I don't know. He tell me the message maybe an hour ago."

"What did they say?"

"They said the gunman, Mr. Jones. He's disappeared."

"Disappeared?" Felipe yelled into his com-set. "When?"

"I don't know."

"Well, get the doctor on the radio so I can find out!"

"Sí. I will call you when he gets here."

Felipe bit back the expletives he wanted to voice and growled at the night. How could an unconscious man just disappear from a clinic?

Didn't anyone see him leave? He stared into the darkness toward the glow he knew was the lab, and picked up the walkie-talkie—then hesitated. Should he tell Julia that Mantis had disappeared? No, he decided. There was nothing they could do about it anyway, and she didn't need another worry right now.

Roughly thirty minutes later, his radio buzzed with an incoming transmission.

"CIST helo. Felipe."

"Felipe, this is Dr. Henry Esparza. Sorry you couldn't make it here tonight, but I'm glad you and Julia are safe."

"Tell me what happened," Felipe said without preamble.

"Sure. As you know, Mr. Jones was unconscious when you left. Because of his injuries, the doctor deemed him 'not a threat,' and he was left unguarded. When he went to check on him two hours later, he was gone."

"Two hours later? Are you telling me he's been missing for over four hours already?"

"Yes. I am very sorry. But I believe they are still searching for him. They have instructions to contact me the minute they find him."

Felipe thought furiously. "Okay—he said he was heading to Columbia. Have someone search the docks. He may have already rented a boat."

"Will do."

CHAPTER 71

JULIA SAT ON HER COT, staring at her clasped hands. A million questions harried her thoughts. She wasn't sure which to address first. Perhaps the most important was securing the lab. Tackle one thing at a time.

With the generator running, everything hummed at peak efficiency. More than anything, she wanted to get out of the heavy biohazard suit. It was suffocating. Reasoning that since she hadn't been infected—even though she'd been exposed to the fungus many times before—she decided she could go back to the gloves and mask she'd worn earlier.

Unzipping the headpiece, she lifted it and winced. The oppressive, noxious odor permeating the lab was overwhelming. Fighting the urge to vomit, she stumbled to one of the tent windows and tore it open. The storm was in full swing and spat huge drops of rain through the screens, but she didn't care. She needed to get fresh air in the lab. After a few minutes of breathing in the moist night, Julia donned a paper mask and set about evaluating the lab.

The floor was littered with leaves and other debris. She needed to give the place a good hoovering, but that could wait. First things first. The battery level read ten percent and rising. That was good. Why hadn't the solar array kept the batteries charged? Perhaps it was covered in debris. One of their daily tasks was removing leaves and dust so that sunlight could excite the cells, thus generating electricity. Were their samples okay? She looked in the glass-faced refrigerator. The thermometer read 7.81 degrees Celsius. Not good, but it was well below room temperature. With any luck, their samples were still viable.

She began a backup cycle on the computers, sending the data to internal and external hard drives. While they ran, she grabbed a broom and began sweeping out the sleeping area. Spots of dried blood crusted the floor. Her blood. She touched her jaw. It was still tender but no longer throbbed. Moving to the kitchenette, she cleaned and swept with focused efficiency. Setting a pot to boil on the hotplate, she dropped her toothbrush into the water.

When she got to the dissection table, she stopped short. Yellow spores dusted the floor. Cordyceps spores. She could see the outline of Brandon's flip-flops in the dust. A soft smile creased her lips as she thought about his beach-boy attire. The sample he'd been studying was still on the scope. It was black and desiccated. His notebook lay open. She stared at it, wondering. Was the answer in there?

She shook her head. She'd already read through it. Nothing had stood out. But then, she'd been under a lot of stress and confusion— more so than she was now. Perhaps after cleaning up and getting a good night's sleep she could start over.

Carefully sweeping the spores into a Ziplock baggie, she noticed they didn't fluff into the air as a pile of dust might. She'd been calling it "dust," but it wasn't really. The spores also wanted to cling to whatever they touched. They were dense, heavy—tacky but not necessarily sticky. She shrugged and sealed the bag. She also bagged up the decomposing sample Brandon had been studying. She then labeled both baggies and stored them in the fridge.

It was two a.m. by the time she finished tidying up. Exhausted, she brushed her teeth, turned off the lights, then crawled onto her cot. The storm had lessened to a drizzle. The soft patter against the canvas roof helped lull her to sleep.

CHAPTER 72

MUCH TO MEGHAN'S SURPRISE, CARLOS was waiting at the door to the CIST that morning. He wore casual clothes, so he wasn't heading to work. But he hadn't knocked or indicated he wanted in; he just sat on the steps, staring off at nothing in particular.

She quickly spruced up, tying her hair back in a ponytail, and put on a low-cut tee and some yoga pants. She opened the door and feigned surprise.

"Carlos! What a nice thing to wake up to." She sat beside him and gave him a tight hug and a peck on the cheek. "To what do I owe this honor?"

She knew why he was here. She'd left a message at the police station for him, insisting he call her first thing in the morning with information about her mushroom. The fact that he'd shown up personally could only be a good sign.

"I had a phone call late last night. There is a delay."

She instantly dropped her happy facade. "A delay? Holy moley. Again? I thought I warned you about delays."

"He say there is bad weather there. It make travel difficult. He can maybe be here today at nighttime or perhaps tomorrow."

"No! That's not acceptable," she snapped, rising to her feet. "I warned you. Now I have no choice but to go to your superiors and tell them what you did to me—several times."

Carlos stood slowly and dusted off his jeans. "I have already tell them about you. They say they cannot wait to meet you."

"What do you mean? What did you tell them?"

He stretched. "It is a beautiful morning, sí?"

She narrowed her eyes at him. What game was he playing? "Carlos," she said evenly. "What did you say to them?"

"That you are very pretty," he said, smiling. "That you are very fun and persay—persayive—"

"Persuasive?" she suggested.

"Sí. Yes. Persuasive."

"Persuasive . . . how?"

"I say you care about the rain forest. You are rain forest soldier."

Rain forest soldier? As angry as she was with Carlos, she did like the way that sounded. Meghan Muir, rain forest soldier. Champion for the jungle. Crusader for the cause.

Bumping her shoulder with his, she said, "That's silly."

Meghan waited for him to say more, but he seemed lost in the sunrise. Well, *he* may enjoy it, but it was already too hot and muggy for her.

Smiling, she opened the CIST door. "Would you like to come in?"

"No, thank you. I have other plans."

Her smile faded to a pout. "Other plans that don't include me?"

"Yes." He stepped off the landing and headed toward his pickup.

Meghan couldn't believe he'd turned her down so quickly and easily. She must be losing her skills. It was probably the conditions here. She needed to get away as soon as possible. This place was ruining her looks. Her spirits were at an all-time low. She was getting desperate. "Baby, what's wrong?" she called to him.

"Nada. Good-bye," he said, climbing into his pickup.

"Hey! Call me when you hear something!"

She wasn't sure if he'd heard her last words, but it didn't matter. She'd send an e-mail to her superiors explaining the situation. They knew she was dealing with primitive people. They knew the weather here was atrocious and unpredictable. Surely they'd understand this delay wasn't her fault. She needed one more day. One more! What could that hurt?

Logging into the e-mail account, Meghan typed:

Experiencing severe weather. Product delivery delayed one day.

She stopped and stared at the screen—suddenly realizing something very strange. There was nothing new in her in-box. The only time there *was* a massage it'd been from Ricardo or Felipe or sometimes a note from her mom or friends back in the States. She got news flashes from several environmental groups, and of course there were the constant Facebook updates. But there were no replies to her contact in Europe. She was certain he received them because she never got a rejected e-mail notification. Was it a glitch in the system? Was he trying to remain clandestine? Or was he simply not interested in what she had to offer?

If the last question was the accurate one, then she'd just wasted a year of her life.

Returning to her room, she flopped onto her bed. Her life was a shambles. She needed to get out of here. She needed to disappear. Daddy and his money would just have to cover her mistakes in Switzerland. He was the one who had sent her there, so ultimately it was his fault. Right?

CHAPTER 73

THE FOLLOWING MORNING, JULIA LET Felipe wear the biohazard suit as they moved Brandon's body to the helicopter. As soon as they finished, he ditched the suit and spent five minutes with his hands on his knees breathing deeply. She didn't blame him.

They also took an hour cleaning up around camp. Just as she suspected, the solar array was covered with leaf litter. They dusted it off and fixed a few other things that had fallen into disrepair. Felipe worked hard, but he said little. Julia suspected he'd slept poorly, yet he claimed to have slept like a log. After a while she gave up talking to him and focused on their work.

After locking the lab and the shed, they stood at the edge of the clearing, next to the trailhead to Goliath.

"I think you left some climbing gear on the kapok. You feel like fetching it?" Julia asked.

"Not particularly," he replied. "You?"

She snorted. "If I never see that kapok again, it'll be too soon."

They walked to the helicopter without further word. Buckling into the copilot's seat, she closed her eyes and tried to relax. As much as she didn't want to relive any of the terrors of the lab, she knew she'd have to return. The answers she'd hoped to find were still in there; she was certain of it.

After lifting into the air, Felipe switched on the transmitter. "La Esmeralda Airport, this is CIST helo Romeo-Quebec-two-five-niner-six-one. Come in."

"CIST helo, this is La Esmeralda receiving you loud and clear. What's your twenty, CIST?" It was Ricardo.

"Good morning, Ricardo. We survived the storm. Ended up being not so bad. Is everything okay there?"

"Yes, sir. We are operating according to international air regulations as per usual, sir."

Felipe shared a confused look with Julia and mouthed the word *sir?* Ricardo was being strangely formal, following SOP to the letter.

"That's good to hear, Paz. Just letting you know our ETA is roughly ninety minutes."

"Ninety minutes, copy that. We'll watch for you on the radar, sir."

"Great. Thanks," Felipe said, frowning. "CIST helo out."

Sensing a problem, Julia said, "Felipe. Is something wrong?"

"I'm not sure. Ricardo *never* talks that way. In fact, he's usually *too* lax when it comes to air chatter. He never follows protocol to the letter."

"No, not with Ricardo. I mean with you. You've been an ornery brumby all morning."

He took a deep breath and let it out slowly. "I'm sorry about that. I just got some bad news last night."

"Welcome to the party," she scoffed. "Anything I can help with?"

He turned and gave her a look of sad frustration. "Mantis is gone."

She considered his words briefly before saying, "Well it serves him right. The bloke was a dill weed, a total nut job. His actions led to the death of a father and son, so I'm not sorry he's dead."

"No, not dead. He's gone. Missing. No one knows where he is."

Julia couldn't believe her ears. "What—when?"

"Yesterday, a couple hours after we left. They've put out a search on him, but I haven't heard anything yet. Sorry I'm so moody. I just can't figure out what I can do about him."

"But where could he go?"

"Columbia would be my guess. That's where he was heading, right?"

"Yeah," she said blankly.

She was vexed. Having a madman like him on the loose added to her list of worries. What if he hired another thief? He knew about the two infected bodies. He could guess it was only a matter of time before they grew stromas. If he had unlimited funding like he claimed, he could hire an army to come after them.

She turned to Felipe. "We need to get to La Esmeralda as quickly as possible."

He nodded. "We've got a bit of a tailwind, so we're making pretty good time."

"No. I mean floor it, full throttle, full speed ahead—whatever you pilot blokes say. I think Mantis may be headed back to La Esmeralda."

CHAPTER 74

"UH-OH," FELIPE SAID AS THEY crested a hill on approach to La Esmeralda.

"What?" Julia asked, looking forward.

"There's an official-looking plane parked at the pumps. I don't recognize it."

"So?"

"They don't get a lot of traffic here. Hardly any, in fact."

"You think it's Mantis? Crikey! Could he really get here that fast?"

"Why else was Paz acting so strange?"

They stared in silence as Felipe slowed his approach. He toggled his transmitter. "La Esmeralda Airport, this is CIST helo Romeo-Quebec-two-five-niner-six-one, requesting clearance to land."

"Felipe? Ay caramba, you got here fast. Amigo, turn around. Get away from here quickly," Paz said in an urgent whisper.

"Hold on, Paz. You're acting very strange. What was going on? Are you in trouble?"

"We both are, mi amigo."

Felipe again glanced at Julia. "Do you need help?"

A heavy length of dead air hissed over the radio. Then, "You should go."

"Wait. There's a plane I don't recognize. Whose is it?"

"That's what's wrong. Paz out."

Julia gawked at Felipe. "Should we land?"

"If Mantis is here, then Ricardo needs our help. The whole town does."

She faced forward; her expression was anxious and angry.

Felipe cautiously landed on the helo pad next to the control tower. No one greeted them. He got out and approached the tower with his gun drawn. Julia followed close behind.

Entering the first floor, they were met by two men in collared shirts and ties. They wore name badges on their breast pocket. They both froze, frowning at the gun.

Felipe kept the gun lowered. "Who are you?"

"Lieutenant Antonio Escobar." The man tapped his pocket badge. "Venezuela Air Traffic Enforcement."

Finally recognizing the badge, Felipe quickly holstered his gun. "Sorry about that. Felipe Pascal, director of the Centro Investigación de la Selva el Tropical out of Caicara del Orinoco."

"Yes, I recognized your helo when you flew in." He clicked his tongue. "The MD600N is a sweet bird."

"Thanks," Felipe said, still unsure why they were there but understanding why Ricardo was acting so formal. "Is there something I can do for you?"

Escobar looked over Felipe's shoulder at Julia. "Hola," he said.

"Hello," she replied in English.

"Oh. Sorry. Are you American?"

"Australian."

"I thought there was an accent. Do you speak Spanish, Miss . . . ?"

"Fatheringham."

"*Doctor* Fatheringham," Felipe added.

"Ah." Taking her in with an indifferent gaze, he extended his hand as if it were something he'd rather not do. "Lieutenant Antonio Escobar."

"A pleasure. And no. I only know enough Spanish to embarrass myself."

He gave a courtesy chuckle. "I see. May I borrow Director Pascal for a moment?" His English was quite good with only the hint of an accent.

"No worries. I'll just head upstairs."

"No," Escobar said abruptly. He offered a patronizing smile. "We'd prefer it if you stayed here in the lobby."

"Why?" Julia and Felipe said simultaneously.

Escobar came close to rolling his eyes. "As Director Pascal can tell you, only authorized personnel are allowed in the control tower. It's international law. I'm sure you understand."

"Fine," she replied with a shrug of her shoulder. Turning to Felipe, she said, "I'll be at the hospital. I need to confer with Dr. Esparza about that patient we discussed."

"Who is the patient?" Escobar cut in.

Julia adopted his supercilious smile. "That's confidential patient information, Lieutenant. I'm sure you understand."

Escobar bristled—then smiled again. "You are free to go, Miss Fatheringham," he said, as if she'd been awaiting his permission.

Felipe could see Julia tensing for a fight.

"That's a good idea, Julia," Felipe stepped in quickly. "Perhaps you can see where Dr. Esparza is on your combined research."

Julia held Escobar's gaze for a moment before nodding. "No worries. Cheers," she said, turning and marching out of the lobby.

Switching back to Spanish, Escobar said, "Touchy little thing, isn't she?"

"Only when her integrity is questioned."

"Ah. Speaking of which, I need to ask you a few questions. Please," he said, indicating a bench to one side of the lobby. Felipe sat, but Escobar remained standing, maintaining a position of superiority.

"I'll get right to the point, Mr. Pascal. There has been a complaint leveled against you for erratic and dangerous flying, leading to the crash of a Harbin Y-12 at San Fernando de Atabapo late yesterday afternoon."

CHAPTER 75

HAVING COLLECTED HER SATCHEL FULL of files from the helicopter, Julia approached the hospital in a wash of angst. The shattered window had not yet been replaced. Dried blood stains dotted the walkway to the door. None of her memories of this place were pleasant.

A new woman sat at the reception desk. She was older than Consuelo, with gray-streaked hair and several extra pounds. Julia hoped that didn't mean the younger woman had died.

"Hola," the receptionist said with an even smile.

"Hola. El doctor, por favor," Julia said.

"*¿Tienes una cita?*"

"I'm sorry. I don't speak Spanish."

The woman frowned. *"Un momento,"* she said, going into the back.

"Julia?" Henry said before he'd even entered the foyer. "I'm so very relieved you made it back unharmed." He limped straight to her and wrapped her in an embrace. The receptionist looked displeased by the informality.

"Me too. How's your leg?"

"It'll be a while before I can . . . how did you put it?—go 'gallivanting through the rain forest.' But it's healing well. How about you? What happened to the gunman?"

"I'll tell you about that later," she hedged. "First, have you implemented the biohazard precautions I gave?"

"Yes, of course. Where is Felipe?"

"Some government air force blokes are questioning him at the control tower. Can I see Marco?"

"Sí. Follow me." Glancing at the receptionist, he said something in Spanish. She returned to her station without comment.

Marco's body lay in a tin watering trough Henry had moved into the procedure room. He was sealed in a body bag and covered with a layer of ice cubes.

"Sorry," the doctor said, seeing her worried expression. "It is the best we could do for now."

She nodded, offering a weak smile. "No worries. Can we get him on the exam table, please?"

"Yes."

Together they cleared away the ice cubes and hefted him onto the table. Esparza offered gloves, a paper gown, and a mask, and donned a set himself. Julia steeled herself as he unzipped the long black bag down to the feet. Marco's milky skin was mottled with faint, green-black splotches. His eyes were opaque and cataracted. The odor wafting from the open bag was fetid and rank. Henry slid the bag off the corpse's shoulders and rolled Marco over on his face. The trailing arm flopped against the table, causing a droplet of something to splat against Julia's forehead. She flinched and fought the urge to claw at it. Calmly wiping it off with a napkin, she closed her eyes, took a quick breath, and let it out slowly.

The stroma looked exactly like the one Brandon had. A barrage of horrid memories caused her knees to buckle. She teetered and fell against the table.

Henry quickly rounded the table and grabbed her before she collapsed to the floor.

"I'm okay," she whispered. "I'm okay."

"Are you sure?"

"Yes. It just brought back . . ." She took several deep breaths and regained her footing.

"We don't have to do this now," Henry said.

"Yes. We do." Gathering her courage, she straightened out her gown and forced herself to examine the stroma. Thankfully, it had yet to form a sporangium. "Brilliant. It looks like the ice bath slowed its development."

"Yes, I agree. I measured its growth rate at eight millimeters per hour."

"Crikey, that's fast."

He nodded. "The kelp off the coast of California has been measured to grow over thirty centimeters in twenty-four hours."

"I know. I've seen it," Julia said. "Some fungi have a similar growth rates, but I've never seen any grow *this* fast."

"What does that mean?" Henry asked.

"It means this stuff is deadly. Were it a slow growth rate, we'd have time to eradicate it. But something this fast—if it gets out—it can spread like wildfire."

"Agreed. Containment is key."

"As it is with all pandemic infections."

Henry folded his arms, thinking. "I did some reading up on zombie ants last night," he said, bending to examine the stroma a bit closer. "The fungus typically infects the carpenter ant *Camponotus leonardi*."

"For *Ophiocordyceps unilateralis*, yes. But there are roughly four hundred species of cordyceps fungi worldwide, maybe more. But not all cause zombiism."

"So is that what this is?" he asked, nodding at the stroma.

She shook her head. "I haven't had time to determine its exact species."

"Huh. Then perhaps that is where we should begin?"

She huffed. "It's one of a hundred questions we need to answer. *My* first concern is transmission. How is it vectored? What's its mode of infection?"

"Then let's put this one back on ice and go to my office. I have my medical journals there. Perhaps if we dig a bit we'll stumble onto something."

"Okay," she said dully, not feeling overly excited about their prospects. This was her field of expertise. She knew fungi had more dispersion and biodiversity than any other organism on earth. Fungi and mold were literally found everywhere and in nearly every epoch of time. Millions of species thrived today, and yet only about five percent were classified. The chance that there was information on this particular cordyceps was very slim.

She stood back as Henry turned Marco's body back over and zipped up the morgue bag. Together, they settled him back in the trough and covered him with ice.

"We really need to get Marco and Luis to a better facility," she said, looking over the makeshift accommodation.

"I have called for a transport to do just that," Henry said.

"Um." She paused and looked up. "To the university? I don't think that's such a good idea. Look, I'm sure they have a great facility, but until we know the exact mode of infection, we need at least a BSL-3 environment to study it. Do they have a lab with that level of bio-containment?"

"I believe so."

"Right. But I'd still feel better if we made arrangements for transfer to a CDC facility in the States."

"Agreed. Come with me," he said, leading her out of the room.

Julia followed Henry into the second exam room. There was a door on the back wall she hadn't noticed before. Opening it, Henry walked into an office that was little bigger than a storeroom. He switched on the lights. A desk cluttered with papers and a computer, a tall filing cabinet, and two modular bookshelves filled the space. He pulled a chair from under the desk and motioned for her to sit, then quickly cleared the papers from the desktop.

"I brought the notebooks Brandon kept," she said, opening her satchel. "I've glanced at them but haven't studied them in depth. Maybe there's something here."

"A great place to start," Henry agreed. "You get started. Feel free to switch on the computer. There's no password, but I'm afraid all prompts are in Spanish."

"I'll figure it out. Maybe I'll just do some web searches. You never know what you can find by following random links. That's the beauty of the Internet. You search *miracle mushroom*, and you'll find a girl posting on Pinterest the recipe for tea her grammy made with toadstools that cured her zits."

Henry laughed and turned to leave—then froze. He spun back around. "What did you just say?"

She smiled. "Which part? A girl posting a recipe for tea her grammy made with toadstools that cured her zits?"

He snapped his fingers. "Exactly!" he shouted, sprinting out of the room.

CHAPTER 76

WHEN HENRY DIDN'T RETURN RIGHT away, Julia took a few minutes to organize her research materials. Brandon's notes were a hodgepodge of random thoughts. It was like reading the freeform writing of someone with ADD. Nevertheless, she'd long since learned to decipher his mindless scrawl.

Starting at the beginning, she read through his solo forays into the underbrush searching for fungi. He'd always worn gloves when harvesting samples. If the fungi had a sporangium ready to release its spores, he donned a mask and encased it in a baggie. She recognized nearly all of the species he notated. She'd helped catalog and run tests on them. Nothing she read indicated he was careless in any way. So why had he been infected?

Finally, she got to his notes on the cordyceps.

New specimen. Found thirty meters from camp, growing from a dead capuchin monkey. Yellow spores found on hands, feet, and lips. Unknown fungus. Suspect cordyceps sp? Unilateralis? Multiformis?

Sporangiophore 11.5 cm length. 1.8 cm diameter.

Morphology consistent with o. unilateralis. Species only found on insects. Highly infective. Creates "zombie ants."

Method of infection into monkey host? Unknown.

Transmission? Unknown. Spores airborne in nature? Unknown.

New species or a mutation of o. unilateralis? Possible cross speciation—Insect to primate? To human?

Am I already infected?

Dear God, I hope not.

Oh, Brandon, Julia thought. *What happened? Why can't I see what I need to see?*

She shook her head forcefully. She was not going to wallow in negative thoughts. She could figure this out. It's what she did.

Turning to a blank page in Brandon's notebook, she roughed out a spreadsheet and began jotting down every argument she had that disproved an *ophiocordyceps* infection.

ROUTE OF INFECTION	REASONING
Inhalation	I'm not infected. Felipe is not infected. Both had ample chance of inhaling spores. Masks always worn. Not all ants in colony are infected—all breathe same air. Noely not infected. Heavy spores, not readily airborne.
Ingestion	Evidence of B. eating at dissection station. Not all ants in colony infected. No evidence of C. Leonardi eating spores. Some ant sp. known to grow and harvest fungi as food. I possibly ingested spores.
Contact with skin	Doubtful. Gloves always used when handling. Sterile technique—hand washing and alcohol sanitizer always used.
Other?	

She paused, her mind searching. Nothing was coming to her. Inhalation, ingestion, and skin contact were the three most common routes of infection. The next was blood contamination, but that usually entailed piercing the skin, as in needle sticks or via bloodsucking insects. There was no evidence of either.

"Julia?" Henry said before entering the exam room. "I brought your answer."

Looking up, Julia was surprised to see Noely standing in the doorway. Her heart swelled with gratitude that the little girl was still alive and healthy. "Noely!" she cried.

"Hola, señora médico," she said, wrapping her arms around Julia's neck. She then rattled off a litany of Spanish, gesturing wildly with her hands as if that would help Julia's comprehension.

"Lo siento, Noely," Julia said, tenderly interrupting her.

"She's explaining how the fungus infects people," Esparza said, grinning. "It makes perfect sense."

"Blimey, how could she know? I mean, this species has never infected humans before."

"Remember when we were discussing this in the foyer, just before the gunman came in? You'd asked Noely if she knew what caused her father and brother to become sick."

"Right. I remember."

"We ended up going off on a different tangent, but before we did, she'd said yes."

"She did?"

"Sí. But then the gunman came in, and, well, you know what happened after that. The point is, when Noely said yes, I assumed she meant that she knew how her father and brother had *died*. But what she really meant was she knew how they'd become *infected*."

"Bleeding bollocks," Julia gasped in awe.

"She didn't give specifics, but what she says makes sense."

Julia took her pencil and Brandon's notebook in hand as if ready to take dictation. "I'm all ears."

Henry asked Noely a question, to which she replied by sitting on the floor and removing her shoes. Speaking nonstop, she began pointing to different parts of her feet, between her toes and around her nails.

Julia frowned.

"She says the infection enters through the feet," Henry said as if it was the most obvious answer there was.

Julia's frown deepened. "What—like hookworm?"

"Hookworm, jiggers—there are many parasites that enter through their host's feet."

"But this is a fungus, not a worm," she argued.

"True. But in my research I found that *o. unilateralis* infects ants through *their* feet. The outer membrane of the spore secretes an enzyme that dissolves the cuticle of ants."

"The cuticle?"

"Sí. The cuticle is the thick, flexible tissue in the joints of animals with exoskeletons."

"But mammals—humans don't have exoskeletons."

"Of course not, but ant cuticle is very similar in construct to the cuticle and the nail bed in humans, apes, and monkeys."

Clarity filled Julia's mind like an evaporating fog. The spores had enzymatic action! Such enzymes are typically substance specific. In other words, they wouldn't work on all tissues. If inhaled, they'd be coated with sputum and expelled through coughing, sneezing, or simple exhalation. If ingested, they'd be neutralized by stomach acid. They might work on bare skin, but skin had natural antibacterial properties that often eliminated such topical pathogens. The point of infection was the cuticle around the nail bed!

Julia's mind scintillated with confirmation. It didn't come through their fingernails because she and Brandon always wore gloves and used hand sanitizer, but Brandon rarely wore shoes. He loved going barefoot and only occasionally wore flip-flops. She, on the other hand, always wore shoes or boots. Then there was the yellow outline of Brandon's footprint in the lab. He *had* gotten spores on his feet.

She looked at Noely's bare feet. They were clean and pale. They rarely saw the light of day. That was unusual for third-world children; shoes were a luxury for them. But Noely had a pair and clearly liked wearing them.

"Ask her if she ever goes barefoot," Julia said.

Henry did. Noely answered with a long explanation.

"She says only when she bathes or swims. She says every time she's seen pictures of American children, they are wearing wonderfully colorful shoes. She wears any shoes that fit her so she can be more like them."

"But how did *she* know the infection was through the feet?"

He asked. "She says they once were visited by two missionaries who taught them about cleanliness and sanitation. She says most of the people ignored their advice; they only listened to get the free bottled water and packages of food. But she listened."

"And her father? Did he ever go barefoot?"

"No. He always wore shoes. But when I examined his body, I found the yellow spores under his fingernails and along the cuticle."

Julia swallowed. "And Luis?"

"He also had spores around his cuticles. Noely says he never wore shoes, but I believe he was infected through his fingernails. They both had touched the plastic bag carrying the fungus and came in contact with the spores."

"But Noely had touched it too. I saw her."

"No, she was carrying it with a stick, remember?"

Everything lined up. Julia began scribbling furiously, her hands barely keeping up with her thoughts, writing down answers to every question she'd had. She turned back to the desk and switched to a fresh sheet of paper. Itemizing factors surrounding the infection process, she began drafting a letter to the CDC, listing knowns and unknowns and suggesting things to research about this new species of cordyceps.

Three hours later she sat back and stretched. Both Henry and Noely were gone. She had no clue when they'd left. She got up and searched the hospital. The receptionist was there but no one else. Stepping outside, she was surprised to see the sun low in the sky. She walked to the airstrip, strangely aware of each puff of dust her feet kicked up.

As she neared the control tower, she heard an aircraft engine revving up. The airplane they'd seen earlier lifted into the sky and headed toward the setting sun. A sharp pang of worry coursed through her. Had the authorities taken Felipe with them?

CHAPTER 77

As Julia entered the foyer of the control tower, she saw Noely sitting alone reading a magazine. She approached the girl with a smile.

"Hola, Noely."

She looked up. "Hola, señora médico."

Julia sat beside her. "Noely, soy *Julia*. Not señora medico."

The girl blushed. "Julia?"

"Sí." Unexpected tears filled Julia's eyes. She took the magazine from the child and held both of her hands. "I wish I could speak enough Spanish to tell you how truly grateful I am for your help. And how sorry I am for the loss of your brother."

Noely smiled back at her, saying nothing.

"I believe she knows how you feel," Henry said, coming down the stairs.

"Henry. What's going on? Where is everyone?"

"Felipe and Ricardo are in the control tower arranging everything for transporting the bodies."

"What about the air traffic authorities? What did they want?"

"I'll let Felipe explain that. Come with me."

When Julia stood, Noely picked up the magazine and started reading again. It was then that she noticed the magazine was *National Geographic*, written in English.

"Oy. Can she read that?"

He chuckled. "No. She just likes looking at the pictures."

Julia stroked Noely's hair once before following Henry upstairs. Felipe and Ricardo were bent over a map spread across a table. They were talking very fast and laughing hysterically.

"Julia!" Felipe said, looking up and wiping tears from his eyes. "Dr. Esparza tells me you've figured out your fungus."

"Noely did, actually. Her hypothesis makes sense, but there is still a ton of research to do. The good news is I can guarantee you're not infected. Neither are you, Ricardo. The spores enter through cuticle, and you both wear shoes and wash your hands."

"Yep, that's what the doctor told us," Felipe said with a smile.

"Sí." Ricardo nodded enthusiastically. She could feel the happiness radiating from his face.

"What have you got going here?" she said, gesturing at the map.

"We're trying to figure out where Mantis may have gone. There are lots of ports up and down the Orinoco, many with small airfields like at San Fernando de Atabapo. If he had enough money, which I suspect he did, he could be anywhere by now. The only way to find out is to start asking around."

"And that's funny?"

"No, no. We were sharing Meghan stories."

"Brilliant," she said, grateful for a reprieve from her angst. "Care to share?"

"Sure," he said, wiping his eyes as if in preparation for more tears. "The air authorities that were here earlier? They came here to question me about ramming the Harbin into the ground. I explained everything to them, but they didn't believe me."

"Even with your government rating and directorship?" she asked.

He scoffed. "The Venezuelan government is trained not to trust anyone, but they especially don't trust each other. Unfortunately, this country has a lot of corruption in its history."

"So I've read."

"Anyway, Ricardo came down when they were interrogating me, and he saved me."

Ricardo shrugged. "I only help."

"See, in spite of the craziness of the past few days, he was smart enough to record all the chatter between my helo and the Harbin. He even caught some of the conversation between Mantis and you when he forgot to release his transmit switch. It incriminated him in everything."

"That's great news," she said. Then, turning to Ricardo, she added, "Good on you, mate."

He shrugged again. "I only help."

"So how does that include Meghan?"

"Lieutenant Escobar called the CIST to confirm that I'd filed my itinerary. When Meghan answered, she was her usual rude self. She said she had no idea where I was, only that I was raping the rain forest and dooming the planet to extinction. Every time he asked a legitimate question, she came back with vitriolic environmental indictments. She even started screaming at him for not taking her seriously. So Escobar finally said, 'Miss Muir, does your head sound like a rain stick when you tip it to one side?' And she said, 'I love the sound of rain. I wouldn't mind if it did.'" He started laughing again. "She had no clue what he meant."

"She has no clue about a lot of things," Julia added.

"Yeah, well, it gets better," Felipe went on. "She started berating *all* government associations in Venezuela, including air traffic control. That really pissed Escobar off, so he hung up and phoned the police in Caicara about Meghan's activities outside the CIST."

"How would Caicara know that?" she asked.

"It's not a big city. Almost everyone there knows Meghan one way or another. Anyway, he talked to an officer named Carlos. I guess this guy has been in contact with Meghan quite a bit. She'd asked him to secretly send e-mail for her. She thought she was being sneaky by not using the CIST router, which records everything. But it's a police station, for heaven's sake! Of course they're going to have records of all electronic communication. Apparently, she was promising someone in Switzerland a new mushroom worth millions of dollars."

Julia's jaw dropped. "You're kidding?"

"Nope. Meghan, Miss Ultimate Environmentalist, was planning on making millions off the rain forest—off your fungus!"

"What a bleeding hypocrite!"

"Exactly. Anyway, she asked this Carlos guy to arrange for someone to come steal your fungus from Ascom base."

Julia sucked in a breath. "You mean . . . ?"

Ricardo's smile vanished. He hung his head. "No. It was Marco who stole your mushroom. I sent him, not her."

"Yeah," Felipe continued. "It turns out Carlos never sent anyone to Ascom. He was going to, but Meghan made him very angry over something, and he didn't contact anyone. He only pretended to."

Julia sat heavily into a chair. This was almost too much to take in. "So what happens to her now?"

Felipe tugged on his ear. "That's something I've been stewing over for some time. See, I've never liked Meghan. Heck, I don't think anyone did. I've been trying to think of a way to get rid of her, but . . ." He paused and tugged harder. "Well, her dad has been dumping truckloads of money to our Interior Department. That's why she got clearance to work at the CIST. I'd never have hired her."

"I've always wondered about that," Julia said.

"I was about to say the heck with it and fire her anyway, but now there's enough documented wrongdoing to have her deported without me even getting involved."

"Brilliant," Julia said—but with little enthusiasm.

Felipe's brow furrowed slightly. "What's wrong?"

"Look, I'm elated your problems are sorting out, but what about Mantis? What about Ascom base? What about the killer cordyceps that's still out there in the wild?"

Felipe pulled up a chair next to hers. "We'll keep searching for Mantis. So will Lieutenant Escobar. If Mantis is smart, he'll flee the country. I'd love to bring him in, but honestly, a murder charge would be hard to pin on him. As for Ascom, I'm still at your disposal. If you need help breaking camp or continuing with your research, I'll see that it happens."

"And as for the cordyceps," Henry chimed in, "there are thousands of unidentified species in the rain forest. You know this. Your cordyceps may be a fluke, a genetic anomaly that infected a monkey and, regrettably, a few humans. I looked over your notes. You said the spores were very heavy. Perhaps they have not spread far. Only time will tell. But if you ask me, it is a perfect reason to continue your research."

She scoffed. "I'm not sure I want to continue at this point."

"But you must," the doctor insisted. "Look at how far you've come already. Look at how much you've learned."

"Señora—er, Julia?" Noely spoke up.

Everyone turned to see her standing in the doorway. She said something in Spanish that brought a smile to everyone's face. Everyone, except Julia.

"What did she say?"

"She says she's very glad you're here," Felipe translated. "She says you are the best one to find out how her brother died."

"But she knows how," Julia argued, feeling her throat tighten.

"No, Julia," Henry said. "She means *how*—as in internally, as in the fungal mechanism of action. She feels once you learn how, you will be able to stop others from dying."

Noely went straight to Julia and wrapped her in a hug. She mumbled another line that ended with, "Por favor."

"She says you are her best hope. And that she trusts you."

With tears spilling, Julia said, "Tell her I will. I promise."

CHAPTER 78

THE TRIP HOME HAD BEEN fraught with close calls. Mantis had cashed out all his liquid assets, taking short, hopper flights and even boarding a fishing trawler to cross the US–Mexico border. He'd ditched his phone at a Greyhound bus station in San Diego. He'd get a new one when he got back to Washington. He still had the reserves in his offshore account, but he couldn't access those without his home computer. The Internet bank had established an IP address verification tool that blocked access from any computer but his. Once he got in, he'd cash out his reserves and move to the East Coast—perhaps up to Maine. Sure, it was colder than Seattle, but it had more heavily forested land than any other state. Once there, he could buy a small cabin in the middle of nowhere and work out his next option for saving the planet.

Suffering from jet lag, hunger, and thirst, Mantis took a cab to his apartment in the low-rent district and slinked up to his front door. Scanning the neighborhood, he saw nothing untoward. He'd pinned a toothpick between the door and the jamb, a security measure he'd seen on a TV show. If the toothpick was missing or on the ground, it meant someone had opened the door. The toothpick was right where he'd left it. He crept into his apartment and cased the area. Everything looked just as he'd left it. Easing from room to room, he found nothing amiss. Relaxing, he allowed himself a huge sigh of relief. He'd made it.

Stretching, he puffed out his chest. Of course he'd made it. He was Mantis. He was a master of camouflage and fast attack.

Turning on the small light over his electric range, he took a glass out of a cupboard and moved to his refrigerator. He noticed the LED illuminating the water dispenser was off. He hoped it hadn't stopped working. He could only imagine how disgusting his milk would be. Opening the door, something inside made a loud pop. He flinched and gasped in surprise—and in doing so inhaled a rancid-tasting powder. He gagged and spit but could not get it out of his mouth. Stumbling to his sink, he rinsed his mouth out several times and gargled till he gagged. Looking back, he noticed there was a dusting of white powder in the fridge and on the floor. Motes of the same powder stuck to his black T-shirt. Inside the fridge was a small box with a face that had been blown open. Attached to the box was a note. With trembling hands, he opened it.

You failed. Enjoy the anthrax. Green Blade.

Meghan Muir entered the United States in handcuffs. She'd been deported from Venezuela under international law, accused of money laundering and bribery. Her parents waited for her at the airport terminal. They weren't smiling. She wasn't nearly as afraid of them as she was of her contact in Switzerland.

"Mommy! Daddy!" she said, busting into tears. "They've been so mean to me. Please help me. I've been accused of the most terrible things. It's a lie. It's all a lie!"

Her dad's jaw clenched several times. Angrily, he hissed, "Don't embarrass yourself any further."

She bawled loudly. A number of people turned and stared. "What do you mean? I'm innocent. I didn't do anything wrong."

"Oh shut up, Meghan," her mother said, exasperated by the scene. She held up an envelope with a postmark from Switzerland Bank.

Meghan stopped short. Her tears instantly shut off as if by a spigot.

"This came yesterday," her mother continued. "You have some explaining to do. And please try to do so without all the melodramatics."

Julia entered the research tent at Ascom base with new resolve. Felipe was at her side. Behind them were two students from the Universidad Central de Venezuela and a Dr. Benjamin Boyer, a research fellow from Emory University in Georgia.

After Henry had arranged for transporting the bodies of Brandon, Marco, and Luis to the Centers for Disease Control in Atlanta, Julia had requested a cadre of new equipment and supplies—including an advanced satellite radio with which to communicate directly with the CDC. The coordination took place without a hitch. The CDC promised to relay all information they could find on the cordyceps. If it turned out to be a new species, they offered to name it *Ophiocordyceps fatheringhamis*, just as Mantis had teased. She declined the offer, suggesting instead they name it *Ophiocordyceps udyensis*, after Brandon.

After organizing a new tent to be used as a housing unit, Julia set about opening the various containers that Felipe had airlifted in. She was looking for one small box in particular. When she found it, she announced to everyone that she was leaving.

"Leaving?" Dr. Boyer asked, surprised. "Seriously?"

"I'll only be gone a few hours, maybe overnight. I need to make a quick delivery to El Desvío."

He took in the dense rain forest surrounding them. A bemused smirk played across his face. They were, after all, in the middle of nowhere. "A delivery to whom?"

"A dear friend." Without further explanation, Julia lowered herself into her kayak and nestled the Dora the Explorer shoebox between her feet.

TO THE READER:

NEARLY ALL OF THE FUNGUS facts mentioned in this novel are accurate. Molds and fungi are involved in every aspect of our lives, although not all of them are detrimental to our health. Some, in fact, are quite beneficial. They have long been used as a direct source of food as mushrooms and truffles, as a leavening agent for bread, and in the fermentation of various food products such as wine, beer, and soy sauce. Since the 1940s, fungi have been used for the production of antibiotics. More recently, various enzymes produced by fungi are used in detergents. Fungi perform an essential role in the decomposition of organic matter and have fundamental roles in nutrient cycling and exchange in the environment. All things considered, we can't live without them.

In this novel, I show a mind-controlling cordyceps fungus jumping species. While this is an actual occurrence in nature, it has yet to be seen in humans (emphasis on *yet*).

For those interested in *Ophiocordyceps unilateralis*, see:

- http://en.wikipedia.org/wiki/Ophiocordyceps_unilateralis for general information,

- http://www.scientificamerican.com/article/fungus-makes-zombie-ants for specific research on chemical mind control in insects,

- and https://www.youtube.com/watch?v=XuKjBIBBAL8 for a creepy video clip from BBC's Planet Earth.

ABOUT THE AUTHOR

Gregg R. Luke, RPh, was born in Bakersfield, California, but spent the majority of his childhood and young adult life in Santa Barbara, California. He served an LDS mission in Wisconsin then pursued his education in natural sciences at SBCC, UCSB, and BYU. He completed his schooling at the University of Utah, College of Pharmacy.

Gregg currently practices pharmacy in Logan, Utah. He is a voracious reader and has been writing stories since childhood. He has been published in *Skin Diver* magazine, *The Oceanographic Letter*, *Destiny* magazine, and the *New Era* magazine. His fiction includes *The Survivors, Do No Harm, Altered State, Blink of an Eye, Bloodborne, Deadly Undertakings, Twisted Fate,* and *The Healer,* six of which were Whitney Award finalists.

Find out more about Gregg's novels at www.greggluke.com.